Casa Al Mare

A Jimmy Reeves Adventure

Featuring the Quiet Stranger in the Black Hat

Paul John Hausleben

Cover design by Jacqueline Sweet Design
All photographs by Paul John Hausleben

Published by God Bless the Keg Publishing
Somewhere, U.S.A.

ISBN: 978-0-9986300-3-8

Dedication

To the view through my lens

Casa Al Mare

A Jimmy Reeves Adventure

Featuring the Quiet Stranger in the Black Hat

Paul John Hausleben

Contents

Acknowledgements

Thank you to my family and friends for the support and encouragement in my writing adventures. Thank you to Mr. Jeremy Hess for his expert consultations on the various weapons depicted herein this story. A special thanks to NAVMARCORMARS for the training and years of mutual service to our country. A warm thank you to Ms. Lydia A. LaGalla for her invaluable assistance and encouragement with this project.

The stranger stopped, turned around and said, “I am who you want me to be and what you can never imagine that I am.”

Paul John Hausleben

July 2018

Preface from the Author

Every time that I feel as if I will take a little break from writing and that any inspiration that is flowing around in my mind can either wait or is weak in nature, a little spark arrives.

It does not take too much, a few words with someone, a view through one of my camera's viewfinders, a favorite piece of music, and off I go!

In the late summer of 2016, I attended a business conference in the San Francisco Bay Area of California. The organizers held the conference in a historic hotel and resort property that is full of grandeur. Fantastic is the only word that I can use to describe the property, and for a man who has spent most of his life admiring and tinkering with properties and facilities, it was a slice of Heaven to me. Spas, towering white clapboard spires reaching into blue skies, magnificent gardens full of exotic plant materials, swimming pools, tennis courts, and inside, the architecture and décor were breathtaking.

Oh yes, they also had three full-service restaurants and four cocktail lounges on the site! My kind of joint!

I also need to mention the overhanging balcony, which cost me a few bucks in a payoff to a maintenance guy, who allowed me to venture out there with my cameras to take pictures of the Pacific Ocean and fabulous scenery from the balcony. You can tell that I am from Paterson, New Jersey; I can work a back-door deal anywhere!

It was photography heaven, and I walked away with tons of photographs for the PJH photo vault. Just to add to the mix, the conference was fabulous, no snoozing, I learned a wealth of new information, met wonderful people and drank some amazing Scotch too.

Anyway, the setting in California stuck in my mind as the perfect setting for a potential plot and storyline. Within a few days of my return from the trip, I performed some outlining and after a few hours of work; I had a basic storyline worked out along with the setting. I felt it was a solid basis for a project. However, which of the many casts of PJH characters should we drop into the book?

A Harry and Paul Adventure?

Maybe.

In the latter half of 2016, I wrote a story for inclusion in one of my short story collections for the popular, quiet stranger in the black hat books and alongside the mysterious stranger, I created some new characters. The story featured a hard-boiled New Jersey Attorney General, some beautiful women and a faithful sidekick-bodyguard and all-around tough guy, and friend to the attorney general named Jimmy Reeves. Jimmy is an ex-United States Marine, a combat veteran, an expert sharpshooter, a sniper, a covert informant for the good guys and most of all, Jimmy is a general all around, badass, tough guy from the tough, yet, fictional streets of the very real, Paterson, New Jersey.

Yes! Jimmy was awesome, and I enjoyed the character, as well as the character of his boss, Attorney General Charles, "Chuck" McCracken, and the rest of the cast that I created for the story.

The story, titled "When the Night Closes In" was very popular and readers enjoyed the characters. The story's genre is crime and fantasy mixed, and of course, when it all goes poorly for the heroes, but just in the nick of time, the mysterious stranger arrives to save the day.

The stranger is very much like my character of Paul John Henson is, very versatile, and I can drop him into many situations and settings and he is effective and adaptable.

Here we go now. I threw all of these characters and the

recent inspiration from the trip along with a dose of poppycock into the Hausleben mind-mixer and many ideas for this book popped out. The luxurious property, the fantastic hotel and resort, a switch of locations, a dashing hero, the mysterious stranger, and this novel suddenly came to life. I placed the property in an old city along the New Jersey shoreline, created a few evil and ruthless New Jersey based mobsters, added a complex plot line of crime and general mayhem, a grisly murder, a wily police detective, beautiful women, along with some covert military radio operations in a gentle nod to my own background. Finally, I dropped in the courageous, handsome and dashing Jimmy Reeves with his guns and assorted weapons, and his convoluted crime fighting gizmos and gadgets.

Of course, even as cool and tough as Jimmy is, I knew that he would need a bit of help. I looked around the room in the writing command center. And there he was, hiding in a dark corner, wearing his black hat and his immaculate black attire. I gave him a nod and the quiet stranger jumped into the pages too. He is a tricky one.

Crime and fantasy mixed.

The inspiration rolled, and this novel had a life with three weeks of some intense and very long writing sessions.

Go get the bad guys, Jimmy, and maybe fall in love along the way too! It is all great fun.

I hope you enjoy reading this novel as much as I have enjoyed the experience of writing it. Thank you for reading it.

Paul John Hausleben

01 July 2018

Prologue

On a hazy, hot, and humid day on a side street off a main drag, in a seedy and unscrupulous section of Clinton City, New Jersey, two men stood and argued with each other. One of the men was a few years older than the other man was, and from a few feet away, a beautiful young woman watched the scene unfold and, in her mind, she carefully recorded the words.

"I don't care about the danger, Kenny! I just don't care. You have to understand that you are my kid brother and I love you with all my heart. I am not going to stand around any longer and let you ruin your life and your wonderful girlfriend's life, too. She loves you, Kenny. Not sure why we both do, but we do!"

The older man jumped into the face of the younger man, who was his blood brother.

"Robbie, I am gonna clean up. I swear that I will. Soon. We need the dough and I have to get off the stuff. I am trying. It is hard to do. Do ya think that I like sharing my girlfriend with disgusting slobs who drool all over her? I want out of this life and Donna does too."

The brother nodded his head and looked over at the young woman, who did not say a word. "Ok, well, I am gonna help you. Together or alone. I am gonna take them all down. End it all. This is what I have to do. For you, for Donna, for this shitty city, for all the good people. Someone has to do it. Someone has to have the guts to stand up to them. To him!"

The young man grabbed his older brother by the arm and tugged at him, "Don't do it, Rob. These are badass men and here in Clinton City, ya can't trust anyone. Not even the police."

The older brother shook his head, pulled his arm away from the grip of his younger brother and said, "I have to do what is right. It has to end."

Without another word, the older brother then turned and walked away while the woman and the younger man watched him turn a street corner and disappear.

Watching the scene between the two brothers unfold and listening to the words exchanged, was a man. An immense man. Tall, lean, but powerfully built. He stood out of view, within the dark shadows between two buildings on that same side street.

Watching and waiting in the shadows of the grit and evil of the old city.

He stood silently, his dark eyes piercing the air as they focused on the situation. The man standing there between the buildings in the dark shadows was dressed all in black, he wore a black vest, covering a perfectly pressed, black buttoned-up shirt, and his sharply creased, black trousers had not a single ripple or a wrinkle in them. There was nothing out of place on this man. Not a wrinkle of his clothes, not a hair on his head, nothing at all. His appearance was impeccable and immaculate. His features were dark; he wore on his face, a finely trimmed beard, closely framing a perfectly chiseled face, and he stood silently while watching with dark, piercing black eyes. Dark eyes that were staring straight ahead, emotionless, expressionless. On his head, he wore a black hat with a wide brim, pulled down to where his facial features were not easily seen, but still visible. On his feet were highly polished black boots, buffed to a mirror shine. If you bent down and looked at them, you could see your reflection in them.

He was the quiet stranger in the black hat.

When the younger brother and his girlfriend held hands, and they slowly walked across the street and entered the front entrance of a shabby apartment on the same side street, the stranger turned and he walked briskly away.

His boots had metal tips on them and while he walked, they made a loud and distinct clicking noise as they struck the pavement in rhythm to his walking.

The noise from the tips of his boots sounded loudly and echoed along the city street until the stranger faded from view and the noise of his boots was lost in the madness and noise of the city.

Casa Al Mare

Chapter 1

Evil Has No Boundaries

In this tainted and complicated world, evil does not only lurk in dark, seedy alleyways in the rundown old cities, framed on a backdrop of illegal drug deals on the corners and gunshots in the streets.

Evil has no boundaries.

It permeates all of our societies.

It exists in the palatial executive offices of corporations, in the opulent mansions and wealthy lifestyles of high society and in the hearts of leaders and politicians. It exists in almost every walk of life imaginable. Wherever those with evil in their hearts feel as if they can inflict their ways to connive, cheat, kill, steal and make money off their evil plans. It is always about the money that they can make, as well as the greed and the power that they consume their very souls with every day. Every act of malice, every evil deed, consumes their souls. A piece at a time. It is not about the lives they ruin, or the evil they spread, it is only about their dastardly plans.

Yet, in this world, hiding amongst some of those same shadows and circles, there are the guardians of good. Guardians whose identities are unknown, yet they do exist. Men and women, who are willing to infiltrate evil and bring justice to those who seek to destroy lives and spread their evil ways. Together, when the need arises, the good persons of this world join forces and they all become allies. When they do so, they fight evil at every opportunity. They fight the darkness with the light of justice, with the power of the law and with all the elements of the goodness and kindness that remain in this world.

These forces of good remain powerful, they remain diligent, and in the case of one strange and mysterious figure, more powerful than all the forces of evil combined. With a power not of this world, but with a power beyond anyone's wildest imaginations.

In the upstairs hallway of a seedy apartment house in Clinton City, New Jersey, a single man stared down the drawn gun barrels held by four henchmen working for the notorious son of the even more notorious mobster, Tony Michanetti.

Tony Michanetti Senior went missing a few years earlier. Since no one ever found his body or any trace of him anywhere, the law enforcement authorities and many other people considered Tony Michanetti Senior to be a victim of a rival mob hit, or of someone or *something* else.

Clinton City was one of the few urban cities found along what is usually a peaceful and tranquil New Jersey coastline. A coastline full of resorts, legendary beaches, boardwalks and locations famous for family getaways and fun. Yet, in Clinton City, life was generally not fun. It was home to organized crime, to illegal drugs, a haven and launching point for the criminals to market and peddle their drugs and wares to the bustling shore traffic, teenagers and the ever-growing drug addiction plague now haunting America's youth and others.

"Cut his fingers off and then let me shoot his ass full of bullets," Tony Michanetti Junior said as he took a handgun from one of his henchmen, loaded the bullets into the barrel and pointed it at the young man standing in front of him. Tony Junior waved at one of his henchmen in order to designate this particular henchman to be the man to perform the grisly amputation. A henchman who was severely overweight, very sweaty and nervous, and who wore a suit that, right now, was ten sizes too small for his huge body. He also was a henchman who was unlucky enough to be standing closest to Tony Junior and the impatience in Tony Junior's soul and in his eyes grew in intensity, when the big henchman did not move quickly enough to satisfy Tony Junior.

"You stupid, or deaf? Gotta knife?" Tony Michanetti Junior asked.

The henchman nervously nodded. He pulled the leg of his pants up and revealed a sheath strapped to his leg, and pointed at it. The knife inside was at least a foot long.

"Good, chop his fingers off on one hand. His right hand. Chances are that he is right-handed, and he pisses with his right hand. Not that pissing will be a problem anymore, but I bet he is pissing his pants right now. Yeah, man, cut the fingers off his right hand. That way everybody will know he stole from me."

The knife was drawn, and while the other henchmen held the poor man down hard on the floor of the hallway, and forced his hand outward, the knife struck, and blood, screams, and agony filled the air. The young man staggered and tried to get to his feet when the henchmen released him. There was blood spurting from the young man's hand in all directions. His screams of agony died off as his eyes widened at the sight of the gun barrel.

"Go ahead and say your prayers, ya double-crossing punk. No one steals from me and gets away with it. Since ya won't tell us, where the money is and my stuff is, well then, tell it to the Devil. We will find it without ya help."

With those words, Tony Junior pulled the trigger and fired three shots into the young man. The young man collapsed and fell into a heap in the middle of the hallway. He rolled on the floor while gasping for his last breaths.

Tony Junior and the henchmen gathered around the

dying young man and watched as the young man struggled to smile and whispered with his last breaths, "Ya wrong, ya dirty asshole, I am not pissing in my pants. Besides, I am left-handed. Ya sorry ass will never find the bear. Never. If ya do, it will be too late. The good guys will find everything and you will rot in jail."

"Piss on the good guys. I control everything and now you are the one who is rotting," Tony Junior said with a sneer.

"No, Tony Junior, you only think that you control everything. In the end, you will lose and the good guys will win. I will smile from Heaven while you burn in Hell."

With those last words, the young man drew his last breath, and he died.

"Should we drag him somewhere, boss?" One of the henchmen asked.

While handing the murder weapon off to the sweaty and overweight henchman, Tony Junior shook his head and said, "Nah. Ha! I hope he has fun in Heaven strumming his damn golden harp. Asshole. Check his pockets. Strip him of everything he has and take anything ya find on 'em. Then, leave his dead ass there. I own all the cops in this shitty city. No one cares about this punk dying. Not sure what the hell the bear bullshit meant, but ya guys need to find the dough and stuff he took. Now! Now, means, now! Turn what used to be this guy's world inside and out, in order to find it. Knowing this double-crossing bum, he left some kind of trail back to me. We have to find it and my stash and dough, too. Stop at nothing or anyone. Kill anyone who gits in ya way. And you, fatso!" Tony Junior pointed at the overweight henchman and with a sneer on his face and while the henchman looked up, Tony Junior said, "Lose some damn weight. Will ya?"

The henchman nodded, but did not say a word.

What Tony Junior did not realize as he stood over the dead man's body was the pooling blood spilling out of the lifeless body managed to lick the edges of the soles and heels of Tony Junior's very expensive hand-crafted shoes. On the other hand, perhaps, he did notice the blood and simply did not care because as Tony Junior said, "He owns all the cops in this shitty city" and the law was the least of the things that Tony Junior cared about or feared.

Tony Junior and his group of henchmen, made their way down a back staircase of the apartment house. They hustled along inside of a maze of interconnecting alleyways and fled to a luxury black sedan, parked in an obscure alleyway next to a Chinese restaurant.

Standing outside the alleyway, watching and waiting in the shadows of the grit and evil of the old city, was a man. Not an ordinary man in appearance, or in any other manner. He stood silently, his dark eyes piercing the air as they focused upon the alleyway and all the dirty secrets it held within its grasp. The man standing on the sidewalk outside the alley was dressed all in black, he wore a black vest, covering a perfectly pressed, black buttoned-up shirt, and his sharply creased, black trousers had not a single ripple or a wrinkle in them. There was nothing out of place on this man. Not a wrinkle of his clothes, not a hair on his head, nothing at all. His appearance was impeccable and immaculate.

His features were dark; he wore on his face, a finely trimmed beard, closely framing a perfectly chiseled face. He had piercing black eyes that stared straight ahead while remaining emotionless, expressionless. On his head, he wore a black hat with a wide brim, pulled down to where his facial features were not easily seen, but still visible. On his feet were highly polished black boots, buffed to a mirror shine. If you bent down and looked at them, you could see your reflection in them.

He was the quiet stranger in the black hat.

The gang quickly hustled Tony Michanetti Junior into the rear seat of the sedan, then they all jumped in the car and the driver started the engine and slammed the vehicle into reverse. While the car moved to back out of the alleyway, the large open-top trash dumpster utilized for rubbish by the neighboring Chinese restaurant that sat at the end of the escape path suddenly moved. It glided slowly across the asphalt, screeching a path of scorched asphalt underneath its own weight. How it moved remained unknown, but it was as if an unseen hand guided it along the way.

BANG!

The limo lurched to a stop when the rear driver's side of the vehicle collided with the dumpster.

Tony Junior turned around and frowned, then screamed at his driver, "What the hell! Are ya friggin' blind? Get us the hell out of here, you asshole!"

The surprised driver nodded, swung the wheel and deftly maneuvered the vehicle out of the way of the errant dumpster.

The driver apologized and then mumbled to his fellow henchman sitting in the passenger's seat next to him, "Damn. Where the hell did that come from? I swear it was clear a second or two ago."

His partner did not speak or acknowledge his testimony; instead, he frantically waved and then pointed for the driver to make the escape up the road. The vehicle screamed in the roadway, the driver spun the steering wheel and the limo sped off into the night.

While police sirens wailed in the distance, from within the shadows of his watch post, the quiet stranger in the black hat peered into the night. He stood for a long time until the taillights of the escape vehicle disappeared from his sight and all that remained of the vehicle was a whiff of burned gas from the exhaust pipe. The stranger walked over to the spot where the car collided with the dumpster, and his dark eyes studied some plastic debris from the destroyed taillight scattered around on the ground. The stranger bent over, reached out, and gathered the plastic parts up in his hand and he studied them carefully. He then placed the parts inside his vest pocket, stood up, then turned and quickly walked off into the night.

While his boots struck the sidewalk, they made a loud metal clicking noise as the metal tips of his boots struck the sidewalk hard and clean. The echoes of his boots carried far into the night. The noise bounced off the walls of the old buildings and the sharp clicks resounded all the way to Heaven.

"Say, tell me sumthin', Jimmy? When was the last time that ya ass took a vacation? Do ya know what I mean by an actual vacation? Where ya sat around a fancy pool, sipping top-shelf cocktails, and ya sit there and check out all the asses and mighty chests of the pretty gals in swimsuits that are jumpin', wigglin', and jigglin', around the pool."

State of New Jersey, Attorney General, Charles "Chuck" McCracken took a long sip of a fine, single-malt Scotch served neat and as he sipped, he waited for an answer to the question that he had asked his longtime friend, the limousine driver and bodyguard, Mr. James "Jimmy" Reeves.

Jimmy Reeves looked somewhat puzzled as to the nature of the question that his boss asked and he answered with a laugh, "Never. Marines don't take vacations. We are always on duty. When my watch is over, then I will take a vacation."

It was a Friday evening and Charles McCracken and his wife, Michelle McCracken sat on one side of the table and Jimmy Reeves sat on the other side opposite them, while the three of them nestled into a quiet corner of their favorite, exclusive, French restaurant, "Nous Somme Du Soleil." These days, it was not easy for Chuck McCracken to appear in public anywhere within his home city, but the management of this restaurant knew how to clear a corner out for their most famous patrons and their bodyguard. Besides, with Jimmy Reeves around, there was not too much to fear. When you are the head of all of law enforcement for New Jersey, well, you tend to make many enemies and since taking the attorney general position about three years earlier, Chuck had locked up his fair share of criminals.

Jimmy Reeves was a former United States Marine, having served multiple tours in combat in the thick of many battles in a number of different wars and conflicts. He was a sharpshooter in the United States Marine Corps and not only did he never miss when he fired his weapon, he did not miss when he swung his fists, too. His hand-to-hand combat skills were the subjects of legends and his fearless courage and impeccable service records told all you needed to know about the character of the man.

Jimmy was tall, extremely muscular and powerful, and outstandingly handsome with a close-cropped full beard and mustache, along with short black hair, steel-grey eyes and dark features reflecting his Irish heritage. Even approaching fifty years of age, Jimmy turned the heads of women half of his age.

He was striking in appearance and Michelle McCracken kidded Jimmy many times by telling the faithful bodyguard that, "He oozes sexiness."

Jimmy never married, had an occasional gal pal or two along the way, but never committed, nor settled down with anyone special.

Jimmy grew up rough and tough in the north end of the city of Paterson in northern New Jersey. He was the product of hard-working parents whose families originally came to New Jersey from Ireland with nothing more than their dreams, strong backs, iron wills and a fistful of Irish grit. Jimmy Reeves was fiercely loyal to Charles and his wife and when Chuck took the position, he knew that he needed his longtime faithful and loyal assistant to ride along with him on the adventures. They were a team. Jimmy had served in the same position when Charles McCracken was working in the Prosecutor's Office along with their mutual friend and business partner, and now, United States Senator Gordon Tolland.

"I knew that is what you would tell me. Same old, Marine Corps bullshit. Ya will take a vacation when ya pushing up daisies," Chuck said while he smiled at Jimmy's reply.

Michelle asked her husband, "I might add, and ask, when was it that we enjoyed our last vacation, my dear Chuck? If I recall correctly, there was some type of hint of a retirement that lasted all of about three months or thereabouts. Now, we are back in the midst of keeping our heads on a swivel as you like to tell us all the time."

With her voice laced with hints of sarcasm, Michelle commented on her husband's short-lived retirement of a few years earlier. Chuck frowned at his wife and her accurate recollections of when Chuck, as he preferred to call it, "Paused his career."

Michelle McCracken was a gorgeous woman, with a glorious female figure, high cheekbones and gentle facial features and dark brown eyes. Michelle wore an impeccable hairstyle, which was very fitting for her facial features and unlike many women, Michelle chose not to dye her hair color, and instead, allowed her natural aging to shine through, while her brown hair touched the edges of grey and she stunned every male who gazed upon her with her beautiful appearance. Michelle also deeply loved Chuck and this solid and amazing woman was first in line for receiving patience.

Being married to Charles McCracken required immense patience.

"You are correct, baby doll. However, all I did was hang

around the house home, drink gallons of Scotch and drive you crazy. Well, I slapped your gorgeous ass on occasion too, and we wore out a few sets of bed sheets here and there. But. . .."

Jimmy playfully put his fingers in his ears, and Chuck cut off his comments and winked playfully at his wife, while Michelle blushed with a deep red color filling her cheeks. Even after all of these years being married to the outrageously outspoken, Charles "Chuck" McCracken, his humor and lack of a "mouth filter" caused his wife to blush at his comments. Michelle recovered; she then smiled and playfully slapped her husband in the arm for his lewd comments.

Charles "Chuck" McCracken was a legend amongst law enforcement and legal circles. The man did not play by too many rules and he constantly tested the edges of the legal systems. If you looked up the definition of the word, "Hard-boiled" in the dictionary, then it might just have a picture of Chuck McCracken aligned with it. No one questioned his intelligence level since he was without peers in legal interpretations and knowledge, and while his New Jersey accent resembled more of street talk than it did his polished legal education, he always got his point across. He was older now, his hair was all grey, he walked a little bent over, drank too much Scotch and chain-smoked too many cigarettes, but his chiseled good looks still remained, and despite the fashion and current styles, Chuck still wore his same old flattop haircut. The public loved him and the criminals feared him. He was a celebrity; the media absolutely loved his controversial press conferences, where he spewed whatever was currently on his mind, while the governor cringed at his latest televised rants. Indeed, his mouth had no filter. There he was, rising through the ranks as a heralded trial lawyer, with a knack for conducting his own behind the scene investigations. There was no doubt that he had a flair for crime solving. Chuck was a lawyer who lost very few, if any, cases and his success followed him when he moved to the prosecution of countless high-profile cases involving organized crime, gangs, and other factions of New Jersey's seemingly endless parade of criminals who tested the system and lost.

Chuck feared no one or anything, and he proudly proclaimed his famous battle cry of the fact that he, "Despised crooks, connivers, chiselers, and thieves!"

Hard-boiled might describe Charles McCracken, but the other definition that clearly defined Attorney General Chuck McCracken was that he was the epitome of honesty. Many had tried to buy his interests, and it only resulted in jail terms for them.

His honesty and his integrity were not for sale.

After all, this was New Jersey, and the attempts to buy the influence of an official in charge of something were common and abundant.

"Sorry about the short-lived retirement, baby doll. However, someday, we will float around on that yacht. You topless and most of the time, bottomless too. I promise. Right now, there are too many evil sons-o-bitches to catch. Jimmy, seriously, I think you need to take a week or two off in order to relax. Regroup a little, breathe deeply, and take in some beautiful ocean views. Get ya mind off guns, weightlifting, and kicking the livin' hell outta bad guys. Ya know, I am thinking that ya need to take a little break from keeping an eye on my gorgeous baby doll and me."

The legend of Charles McCracken extended to this establishment and most every Friday and Saturday evening found them dining here, at their favorite table in a quiet corner. With the prestige, came a dedicated server too. Jean-Marc Richard fit the bill and provided the top-flight service. Fluent in French for menu interpretations, he also spoke fluent "New Jersey." Trained in France under the most demanding and watchful eyes, Jean-Marc was the class of all servers, well versed in when to check on the table, how to interpret the body languages of his most famous customers and he knew when the Scotch of Chuck McCracken required an "ahead of time" refill. Jean-Marc also knew that any tidbits of conversation that he might overhear in the conducting of his service, the server needed to hold within the strictest of confidence. Years before, Chuck checked Jean-Marc's background out and he passed the tests with flying colors. Jean-Marc was part of the team; Chuck knew he could be trusted beyond any boundaries. Chuck paid top-dollar, and he allowed no one else other than Jean-Marc to serve his table.

The server glided over to the table to check on the dinner status and spoke in his glorious French accent, "Mr. McCracken, I see that a drink refresh is in order. I think that I see that everyone else is good."

A nod of the heads confirmed the facts of the drink order. Chuck did not miss a beat and nodded, and when Jean-Marc turned to obtain the drink, Chuck gently grabbed the server's arm. Rather determinedly, Chuck called upon the other team member to reinforce his mission for this evening.

"Jean-Marc, I was just sayin' to Jimmy, here, that he needs a vacation. Don't you agree with me that it is time?"

Jean-Marc carefully listened to Chuck's statement, then he adjusted the towel draped over his folded arm, looked first at Mrs. McCracken and then at Jimmy.

"Oui. Without a doubt. Overdue, I might add. I am sure that it will be a relaxing, yet, interesting mission, ah, I mean, an interesting vacation."

Chuck relaxed his grip and smiled while the server walked away to obtain the drink order. No doubt, Jean-Marc was part of the team.

Jimmy Reeves knew his boss too well. He could tell by the posturing, the out of context questions and his general tone that while Chuck might actually sincerely desire to see him take a few days off, there was a particular location that he rather strongly was going to suggest for the vacation destination. In other words, he was sending his faithful assistant on a fact-finding and unofficial "investigation" under the disguise of a vacation. A vacation that was actually a mission. A mission that Jimmy Reeves knew was miles ahead of not only the targeted criminals but many others, too. Jimmy set his fork aside, wiped his mouth, and leaned back into his chair with a wide smile plastered over his face.

"I sense ya got concern 'bout me overworking, but ya also need me to check sumthin' out. Whatcha got? Where is the mission? Or, ah . . . the vacation?"

Michelle McCracken listened carefully to what Jimmy said as well as what he sensed, and Michelle was horrified at her husband's behavior. When Michelle observed and made careful note of the look of satisfaction on Chuck's face at the fact that Jimmy was correct in his intuition, Michelle scolded her husband.

"Chuck! You mean to tell me that, what I thought was going to be a nice getaway for Jimmy, is really a mission in disguise. I swear that you are despicable, sometimes. You really are!"

Michelle folded her arms across her mighty chest, while Chuck laughed, leaned over, kissed his wife's cheek and then reached into his suit jacket pocket. He pulled out a colorful brochure, which was a typical travel destination type of brochure, and handed it to Jimmy Reeves.

"It is a vacation, my baby doll. We are payin' for it too. A vacation, where I need Jimmy to check out some activity and see what he can sniff out while he checks out the babes by the pool."

"Some vacation! Let me guess, Chuck. That Jimmy needs to keep his head on a swivel and make sure he is packin' too."

"Well, yes, of course. While ya study that brochure,

Jimmy, old Chuck has to mention one name. Tony Michanetti Junior."

Jimmy studied the brochure. He whistled a low whistle and looked at Chuck.

"Fancy joint, huh? I cannot even pronounce the name of the place. Let's see. Outdoor and indoor tennis and racquetball courts, indoor pools and heated outdoor pools, Oceanside views, bay views, the joint has restaurants and fancy-ass bars and cocktail lounges inside of the place. Health spas, workout rooms, running tracks. Geez, hell, look at these pictures of these fancy gardens and grounds." Jimmy looked at Chuck for his reaction, but his boss simply stared at his bodyguard. Jimmy knew that Chuck was waiting for his next intuitive move. Chuck never stopped testing those around him to make sure they all were on the same page.

Jimmy was up for the task, "Ok. I am in. All ya had to say was that one name, Tony Michanetti Junior. Let me guess, he owns this place, and it is a front for his operations. Interesting, very interesting . . . ah, say, Jean-Marc." Jimmy waved the server over to the table because he required a translation. Jean-Marc hustled over to the table and leaned in, while Jimmy held the brochure up for him to read the cover. "Jean-Marc, how do ya say the name of this dump? I think it is French, ain't it?"

The server studied the brochure and smiled while explaining, "No, Jimmy. That is Italian. Casa Al Mare. House by the sea. In French, it would be, Maison de la Mer. In New Jersey, speak, well, it is a fancy joint by da beach. It is quite a famous and historic hotel and resort along the Jersey Shore. Quite famous, indeed. Full of high rollers. Many connections. Some good and some very bad. No doubt, it is a fascinating destination for a holiday for the legendary, Jimmy Reeves. I have a feeling that Casa Al Mare will never be the same after your visit, Jimmy. It is an interesting place. Amongst other things. Refills?"

Jean-Marc was not only a server to the team; he was also a consultant of sorts.

All three nodded at the drink request. Jimmy mumbled, "Thank you. Shit, I was sure it was French. Should'a known that it was Italian."

The replacement drinks arrived, Chuck leaned into another double Scotch, poured neat and after a long sip, he finally revealed the inside information of the "vacation" planned for Jimmy.

"Clinton City is a crime-infested dump. A sore spot on one of our greatest natural resources, a pimple on the ass of New Jersey. Organized crime moved in when the little number of legit businesses left there went belly up. They use it as a launching point for drugs, crime, guns, and all kinds of illegal activities. Feed off stupid college kids and wealthy folks vacationing on the shoreline. I hate the place, but it has been hard to focus on it. Until now."

"How so, dear? Why now?" Michelle asked her husband while she sipped her martini.

"Cuz, I think Tony Junior has moved out of the north here and settled into Clinton City as his new base of operations. It is not too far from the Interstate Ninety-Five Corridor for drugs and weapons running, and my inside scoop info tells me that the evil thug has bought out the police force there. The police force is full of corrupt bastards that I want to nail. The last weeks or so, I picked up some more inside words from a few informants that we have on the streets there, and the word is that Tony Junior bought the fancy resort to use as a front and to meet the people he wants to use and manipulate. He brings in the high rollers and fills the joint full of rich assholes and milks the fat wallets of them all, while making the connections and fronting things the way he needs to, in order to rule his little world of evil. Business is lucrative. High-end prostitution, drug running, unprecedented heroin and other types of opiates in full distribution. He runs countless illegal gambling and number games. Yup, good ole, Tony Junior is living the high life of crime down there. Opiate-based addictions are dropping American youth like moths around flames. It is an epidemic and Tony Junior, in many ways, is even more of a ruthless asshole than his father was."

Jimmy nodded, but he did not comment. Chuck could tell that his bodyguard's demeanor was changing. Jimmy was intense, his skills now itching for some action.

Chuck McCracken knew what buttons to push, and he continued to do so, "I have a connection on the city police force. He feeds me intelligence. Might be the only honest cop left in the entire city. Detective Oscar Campenella. Oscar is a homicide specialist. I knew his old man. We worked together, many years ago, on a task force team. In old Paterson city. His old man was the best and if his son is half the detective that his old man was, then he is onto sumthin'. There is another sure sign that Tony Junior is workin' the city and the shore."

"What is that, boss?" Jimmy asked.

"Dead bodies are showing up. Lots of dead bodies. All full of bullets and drug overdoses."

"Yeah, that sounds like a Michanetti operation, for sure. I am ready. When do I leave? I am guessin' this Detective Campenella is my tour guide."

"Yes, he is. Oscar is tough, brave, and fearless but he tends to be overzealous and he does not keep his head on a swivel. He will need your smarts, Jimmy, but he also will need your protection. Once you get into town, then I will ensure that you two connect quickly. I think that time is short now. We need to move on this one. This is an unofficial, yet, an official mission, Jimmy. I need info and Oscar needs help. Above it all, I know that you are the man. You can leave next week. Relax over the weekend, eat and drink well and in your spare time, well, do what Marines do and pack your seabag and your gear. Ya gonna need all your gizmos and gadgets too. Head on a swivel, my old friend. Head on a swivel. And make that you are always packin'.'"

"Understood, boss. Ya can count on me. Do you think Tony Junior or any of his thug punks will recognize me? I never ran into Junior, only his dad."

Chuck seemed to ponder Jimmy's questions for a few seconds before answering, "I don't think so. There might be some hold over thugs who still hang with the kid, but that is a chance ya will need to take. You are smart and you will maneuver. By the time, they figure out who ya are, then hopefully, Oscar has enough on him to call me in and we can nail 'em. Rent a high-end sports car, pack fancy suits. Expensive sunglasses. Ya gotta be da bomb. The women will faint at the sight of ya handsome ass. Ya need to fit in and blend in with these high-rolling jacklegs. Invent some cover bullshit. I dunno, maybe, a fancy businessman of some sorts. Ya own a factory or sumthin' up here. Near Paterson." Chuck smiled, and he knew that in his mind, Jimmy already was spinning the yarns that he required for his cover.

"Okay, boss, gotcha covered on that, but I will worry about who will be watching you and Mrs. McCracken, while I am gone." Jimmy smirked a little and finished his thoughts, "Ya know, while I am on my vacation."

"Oh, don't worry about bullshit like that. I will have a group of police officers hang around. Gonna hang around the home office for a while. Stay away from the main office and the streets for a bit until the heat dies down and we nail these suckers. You hand pick the officers for me. Guys that you trust. Okay?"

"I like that. Will do, boss."

"Yeah, we all need to lie low right now. Trust no one or anything. No cell phone bullshit or texting, or email nonsense. These evil suckers are the real deal and everyone is on the take. These boys can infiltrate everything and I trust nothing but old school stuff. Pay phone landlines in the middle of nowhere will be our preferred means of communications. All that technology nowadays is bullshit, anyway. Why do we have a need nowadays to be in constant communication? The old ways worked for a helluva long time. All those fancy-ass phones sure make it easier for the crooks to stay in touch. It's all 'bout sellin' stuff to you twenty-four-seven-three-sixty-five. Wireless crap is big business."

Chuck paused from his rant, ran his hand over the top of his flattop and waved his hand in little circles in the air while pointing in the direction of Jimmy Reeves.

He displayed a typical New Jersey manner of expression with the dramatic wave and while remaining waving, Chuck continued with his directions, "Bring all that covert military radio shit with ya. We might need it all. Pull out all the gizmos, and weapons, Jimmy. Secret weapons or otherwise. Ya get my drift. These guys are the real deal and they don't play. Don't need me tellin' ya this bullshit, cuz, ya already know that, Jimmy. This ain't ya first roll in the mud."

Chuck smiled, knowing that Jimmy understood and that he agreed with his plan. Chuck waved Jean-Marc over to collect their spent dinner plates, order desserts, and another round or two of after-dinner cordials and drinks.

When Jean-Marc and his crew cleared the table and the efficient server began to walk away from the table, Chuck had another request that popped into his mind, "Please bring the house phone, will ya, Jean-Marc?"

"Certainly, sir. Oui. I understand . . . no cell phone usage."

Jean-Marc was on his game.

Within a minute or two, Jean-Marc delivered the phone to the table, and Chuck pointed to Jean-Marc for the server to leave it in front of Jimmy for his use.

Chuck told his longtime driver and bodyguard, "Make

the call for a back-up driver, Jimmy. Our driver needs a driver tonight. It is one of those, long-ass Friday nights. Much more to tell ya. Too much, booze. Ya ain't drivin' tonight. After all, ya on vacation now."

Jimmy nodded, picked up the receiver, and began to dial the number.

While he worked at the buttons of the phone, Jimmy said, "Say, boss, any idea whatever happened to Tony Senior. I mean, poof! Gone, without a trace. Kinda weird, even for a rival hit."

Chuck stirred what remained of his Scotch with his finger. His face showed just a hint of a smile, and his eyes lit up.

"I have a damn good idea. No proof, but a gut feeling and a damn good idea."

Jimmy listened while he held his fingers over the last number that he needed to dial and he smiled too.

While pushing the final digit, Jimmy asked, "The quiet and elusive stranger? Our friend in the black hat?" Chuck nodded and Jimmy asked, "Ya seen him as of late?"

"Nah. But don't worry, he is out there watching and waiting. Too much, damn evil for him not to be out there somewhere. I know that in my heart, he will show up at just the right moment. Believe me, he will, and when he does, it will be right when this sick, tired, old world needs him the most."

Chapter 2

On the Trail

Detective Oscar Campenella was a driven man. Above all, he was a cop's cop. His father was a police officer and after years of walking the street beat, he became a detective. A homicide detective and a damn good one, too. Detective Campenella's father had unparalleled street instincts, and he passed his instincts along with his genes to his son. On top of his father's career, Oscar's grandfather, his father's father, well, he was a police officer too. All the Campenella officers served their duty in the old and hardened city of Paterson, New Jersey. Mostly in the northern wards of the city, in the rough neighborhoods that bordered the northern boroughs of the city's outskirts. Understandably, and with fine reasons to do so, Oscar was proud of his bloodline and his family.

When his father retired, the family moved out of Paterson and they relocated to south Jersey. Oscar moved with them and he secured a job as a police officer on the police force of Clinton City. Not quite as rough as old Paterson was, but as of late, crime was growing at an alarming rate. In the last year or thereabouts, something changed here in Clinton City, and it became a very dangerous place.

Oscar received his promotion to the position of a detective at the age of forty-two, which was now about three years ago, and his pride in following in his father's footsteps overflowed. Oscar was the first Latino detective in the history of the Clinton City Police Department. His dad warned him of the dangers, and Oscar knew the ground rules when he accepted the promotion. He did not care because he was smart, brave and diligent and with his medium stature, his close-cropped brown hair shaved in a military style and sharp green eyes that did not miss a trick, Oscar knew that he was not a Hollywood movie star, but he was a damn good detective. Oscar was determined to make a difference. He was going to be exceptional in his work, despite the obstacles. He had a pretty wife and two young children and although he feared for his family if something happened to him in the line of duty, he never feared the duty itself. His wife was good and kind and she knew the risks before they married. Their love overcame the risks. Oscar hoped that it could overcome evil, too.

It seemed, as of late, that Oscar could not trust anyone on the police force. His commander provided him with poor advice, and Oscar felt as if he misled him on purpose with the investigations of cases. When he knew it was the wrong thing to do, and crime was obvious, Oscar's fellow police officers encouraged Oscar to look the other way a number of times. It seemed as if the tide turned on the police force of Clinton City and something or someone had taken control of the streets and the police force too. Oscar knew the warning signs of what might be happening and rather than elevate it through his chain of command and risk further alienation, he discussed this situation with his father. At this point, Oscar could not be sure where the good guys began and the evil ones took over!

His father had seen it all before and his father knew all the signs, too. His dad had traveled many roads and dark situations in his career, and he warned his son of where he was venturing. Into a dark world of corruption, of payoffs and of battles for control. Organized crime had very few boundaries. His father knew people, or in fact, one person in particular. A person who he trusted explicitly, above all others, and a person who was now in a very high place. In fact, in New Jersey law enforcement, there was no one higher. A phone call to Attorney General Charles "Chuck" McCracken yielded the assistance, as well as the attention required, mostly because of the fact that Oscar's father's reputation for goodness and honor preceded him. Oscar's dad and his old friend made the connection. Chuck told them that help was on the way and both Oscar and his father knew that if Chuck McCracken said it, then it was going to happen. Since the conversation with the attorney general, Oscar Campenella circled the wagons and kept a low profile. He did his job, but only reported what facts he needed to report to satisfy his commanding officer. Lately, the facts that the command required were few and far between. Behind the scenes, Oscar observed everything, and he missed no details. It was a difficult situation, and as of late, there were growing concerns in Oscar's heart with the numerous dead bodies that kept showing up all over the city.

The growing body count of dead people from drug overdoses was disturbing enough, but now there were dead bodies riddled with bullets too. In particular, a dead body of a young man with all the fingers on the right hand of the corpse chopped off in a gruesome and heartless manner, along with three bullets buried in the body.

On the same Friday evening, that Attorney General Charles McCracken was enjoying some fine dining with his wife and faithful bodyguard, Detective Oscar Campenella was still working late. . ..

"You mean to tell me that right here in an apartment house hallway, a hallway with, ah, let's see, 'bout fifteen apartments up and down the hallway, no one heard gunshots, heard screams of agony, or saw anything? We have a dead man here on the floor, many bullets stuck in him, his fingers cut off and spread all over Hell, blood running all over the floor and until someone finally stumbled upon the body, what appears to be twelve hours or so later and called the police that no one, not one single person, saw or heard anything."

Oscar Campenella spoke while he stood over the dead body of the man, who earlier that same evening, Tony Junior and his men, sent to a different world. Two police officers stood listening to Oscar's questions and rant, while a police photographer snapped picture after picture of the crime scene and a team of crime scene technicians poked around while gathering scientific clues.

One of the officers looked at his partner, shrugged his shoulders and answered, "Most people will not even answer the door when we knock. So far, only three people have been willing to answer the door and speak and all of them say, they did not hear or see anything. Only one guy told me that he thinks the dead guy lived a few doors away and he would occasionally come and visit someone who lived here. That is all that we have."

"Who called in and reported the dead body here in the hallway?" Oscar asked the officers.

The officer who appeared to be taking the lead in the conversation answered, "Anonymous. Called in from a pay phone down the street from here. No one wants anything to do with this scene. They know the guys involved here and these people might be poor, but they ain't stupid. They closed their eyes. We have tried. Dead end. It is a waste of our time."

Oscar shook his head, bent down, and examined the body and scene. "Well, try harder. Expand your search. You need to find someone willing to make a stand. Not every person in this crummy city is under the thumb and on the take with the bad guys. We have nothing to go on. No identification on this guy, no wallet, nothing. No keys to a house, an apartment or a car. We will need medical help to identify him."

Once more, the one police officer looked indifferently at

his partner and it appeared, as if the team of officers were not interested in any further legwork or investigations.

The same officer spoke again, "Okay, detective, but we already checked everyone out here and no one is cooperating. Why should we keep trying? This guy is most likely a bad guy, rubbed out by other bad guys. Same scene, different body and day."

When he heard the officer's words, Detective Oscar Campenella sighed deeply and slowly stood back on his feet. Even the crime scene technicians and the photographer paused when they heard the officer's testimony.

Oscar looked around, shook his head, and said, "Why should you keep trying? Because he is dead, I am a homicide detective and you are police officers. Really? WHAT THE HELL? ARE YOU FRIGGIN' KIDDING ME?" Oscar then mumbled in Spanish, "Qué montón de idiotas."

He waved his hand in disgust and peered in at the officer's name tags and badges.

Oscar then took out his notepad and pen and said while writing down their identification, "Ya know, sumthin'? Forget it. I will take care of this on my own. Go and write parking tickets for the expired meters along the boardwalk. Ya know, do some very important stuff. Dead bodies ain't important to you two. You are both relieved."

Upon hearing Detective Campenella's words, the officers both smiled; actually, they smirked, turned, and walked away. For a brief moment, Oscar thought that he would seek out their sergeant and make a formal complaint. Then, after some additional thought, he decided against it. What for? Once more, where do the bad guys end and the good guys begin? Detective Campenella returned his attention to the body in the hallway and the work of the crime scene technicians who were gathering evidence.

"Whatcha seeing, guys? Anythin'?" Oscar asked as he

leaned into the work.

The lead technician pointed with his examination tool, which was a long steel pointer, and explained, "Lots of stuff here. The doc already pronounced him dead on the scene, but we are already onto lots of evidence here. No cooperating witnesses or patrolmen, but we carry on with our work. My team and I are on your side, Detective Campenella. We gathered the severed fingers up. At least it will be rather easy, but slightly gruesome, to pull prints off of 'em." The lead technician held a clear plastic evidence bag up in the air and pointed at the collection of fingers contained within the bag. He added, "Sorry, but I know you ain't squeamish, detective."

Oscar nodded and patted the technician on the back while telling the team, "Thank you. No, after these past few weeks of checking out dead bodies strewn all over this city, squeamish is the one thing that I am not feeling any longer. I appreciate the assistance and teamwork. Believe me, I do."

The technician nodded and continued, "We need the doc at the medical examiner's office to confirm, but what our team is seeing here is that after chopping off his fingers with a wide-blade knife, they shot him multiple times and we are thinking that he died about twelve hours before we arrived. Despite the number of bullets filling him up, this poor guy, did not die right away. You can see that he rolled around for a bit, in his own blood. The bullets must have taken out a main artery because there is a ton of blood loss. The blood trail here shows that he thrashed around a bit. I have to say that it was a pretty, damn gruesome death."

Oscar nodded and ran his fingers through his thick hair.

With a voice showing signs of compassion at the thoughts of the scene before them, Oscar said, "Shit, I'll say it was gruesome. These guys don't play. Chopping the fingers off is symbolic. It is a warning to the street. The bad guys must feel as if this poor guy stole from them. Despite our efforts, the word will hit the street, not to steal from these assholes."

The technician nodded in agreement, and then he pointed with the steel pointer to a trail of blood on the dead man's coat and on the floor on both sides of the body.

The technician explained, "This is where he thrashed around in agony. See the path of blood?"

Oscar whispered, "I do see that. Yes."

The good detective was not a forensics expert, but he had seen enough dead bodies in his career to understand the evidence. The lead technician continued to explain as the photographer zoomed in for close-up shots of the evidence.

"They shot him from the direction from where you are standing, right now, Detective Campenella. I am no doc, but the angle of the bullets seems to indicate that the killer was standing over him and shot him from about three to five feet away. Interesting to note, Detective Campenella, is that as his blood spilled, the killer or someone else who was standing close had some of the dead man's blood lick out and touch his shoes."

The head technician turned and pointed to the crime scene photographer and asked, "Say, can you please take some close-ups of that faint shoe imprint there on the floor? Will you be able to pick it up? It is just an outline in the blood, but I am sure, it is a man's shoe. Look at the imprint very carefully. See if youse guys agree."

"I agree. I see it too," Oscar agreed, while he carefully studied the imprint from a few different angles and by using his flashlight to illuminate the outline.

The photographer nodded, fished around in his vest and pulled out a different type of lens, and while he mumbled, he said, "Gotta change to a macro lens. I think that I might be able to pick most of it up in the shots. The lighting here sucks but I will do my best."

The photographer took many shots from many angles

and he nodded his head in satisfaction at his confidence that he captured the imprint and evidence that the head technician requested. The crime scene team also worked on the imprint with some type of high-tech plastic sheet, and they carefully worked over the imprint in an effort to gather more evidence on the shoe's makeup and origins. While Detective Oscar Campenella carefully observed the scene and the ongoing work, he made notes on his pad and tried hard to forget the lack of cooperation by the police officers. He knew that he would need to pound some shoe leather on his own to gather any evidence needed. The team wrapped up the work. The 2-way police radios on the crime scene technician's belts crackled with radio chatter and the calls announced the arrival of the coroner's wagon.

"I think that we are done here. We have gathered all we can gather, Detective Campenella. Okay, to move the body to the morgue?" The head technician asked the detective.

"Sure, yes. Thanks for everything. Not much to go on, but we have a little something. Appreciate the effort, and the loyalty, men. I really do. Youse guys are awesome."

The men shook hands; the photographer packed up his gear and left after explaining to the detective when the photographs would be available.

"Youse guys can leave. Since I am the detective investigating the case, I will stay and sign off on the transport of the body. Thanks again."

Oscar stood and watched the body loaded and when he had taken care of the paperwork, and the coroner's team had moved the body out and they were on the way to the morgue. The detective stood in the hallway for quite some time. Not one resident opened their doors. He could hear radios and televisions playing behind closed doors in the various apartments, but not a single person even peeked out their doors with the slightest curiosity as to what happened in the hallway of their home. Not even the maintenance person or superintendent for the building made an appearance. No one. Who has this entire neighborhood, and in fact, what seems to be all of Clinton City under their control? As Oscar slowly tapped on doors, and he announced that the police were requesting any information on the murder, he knew the answer. Between the, "Go away, I did not see or hear anything" shouts from behind the doors, to the silence from behind the others, he knew.

Tony Michanetti Junior.

That was the only name that he needed to know.

Despite working the hallways and knocking on every door, the detective could not find any residents to cooperate with the investigation or even speak to him, and he thought for a moment about contacting the uncooperative police officers. Oscar had a thought that he wanted to question them some more as to which resident gave them the information about the dead man visiting someone who lived in the apartment, but he quickly dismissed the idea. Since he was still fuming at their indifferent attitudes, Oscar decided against speaking with them right now, and instead, he headed for the main lobby of the apartment and decided to call it the end of the day. Another long, long day. His only hope now was the conversation he had a few days earlier with Attorney General Charles McCracken, and his promise to investigate what was going on here in Clinton City, both behind the scenes and on the front lines too. Oscar was curious as to whom or what, the help consisted of that the attorney general promised to him.

Just as he descended the main staircase and turned to leave out the front door, Oscar Campenella stopped as the front door of the apartment house opened and a man walked in and stood in front of Detective Campenella. Not an ordinary man, but one of the largest men that the detective had ever seen. Oscar stopped in his tracks and for reassurance; he tapped the top of his suit jacket to ensure that his service weapon remained tucked in the shoulder holster under the jacket. The man walked in and closed the door gently behind him while he stopped and intently stared at the detective. He was a very tall, lean, yet very powerfully built man, standing there in front of the detective, and he showed no emotion, nor did he say anything. The man standing in the vestibule of the apartment house was dressed all in black. He wore a black vest, covering a perfectly pressed, black buttoned-up shirt, and his sharply creased, black trousers had no ripples or wrinkles. On his head, he wore a wide-brimmed black hat and on his feet, he wore highly polished black boots. His attire was immaculate. Nothing was out of place on the man; even the hair on his head that Oscar could see from under the wide-brimmed hat was perfectly groomed, trimmed neatly and clean along the edges. His face sported a black beard and full facial hair and once again, it was neat, clean, and trim. His eyes were black. Dark and piercing eyes that sent shivers down the detective's spine. Detective Oscar Campenella did not exactly know what to make of the huge man who was presently standing in front of him. It was difficult for the good detective to assess the situation and all he could think of was the old battle cry of "Friend or foe?" Oscar was a brave and courageous man, who prided his honor on not running from anyone or anything, but the sight of this immense man dressed as if he arrived from another time, place, and era, unnerved Oscar a bit more than he wanted to admit.

Recovering from his swoon, Oscar suddenly had a thought that perhaps he needed to do his job and this stranger in black might live here or know something of interest to the detective's new case. Even though his attire seemed to place the stranger slightly out of date, there was no doubt that this stranger wore fine and expensive clothes. He seemed too well dressed to live in such a run-down building, but you never know. Regardless, it was time to do his job.

While he reached for his wallet and displayed his detective badge to the stranger, Oscar said, "Say, hello, there, amigo. I am Detective Oscar Campenella of the Clinton City Police Department. Do you live here? You see, there has been an unfortunate incident here today, and I was wondering. . .."

The detective stopped speaking as the stranger took a few steps closer to him and continued with his piercing stare. The stranger stopped. He reached into one of the pockets of his vest, and the detective paused and once more, Detective Campenella's hand reached across his chest and Oscar stood poised to draw his service revolver out of his shoulder holster. The detective eased back from his defensive posture when he saw that the strange man dressed in black, pulled out some small pieces of what appeared to be broken pieces of red plastic, he then held out his hand and nodded his head to Detective Campenella to indicate that he should take the pieces of broken plastic. Now, the detective fully relaxed, as he felt as if this immense and quiet stranger was an ally.

There was now an answer to the friend or foe's question.

Friend.

Oscar was sure of it.

This was someone who arrived out of the midst of the madness of what Clinton City had become, who just might be on his side. Oscar took the pieces from the quiet stranger, and he carefully studied the pieces. It was easy to see that the broken pieces of plastic were from the taillight of a vehicle. Still, the ominous stranger did not speak, but he continued to stare at Detective Campenella.

"A broken taillight with pieces from a car or truck, huh? I guess you found this somewhere close by. Sir, do you know something about what happened here today? Do you have any identification?"

The quiet stranger ignored the detective's questions. He

pointed first to the plastic pieces in Oscar's hand, and then to the outside world.

He finally spoke; his voice resonated in a deep melodious tone, in a voice of authority, "A short walk from here. Next to the Chinese restaurant is an alley. The trash dumpster on the side of the restaurant has evidence that will tie those pieces in your hand to a vehicle. Find the vehicle and find the shoe that made the imprint in the hallway and you will be on to someone. You also need to find the dead man's brother. Quickly, or he will be the next victim. You have a long road in front of you. You will succeed. However, be very careful, Detective Campenella. This all runs deep and evil. You will encounter evil people who will stop at nothing to control what they perceive to be their world. That dead man was a good guy. Circumstances forced him into a situation, but he planned to help. He was going to turn the tide in your favor with some evidence. You need to unlock his secrets. You are a very smart man. A man of great honor, you must not falter, and you must stay the course. This old city and many good people are counting on you. I am counting on you too and please keep in mind that I only partner with the best of the best."

With that, the stranger tipped his hat, smiled, and turned to walk away. His boots made a sharp clicking noise when they hit the floor, and it was then that Oscar noticed that his boots had metal clips on the bottoms of them. Clips that sounded the coming and going of the dark stranger in a very distinctive manner.

"Hey, wait! C'mon, pal, you need to show me some identification. I *am* the police around here, and I just asked you for your credentials. You need to listen to me. Please, thanks for the tips and words of encouragement and the inside scoop, but whom the hell, are you? It is obvious that you know a great deal about all of this. Ya just can't tell me bits and pieces and then tail ass out of here. I am the police!

So, once more, who the hell are you?"

The stranger stopped, turned, and spoke once again, "I am a friend of Attorney General Charles McCracken. Call him and tell him that you met me and that I told you that I despise crooks, connivers, chiselers, and thieves. He will explain. He is sending you help. Sending you a good man, a man beyond reproach, and a man, of immense strength. A man, who has stared many times into the faces of evil and a man who always wins. He is a man of enormous courage and you two will make an excellent team. As far as my identification, I am whoever you want me to be, and Charles tells you that I am. My allowance for intervention can be, at times, somewhat limited, but always remember that I am out here. In the shadows, watching and waiting for the right moment. Detective, please, hold on to your hope throughout the darkest of nights and days, because I can assure you that in the end, good will always conquer the evil. There are still more of us than there are of them. You are not alone. Ever."

Once more, he smiled, tipped his hat, and disappeared into the night air. Detective Oscar Campenella did not answer the stranger, nor did he press him for any more information. Once the stranger mentioned Attorney General Charles McCracken, then despite the mystery of the strange encounter, Oscar knew that this dark stranger was indeed on their side and he was part of the team. A strange part, indeed, but he just might be the most important part of them all.

Oscar mumbled under his breath while repeating the stranger's motto of a statement, "Love that he despises crooks, connivers, chiselers, and thieves. Love that, because I despise them too."

Oscar then smiled. He stood, watched, and listened until he could no longer see the stranger or hear the clicks of the metal tips of his boots striking the pavement.

Chapter 3

Tilting the Odds

Detective Oscar Campenella did follow the instructions of the quiet stranger in the black hat and he found the dumpster in exactly the location that the stranger told him he would find it. He also found additional plastic pieces on the ground from what were obviously remnants of damage to the rear taillight of a car. Oscar also found evidence that a vehicle must have struck the side of the dumpster, due to the distinct mark from black paint on the side of the trash dumpster.

"Okay," Oscar mumbled aloud, while studying the paint mark carefully, "this is something to go on. Looks as if some driver was mighty nervous about getting the hell outta here as quickly as possible. The dumb-ass backed into the dumpster."

After some careful study from numerous angles, the detective confirmed in his mind that the accident occurred when the vehicle backed down the alley in haste in order to make a quick getaway after the murder. A vehicle that the perpetrators and the murderer used to escape the scene of the crime. Oscar made a quick call and dispatched the crime scene team to the scene.

After gathering the evidence and returning to the crime lab, the team assured Detective Campenella that they would have some identification and additional information within a few hours.

Oscar was at home relaxing while this incredibly long

day finally wound down when the phone call arrived. The forensics team was able to determine make, model, and year of the vehicle from not only the pieces of the broken taillight, but also from paint samples extracted from the trash dumpster. They were looking for a newer model black Galaxy 5000 vehicle, which was a luxury sedan and a vehicle of choice for many of the organized mobsters currently roaming Clinton City.

Now, in the words of the quiet stranger in the black hat to Detective Campenella, he needed to find the vehicle, as well as the shoe with the traces of blood on it from the victim. Oh yes, and the brother too.

Easier said than done.

Chances are that the car already had repairs performed to it and the shoe, well, that might be long gone too.

By Saturday morning, the reports filtered into the hands and the mind of Detective Oscar Campenella. The good detective was now hot on the trail and his blood boiled with the thought of the wave of crime, and now, cold-blooded murder that currently enveloped Clinton City.

In *his* city.

On *his* watch.

Right down to his very soul, through his inherited genes, there was no doubt that Oscar was a detective. A homicide detective. The bad guys were in for a rude awakening, because Detective Oscar Campenella was fearless, and above all, he was exceptionally good at his job. In the words of the mysterious stranger, Oscar was the "Best of the best."

The medical examiner determined the identity of the murder victim from medical and dental records as well as fingerprints and records from his previous criminal activity. The victim, Mr. Robert Mercurio, was a young man who had a troubled past as a youth, but in recent years, he remained out of trouble. His previous criminal records were older now, from his late teen-age years and as of late, it seemed as if he turned his life around. He had a full-time job at the famous resort and hotel on the shoreline and the far outskirts of Clinton City, Casa Al Mare, and he lived what appeared to be a quiet life. His apartment was a short distance away from the apartment where he met his demise. Unfortunately, by the time that Detective Campenella obtained a search warrant (Oscar felt as if his chain of command purposely stalled on the paperwork to allow the thugs access first) and he arrived with his forensics team to check out the apartment, the crime scene investigation team found it already ransacked and combed through. Someone beat them to it and Oscar knew that whoever killed Robert Mercurio had been there first and they were looking for something. Truthfully, there was very little in the way of anything in the apartment. Mr. Mercurio lived a modest life. His parents were both dead, no girlfriends, no pets, no evidence. He was a guy who appeared to live a low profile; he went to work and came home to a quiet life. A quiet life that ended violently.

Of course, no one in the adjoining apartments knew anything, or if they did, they told no tales. But one thing that Oscar Campenella confirmed was the testimony of the mysterious stranger in black because the stranger was correct in all of his statements. Not that Oscar was going to doubt anything that the stranger in black told him then or hereafter. Oscar needed to call Attorney General McCracken and report his encounter with the stranger, but right now, Oscar felt as if he needed to obtain some more details and be in a better position to report them to his superior.

Indeed, in keeping true to the testimony of the stranger in black, Robert Mercurio had a brother named Kenneth. He too worked at Casa Al Mare and while he did not live with his brother in the apartment, they did apparently work together. Oscar knew that if the killer or killers knew of the relation, then chances were very high that whoever murdered Robert for whatever he did, or had his apartment ransacked over in search of, then they also knew of Kenneth's relationship to Robert. It might be a very dangerous world for Kenneth Mercurio right now, and Oscar was determined to find him before someone else did.

The good detective took Sunday off. The Campenella family attended church services together and then they shared their usual Sunday family meal and gathering. His family needed to see him, and his mind and body required rest. Besides, there was not too much more to go on right now, and he did not want to conduct business on a Sunday unless he really had to.

Oscar was going to need God on his side for this one. Perhaps God was already there.

On Monday morning, Detective Campenella found a pay phone in a remote end of the city and he dialed the number of the New Jersey Attorney General's office. The good detective had a feeling that using anything other than a remote pay phone was too high of a risk. At this point, Oscar trusted very few people, and he was taking all precautions. Oscar spoke with Attorney General Charles "Chuck" McCracken on the telephone. Oscar told Chuck about the latest murder and about his strange encounter with the quiet stranger in the black hat and while Chuck remained mum on whom or what the mysterious stranger is, or might be, the cagey old attorney general assured Detective Campenella that above all, the stranger was a good guy. In fact, Chuck McCracken testified how he was not surprised that his strange friend made an appearance in Clinton City and was apparently tracking the criminal activity going on there.

Chuck explained, "He always shows up when we and the rest of the world need him the most."

"That is nice to know, Attorney General McCracken. I can testify that he showed up at the right time the other day. I had nothing to go on at all and now, well, I have a little something to track down. The stranger told me that his allowance for intervention is limited. What does that mean, sir? Whom does he answer to?"

"I dunno and I dunno. He told me the same thing, and then a few weeks later, Tony Michanetti Senior disappeared from the scene. Honestly, I just dunno."

Oscar was shocked, and he did not hesitate to ask Chuck, "You think the stranger had something to do with the disappearance of Tony Senior?"

"Look, Oscar, let's not get off in the weeds here. You need to cool your jets a bit. The stranger is exactly who he is and says he is. He is our friend and ally and whomever we think, he is. All I know is that as weird as it all is, if the stranger is there, he is there for a good reason. Most of all you have to understand that the stranger is there to help us."

Chuck paused and spoke again because he could tell that Oscar had shelved his overzealous mannerisms and he was listening, "Look, Oscar, from here on in, ya gotta trust no one other than anyone from my office, Chuck McCracken, the man that is heading your way to help you, and the quiet stranger in the black hat. No one else. If the stranger tells you to do something, even if it contradicts my orders, do it. Without hesitation, do it. I have my covert task force assigned to investigate your top brass there in the department, and let me tell you that they have already discovered enough for me to continue the investigation. Your hunch and your father's hunches were right on there. Some of their bank accounts have an awful lot of dough in them for police officers, and the mayor and his council, well, it is not looking too good for them either. It seems as if they all have very lucrative part-time jobs. Who is this Lieutenant Davis character to you?"

"Well, he is my chain of command. That is ultimately the officer that I report to as you go up the ladder."

"Gotcha. That really sucks. Okay. Oscar, I have to tell

you that his bank account is particularly overflowing, and he has some cash hidden away overseas too. He has a vacation house in Florida that would make a movie star proud. He earns a nice salary as a lieutenant, but not that generous. Be careful of that clown until my task force can sniff out some more on his activities. Keep your chain of command satisfied, but do not tell them jack shit of what you are actually doing. Write generic reports full of bullshit. Write reports that show dead end after dead end on all the cases. Act as if you are some stumble-ass, loser, detective that cannot even tie your shoes. Come up with a cover story. The job is getting to you and you are lost . . . drink too much . . . wife is driving you nuts. You know, whip up bullshit with all the usual cop troubles. Make out as if all this personal burden has made you clueless. Not sure how deep this all is, but it is deep. Do you understand me, Detective Campenella?"

"I do. I understand, sir. You can count on me."

"I know that I can. Your old man was the best and I know that he trained his son to be the best, too. The man that is coming down to help you will be on unofficial, but official, business. His name is Jimmy Reeves, and he is my bodyguard and assistant. There is no braver man in this world. He is a retired United States Marine, from the hood of the north end of Paterson city. Every bad guy's worst nightmare. Jimmy is the ultimate badass. A Marine, born and raised in the hood who just so happens to be a good guy. He is a sharpshooter. A sniper. A trained assassin who spent time in the thick of some badass shit-storms. Seventeen combat kills. Seventeen enemy officers confirmed as kills, but who the hell knows how many he really nailed. No one is sayin' and dead men do not speak very well. He will protect you and watch your back. He is very smart and he can help you with clues and gathering of information. Jimmy has worked with me forever and he knows what to look for. You will make an excellent team."

Oscar laughed and told Chuck, "That is exactly what the stranger said. He told me that we will make an excellent team."

Chuck paused, and he laughed too. The humor of Charles "Chuck," McCracken helped Chuck to keep going, and it was always present, "See, we think alike. I will celebrate that fact with another double Scotch. Neat. I need to puff on a few cancer sticks, too. After I take a few sips of this glorious mixture of liquid, I have to find my wife and squeeze her gorgeous ass, too. I am working from my home office today for a good reason."

With a smile on his lips and a chuckle in his voice, Oscar admired the crude mannerisms and words, yet the amazing personality of Chuck McCracken.

Oscar recovered and said, "Works for me, Attorney General McCracken. Works for me. When will Jimmy be here and where do we meet?"

"He is rolling there right now. He will stop along the way, call you, and work out a plan. Just remember that he is now Jimmy O'Shaughnessy. Forget the Reeves name. You need to remember his new identity. Jimmy knows how to work the angles. He has a fancy sports car and a new identity. And weapons and a variety of gizmos and gadgets. Lots of tricks these crooks never seen before and lots of cool weapons. He is a walkin' weapon of good, but 'member, he is the ultimate badass. He is going to try to blend. His mission will be to pretend as if he is just another high roller, wealthy and conceited jackass, looking for high-end prostitutes, and whatever the hell else, goes on in that fancy joint on the ocean there on the far end of the city. Casa ah bullshit, or whatever the name of it is. That is a front joint for Tony Junior. I am sure that he uses that dump for connections and washes the money that he makes illegally through the books of that dump. It smells like organized crime and Jimmy will sniff it all out. That is where we need to focus. Jimmy will check in there and you two can make the connection. Very carefully, Oscar. Very covertly and carefully."

"I understand, and you are correct. The murder victim, Robert Mercurio and his missing brother both worked at Casa Al Mare. That was the next stop on my investigation."

"Good, just be careful and keep your head on a swivel. The brother is missing, huh? Sounds as if the dead brother might have taken the bullets for his brother. Didn't the quiet stranger tell you that the dead man was a good guy?"

"He did, yes, he did."

"Okay, well then, ya have to find the missing brother, before Tony Junior does, Oscar. It is a race. Chances are that whatever these brothers were involved in, you and Tony Junior, are on the same path to find out. Beat him there or you will have more dead bodies to deal with. Good luck. Jimmy will contact you later this morning."

"Thank you, sir. Thank you. This, Jimmy Reeves, or O'Shaughnessy, I gather that he is not a sworn police officer, or a sworn law enforcement official of some rank? He is working as an informant?"

Chuck paused and laughed once more, "As I said before, don't go gettin' hung out in the weeds, Oscar. No. Jimmy has no law enforcement badge pinned on his ass. I deputized his ass. But it ain't official. Yet Jimmy has sumthin' a lot better. Jimmy has a badge of honor. He swore a long time ago, to his own honor, to the honor of the people and our country's honor and yours and mine too. And to the stranger's honor. Always remember the honor. He is simply on a planned vacation. I ordered him to take a few days off and he chose that fancy dump by the ocean for his vacation. Repeat after me, it is a vacation. Please understand that Jimmy has a license to kill. He earned it in places that we can never even dream of, by wadin' through horrible shit, which no one wants to talk 'bout. You are dealin' with very bad people that do not play by the rules. Sometimes, when you deal with evil bastards, you have to bend the rules, even the score, and tilt the odds in your favor. Guys like Jimmy Reeves and the dark stranger overwhelmingly tilt the odds over to the good guys. One more thing, Oscar. It was very smart thinking on your part to call from a pay phone. Feed the hungry sons-of-bitches coins, but stay low and keep ya powder dry. No smartphone and email or texting nonsense. From now on, only call me from pay telephones. Not your home phone, not your dad's phone, and never from your office phones. Trust no one and nothing unless we all agree it is secure. Do you understand?"

"I understand. Mostly, I assure you that I understand that Jimmy is on a vacation. No more hanging out in the weeds and being stuck hanging on the official rules. I promise."

Chuck sighed. He was not too sure that he had fully convinced Oscar, and after a slight pause, he rolled the dice and decided to show some faith in the young detective.

Chuck told Detective Campenella, "Good work. Now, I have to go and find the wife and that double Scotch. Neat."

"It is only ten in the morning, sir."

"Exactly. I am late. Overdue for Scotch and for lovin'. Besides, I need to soften the blows of this screwed-up world cuz I despise crooks, connivers, chiselers, and thieves. Keep me posted and be careful. Keep ya head on a swivel. Always."

"Click." The line went dead.

Oscar smiled widely because he had heard that line before, and he knew that he was in good hands. The young detective enjoyed speaking with Attorney General Charles "Chuck" McCracken. No nonsense, hard-boiled, hard drinking, chain-smoking, but just as his father told him, there was no better or more honest man on the face of the Earth.

Mr. James "Jimmy" Reeves, or as he was now known as, "James O'Shaughnessy," pulled up to the front entrance of the exclusive Casa Al Mare Hotel and Resort. He gunned the engine a little to navigate the hilly driveway, and the big engine of his sports car revved and increased in RPM. Jimmy shifted the car's manual transmission into a lower gear and the engine roared into a deep throttle, turning the heads of all the bystanders hanging out in front of the hotel. Chuck had fixed Jimmy up to the maximum. Jimmy drove a brand-new, foreign-made, black, two-door sport coupe with all the options and a special license plate hanging upon it. "J.O.S.1" stamped on a New Jersey plate and the new plate matched the new identity that Jimmy required to blend into the mix of other high rollers.

Phony or otherwise.

Even inside the car and from behind the windshield, glints of sunlight reflected off Jimmy's dark sunglasses, immediately enhancing and establishing his "ultimate cool" appearance. Jimmy dressed all in black, with a black suit, black shirt and tie, shiny black boots, and in a place used to high rollers and fancy guys driving sports cars—Jimmy hoped that he fit the bill. Jimmy stopped the sports car under the portico entrance of the hotel and watched as a team of young men working as valets sprinted out to meet and greet him. Jimmy also watched a tall man, an older man, watching his grand entrance from a dark location next to the parking station. The tall man wore a black suit too, and he had the look that Jimmy knew so well.

This guy was the forward watch of the "operation."

Above the forward watch and his post were two security cameras and Jimmy's eyes took notice of three more cameras mounted in strategic locations in and around the front entrance. Even the forward watch had a set of back-up eyeballs. As he shut off the engine, Jimmy reached down to his ankle and confirmed the presence of his trusty knife, strapped in a black leather sheath in its familiar place under his pants and above his boots. The knife was the standard issue, make and model knife in the Marine Corps, with "Jimmy Reeves" custom modifications.

Chuck convinced Jimmy to trade his usual jump boots in for a fancy pair of side-zip military boots in an attempt to, as Chuck told him, "Not to be a complete fish outta water, Jimmy."

Jimmy agreed, but his comfort level was off just a bit. Under his fancy black suit, his shirt and tie, and for old time's sake, his dog tags hung around his neck. Once a Marine, always a Marine, but the dog tags and chain had a dual purpose. Concealed inside another small holder hanging from the same chain was a small, custom-made knife. It was small, but sharper than the finest razor and the blade tucked neatly in the smallest of sheaths. This knife was a backup that Jimmy used many times in hand-to-hand combat, as the last line in defense, a concealed knife, hung in the last place that an enemy would think of a knife to appear from during the heat of battle. The rest of his weapons and gear, Jimmy carefully packed inside of his luggage. His sea bags and duffels, now, traded in for fancy, high-end luggage. Jimmy Reeves, with some help from his boss in a very high place, now magically transformed into Jimmy O'Shaughnessy. Mr. O'Shaughnessy, the son of wealthy Irish parents who established a dye factory business in the once thriving Paterson, New Jersey, clothing and garment industry. Now that his parents were both dead, and the factories all sold and the wealth banked, Jimmy lived the life of a handsome and dashing playboy. Here he was, arriving at the historic Casa Al Mare for a week of fun in the sun, mixed in with fine booze, fast and hard living and fine women.

Now Jimmy Reeves simply needed to believe it and play the part.

"Welcome to Casa Al Mare, sir. Ah, Mister, ah. . .." A young man working as a parking valet smiled at Jimmy as he greeted him next to the sports car.

"O'Shaughnessy is the name. But, hey, youse guys just call me, Jimmy. Okay?" Jimmy said, while he opened the door and the young man stood back at the sight of the large, imposing and muscular Jimmy O'Shaughnessy. With a quick toss, Jimmy tossed the valet the keys to the car. The valet caught the keys in midair and smiled.

"Okay, very cool, Jimmy. I am Teddy. I am the Head Valet, during the day shift. My brother, Michael, takes over for me during the night shift. He and I are a team, and we will take good care of you and your car, too. Nice ride, love the black color and the black and silver interior. Brand-new, right?"

"It is. First real roll for it. I drove down from north Jersey today. I have two of 'em. One black one and one silver one. Please, do take care of the wheels, and here, you are on my payroll now. I will take care of your brother later. I like teams."

Jimmy peeled off a fifty-dollar bill and tucked it in the top pocket of the valet's suit jacket.

"Wow! Fifty bucks, huh? Thanks, Jimmy, and man, I gotta say that, damn, you are one big, strong lookin' dude."

"It ain't just a look, Teddy. It is real. Very, very real."

Teddy smiled and nodded while scanning Jimmy's physique and acknowledging his presence, and then asked, "Can I pop the trunk and my team, grab your luggage? We will bring it to your room."

Jimmy kept his dark sunglasses on in order to avoid the forward watch or anyone else from following his eyes. He paused for just a moment, knowing full well the arsenal of weapons, as well as the various gizmos and gadgets that he packed for the trip. In Jimmy's line of work, you did not travel light. He needed to be careful here, not to risk anything or cause any early alerts, but he knew that those weapons and assorted devices could not leave his sight. Jimmy's eyes darted over to the man standing as the forward watchman and the man stood stoically, watching the scene unfold.

Two minutes into the adventure and already Jimmy faced the first test. . ..

Luckily, Jimmy Reeves packed two bags, and he had some foresight too. The smaller bag contained the covert items and the weapons, too.

"Ah, yeah, sure, Teddy. Take the large bag, the smaller bag ya gotta leave that one, because it has my identification and my credit cards in there. Need them to check in."

Teddy nodded in understanding. Valets joined Teddy in unloading the luggage, and the team of valets had the trunk opened already.

Jimmy moved over there quickly and grabbed the handles of the smaller bag while planting a diversionary tactic, "Say, Teddy, I know that it is still early in the day, only ten in the morning or so, but please tell me that you have restaurants and especially, some bars open inside of here. Been a very long drive."

Teddy smiled widely and without any hesitation he answered, "Sure thing, Jimmy. We have three full-scale restaurants all serving the finest foods and all of them are equipped with lounges and bars. However, we also have three exclusive bars and lounges. They never close, except from three to eight in the morning and even those hours, for da right price and for a guy like ya, if ya know what I mean, are negotiable. Honestly, that is where ya want to be. Ya can get some bar food and wow, the chicks that hang out there. Man, ya gonna break some hearts and score big time, here, Jimmy. The muscles, the look, the car. Ya are gonna love it here at Casa Al Mare."

It appeared as if Teddy rather easily fell for the disguise of Jimmy Reeves because he showed his motives and "side job" right away. It was obvious to Jimmy that Teddy, his brother and his team, were the first to feed info and intelligence on suckers checking into Casa Al Mare. The valet team and the forward watch planted the initial seeds. From there on in, the rest of the operation preyed upon the wallets and the bank accounts of these rich stiffs.

"Say, there, ah, Jimmy, if you are looking for some stuff, you know, other than booze to pass the night away on the wild side with, be sure to come see us. My brother or me. If you know what I mean. If you need a plug."

Jimmy thought, 'Ah yes, and a little drug trafficking too. What a bunch of amateur losers playing tough guys. They played their hand and showed their cards right away.'

Jimmy smiled, lifted the bag with the hidden tools of Jimmy's trade packed inside and the big man patted the young valet on the back while saying, "I knew you were the man. I usually stick with my top-shelf Scotch, but I will keep that in mind. Please bring that larger bag to my room and I will check in at the desk. If it comes down to what I need, please know that I will hit ya up and be sure to take care of you for the effort."

"Sure thing, Jimmy!"

As Jimmy O'Shaughnessy carried his bag and followed the team of valets into the fabulously elegant front entrance of Casa Al Mare, the man standing watch at the front door stared at Jimmy and nodded.

Jimmy nodded back and the forward watch whispered to Jimmy, while he passed by, "Nice wheels, big man."

"Thanks," Jimmy answered.

While he walked by the man, Jimmy held back a little smile and even a bit of laughter. He thought how he knew they would meet again under different circumstances; he could tell. He knew it and the fancy ride would not matter then. Oh no, Jimmy knew that the ride would not matter at all.

You could use the word elegant to describe Casa Al Mare, but chances are that it will be a description that is vastly understated. The words, opulent, ornate, and exotic, might work a bit better, but suffice it to say that Casa Al Mare overflowed with the best of everything. Marble floors, crystal and gold chandeliers, elaborate statues and flower vases filled with not only freshly cut flowers but also the vases, which held the flowers, were cast out of gold and silver.

Casa Al Mare was at one time, in an era long since passed, the mansion home of an extremely wealthy man. A man whose family made a fortune in the railroad business and after searching for the perfect place to build their retreat home, the family selected this tip of the marvelous seacoast of New Jersey to build their elaborate mansion. After years and years of serving as the family home, with the home passed from generation to generation within the same family, the home eventually ran its course, and the family sold the mansion to an investor. An investor who saw the potential for the mansion to receive an expansion to accommodate numerous hotel rooms and to turn it into a world-class resort and retreat. After all, in real estate it always comes down to the location, and the mansion and property sat proudly on a sandy cliff, overlooking a gorgeous ocean view, and it sat on the furthermost point of the edges of Clinton City.

Now, many years later and after many expansions, adjoining land acquisitions, construction projects, and alterations, the hotel and resort boasted the best of everything, from tennis courts, to luxurious spas, to world-class fitness centers, to the many fine restaurants contained within, along with the famous cocktail lounges. As far as the hotel rooms went, they all seemed as if they had golden trim and golden linings.

Literally.

The best of everything is a perfect description. Marble-tiled showers and bathtubs with golden fixtures, deep pile carpets and rooms equipped with wet-bars stocked with top-shelf liquors, beer, and wine.

Despite the pressure and stigma associated with the decline of the surrounding area combined with the collapse of the once bustling casino business of Clinton City, the resort remained a shining star along the New Jersey shoreline.

A shining star, hiding a dark interior full of evil and deceit.

The rumors swirled over the resort that a recent sale of the facilities and properties was to investors, heavily rooted in New Jersey's legendary affiliation with organized crime members and the resort now served as a front, and "home base" for mobsters, but the fact remained that whoever the owners were, the property remained a world-class property. The hotel and resort attracted visitors from far and wide, from Canadians seeking escape from the land of ice and snow to the sandy beaches of New Jersey, to visitors from California to Maine and some Europeans seeking a fine resort and hotel for an authentic American adventure.

The main facility towered above the ocean in expansive glory. Floors and floors of stacked and glorious white wooden clapboard towered into the sky, dotted here and there with the windows of the various hotel rooms, combined with balconies and ledges for visitors to enjoy the glorious views of the oceanfront. Proudly perched on the highest point of a tower of the main facility flew an American flag. Waving proudly and elegantly, the flag announced the freedoms that it stood for, in such a breathtaking manner that it was hard to imagine that such a glorious symbol of honor, actually masked the elements of dishonor and the danger hidden deep within the bowels of this remarkable resort and property.

"Welcome to the world-famous, Casa Al Mare resort and hotel. Are you checking in, sir? Please, sir, your name."

"James O'Shaughnessy is the name. Yup, I am checkin'

in today," Jimmy proudly and effortlessly announced to the desk clerk, who was working the front desk in the lobby of Casa Al Mare. "House by the sea," Jimmy added with a gentle laugh.

"Yes. That is correct. Do you speak Italian, Mr. O'Shaughnessy?"

"Nah, hell, no. Do I sound as if I do? Nah, I only speak, New Jersey. Some guy that I know told me what it means in Italian."

The desk clerk smiled, laughed, and said, "I see. Interesting language choice."

The desk clerk was a short, very attractive young woman who had broken away from a group of desk clerks that she was chatting with in order to serve Jimmy. No doubt, his handsome appearance caught her eye, because her face lit up at the sight of Jimmy and the young woman rather willingly broke away from the group in an effort to serve Jimmy first. Jimmy immediately admired her incredible attractiveness. Short brown hair, diminutive, white gold hoop earrings, wide, doe-like green eyes, and a perfect smile. Jimmy's eyes wandered about her shapely figure and even in the uniform of the hotel, her amazing figure inspired visions of grandeur within the hardened bodyguard's heart. This was an extremely attractive young woman and her stunning beauty, as well as the impact of meeting her, had an immediate and profound influence upon the previously impenetrable heart of Jimmy "O'Shaughnessy" Reeves.

"Hello, Mr. O'Shaughnessy. I am, Vanessa, and it is my pleasure. . .."

"I see that on your nametag there. Ya gotta have a last name too, right?" Jimmy cut the young woman off as he pointed to the nametag on her uniform.

Vanessa laughed and her face turned a little red, as she first turned and checked on the awareness of her fellow desk clerks, then she leaned in and said in a low whisper,

"Yes, of course, Vanessa Michaelson. I know that the greeting is somewhat dumb. Isn't it stupid? It is a silly canned speech that the management tells us that we have to say."

"I don't see how anything but gorgeous words could ever come out of such a glorious mouth as yours is," Jimmy answered with a wink and a lean and tilt of his head.

Before Vanessa could request his identification and payment options, Jimmy presented them to her, along with a seductive and coy smile. Jimmy was working the angle of the rich and dashing playboy right from the get-go. He knew the first few minutes here were critical to the success of his mission. There was little doubt that the word of his arrival would spread as if it was a fire within the workers at the resort. Especially female workers.

"Who is that rich, good-looking stranger? Did you see his muscles, his car, and the wad of bills he flashed?"

From the front-line of the valid workers and with the help of the valet team, the word of Jimmy's arrival and presence would work its way into the not so valid workers. From here on in, this all was going to be a dangerous game. Yet, Jimmy was just as his boss was because they both possessed an uncanny sense of criminal activity and of enemies. Right now, Jimmy knew what this fancy joint actually was. A front for crime. Jimmy knew it as soon as he pulled in front of the building, he smelled the evil, the criminal odor. It was here, hidden behind ornate displays of opulence. Jimmy knew how this had to go down and he planted the seeds along the way to produce the smokescreen that he needed.

Vanessa glanced at the identification and credit cards that Jimmy presented to her. The driver's license that Chuck McCracken produced for Jimmy would easily pass as authentic with anyone. It was a perfect replica of an authentic New Jersey driver's license.

Vanessa smiled, swiped the credit card through the

reader, and asked Jimmy, "Mr. O'Shaughnessy, we have you staying for a week. Am I correct?"

"It is, might extend it a little. 'Pends on da action. Say, just call me, Jimmy. After all, I am calling you, Vanessa. Right? I am losing the Michaelson right now." She smiled again and returned the credit card and identification to Jimmy.

"Certainly. Jimmy, it is then. Action, huh? Oh, no doubt, if I think I am correct in interpreting your definition of what action is then I think you will find your stay enjoyable, Jimmy."

Jimmy thought, 'Oh, baby, you actually have no idea of what action is to me.'

He quickly shifted gears.

"Maybe, we can hang out together, Vanessa. I will be at one of the bars. Please, come and find me after your shift ends."

She smiled again and winked, "Officially, we are not supposed to fraternize with our guests, but unofficially, I know the right person to ask beforehand. I will keep your invitation in mind." Vanessa held an ink pen in the air and explained, "This will just take me a minute to prepare these papers. You need to sign for the room and such."

Jimmy nodded and smiled while mumbling, "Ok. I am in no hurry. I can hang here and stare at you for a little. Ya, a gorgeous gal for sure. Yes, ask the questions first and get the permission. I do not want you to be in any trouble."

While Vanessa moved to a different post to work on the papers, Jimmy leaned on the counter and thought, 'Shit, he was really turning this phony act on to a full-speed.'

Jimmy still wore his dark sunglasses, and he never lifted them from over his eyes. The lobby was very bright, and the day remained perfectly clear, with bright sunshine. Therefore, wearing the sunglasses even while inside, seemed to work for not only enhancing Jimmy's smooth image but it also did not seem out of the norm. As Jimmy leaned on the counter, he carefully studied the lobby and the surroundings. In his military-trained mind, Jimmy captured every detail for use later on, when and if there was little time for studying. Jimmy's eyes floated around the area taking in all of the features and details, from a high ceiling in the lobby, leading to skylights, what appeared to be a wine room and wine cellar entrance, a bar and lounge directly across from the lobby desk. A few patrons already sat on bar stools, with a black suited bartender leaning in and working the early crowd. Jimmy noticed what appeared to be a hallway off the main lobby and the signage posted there revealed that the hallway led to conference rooms and large banquet rooms. No doubt, gatherings here must cost a small fortune to hold, a wedding might bankrupt a small city's yearly budget. Jimmy could not even imagine how much money floated through this joint. The lobby was the same as the front entrance was, loaded with security cameras. Cameras that pointed in every direction and covered every inch of the lobby and beyond. Jimmy noticed a small store, or what Jimmy thought was a gift store, tucked over in the corner of the lobby.

While Vanessa still fiddled with papers and such, Jimmy wandered over in the direction of the store. For the first time since he entered the building, Jimmy lifted his sunglasses off his eyes and perched them atop his head. There were no lights on inside the small storefront and the small sign on the door stated, "Closed" in block letters. From the display in the small window, Jimmy could see that the store sold various tourist type items, some collectibles, along with convenience supplies such as suntan lotions, toiletries, sunglasses and other items often forgotten or required when on a vacation holiday. There also was a display of fine cigars, fine wine glasses and liquor glasses and champagne glasses. Everything required for a fine celebration while visiting the resort. The display was very tasteful. Jimmy could see that in addition to some essential and convenience items required for travel, this little nook only sold high-end items. No plastic tourist junk here. High dollars only.

"Hello there, Jimmy! You are all set. Did you need something from the store? Did you forget something at home? It is closed, but I can open it for you, if you need something."

Vanessa's voice returned Jimmy to the checking-in process, and he turned and walked back to the lobby desk.

"Yeah, okay, not right now, but the cigars caught my eye. Maybe later, after I sip sum booze. Why is it closed?"

For some reason, Jimmy felt the store was important. He did not know why; it was just a feeling he had. The closure of the store at the height of check-in time seemed to be out of character with the rest of the operation. Nothing was out of order, or did not operate perfectly here, except for the store. The closure of the store seemed out of the ordinary realm of operations of an otherwise perfectly fine-tuned business. Vanessa studied Jimmy's face for a few moments, her eyes meeting Jimmy's eyes. She then smiled, handed Jimmy a pen, and she placed a paper on the counter of the front desk, while pointing at various locations that she required Jimmy to sign.

"Please, Jimmy, sign this line, initials here and here, and then sign at the bottom, along with filling out the information for your vehicle on that bottom line. By the way, now that you took off your sunglasses and I could see them—you have amazing eyes."

Jimmy took the pen and nodded while filling in the information.

"Thanks, Vanessa. Your eyes are gorgeous. In fact, I am looking forward to studying them, as well as, sum 'udder parts and pieces of ya, a little more carefully later on tonight."

Vanessa swooned at Jimmy's comment, but she did not

answer his compliment.

Instead, she watched while Jimmy completed the papers and explained, "Yes, sorry about the store. We can obtain the cigars for you. I will have the houseman bring a selection of the finest cigars to your room for you to choose from our selection. We are working on filling the manager position for the store. Unfortunately, the manager passed away tragically and suddenly a few days ago and it all has been a bit of a shock. Rob was such a great guy, and it has been a terrible struggle for us."

Jimmy tried hard not to react to Vanessa's statement and explanation. His training kicked in and he remained smooth and did not react. Indeed, he held a smooth and cool demeanor and image, even though Vanessa's words told Jimmy why he had such intense focus upon the store. Jimmy had made the initial connection with Detective Oscar Campenella before he left north Jersey and he knew the details of the case. A recent murder victim was a certain Mr. Robert Mercurio and Jimmy knew that he had made the first piece of the puzzle fit. Vanessa named the manager as "Rob," and she used the words, "Passed away tragically and suddenly."

'Okay, I am on to a little part of this mess already.' Jimmy thought. He also knew that there were many more pieces to figure out and place correctly.

Vanessa changed the subject. The gorgeous desk clerk pointed out some lines on the paper for completion and she pointed with polished, red nails of a deep luster to some lines on the form in front of Jimmy. Jimmy's mind wandered, and he tried hard to shake off an image of Vanessa's glorious nails and hands holding onto various parts of his body. Vanessa's soft voice shook Jimmy into reality.

"Please, Jimmy, be sure to fill in the information for your vehicle . . . right there."

Even though it was not his own car, Jimmy memorized

the information about the vehicle and in an effort to deflect any attention and continue the role of smoothness, Jimmy filled in the vehicle information and smoothly added while speaking aloud, "Great nails. Sexy as all hell. Okay, yeah, yeah, yeah, license plate, yeah, ah, J.O.S.1. Ah, yeah, too bad about the manager. Sorry to hear 'bout that. Died tragically, huh?"

Jimmy completed filling out the form, handed the pen and paper back to Vanessa and she smiled and said, "Yes, someone shot him. Robbery, I guess. Clinton City is a dangerous place. Not this end, we are high class here, ya know—over in the city." Vanessa glanced at the information on the paper and proclaimed, "Wow! That is what *you* drive? I always wanted to ride in one of those."

The make and model of Jimmy's vehicle caught Vanessa's eye, and her reaction was just what Jimmy desired to see. His plan to be a high-rolling playboy worked to perfection. He found Vanessa to be entirely captivating and actually, even though his guess was that she might be ten or so years younger than Jimmy was, Jimmy found her extremely attractive and very intelligent. Jimmy did not feel too good about using her as a ploy, but that is the way things rolled sometimes.

"Shot, huh? That's too bad. Very sad. I am sorry to hear about it. The world sucks, full of bullshit and bad guys, but anyway, yeah, that is my car. Brand new too. It is what we roll in. Like, I said, come find me later and we will go for a roll." Jimmy paused for a second while gauging Vanessa's reaction to the invitation and after the pause Jimmy asked, "Ah, say, Vanessa, is there a safe in my room?" Jimmy planned the next step beforehand and when he finished asking Vanessa the question, he reached into his pocket and pulled out a huge wad of rolled money, held it out and smiled while saying, "Yeah, have to lock up a few green stamps and other stuff."

Vanessa glanced at the money and smiled.

"Oh, yes, wow. There are two safes. No extra charge for you, Jimmy. We keep the keys to the safes in the main office, your room number is on those papers and here are the room keys. The valet team brought your luggage to your room and your car keys, too. Your car is safe and sound in the parking garage. Let me go and pull the keys for the safes. I will be right back."

She handed the room keys to Jimmy, and he glanced at the room number. He was on the sixth floor. Vanessa dashed off to an office behind the curtain wall of the front counter. Jimmy watched her carefully, and he sighed at the thoughts of how lovely Vanessa was. No doubt Vanessa was a knockout chick. Too bad, there remained high chances that he would have to use her for some inside info. She seemed as if she was quite a bit of fun and the rear view of her was amazing. . .. He would try his best not to hurt her emotions in the process.

Vanessa quickly returned with the keys and a wide smile upon her face, framed with sparkling eyes.

"Here you go, Jimmy."

She handed the keys to Jimmy and smiled, looked at her co-workers again, while slipping a piece of paper to Jimmy and whispering, "I will work on things on my end, but yes, I plan to come find you at the bar after my shift. Around six o'clock or so. Renaldo is the houseman on duty. He will bring the cigar selections to your room in a few minutes. If you need anything, I do mean, anything, then please ring me. Elevators are down the hallway to the left. Sixth floor, Jimmy. Ocean views. Breathtaking."

"Got it. Sixth floor, ocean views and breathtaking. Speaking of breathtaking, I gotta say that you are breathtaking. Thanks for everything. I will be in touch. Looking forward to seeing you later. Yeah, six o'clock is good for me. Perfect." Jimmy turned around and pointed at a cocktail lounge and bar area directly across from the lobby desk. He read the name on the sign mounted above the door to the lounge aloud, "Reflections. Yeah, let's go to this place. Reflections. Is this a good joint or are there others?"

Vanessa smiled and nodded her head while commenting, "They are all the finest of the fine inside of Casa Al Mare, Jimmy. World-class. However, yes, Reflections is very cool. Top-shelf drinks and bar food, but it is always hopping. Six is good. That leaves me time to go off my shift, ride home, freshen up and change into something attractive."

Jimmy looked at Vanessa and winked his left eye, while seductively changing the tone of his voice, "I cannot imagine you looking anything but gorgeous. See ya later. Six it is. Yes, indeed, I will see you later, Vanessa."

Jimmy glanced at the paper and noticed it had a phone number on it and an address. He tucked it in his shirt pocket, flipped the sunglasses down and, while clutching his small bag tightly in his grip, made his way to the elevators. So far, this was working out quite well. He planted seeds and knew that they would sprout quite well.

Vanessa swooned as Jimmy walked away. She could not believe her luck at attracting the attention of such a captivating and stunning man as Jimmy O'Shaughnessy was. Her heartbeat raced, and admittedly, she felt a tingle in other parts of her body, too. The smile on her face and the dull ache in her loins remained long after she admired the rear view of Jimmy as he strode down the hallway and gradually disappeared from her sight.

The hotel room was amazing. Two soaking tubs with showers and gold fixtures in the sinks, tubs, and showers. The room boasted wide glass windows facing to the east and a slider to the deck, which Vanessa described quite perfectly. The ocean view was glorious; this room had the best of everything. Deep pile carpets, a solid oak desk, a bed for a king, a wet-bar, fully stocked with top-shelf booze, beer and wine. It was all here.

Jimmy sighed and spoke aloud, "Damn. Thanks, boss. This is some joint for a vacation. Somehow, I know there is not going to be much in the way of relaxing. Despite the booze, gorgeous young women, cigars, and all the fluff and bullshit."

Renaldo dropped off the cigar selection. Jimmy picked some top-shelf cigars, asked Renaldo to put it on his room tab, signed for them, gave the houseman a nice tip and let him ride. The young man seemed pleasant enough and Jimmy's criminal radar did not activate around him, but right for now, Vanessa might be of more use to Jimmy than the houseman would be. Time will tell, and Renaldo might prove useful, but Jimmy did not want to open up too many fronts and connections too soon. Besides, Vanessa was gorgeous! Jimmy just had to find out if she was trustworthy or not. In his heart, he felt as if she was rock solid and honest, but in Jimmy's line of work, he learned to be overly cautious. Jimmy lived with, "Trust but you need to verify." Right now, despite the intensity of the mission and the need to get right to work, Jimmy found it difficult not to dream of Vanessa. Her beauty and her soft voice and captivating personality etched into his mind and might have worked into the edges of his soul too. Jimmy tried hard to shake off the thoughts because he knew that it was time to get to work now.

Once Renaldo left, Jimmy quickly went to work. The safes would work out well for some decoy items and a bit of the money. Jimmy was not entirely comfortable using them, but at this point, he had little choice. He knew that the thugs would check his room and that he needed to plant some things, but he could not carry all of this weaponry with him all the time. He needed primary weapons, but he required backup weapons, too. Detective

Campenella had his own weapons, but Jimmy knew there might be an ally that he would recruit and they required self-defense, too.

First, he found hiding spots for the handguns. He was not going to trust the safes for the weapons. His weapons of choice for this mission were rimfire twenty-two caliber semiautomatic handguns with a stock of suppressors. Being an old school, combat-hardened Marine, he preferred forty-five caliber handguns, but for this mission he chose the twenty-twos. He had two of them, and two, nine-millimeter, semi-automatic handguns for use in firefights. Jimmy knew the twenty-twos with the suppressors would work for close and silent kills, but if the action became heavy, then he required the nines. In addition to the knives already safely in place on his body, Jimmy would carry two handguns in shoulder holsters on his person at all times. One twenty-two and one nine. The knives on his body never left him.

The other two guns required strategic hiding within the room.

Jimmy knew there were always places to hide things, and he quickly found his tool kit from the small bag and went to work. He took apart the ceiling air-conditioning supply air duct diffusers and the return air diffusers, and stashed some back-up ammo and the guns, all in different duct locations. Some money would go into a safe, but a small amount of the money, Jimmy strategically hid underneath one of the open pedestals of the desk. Actually, this was a little decoy ploy on Jimmy's part. The underneath of desk drawers were poor hiding spots. The thug's room reconnaissance always pulled them out and checked for money taped on the underside, but Jimmy knew better. The planted money stash went deep into the bowels of the desk. They might find it, but they would need to look hard. The motive here was to make the thugs think that Jimmy was a cut above the ordinary rich punk.

Maybe a rich punk, but a smarter one than the usual jackasses that passed through here.

If they hoofed the dough, Jimmy did not care. It was worth the ploy, and he had plenty of green stamps. Even if money became an issue, he knew that Chuck would send more.

The rest of the money Jimmy would carry in his wallet or he placed in a pouch that he taped to the upper part of his leg.

Jimmy felt sure that the room examiners would check and examine the safes. Despite the legal disclaimer stating that Jimmy held the only keys, Jimmy knew better.

"Ain't nuthin' on the up and up here in this joint," Jimmy mumbled.

He knew there remained a grandmaster key to the safes kept by management and the thugs, so along with the money, he left an expensive watch and a men's gold necklace inside the one safe. He left a decoy wallet filled with credit cards stamped with his new identity in the other safe to allow the forward probing to find some items that would fit his image and deflect suspicion.

Jimmy's tool kit had everything from super-grip tape to lock picks, to subminiature drills, to hand tools, and Jimmy made quick work of hiding his weapons and various items. Jimmy might need to use his electronic eavesdropping equipment, a voice recorder and a miniature camera, later on tonight but for now, and as a test fit, Jimmy found that it all hid quite easily into a corner of the room, under the deep pile carpet and underneath, an easily, pried up floorboard. Jimmy was very pleased with how the equipment along with two silencers for his handguns tucked neatly within and between some wooden floor joists. It was a good thing that this building was old and built so long ago in the past that the hotel rooms still had wooden floors. The underside of the frame of the bed was useless for hiding weapons, but it worked well for some more decoy items. Jimmy taped another expensive necklace there.

The electronic bugs he would stick into his pockets for strategic planting, and the rest of the bug collection, Jimmy hid behind an access plate for the plumbing for the restroom, deep in a recess where even if the maintenance crew made repairs, they would not see them. The tool kit would fit quite nicely in another floor joist in another far corner of the room. His field glasses seemed as if they could be a typical tourist item for a vacation and Jimmy made sure he had a high-quality pair, but he did not bring the standard military-issue field glasses that he generally used. After all, Jimmy was just a hotshot playboy on a vacation. He sat the field glasses on an end table next to the slider for the deck and made a careful mental note of the exact position on the end table. The infiltrators to his room will think that he used them for long-distance girl-watching of the beach-going gals. . ..

Chuck McCracken's topnotch, technical crew had outfitted the sports car with more hiding places and hidden deep underneath the spare tire compartment was his coveted sniper tool, which was his prized long-range rifle, a scope, more ammo, body armor, and two more twenty-two caliber handguns. Under the passenger's seat in a hidden compartment that required you to flip a complex series of levers, were two very high frequency portable radios and one miniature, battery-powered, high-frequency military-issued radio with a miniature antenna tuner to tune anything from a rain gutter to a random section of pipe, into a transmitting and receiving antenna. Initially, Jimmy felt as if the communications and extra weaponry might be overkill, but then he acquiesced and stashed them along for the mission. They might be required in a pinch, but chances are that he would be fine. Yet, thanks to the technical crew's efforts, the items did not take up any valuable room. Besides, Jimmy Reeves never doubted and prepared for the worse and hoped for the best.

Jimmy now only had a little more preparation work to finish, and this phase of the mission would be complete. The last pieces of the puzzles included two more items and a trick or two to confirm his suspicions that the thugs would arrive in his room and poke around a little. First, Jimmy needed to plant another decoy and then work on the final piece of his arsenal. Then, finally, the tricks. Out of his luggage, Jimmy took a box of extra-large size condoms, opened it and put two of them into his wallet. He would ditch them in a wastebasket somewhere in the hotel. He then placed the box in the top drawer of the end table next to the bed.

The playboy image had to remain paramount, and he wanted it to seem as if he already had hooked-up with a chick.

Next was a portable, multi-tool kit, a kit that contained assorted screwdrivers, a selection of wire cutters and a variety of lock picks. This kit was much smaller than the larger kit, which Jimmy had already used and hid. This miniature kit was for field use, and Jimmy knew that it could be a lifesaver to him and his allies. It fit into a small sheath, and Jimmy strapped it around his left ankle. The knife remained strapped to his right ankle. Next, from his bag of endless tricks, Jimmy opened a small sewing kit with a selection of threads and sewing needles. After carefully selecting a fine thread that closely matched the color of the carpet, Jimmy opened the safes and after cutting small sections of threads, he placed the threads in strategic locations alongside and on the tops of the ledges of the safe's front doors. Jimmy called these little threads, "Tattletales." When the thugs swung open the doors to the safes, they would disturb the threads and they would land on the carpet, where the thugs, in their haste to search the room and leave quickly, would not even notice them. If they did notice, the threads seemed innocent enough. As if they were merely random carpet or clothing threads. . ..

After placing the Tattletales within the ledges of the safes, Jimmy did the same to the desk drawers, as well as the drawers on the end tables next to his bed.

Jimmy felt confident about the situation and he glanced at his wristwatch and noted the time. Right on course. Plenty of time left to gather some information and obtain a feel for this joint and the players of the operation. Yes indeed, phase one complete and on target. Settled in weapons, gizmos, and other items carefully hidden and in place.

He was ready to roll.

In about two hours, today's plan included Detective Campenella to find him. They were to meet at one of the bars when he began his investigation into the demise of poor Mr. Mercurio. They worked it all out beforehand; they would meet innocently, but strategically. Jimmy's hope was that the gorgeous Vanessa would stick with her promise and meet him tonight for some drinks and company. He sorely needed her to enhance his playboy image as well as to milk her for some inside information, and with that in mind, he felt as if Vanessa was going to work out quite well in that role. It might take Jimmy a little bit of extra effort at romance to make sure he could trust her, but in his heart, Jimmy felt as if she was honest and not part of the hidden world of Casa Al Mare. At the thoughts of the amazing Vanessa, Jimmy sat on the edge of the bed. A shake of his head, and a hapless attempt at dismissing the immediate connection between Vanessa and him, brought reality to the forefront. Jimmy's initial plan and thoughts were to use Vanessa as part of the mission. Yet, as he pondered the images plastered in his mind's eye, Jimmy knew that it was much more than just meeting and utilizing Vanessa as part of the mission. Despite the fact that they just met, and despite his best efforts, there was no way for him to deny the fact that Vanessa was now front and center in his mind. This was somewhat shocking to the soul and to the mind of Jimmy Reeves. A woman never deflected his thoughts before, but this was not an ordinary woman. Jimmy immediately sensed their deep connection, and he tried to dismiss the emotions as foolhardy and straying from his training. Yet Jimmy already knew that he did not want to use Vanessa as part of the mission and then heartlessly cast her aside. That was not Jimmy's style and the thought of doing so, even for the good of the mission, ached at his heart and soul. Jimmy wanted to see her again, spend time with her, share in conversation with her, and maybe, just maybe, the two of them could share a little more than just time.

Jimmy recaptured his thoughts of sticking with the mission plan, and he stood up from the edge of the bed and went back to work. He triple-checked the room and the hiding spots for missteps and evidence of his disturbing them, and after some touch-up; he felt satisfied.

It was time to relax just a little now before beginning the next phase of the operation. He checked out the wet-bar, selected a glass, some top-shelf Scotch, and poured a drink. Neat. Jimmy glanced at his watch. Just a few minutes past the noon hour. Now, he just needed to kill an hour or so. Then it was time for him to move on with the next steps in the plan.

With a tilt of the glass and a nod to the north, Jimmy took a deep sip of the Scotch and spoke aloud, "Here's to ya, boss. I know ya are already into a few and now, I am right behind ya."

Jimmy smiled, because in his heart, for sure, he knew that the team had just tilted the odds in favor of the good guys. And, in thinking of those amazing eyes and other glorious assets of Ms. Vanessa Michaelson, they tilted the odds in favor of the good gals too.

Chapter 4

Ms. Hillary Thornburg

Ms. Hillary Thornburg had some difficulty finding Casa Al Mare. She did well enough on the New Jersey Turnpike and then on the Garden State Parkway, but after that, it became a bit confusing. Hillary Thornburg was not used to navigating along the complex roads of New Jersey, nor was she actually used to driving on her own. Most of the time, she had a driver and sat in the rear of a limousine. Once she left the highways, the side roads provided her with some additional misdirection and some wrong turns resulted in frustration and turnarounds here and there. Clinton City was not what she expected. Parts of it were not ideal for wandering aimlessly in. Especially so, when you are driving an expensive luxury vehicle and you looked like Hillary Thornburg did.

Hillary Thornburg was on top of the world. A world-famous socialite, famous enough to make all the front pages of the gossip tabloid headlines and famous for doing nothing much more than being famous. When you carried the mountains of wealth and the Thornburg name as well as Hillary did, well, the rest of it came rather easily. People fell at her feet and gasped at the sight of her. It was an interesting world that she lived within and Hillary was accustomed to being at the center of it all. Ms. Thornburg was the heiress to her family's fortune and quite the opposite of her reclusive brother, with whom she, someday, would share the family fortune. A fortune made in the cosmetic's business and passed down from generation to generation. Wealthy was not an accurate description of her financial status.

Fabulously wealthy would work.

Hillary was tall, statuesque, a perfect figure, long, flowing brown hair with auburn highlights, and perfect facial features. She was stunningly gorgeous. As a young woman, Hillary Thornburg did some modeling work for magazines and such, but the business was not of interest to her. It was too demanding, busy, and it required commitments. Hillary did not do well with commitments and she obviously did not need the money. . ..

The family lived in a famous mansion located in lower New York State in the spring and summer months; they lived in Florida and California in the winter months, and technically, her office within the corporation was in Manhattan. However, Hillary did not actually have to report to work every day. She was more as if she was a figurehead, just a wealthy socialite, jetting around the world, smiling for the cameras and causing another round of gossip within the media circus of madness that surrounded her and the other, "privileged and beautiful people" of this world. Despite this ongoing madness, as of late, something had changed within Hillary's world. She was not exactly sure what changed, why it changed or how it did so, but she felt it and this vacation was a huge part of it, too. Hillary was determined to change things within her life and right for now, she was on a mission to "find her inner self."

Hillary was around forty-five years of age and she drove her parents and grandparents a little crazy with her social activities and stubbornly wayward ways. A few months ago, Hillary met a dashing Italian man who was vacationing in the states. A supposedly wealthy man and a man who apparently had a vague background and a man who did not work at any profession or occupation. This is, unless, attracting gorgeous women and luring them into his bedroom, counts as a profession. The dashing Italian was a little younger than Hillary was, and she fell madly in love with him. Despite the family's best wishes, cries, and pleas, she married, and the tabloids went crazy, tracking the famous socialite, Hillary and her handsome "boy-toy" husband around as the couple globe trotted all over the world.

The family cringed at the pictures of the couple naked on the beach. . ..

The marriage lasted about six months. It seems as if the handsome Italian had a network of gorgeous women spread across the globe. Luckily, Hillary listened to the huge arsenal of attorneys employed by her father and grandfather and the prenuptial agreements were solid, in place, and undeniable. The handsome Italian did not receive even one thin dime after the divorce finalized. He did, however, have photos of all his private parts plastered all over the tabloids, so at least he received some free publicity.

Despite the recent turmoil in her life and the haphazard pitfall of the bogus marriage to the Italian wonder man, Hillary came out of the last few months, unscathed. In fact, she felt more grounded in her life than she had in a very long time. Perhaps more well-grounded and down-to-earth than ever before in her life. She attended a number of one-on-one classes with a world-renowned instructor in photography and took up the hobby, or in fact, it now was a borderline profession. When one took into account that she only recently took up the photography venture, the photos that Hillary captured were impressive. She had an eye for details, for the landscapes, for objects and other photographic subjects. Of course, Hillary was equipped with the best equipment and cameras available; price meant very little to her in this new venture. As a matter of fact, for this, or any other venture.

Now, Hillary was off to the world-famous, Casa Al Mare Hotel and Resort, for a vacation of sandy beaches, photography along the New Jersey coastline, restful days of wandering and snapping photos of the famous property and building that stood proudly while overlooking the ocean. There were a number of very picturesque lighthouses located close by the resort too and Hillary intended to make those lighthouses subjects in many of her photographs. Her parents and personal attendant were not too happy when she told them of her plans to take a vacation on her own, without her driver, without her usual entourage of muscular bodyguards, and other assorted persons that generally tagged along on her wanderings, but Hillary did not care. Hillary felt as if it now was finally time to stand on her own. Off she went, ever remaining headstrong, tooling off behind the wheel of a world-class luxury sedan from her family's extensive collection of fine automobiles. Off to snap photos, to wine and dine in the resort's legendary fine restaurants, to receive body massages in the famous spa, lounge poolside in a skimpy bikini and cause the male species to faint at the sight of her. A vacation getaway to relax in luxurious comfort, in essence, a trip to rediscover and finally, to find the inner being of Ms. Hillary Thornburg in a glorious and redefined way.

Hillary finally found the Casa Al Mare and the gorgeous woman caused quite a bit of a stir when she drove up to the front of the entrance to the hotel in that amazing luxury sedan. Then, when she exited the vehicle, it caused a few of the male populations to swoon. . ..

Tight black pants that enhanced a perfect figure, a black blouse open just enough to reveal stunning cleavage, high heels, a white pearl necklace and matching white pearl earrings, brown hair with auburn highlights reflected in the sunlight tumbling all around her. Her stunning blue eyes remained hidden behind an expensive pair of designer sunglasses, but the lure of those glorious eyes could have burned a hole in the lenses.

Hillary was the real deal.

The entire package.

Teddy and the valet crew would need an entire cooler of ice packs in order to cool themselves down after this meet and greet experience ended. Hillary left the stunned crowd. With a flip of the car keys, a peel of a fifty-dollar bill and a point toward the trunk and her luggage and off she went, leaving panting tongues and broken hearts behind her. Hillary checked in with the front desk, and a young man assisted her with the check-in process (Vanessa was on a break) and Hillary, as Jimmy did before her, noticed the small store located in the lobby.

After wandering over and checking the store out, Hillary asked the front desk clerk, "I see that the store is closed. I might be a little low on film for my cameras and photo shoots. I might have miscalculated and forgotten to grab more film before I left home. My hope is that the store carries film. Can someone open the store so that we can check and if so, then I can buy some more? I do photo shoots with very expensive and the finest digital cameras, but I am experimenting with some older, classic, film cameras on this trip. Film makes them tick and since becoming lost in the digital age, it is easy to forget to load up on film."

The young man working the desk clerk position at the front desk was all too willing to assist the gorgeous and captivating; Ms. Hillary Thornburg and he assured Hillary that he would check in with the general manager, obtain the keys to the store and open it for her needs as soon as he completed the check-in process. As the young man worked on the papers for the check-in process, Vanessa returned from her break. When Vanessa inquired if she could be of any assistance, the young man explained to Vanessa that Hillary wanted to check if the store carried camera film in stock and to buy some rolls if they were there in the store. Upon hearing of the request, Vanessa willingly offered to assist.

"Oh, I love your pearls and your matching earrings! They are gorgeous! Stunning! And your blouse is perfect!" Vanessa pointed at the immaculate jewelry, while she admired the glowing pearl jewelry and the blouse that Hillary wore.

Hillary smiled at the young woman's enthusiasm and comment and mumbled, "Thank you."

"Please, let me find the general manager, obtain the keys, and we will open the store. I will be more than happy to assist you and you can pick out what you need. I sincerely apologize for the inconvenience of the store closure, but we had an unfortunate incident with the store management and we are working on opening it again as soon as possible. I will be right back," Vanessa promised, and she hustled off to obtain the keys and provide outstanding customer service to such an important and prestigious customer as the world-famous Hillary Thornburg was. Vanessa moved so quickly that Hillary could not even comment or thank her for the compliment of her selection of jewelry.

"Ms. Thornburg, here are your room keys and your paperwork. I also have keys to the safes in your room for your valuables. The valet team just checked in and your luggage is in your room. They are asking if your tripods, and other photographic equipment that are stored in the trunk of your car, should be brought to your room too."

Hillary carefully listened to the young man who was falling all over her while working the front desk. The young man nervously felt along the collar of his shirt, puffed out his chest and his eyes desperately tried not to fall upon Hillary's bulging cleavage that was broadcasting waves of allure from out of the top of her blouse.

She smiled at his reactions, but appreciated his

efficiency.

Hillary answered, "Yes, please . . . that will be perfect. My apologies for not providing instructions that were more exact to the valet crew. Honestly, they were so enamored with the views of my ass in these tight pants, and the hints of my breasts that I am not sure they would have heard my words, anyway."

Hillary winked and flipped her hair over her shoulders to expound upon her attributes.

"Please, all the photographic equipment should be in my room. Please let me ask you, will the general manager of this establishment allow me to do a photo shoot from that balcony over there?" Hillary turned and pointed to a balcony, which was located directly off the main lobby, and afforded quite an astonishing view of the ocean.

No sooner had Hillary finished her statement and asked the question when the general manager of the Casa Al Mare Hotel and Resort appeared at the front desk with Vanessa at his side. He heard Hillary's words, as well as the question, and he smiled. Even in an establishment that was used to hosting world-famous guests, the prospect of meeting the famous and gorgeous socialite, Ms. Hillary Thornburg, up close and face-to-face was a bit too much for the general manager to resist. He knew that this particular dose of outstanding customer service required a personal appearance.

"Ms. Thornburg, I do apologize for our valet crew, especially if they were inappropriate in any manner. I am Mike Spence, the general manager of the Casa Al Mare. Please, I can assure you that I will adjust your folio in our system and ensure that there is no charge for the valet service."

Hillary laughed, smiled, and waved her hand at Mr. Spence as if to dismiss his testimony and his offer.

"That is very kind of you, Mr. Spence, but, please, there is no apology required, nor any adjustments of charges. I assure you that I am not offended. In fact, just the opposite. Their behavior was quite charming and flattering to me. After all, they are young men and they have eyes and hormones too. Let's move on, please, can the young woman, gain me access to the store? I need to check on the camera film and then get to my room. It was quite a long ride from the city to here and I do desire to wash up a bit and relax before the dinner and cocktail hour."

"Yes, of course. I understand about the valet crew. Certainly, I will adhere to your wishes. Yes, Vanessa, will tend to your needs within the store. I do believe there is a selection of camera film in stock. We do tend to have quite a number of photographers that still use film, stay here at Casa Al Mare and enjoy the scenery for photo shoots. Our hope is to reopen the store tomorrow, ah, ah, we suffered, an unfortunate loss there. As far as the balcony for your photo shoot, please, it is all yours. When you are ready, please, if you call down to the front desk a few minutes ahead of time, I will make sure that our facilities maintenance crew reserves it exclusively for your use."

Hillary smiled at the genuine and successful efforts of Mr. Spence to provide outstanding customer service. He was very gracious; however, Hillary deeply desired to get to her room, so she whispered a gentle, "Thank you" and politely pointed toward the store. Mr. Spence nodded to Vanessa. The young woman smiled and with the keys to the store in her hand, Vanessa hustled off to unlock the front door of the store. Vanessa slipped the key into the door lock; a quick spin, and the two women entered the store.

"I will find the light switch and turn on the lights, so we can see what we are looking at here, Ms. Thornburg."

"Please, Vanessa, call me, Hillary. I must say, you are so upbeat and eager to assist your guests. And I might add that you are gorgeous too. Such a pleasure to meet you," Hillary commented while smiling at Vanessa.

"Oh my, thank you. I am not gorgeous, but my goodness you are amazing in person! Even more amazing than you look in all of those magazines and tabloid photos and on the television screens."

Vanessa blinked shyly and when Hillary Thornburg remained smiling while standing next to her, Vanessa relaxed and realized that Hillary took her compliment as very genuine.

"Okay, yes, Hillary, it is then. I must confess to being just a little excited at meeting you as well as happy to provide the service. I am also on cloud nine right now. I met this awesome man today. He checked in and invited me to have some drinks with him tonight. He is stunning. Kinda oozes sexiness. He has a gorgeous build and body and I swear that even with a baggy shirt on, you could see that his muscles have muscles. And he has these glorious and truly amazing eyes, steel grey with blue highlights. I have never before seen eyes like his eyes. Chiseled features, with a full beard. Black hair with just some licks of grey here and there. Geez, he is hard to resist! He is older than I am, too. That is the best part because I am so tired of the immature, younger men that I have dated as of late."

Hillary nodded and continued to smile. Her expression broadcasted admiration at Vanessa's good fortune of snagging a date with the handsome man.

"Oh, I see. Lucky girl! You are certainly bursting with excitement, my dear Vanessa. An older sexy man and an invitation for drinks after work. He is stunning, huh? Steel-grey eyes with blue touches. Wow! I can see why you are so upbeat." Hillary looked around and spotted the film display in a display case near the cash register. Changing the focus of the conversation, she then instructed Vanessa, "I need all the color thirty-five-millimeter film that you have in stock, Vanessa. Oh good," Hillary said while picking up a box of the film and studying it, "it is the highest quality brand of film. Impressive."

"Yes, we only have items of the highest quality here. Everything we sell is the best. Please, feel free to look around and you will see what I mean. I will gather the film as quickly as I can for you. I know that you are anxious to get to your room."

"Perfect. Thank you, Vanessa. While you do so, I will look around. It has been a long day already."

Vanessa nodded, reached down and unlocked a display case and while Hillary browsed the items for sale in the store, she continued to comment on Vanessa's date and evening plans, "Well, please be careful, Vanessa. You are quite the gorgeous woman, too. Please never sell your beauty and your love short. The stunning and dashing ones always seem to have an entourage of other women on their arms and in their beds that they conveniently forget to mention to you. However, I do agree about older men. They are, how, shall we say, so much more in tune with your needs and are generally very experienced. The younger ones are often so clumsy. If you know . . . what I mean. The older men are so smooth. They understand more of what a woman requires."

Hillary winked at Vanessa as if to emphasize the inside meaning of her testimony.

Vanessa smiled, turned a little red at the actual meaning of Hillary's words, and nodded as she shyly said, "Thank you for the compliment. As far as the younger men, yes, I do know what you mean."

Vanessa seemed quite shocked that the famous socialite, Hillary Thornburg, was speaking to her so casually and evenly. Speaking to her as if they were old friends. Hillary seemed so honest, well grounded and sincere. Not anything like the usual aloof, high rollers and famous people who visited Casa Al Mare.

"Oh! These teddy bears are soooo adorable." Vanessa looked up from gathering the film and saw that Hillary had been browsing the store and she found a display of teddy bears lined up proudly in a row on a shelf in the rear corner of the store. The socialite was very tall, so the bears were easily within her reach and Hillary plucked one of the teddy bears off the shelf and held it in her hands while she carefully studied it.

Vanessa looked up from her work and smiled while commenting, "They are adorable! Very high quality too. The bears are handmade in New England. The previous manager of the store, Rob, showed me a sample of one of them before he brought the line in, and I loved it. I was so pleased when he listened to my advice and decided to sell some of them. I am saving my pennies for one for myself. They are quite costly, but worth it."

Hillary continued to study the teddy bear while she listened to Vanessa explain the history of the bears and her wishes to buy one, too. She replaced the teddy bear that she first picked off the shelf and after studying them all; she noticed a bear tucked into a dark corner of the shelf, hidden behind all the others. With her height advantage, Hillary reached up and selected the semi-hidden bear. Hillary now held a bear with a red rose necklace around the bear's neck and a bear that was different from all the other teddy bears.

"I love this one! Someone tucked it away behind all the others. I wonder why? My youngest niece collects teddies and her birthday is coming up in the next few weeks. I think that I will take this one, this little girl teddy bear. The red rose necklace is wonderful. I am in luck because it is the only one left here—the rest of them must have sold already."

"Great selection, Hillary. Your niece will love it."

Hillary turned, smiled, and started to walk back to the front counter with the bear tightly held in her hands.

She then said, "I think so. Tell me, Vanessa, can you ship this to my niece?"

"Of course. For you, anything. I will need the name,

address, and particulars, and I will be happy to take care of it for you right away. Do you want to pick out a birthday card for your niece? We have a fine selection right over there. Once again, our old manager, Rob, was exceptionally good at his job. We have the best of convenience items here as well as very cool gifts. I hope the new manager is half as qualified as Rob was."

"I see that and agree. This little store is wonderful. Yes! Thank you for your ideas and suggestions. You are amazing, Vanessa. Of course, I do need a card."

Hillary handed the bear to Vanessa and hustled over to the card display to select a card for her niece. "Please, can you put all of this on my room charges?"

"Yes, of course. I will take care of all of this right away."

Hillary continued with her browsing of the card selection and as she did so, she continued to engage in a general chit chat with Vanessa, "They mentioned at the front desk that the reason this wonderful store was closed was due to some unfortunate incident with the store management. I have heard you speak highly of the manager. A man named Rob. Please, may I ask what has happened to him? I agree that he was very good at his position. This store is not only convenient for visitors to the resort but it is wonderful in its selection of stock and the display of the merchandise. Exceptional. We women do love to shop even if it is within the confines of an exclusive hotel, but this store is so much fun to browse in and enjoy. I dare to say there are very expensive and exclusive stores in Manhattan that the managers could learn a few tips on marketing from Rob."

Vanessa did not answer Hillary right away, and that seemed to be unusual for the usually exuberant Vanessa Michaelson, therefore, Hillary turned away from the card selection and looked over at Vanessa. It was easy to see from the look on her face that Hillary had struck a painful chord with Vanessa's spirit.

"Oh, dear me. I am so sorry, Vanessa. I did not mean to pry."

"No, please, it is fine. It is just such a shock, and it is so very tragic. Rob was a great guy and he, uh. . .. Well . . . he was shot in a robbery in downtown Clinton City last week. He died of the gunshot wounds. What he could have had other than pocket money to steal, I am not sure, but it is such a tragedy. He was such a nice guy. A great worker and it was such a shock to us."

Hillary reacted to the obvious pain of the memory, "I am so sorry. Yes, I can see that he was a good guy. If you liked him, then I have no doubt as to his character."

"Thank you. Please, Clinton City is a dangerous place. Mostly in and around the downtown areas and in the east end of the city. Around here, we are fine, very exclusive. Please stay on the beach or close to the resort."

Hillary selected a card and walked over to the front counter while handing the card to Vanessa. "Oh, I will. I understand. All old cities have their areas. New York City is an adventure, as well as Chicago, and well, all of them. Old urban areas suffer. Once more, I am sorry to hear of the tragedy."

Vanessa placed the card in the shopping bag with the film and she asked, "Thank you. Should I put the bear in the bag? Or should I keep it at the front desk until you can give me the shipping information?"

After just a few seconds of pondering, Hillary answered, "I will take the bear and keep it in my room. I want to take a picture of it with my smart phone and text it to my brother. I am tired and need to relax and to wash up before dinner and cocktails. I will bring the information and the teddy bear down to you tomorrow. I have plenty of time. My niece's birthday is not for a few weeks. There is no rush. Will you be at the front desk tomorrow?"

Vanessa placed the bear into the bag and handed it off to Hillary as she said, "No, Tuesday is my day off. I will see you on Wednesday. I am excited because with the day off, I can stay out a bit later with my date tonight."

"Oh yes, of course. Mr. Sexy! Wednesday, it is then. You are such a dear. Thank you for everything. Please, good luck tonight and we must join up on Wednesday for some cocktails after your shift, so that you can give me the low-down and inside scoop on your date." Hillary giggled, winked and added, "With the entire inside scoop and hopefully, the super-hot details."

The two women turned to leave the store together, and Vanessa locked the front door behind them.

"Hillary, I would love that! Thank you for the well wishes. Yes, I will give you the low-down and the hot details too. Girl talk will be so much fun, especially, when the topic is smoking hot men. It is so exciting to meet you and it has been wonderful."

The two women embraced and left each other with a promise to meet on Wednesday. As Hillary strolled to the elevators in the lobby and turned the heads of every male she passed by, she was quite satisfied. Vanessa was such a darling, and she felt as if she had made a new friend. Hillary also felt as if she achieved her goal of being well grounded and more in touch with the world. Her goal to be less aloof was working, and she felt as if this vacation was just what she needed. She pushed the call button for the elevator and thought how this was all evolving so perfectly. A great location for her photo shoots, lighthouses, sunsets and sunrises over the ocean, a world-class hotel and resort, a historic building full of grand architecture to capture on film and within the digital technology, a new friend, the beach, and perhaps, she will be as lucky as Vanessa was and she would meet a handsome, older, sexy man too!

The gong of the elevator signaled the elevator car's arrival and as the doors opened and Hillary stepped into the car, she smiled widely and thought, yes indeed; this vacation might be very interesting indeed.

Chapter 5

First Instincts

Jimmy Reeves, or as he was now known in his undercover and alternative role, Jimmy O'Shaughnessy, looked at his watch to confirm the time. It was twenty minutes after five in the afternoon. Monday afternoon. Soon to be Monday evening. He knew the plan. Detective Campenella and Jimmy had carefully expounded upon every detail in their telephone call earlier today. They would meet in an innocent and roundabout manner at the Reflections cocktail lounge. Jimmy would be just another high roller guest of the hotel. Tonight, he was a rich, conceited punk, enjoying a few drinks and the company of a gorgeous woman. Their paths would cross, when the good detective would wander by while he began his investigation as to why the manager of the hotel's store, Mr. Rob Mercurio might have been the victim of a murder under the shadowy pretense of a robbery attempt. As well as, where oh where, has Rob's brother, who also happened to be an employee of the hotel, gone off to these days? Both Jimmy and Oscar knew that bartenders and desk clerks of hotels know everything and everyone. They were where they needed to begin in questioning where, who, and what.

They needed to begin with questions and general conversation with all the bartenders, the desk clerks, and the facility maintenance crew. There was a problem with the facility maintenance crew and that was the fact that Rob's brother was a member of the facility maintenance crew and right now, no one could find him. They both felt as if it was a solid plan. A good start.

Thanks to a little innocent flirting, a flexing of his muscles, his fake playboy image and some strategy, they had the hotel desk clerk covered. Still, Jimmy could not help but to think that Vanessa could not, and that she would not, be a mere ploy in this investigation. She continually stuck in Jimmy's mind and she still captivated him. Her smile, her golden voice, the earrings dangling from her ears, the perfect figure, her glowing demeanor and most of all, the unquestionable connection that they had made. Jimmy tried hard to shake it off, after all, he was a bodyguard, a sharpshooter, a gifted sniper, actually, he was a glorified assassin, a Marine on a mission and to allow a gorgeous young woman to derail his thoughts was not what he was accustomed to, nor was it something that he ever allowed in his past. Here and right now, was not the place to start allowing it to happen.

Yet, she was so gorgeous.

The connection is so strong.

Jimmy desperately tried to shake off the wandering thoughts.

He had been hammering down a few Scotches for a few hours, but Jimmy Reeves could hold his booze. It was a good thing that he could hold the booze and that he knew when to knock it off as not to dull his senses too much. Still, it was good, even with all of his experience and "kills" under his belt and notches on his gunstock, to have the drinks knock some edges off. Jimmy Reeves had always lived his life on the edge. And no more than he did right now. Jimmy knew the stakes. He knew that Detective Oscar Campenella and Chuck McCracken counted upon him to wade into very dangerous waters. Waters full of treachery and of evil. He had been there before. This was not his first mission, and he vowed not to make it his last.

Jimmy glanced once again at his watch.

It was now time.

His plan was to arrive at the bar about a half of an hour before Vanessa did, and an hour so before Detective Campenella arrived. He would throw down some more drinks, all top-shelf stuff, play the playboy part to the hilt, tip the bartender like a drunken fool and lure him into the fold, engage the bartender in conversation, see what he was like and to feel the situation out. It would not take Jimmy too long to figure out the bartender. To determine whether he was a good guy or a bad guy. If the forward watch was in place at the front entrance, watching the coming and goings, then Jimmy was confident the bartenders were all working for *the man* too. Bartenders, in some roundabout manner, eventually meet everyone and Jimmy felt that when Vanessa told him that Reflections was the "spot" then the bartender there would certainly be part of the system. Ironically, in his discussion with Detective Oscar Campenella, the good detective picked the cocktail lounge located right off the main lobby as a meeting place for Jimmy and him. Amongst the other restaurants and lounges within the hotel and resort, Oscar picked Reflections by studying the sales brochure of the Casa Al Mare Hotel and Resort. Jimmy recalled Oscar saying, "That will be a hotspot." The detective was a sharp one; this was not his first mission too. Now it was time to see if that prediction was going to prove true or not. A few minutes with the bartender would be all that Jimmy required.

Jimmy had showered earlier, and now, he dressed in a black suit, white shirt, black pants, black tie, and a black jacket just a size or two larger in certain locations than what he needed. Chuck McCracken's tailor had custom fitted Jimmy for this one. Jimmy explained to the tailor that he required a little extra "shoulder room" and some additional inside pockets for "stuff."

He strapped the knife to his ankle and hung the other knife around his neck, along with his dog tags. Jimmy strapped the tool kit into place. The holsters, Jimmy flung over his shoulders and the one holster received the twenty-two caliber handgun, and the other holster received the nine. Spare ammo and a silencer for the twenty-two went into the larger, extra inside suit jacket pockets and into notches sewn into a customized hem of his suit jacket. The smaller inside suit jacket pocket received the eavesdropper and a handful of bugs. He decided to leave the voice recorder and the camera in the room. The bugs were his main electronic tool for tonight's mission. Jimmy tested the bugs for battery life and made sure they were "on-the-air."

They were.

Jimmy perched the designer sunglasses on his head. He needed them for the look but for function too. In case, he had to hide his eyes, and they were actually sniper's safety glasses, as well as designer glasses. The sunglass case with an embedded eavesdropping bug went into a suit jacket pocket. Jimmy also tossed a few of his bogus business cards in his pocket, proclaiming that Jimmy O'Shaughnessy was a businessman from the city of Paterson. He needed all the finishing touches to proclaim how he was just some spoiled, wealthy playboy living off his family's fortune that they made in the once thriving lace and garment industry.

A double-check of the room, the hiding spots secured, the decoys in place, and Jimmy was ready. Jimmy looked at his watch; it was now five-twenty-five. Time to leave and find out exactly who tends bar at Reflections. Jimmy walked over to the counter by the wet-bar, picked up the glass of Scotch, and swigged the last of the drink. He set the glass down, shut out the lights, and grabbed his room key, safe keys, and the keys to the sports car.

You never know when you have to make an escape.

"Hey there, good afternoon. Welcome to Reflections. I am Mick Malzoni, and I am the Head Bartender of Reflections. It will be my great pleasure to serve you this afternoon and I hope well into the evening."

Jimmy nodded at the canned greeting of Mick Malzoni, as he stopped a few feet away from the bar, paused and checked out the bartender as well as the surroundings. The day was waning, but the establishment faced west and the sun still brightly lit the entire cocktail lounge in brilliant light. The fact that the western side of the room had full glass windows only added to the illumination. Jimmy took full advantage of the brilliance of the sunlight and he kept his sunglasses down over his eyes. Underneath the sunglasses, his trained eyes, the eyes of a combat-hardened, expert Marine Corps sharpshooting sniper, quickly took in all the surroundings. In the keen mind of Jimmy Reeves, it only took a matter of seconds for him to capture all the surroundings and to identify escape routes and potential danger, as well as potential allies.

Three fire exits, not including the front entrance. It appeared as if one of the fire exits led directly to the exterior of the facility. The others might lead to inside hallways and then eventually to the exterior of the building. A long bar, with a curve at the end that ended in the hole where the servers picked up drinks for the floor patrons, and where you could order drinks from, if the bar had no available seating room. The rear of the bar had no mirror for the patrons to admire themselves in or check their makeup and hair. Instead, it had rows upon rows of glass shelves stacked rather oddly in a haphazard pattern that some designer somewhere thought was captivating, and on the front of each shelf layer, a low lighting of decorative lights illuminated the bottles and the shelves with a rotating cast of colors. The shelves filled and overflowed with booze bottles, and the broadcast of the various shades of the colors of the lights cast a glow that made the bottles glow in captivating colors and hues. Six security cameras hung strategically over the bar area, capturing every angle, and Jimmy was sure there was a high-tech micro-camera hidden in the air register mounted in the ceiling and positioned directly over the cash register. Jimmy could see the wider hole in one side of the air outlet and in the sunlight, the hint of the camera lens peeking through the hole. Certain things stand out and some of this was too obvious for the trained eyes of Jimmy Reeves.

He chuckled as he thought of one of Chuck McCracken's idioms that are more famous, "Some of this criminal bullshit stands out like a drunken woman dressed in a tight black dress, while standing on wobbly stilettos in a cheap gin joint late on a Friday night. A woman like that pleads for mercy."

Chuck painted pictures with words.

Jimmy's eyes turned to the dining floor of the lounge. A selection of recessed lighting hung in the ceiling over the lounge and Jimmy made a note of where the light switches sat mounted on the wall next to the far end of the bar. You never know when you might require darkness. Elegant décor, with tables and deep plush chairs scattered about the floor, some private, some larger tables for groups to gather. The wine cellar and display that Jimmy noticed from the lobby backed up to Reflections and one of the wine displays faced the interior of the dining room. A grand piano sat in the far corner of the dining area without a piano player tinkling on the keys yet. Four security cameras mounted in dark corners of the dining room kept a silent watch on the dining room action.

The lounge was sparsely populated.

It was early.

A handful of businessmen in expensive suits sat at one of the tables and an older man with a bad comb over and a huge and disgusting belly and rolls of fat spilling over his belt, sat at one of the smaller private tables, with a gorgeous, young chick dressed to the hilt. She smiled and laughed a staged laugh as the large man sweated bullets of goo in a suit that was two sizes too small for him. High-end prostitution, Jimmy nailed that meeting rather quickly.

Good luck to the gorgeous chick, with that sweaty, tubby flopping around her later in the hotel room.

Jimmy thought, “Sometimes, you have to rethink your career thoughts because the pay might not be worth it.”

Yet desperation often leads to stupidity.

Reflections had the menu posted next to the bar, on a golden pedestal. Everything here seemed to be golden. Vanessa was correct in her description of the menu here, in the fact that it was bar food. Food to pick at and to soak up the excess alcohol. Jimmy surmised that the other restaurants and lounges within the property had full menus. The Casa Al Mare had everything at your fingertips, booze, wine, women, food . . . you name it.

It had a smell of crime and evil too. . ..

Within mere seconds, Jimmy had all the surroundings carefully examined and categorized, and now, Jimmy turned his attention to where he was going to sit at the bar and to the smiling bartender staring at him while waiting for his acknowledgment of his previous greeting. Jimmy scanned the bar from one end to the other. Two of the six wall-mounted security cameras pointed directly at the end of the bar where Jimmy initially was thinking of sitting. The cameras were only slight obstacles; if required, Jimmy knew how to disable them. Jimmy noticed that one end of the bar, the end opposite the drink hole, had a landline telephone sitting on a small shelf near the rear of the bar counter. Only one wall-mounted camera focused on that particular spot. That was where Jimmy headed. If the bartender needed to alert the forward watch, then that landline was going to be the communication method. The phone would be just out of earshot of bar patrons, but Jimmy knew that it was within range of his listening bug. The curve of the bar allowed Jimmy to see the entire lounge from this seat and the front entrance too. His back would be against a wall, with only a door close by the end of the bar. A door, which Jimmy surmised, led to the back of the house and into the kitchen. The restrooms for the lounge were off into a small hallway just before the kitchen door and they would be a convenient escape for potential eavesdropping if it was required. Jimmy smiled, walked over to a bar stool near the landline, pulled it out and sat down. He left his sunglasses on as his eyes continued to scope everything out in careful detail.

"That might get a bit busy there. That seat, I mean. The kitchen entrance is there and we hustle back and forth once it becomes busy," Mick Malzoni said while he pointed at the door.

"No trouble. Thank you for the warning. I always sit at bars on the far ends. It is where I get lucky from all the time. I would sit on the other end, but the sun is so strong. I have to leave my sunglasses on because it is too bright in here."

"Yeah, it is bright. The sun will move soon. Gotta leave the window shades up cuz, the manager of this joint says the view is part of the atmosphere," Mick explained while he wiped his hands very slowly on a bar towel. The bartender smiled while leisurely walking over to Jimmy. He was young, maybe, in his mid-thirties, dark features reflecting an Italian or Mediterranean heritage. He was not overly handsome and not at all, what you might call, rugged looking. He wore a black suit; he was immaculate in appearance, as was all the staff here at Casa Al Mare. Everything about Mick was black, from his shoes, to his necktie, to his shirt, to his hair. In addition, his eyes scanned and checked Jimmy out from every angle. A defining moment because other than Vanessa, who Jimmy in his heart now trusted explicitly, and the valet's scene, this was the first real contact for Jimmy. Mick reached out and extended his hand, and Jimmy did the same.

"Nice to meet ya . . . ah, should have been on my game, and know ya name, but I am sorry, cuz I need to confess that I do not. Did ya check in today or what?"

Upon hearing the words, Jimmy felt the sense. The sense that told him what he required. Bullshit spewed from Mick's mouth, and Jimmy Reeves had learned from Chuck McCracken how to detect bullshit. Chuck was the best bullshit detector in the world. Just from the body language, you could tell that Mick already knew who Jimmy was, you could tell this was just a confirmation. A test. The valet team and the forward watch downloaded guests to this guy when he first arrived for his bartending shift. They had to identify suckers, like the huge belly dude. Dopey suckers to drop tons of money on women or drugs or other wild times. In the big picture, this was just a small piece of the huge Michanetti operation, but Jimmy was quite sure that it raked in tons of dough. No doubt that Mick Malzoni was a bad guy. On the other hand, maybe, because he gave it up so quickly, Mick was simply a wanna-be-bad-guy. Regardless, wanna-be-bad-guy or otherwise, Mick was on the wrong side.

When dealing with Jimmy Reeves, you did not want to be on the wrong side.

"No trouble, Mick. Ya must get a shit-ton of guests here. Nice to meet ya. Jimmy O'Shaughnessy is the name."

The two men shook hands, and Jimmy squeezed hard. Mick's handshake was wimpy and the bartender, when faced with Jimmy's power, seemed to try to match Jimmy's grip but gave up quickly. When they released from the handshake, and Mick staggered a bit to recover, Jimmy carefully reached in his suit jacket pocket, grabbed a business card and handed it to Mick.

"Oh wow, strong dude. Nice to meet you, Mr. O'Shaughnessy," Mick glanced at the card and held it up to study it. "From up north, huh? Paterson. Rough city. Can hear the heavy Jersey accent. Northern Jersey accent. Kinda figured ya from up there. Whatcha do for jingle?"

"Nothin' but just chasin' fine women, workin' out in gyms, drinkin' fine Scotch and rollin' in dough from a huge inheritance. My family for many generations owned silk, lace and garment factories in Paterson during the manufacturing heydays, and they sold them all for a fortune. I am the sole heir and they are all gone now, so I banked all the dough and live the high life."

Mick smiled and nodded, "Nice. Very nice plan and life there, Mr. O'Shaughnessy. The workin' out is paying off, ya a big strong dude."

"Thanks. Despite my previous statement, I do actually work on occasion. I am a personal trainer to some athletic dudes that want to look and feel like me. Good luck with that. This took me years to look like this. I have a gym that I own up in Paterson. It gives me play money and makes me some connections too. Have me some guys that I trust to run it for me, but I work these guys out occasionally."

Jimmy played the cocky playboy to the hilt and then realizing he might have overreached with the gym cover story; Jimmy scrambled some names for a gym in his mind. He knew of one on Belmont Avenue in Paterson, and he loaded that in his memory, just in case the bartender asked him for the name.

"Gotcha. Very cool. Say, ya said ya drink Scotch. So ya wanna top-shelf Scotch?"

"Of course, you pick it. Give me da best. Pour it neat. And call me, Jimmy. After all, I am gonna call ya, Mick."

Mick nodded and walked off, stood for a moment or two in front of the assortment of booze bottles. He selected one of the top-shelf brands, grabbed a glass and began to pour the whiskey. Jimmy carefully studied him as he worked at the pour and it was easy to see that he wore a shoulder holster armed with a weapon. When he bent a certain way, his jacket, unlike Jimmy's custom-fitted suit, revealed the outline. Yup. Most likely, a forty-five by the size of the holster, Mick was a bad-guy. And a punk too. Jimmy could sense the change in his demeanor after he nearly popped his eyeballs out of his head with the handshake. This punk did not like to lose at anything. He felt as if he was king-shit.

"Make it a double, will ya, Mick?" Jimmy called out, and the bartender nodded and mumbled, "Sure" as he continued with a long pour.

Mick walked over to Jimmy, waved and held a hand up to an elderly man who just walked in, and sat on the other end of the bar. Mick wanted to indicate to the man that he would be right there. Mick set the glass in front of Jimmy.

"Cheers. Ya gonna start a tab?"

"Yeah, sounds good."

"Ok. I gotta take care of Grandpa here. He packs a ton of jingle so I need to take good care of this old guy, but I will be right back."

Jimmy did not answer Mick or acknowledge his statement. He took a sip of the Scotch and let it slowly drift down his throat while he studied the situation. This was predictable. A glance at his watch told him that it was twenty minutes to six and Vanessa would be arriving very shortly. The elderly man delayed things a bit, but it all was running on schedule. Now, this punk just needed to fulfill Jimmy's prediction.

Obviously, the elderly man was a regular patron of Casa Al Mare. Jimmy's radar did not activate when he studied the elderly man. Jimmy pegged him to be a wealthy retired businessman, a man who simply enjoyed the resort for what its primary intention was. A high roller's wonderland for a vacation spot. Now, Jimmy needed to watch this next scene predictably unfold, and he did so while gently sipping the drink. Sure enough, after some general chit chat with the elderly man and pouring him what appeared to be his regular drink, Mick walked slowly over to the far end of the bar. The bartender did not lift his eyes toward Jimmy or acknowledge him at all, as he walked over to the landline, and picked up the handset, while dialing what Jimmy knew to be an in-house extension. Mick only punched in four numbers. Yes, indeed, a house extension. For a mere second or two, Jimmy almost took out the bugged sunglasses case, and he debated whether to slip into the men's restroom down the hallway and activate the eavesdropper, but he quickly dismissed that thought. No need to take an unnecessary risk. Jimmy already knew what the phone call was about and by the time he would bug the call, it would end. Mick was calling in the particulars of Jimmy O'Shaughnessy, and the henchmen floating in and around the hotel would now search his room to confirm what Jimmy had told Mick. The call was short; the details exchanged in a whisper, and the search was now on and underway. These guys were not only predictable, but they were a bunch of amateurs.

Mick hung up the phone. His eyes quickly checked the elderly man for his drink level, and potential refill, and seeing that he was in good shape, the bartender turned his attention to Jimmy. After all, the elderly man probably tipped very well and, being a flunky in the mob, did not pay all the bills. Jimmy looked at his watch. About ten minutes to the hour. Vanessa should be here very shortly, and the timing was going to work out quite well. The room search would not take them more than five minutes or so unless Jimmy blew it and they did find something.

Jimmy tucked his arms in and felt the bulges of his weapons. Just a touch of reassurance in case he did blow it and all of this went down the drain.

Mick walked over to the washtub in order to wash glasses and to kill time until the call came in. Sometimes, time moved so terribly slow. After what seemed as if two lifetimes passed, and with Jimmy and the elderly man down to their last sips of their respective drinks, the phone rang on the end of the bar. Mick wiped his hands on his ever-present bar towel and hustled over to answer the call.

It was a short call, a few, "Uh, huhs," a yes or two, and a nod of the head and it ended. Jimmy was sure that he just passed the covert inspection. He was now just a loser playboy, living off his family's dough, living the high life. Mick hung up the telephone, turned and checked on the elderly man, who held his glass in the air to indicate his desire for a refill. Mick hustled over to prepare the drink, delivered it, conducted some general bullshit over subjects that he really could give obviously two shits about, but needed to pretend that he cared in order to humor the old bird, and then he turned to his next prey, which was Jimmy O'Shaughnessy. Jimmy looked at his watch. Tick, tick, tick. Almost six. If Jimmy assessed Vanessa Michaelson correctly, she might be a minute or two earlier, or later, but she was going to be pretty much on time for this date. He could tell by the look in her eyes. Promptness was part of her character. Mick hustled over to Jimmy and pointed to the empty glass.

"Refill? Sorry. It suddenly became a little busy."

"Please, yeah, man, sounds good, Mick. Please, yes, a refill. A'nudder double."

Mick picked the glass up and then before he headed off to prepare another drink, he turned back, leaned in closely and just above a whisper, he said, "So, Jimmy, a guy like you, do ya need some company? Ya know, maybe, a fine lady to drink with tonight. I checked the guest list and other than one super-hot chick, who is a super high roller, there might be slim pickins'. Ya never know about walk-ins, but hey, I can make a few calls for ya and fix ya up with a really pretty gal for a nice. . .."

Jimmy thought about how this guy was such an amateur. Mick passed his thug check, but Mick was such a stupid punk that he fell right into the trap. High-end prostitutes on call. Just like the gal working the sweaty dude on the floor tonight. Most likely, these gals were all hard-core drug addicts, polished up all pretty, but working for pocket money and for fixes. Sad. This punk makes the connection, and he picks up the majority of the cut. The evil house takes the next part of the rolled dough and the hooker gets pocket change and a needle for her arm. Now, Jimmy felt his blood boil. He wanted to take this guy out right here and now, but he played it cool. Jimmy was going to play dumb as if he was too stupid to realize that Mick was going to fix him up with a chick for tonight at an incredibly inflated price and that she was going to be a "professional escort." His watch clicked to the top of the hour and he hoped that Vanessa would time her arrival perfectly. . ..

"Oh, thanks, but I have a date for tonight. Gonna meet her here in just a few minutes. Gorgeous chick that I met when I checked in."

Mick paused. He seemed to be out of sorts with the quick and the confident response by Jimmy, but he shook his head and eventually responded, "Oh. Yeah, okay then. You met her when you checked in. Really? I guess when you pack the look that you do, and you are, Mr. Jimmy O'Shaughnessy, then life is good." Mick shook his head a bit and turned to prepare the drink.

Jimmy smiled at the blow to Mick's ego and before he had time to gloat too much, he turned to watch the front entrance of Reflections, and right on time, in strolled, Vanessa Michaelson. In desperation, the highly trained, super cool under fire, trained assassin, Mr. Jimmy "O'Shaughnessy" Reeves held onto his heart and perhaps his eyeballs too. Jimmy had been in many incomprehensibly difficult situations that required him to play it beyond stealth and beyond cool, but right now, it was all he could do not to keel over and fall on the floor while convulsing at the sight of the beauty of Ms. Vanessa Michaelson. He also had a few additional bulges popping out on his body. These particular bulges, Jimmy had little to no control over. Thank goodness, there was the extra room sewn in the waist area of the pants to his suit to allow for extra "stuff."

Out of the corner of his eyes, he watched the table of businessmen look up and all of them glanced over to the grand entrance of Vanessa. Even the elderly man at the bar lifted his eyes and the last time this poor old boy had seen any female action might have been when the dinosaurs roamed the Earth. Knockout might best describe how Vanessa looked, but it would be a gross understatement of her appearance.

Stunning would work much better.

Beyond stunning.

Her beauty seemed as if it first filled the entire room and then expanded to the entire universe. She slowly, but seductively, walked over to where Jimmy sat and smiled a wide smile. She wore a black dress, which gracefully clung to her amazing figure and the dress moved along her body, in gentle waves of allure, while she walked. In her hand, she held a simple, but elegant, black clutch purse, rimmed on the edges with some silver trim. Perfect complement for an elegant evening. Her hair was perfect, her hoop white gold earrings sparkled in the overhead lights, and a matching white gold necklace that hung just above the neckline of her dress gently enhanced them. A neckline that revealed some amazing hints of glorious mountains of cleavage and uplifted breasts. Her green, doe-like eyes, enhanced by eyeliner and makeup that broadcasted their beauty far and wide.

Vanessa Michaelson was beyond gorgeous. Her beauty was indescribable.

"Good evening, Jimmy. I hope that I am on time. I tried very hard to run home, change, and return in time and still allow a little time to make myself presentable."

Jimmy remained stunned by her appearance and at first; his stagger delayed his response, then Jimmy jumped to his feet to greet Vanessa. He was now under her spell. Jimmy gently reached out with his hand, took Vanessa's hand and guided her onto the bar stool next to his.

"I hope you do not mind sittin' here at the bar. I was killin' time. We can move to a table if ya would like to do so. You are right on time." Jimmy could not help it, but despite his elite training, his soul overflowed, and he uncontrollably gushed over Vanessa. "My goodness, Vanessa. Presentable? Really? How about indescribably gorgeous! I do not know what to say, other than you are beyond gorgeous. There are no words to describe how gorgeous you are."

Vanessa sat next to Jimmy. She giggled and smiled and leaned over into Jimmy while whispering, "The bar is fine. No need to move to a stuffy table. Jimmy, you are too kind in your description of my appearance. Your flattery embarrasses me. I am not gorgeous. However, you, sir, are quite the looker tonight. In fact, I dare to say that you are quite the looker every day and night. My goodness, your suit is amazing. Will you take those sunglasses off, so I can see those amazing eyes?"

Bright sunlight or not. Scoping the area and the action out were now in the past, so Jimmy promptly removed them. Right now, sunglasses were not the only thing that Jimmy wanted to remove. He could not resist her allure, because her beauty and personality intoxicated his very soul. Jimmy Reeves was always on duty and even in the wave of intoxicating beauty, Jimmy made sure of the coverage of his suit jacket and the hidden items contained within. But he leaned over and gently kissed her on the cheek. Vanessa loved it.

"Hello, Vanessa. I now see how ya made the connection when you checked in there, Jimmy. Cheers to ya lucky ass. Here is your double."

Mick suddenly had a poor attitude.

After rudely dropping the drink in front of them, Mick turned his attention from a paying customer to the object of his desire and his obstinacy and addressed Vanessa directly, "You do know the rules for drinking with guests and sitting at the bar don't you, Vanessa?" Mick had arrived on the scene and his demeanor was less than cordial. Jimmy knew right away that Vanessa had, at one time, jilted Mick. Perhaps she refused his advances. . ..

"Of course, I do, Mick, and yes, it is nice to see you too. I cleared all of this with Mike Spence. He approved of my plans for tonight and for tomorrow, too. Would you like to check with him? I can excuse myself and go get him for you, if that is what you need me to do. He is still here. Or call him yourself if you need to do that."

Jimmy smiled and leaned over the bar and in toward the direction of Mick. Jimmy needed to play his role to the hilt as well as rub some pain into those wounds that Mick displayed, "Yeah go ahead and check with Spence. By the way, it ain't just *my ass* that is lucky there, Mick. I am thinkin' there might be some other lucky parts of me too."

Mick stood for a moment in front of Vanessa and Jimmy, and his eyes went up and down Vanessa and then over to Jimmy. Inside he was fuming, but he faked his exterior appearance, forced an incredibly stupid looking, shit-eating grin, and waved his hand in the air while glancing at Jimmy. Jimmy had leaned in close and it was easy to tell that this scene could turn south very quickly. Mick could call in waves of henchmen, but something inside of him told him that Jimmy was poised for action and right now, with Jimmy in such close range, Mick wanted no part of the big man. By the time help arrived, Mick imagined that Jimmy could lay a major hurt on him and pulling his weapon here would be a huge disaster. Vanessa was a super-hot chick, and a chick that Mick sorely wanted for his operation, as well as in his own bed, but it would be a very bad scene and cost Mick and the house a lot of trouble, not to mention the loss of revenue. Loss of revenue was difficult to explain to the big boss.

Coincidentally, Mr. Huge Belly came by with his arranged date hanging on his arm; he dropped a huge wad of rolled dollar bills on the bar for Mick, waved and danced off into the evening for a night of sweat and who-knows-what. Mick suddenly cooled his jets. The money paid for more than just food and drink, and it helped to ease his pain and diffuse the situation.

"Nah, we are good. If you checked with Spence, then we are good. Let me guess, you are going to have a martini. Dirty. A dirty martini, right?" Mick did not hide very well his inner agitation in his voice.

"Yes, please, you are correct. Dirty. Thank you," Vanessa replied.

Mick walked away. A few more patrons took seats at the bar and he glanced at them as he went to prepare the drink for Vanessa. Jimmy stood down and relaxed. He leaned into Vanessa and spoke in a low voice.

"Lemme guess. He has come onto you several times and you refused to go on dates and hang with him," Jimmy said to Vanessa as he watched the scene unfold. Vanessa nervously fingered the earrings in her ears, placed her clutch on the bar counter, and she frowned. She nodded her head and leaned back into Jimmy to explain. Jimmy caught a whiff of her perfume and tried hard not to allow it to cause him to swoon, even more than the look in her eyes did.

"You are right on, Jimmy. He is a creepy and disgusting man. I have refused his advances more times than I can count, as too, have many other women who work here. In fact, I refuse to date all the men who ask me out here at work. However, this guy, I have no use for him at all, even to speak with him."

Vanessa rolled her eyes, and her mouth turned into a scowl. With some disgust layered within her lovely voice, Vanessa continued to explain, "He has suggested a number of times that with my looks, and my, as he said, amazing body, I could earn an enormous amount of side money, by, as he smugly told me, doing some certain favors for wealthy businessmen who stay here. Mick told me that what he called the house, and he would only take a small cut out of my earnings from me. He is disgusting. I complained to Mike Spence about this creep many, many times, but nothing ever happens to him. Whenever one of the female staff complains about him, they receive a bonus in their paychecks to offset his bullshit. We kid about it. When you need extra money, complain that Mick grabbed your ass or your breasts without permission. Strange, but he seems to do whatever he wants. Like he is untouchable. I do not know why nothing ever happens to him, but all I can say is that he is a creep."

Vanessa once more nervously fingered her earrings, and Jimmy surmised that she was carefully weighing her words before speaking.

In a slightly lower voice, Vanessa said, "Honestly, there is a dark side to working here at Casa Al Mare. It is all glitz and glamour on the surface and full of allure. But honestly, lately, I am not sure of some of what goes on here behind the scenes. Some of it makes me very uneasy, and it gives me the creeps."

Jimmy did not react to her words, aside from a gentle nod of his head and a gentle reach for her hand, which Vanessa willingly allowed Jimmy to do. Jimmy Reeves now knew that his first instincts were correct. Vanessa was on the good side. She was more than honest and trustworthy; Jimmy knew that she was special.

"Hey, c'mon, let's forget the creepy bartender and have a great time. Right? You are gorgeous and we have the whole night in front of us. We are gonna have a great time." Jimmy squeezed Vanessa's hand tightly, and she squeezed back. Her smile defined her emotions. Jimmy knew that all was well. Mick delivered the martini with nary a word, just a nod of the head, a point of his finger as he checked on Jimmy's drink and he quickly moved over to serve other patrons. The bar and lounge grew busy as the dinner hour approached, and Mick no longer had time for the general discussion. Especially now, since Jimmy O'Shaughnessy proved to be a dead end for some side jingle and working the angles, and he had a date with the gorgeous desk clerk that proved to be so elusive for not only Mick, but all the other men pursuing her at Casa Al Mare.

"Okay, cheers. Here is to a wonderful evening." Jimmy held his glass up and Vanessa did the same. The glasses clinked together, and the drink sips began.

"So, please, tell me all about Jimmy O'Shaughnessy," Vanessa said with a wink in her eye and a deep allure in her voice.

"Well, only if you promise to tell me all 'bout, Vanessa."

She smiled and held her drink up as a testimony. Her gloriously beautiful eyes flickered in the waning sunlight that was now bathing this end of the bar. Her beauty and her spirit glowed from within her soul, and Jimmy captured it and held it within his own soul.

Despite the remaining licks of sunlight still bouncing around the room, Jimmy kept his sunglasses perched upon his head. Suddenly, he loved the sunlight.

"I will promise you that I will tell you all about me, Jimmy. You go first though. My first instinct is that you are more than just this sexy and wealthy playboy who waltzes and dances around America wooing helpless women who fall for your handsome appearance and captivating magic."

Jimmy smiled and thought, 'Wow! This gal is brilliant. However careful, now, Reeves. Oops. Rather, careful there, O'Shaughnessy.'

He then continued with the perpetuating of his fable, "Okay, but a promise is a promise. Gotcha covered here. I am the heir to a lot of dough. You see, my family, owned silk, lace, and garment factories up in the city of Paterson and they made a ton of dough. When the industry began to fade, they sold out, and we banked all the money. Here is one of my business cards. . .."

Therefore, it began. The discussion continued as a prelude to a growing love and deep connection between Jimmy and Vanessa, and in many ways, the words inspired a deep touch of romance within the old Marine's heart. Even old Marines who never found love before might just find room in between missions and in their hearts to fall in love.

After all, they always go with their first instincts.

Chapter 6

Romance and a Dash of Mayhem

Detective Oscar Campenella pulled up to the front entrance of the Casa Al Mare. He checked his watch. It was now ten minutes after seven o'clock in the evening. Right on time. The slow evolution of the plan that he worked out with Jimmy was underway. The forward watch of the behind-the-scenes operation immediately spotted the detective's car. Despite the car being unmarked, the telltale signs that defined the vehicle as being a detective's car remained outwardly obvious. Teddy, the Head Valet for Casa Al Mare, had turned over the duties for valet parking to his brother, Michael, for the night shift. Michael held his arm out to one of his valets to prevent the valet from running out to provide service to Oscar. Michael and the valet team looked over to the forward watchman, and he nodded and waved to them to indicate that he would handle this one. The valets all knew who the driver was. This particular guest was not welcome here at Casa Al Mare.

The forward watchman strode out to meet Detective Campenella as he exited the driver's door and looked around. Oscar, as Jimmy did before him, made a careful note of the location and the number of security cameras mounted in and around the front lobby entrance. Oscar was not a rookie; he smelled the criminal elements in the air, too. His father gave him his genes as well as his instincts. Oscar Campenella and Jimmy Reeves shared many things in common. Oscar also went with his instincts.

"You! Get ya car outta the way here. Park it over in one of da visitor's parking spots. Valet service is for paying guests. Park it over dare. Move it now," the henchman growled in a heavy New Jersey accent to the good detective, while pointing ungraciously at a number of parking spots located alongside the main driveway leading into the hotel and resort.

"How do you know that I am not a paying guest?" Oscar asked the henchman.

The henchman stood stoically in front of Detective Oscar Campenella, and he did not answer his question right away. Despite the fact that the sun had now set and he no longer required sunglasses, he still wore a dark pair over his eyes. The henchman did not even remove his sunglasses, but he continued to stare at Oscar.

Oscar stared back at him and after the henchman still did not answer and the henchman patted his suit jacket to imply that there was something underneath the jacket, Oscar asked once more, "Ah, are you deaf? I asked a question. How do you know that I am not a paying guest?" Oscar was not going to back down from a forward henchman. He was a fearless man.

The henchman finally said, "Cuz, I know ya a copper. Park it over dare, go in, do whatever the hell ya got to do and get the hell outta here. This is private property. Unless ya got a warrant, then I am settin' the rules here. Not ya ass."

Michael and one of his valet team members stood watching the scene unfold, and Oscar held up his police badge for Michael and the other valet to see the badge.

The detective smiled and said to Michael, "Perceptive son-of-a-bitch he is. Grumpy too. Is he always grumpy? Okay, I will park over there."

Michael did not say a word, and neither did the other valet. They simply glanced at the badge and turned and walked away.

"Okay, then. Welcome to the world friggin' famous, Casa Al Mare, Detective Campenella. Where assholes think they rule and evil lurks," Oscar said aloud for everyone to hear as he jumped back into his car, put it into gear, and drove over to park it in one of the visitor's parking spaces.

Meanwhile, as Detective Oscar Campenella parked, then he walked into the main lobby of the Casa Al Mare. At the bar inside of Reflections, Vanessa and Jimmy remained locked in a deep and engaging conversation. Within Casa Al Mare, amongst the evil, and within the throes of the mission, something amazing was occurring here.

It was a strange thing called falling in love.

Jimmy found this woman to be enthralling and captivating. Not only was she gorgeous in appearance, but her personality was exuberant and her spirit captivated Jimmy. Vanessa told him all about her life, her parents, her struggles to find a career in the challenging environment of Clifton City, the story of stops and starts with education at a local college and even honest testimonies of failed dreams. Vanessa was not only engaging, she remained openly honest, and while she enjoyed a few more martinis, her honesty opened up and revealed its honor even more. She came from humble roots, a working family, her father worked in a local food-processing factory and after he suffered an injury on a job, he could no longer work. The disability settlement paid for some bills, but not all of them. Her mother worked at various hospitality jobs within the bustling resort side of Clinton City, doing her best to keep everyone afloat. Vanessa found the job at Casa Al Mare a few years earlier and at first, she could not be happier. It paid very well and the benefits and prestige of the job were astounding.

Vanessa leaned in and told Jimmy in a gentle whisper out of earshot of Mick, "Just like Clinton City, as I mentioned before, this place has a dark and seedier side to it, Jimmy. I am not sure of everyone that is involved, but it is here, and while I am not privy to anything, I have seen some shady and suspicious things here. Things that I am not entirely comfortable seeing and experiencing."

Jimmy kept a neutral response. He spewed something generic about how all old cities had issues these days, and you should see Paterson right now, types of responses. Jimmy felt more than just a little stupid at the vague response, but he felt that it was too early in the game to open up any more to Vanessa. He could not risk giving up too much of the inside scoop just yet.

Mick was very busy now. He scooted over for refills of drinks, delivered some bar food when Jimmy and Vanessa ordered it but he did not hide his anger too well. Between his anger at Jimmy for his presence, as well as his luck at obtaining a date with the stunning Vanessa after Mick's failed attempts to make headway with her, it was obvious that Mick Malzoni wanted very little to do with being cordial or friendly towards Jimmy and his date for the night. Once any opportunities for extra jingle or action vanquished, it was obvious that also long gone were the welcome greetings and friendly demeanor of Mick Malzoni. That suited Jimmy quite well. The farther away that Mick stayed, the easier this acting job of the dashing playboy was.

The atmosphere of the lounge changed, as the crowd grew, and in the corner of the dining room, the piano player began to tinkle soft melodies upon the keys. For Vanessa and Jimmy, the piano music only added to the romance of the evening. As their connection grew, and Jimmy realized how special Vanessa Michaelson was, he felt very uneasy about his lack of honesty, his initial ploy of using a date with Vanessa to gain an ally and information on the inside, and his initial motives. Yet, he did have a mission, and he vowed to be honest with Vanessa just as soon as it was possible to do so. Now, he had to make sure he protected her too, and prevented her from the madness. Jimmy had wanted some information and falling in love was not on the agenda, nor was it part of the plan.

The telephone on the end of the bar was ringing off the hook and Jimmy spotted Mick glance at it, but he was so busy that he could not break away long enough in order to answer the call. The frequency and the persistence of the ringing of the telephone, combined with the time of Jimmy's watch, made Jimmy realize that Detective Oscar Campenella had made his arrival. The forward watch needed to alert the various layers of the operation as to the detective poking around. Jimmy knew it was time to snoop a bit more into what was going on here.

"Well, Vanessa, the sun is long since gone now. Guess I can put my sunglasses away." Jimmy had perched the sunglasses on top of his head and he removed the sunglasses, took out the sunglass case with the bug, and slipped the glasses into the case. The bug looked as if it was an emblem or logo on the side of the case; it was very inconspicuous and barely noticeable. Jimmy strategically set the case on the counter of the bar and made sure the bug pointed toward the telephone. He knew that very shortly; he might need the technology contained therein.

"Yes, long since gone now, Jimmy. The night is here and so far, it has been amazing! Besides, I do not want you ever to hide those amazing eyes," Vanessa cooed.

Jimmy leaned in and continued to play it cool, while gently putting his arm around Vanessa, "Baby, it is only just beginning. I guarantee that tonight will be amazing in every way."

"Hello, I am, Detective Oscar Campenella with the Clinton City Police Department. I am a homicide detective and I am investigating the recent murder of one of Casa Al Mare's employees, a . . . Mr. Robert Mercurio." Oscar held his badge up in front of him as he spoke to a middle-aged man working the front desk duties.

The desk clerk studied the badge and said, "Ah yes, hello, Detective Campenella. Terrible tragedy about Mr. Mercurio. We were all quite saddened to hear of his death. A robbery, right?

"Something like that. Maybe. Say, did you know him?"

The desk clerk shook his head and explained, "No, not really. Just to say hello on a rare occasion. I work the middle shift here. Four to twelve. I would see him around, because he managed the lobby store over there, but for the most part, he was gone for the day when I reported for work. Everyone that did know him said he was a nice guy. The few times that I did interact with him, he always seemed pleasant enough."

"Yeah, that's what I keep hearing. Is that the store he managed, right over there?" Oscar asked, while he pointed to the lobby store tucked in the corner.

"Yes, sir."

"Can I take a look inside there? I see it is closed."

The desk clerk shook his head and explained, "No, I am sorry, but I do not have the keys. We closed the store when Robert passed. The general manager is trying to find a new manager to run the operation. Only the general manager has the keys."

The desk clerk held his hand up, mumbled, "Please, excuse me," while he answered a telephone ringing on his desk. Oscar nodded, and while the clerk tended to the call, the detective wandered over to look through the windows of the store. High-end products on display in the window. No surprise there. This was a high-end joint. Unfortunately, the reality of this twisted world was that money earned in the throes of evil only bought the best of the best. Oscar looked through the windows but without lights on inside, it was difficult to see much. From what Oscar could see it was a pleasant store and for a small nook tucked away in the corner of the lobby of this exclusive hotel, it had quite a large selection of merchandise, some items that a visitor or tourist on a holiday would desire, other things were unusual. Particularly, a row of teddy bears seemed so out of place. Detective Oscar Campenella did not miss anything.

He noticed the row of teddy bears lined up in a single file row on the shelf in the corner and laughed, "Teddy bears that most likely cost a million dollars. If you can afford to stay at this joint then, I guess that it makes some kind of obscure sense." The desk clerk finished the call, Oscar wandered back over and he took out his pen and writing pad from his suit jacket pocket and engaged the desk clerk once again, "The general manager, I guess that he has left for today?"

"Yes, detective. You just missed, Mike."

"Mike? Does he have a last name?"

The desk clerk smiled, and for the first time, he seemed to be a little annoyed with Oscar's rather persistent questions. Until now, he was very pleasant and polite.

"Most of us do, detective. Spence. Mike Spence. He is usually in the office from seven in the morning until around six at night. It is a demanding job."

Oscar wrote the information down and nodded his head. He looked up and around the lobby and noticed the array of security cameras watching his every move.

"I can imagine. I know the feeling. One last question and I will leave you alone. You have been very helpful. Rob Mercurio has a brother. Kenneth Mercurio. It is my understanding that he works here too. Is that correct?"

The desk clerk grew silent for a moment. For some reason, this was a question that he seemed to be a little reluctant to answer, but after what appeared to be a few moments of pondering, he answered, "Well, yes, I guess. I did not know him either. He worked the midnight shift in the maintenance department. He was a general helper on the crew. It is my understanding that he has not been at work since his brother died. No call. No show. Maybe he is mourning the loss of his brother. That is understandable."

Oscar shook his head and said, "If he is, he has a funny way of doing it. Never even showed up for his brother's funeral."

The desk clerk changed the tone of his voice.

Without caution, he suddenly sounded very understanding, "Okay, well, I guess you staked out the funeral. You *are* a detective. Oh well, I guess he is not mourning. That fact is not surprising. Like I said, I did not know him at all, but the word was that he was not as cordial as Rob was. The beat on the street was that he was kind of a reckless and wild guy."

Oscar nodded and asked, "I guess that he reported to the head of the maintenance department here? My guess is that he is gone for today, too. I need to come back tomorrow, ya right, cuz, I was tied up today with the funeral watch."

"He reported to the chief engineer of the building, Mr. Danny Keene. K double e, n and another e at the end. He works days too. Busy guy." The desk clerk smiled, and Oscar smiled too while he wrote the name in his book.

Oscar stared in at the desk clerk's name tag and wrote his name down, then reached out and shook his hand while saying, "Thanks, William. You have been a helpful guy. If the police pull ya over for speeding around here, don't mention my name. They might write you two tickets instead of one."

The desk clerk shook Oscar's hand and said with a smile, "I will keep that in mind. Good luck with your investigation."

"Thanks. Off-duty now. Let me go spend a million dollars for a two-ounce beer over here."

Mick finally shook free, and he answered the telephone. Jimmy carefully studied the conversation and from the nods of Mick's head and the short duration of the call, Jimmy knew it was just a warning that Detective Oscar Campenella was on his way. Jimmy did not have the time, nor the desire to power up the bug, and then escape, walk away and go listen in. However, once more, these guys were predictable. The predictably offset the unnecessary risk. After Mick hung up, he checked on their drinks, and Jimmy ordered another round for both of them.

Vanessa laughed and gently grasped Jimmy's hand and confessed, "Jimmy. My goodness, I am feeling a bit tipsy and lost in the drinks already. I have been babbling endlessly, and you have been kind enough to listen so carefully. Really? Another one?"

"I want to listen to everything ya say, Vanessa. Not miss a word. Learn all 'bout ya. Besides, ya only live once, Vanessa. C'mon, baby, as we just said, the night is just startin'. Who knows where and when it will end?"

Vanessa leaned and swooned at the words, as well as the thought, and Vanessa and Jimmy almost kissed, but Mick delivering the drinks interrupted their swoon. No doubt that their closeness only fueled Mick's inner fire. Mick promptly delivered the drinks and moved quickly on to his work.

The Reflections bar and cocktail lounge was rocking and rolling tonight. In many ways.

Detective Oscar Campenella walked into the main entrance of Reflections, adjusted his suit jacket, tucked his arm into his shoulder holster as if to double-check the presence of his service revolver, and scanned the crowd.

First, his eyes waltzed around the dining floor of the cocktail lounge and then to the piano player, rather mindlessly dribbling a familiar, yet an uninspiring tune on the ebonies and the ivories, and then his eyes slowly moved to the bar. It only took a second for Oscar to identify Jimmy Reeves, seated at the end of the bar, right next to a stunningly gorgeous young woman. Jimmy was exactly as described, but Oscar had to admit that Jimmy was quite a bit larger in physical size than what Oscar envisioned.

Jimmy Reeves was a very imposing man. Geez, he looked as if he could snap a man's neck with an effortless twist of his powerful arms and immense hands.

Their eyes met for the briefest of seconds and despite never meeting each other ever before, they knew each other. Oscar was not surprised at Jimmy's company of the young woman; he knew it was all part of the plan and part of a smokescreen. Yet, he could not help but swallow hard at Jimmy's good fortune of picking one helluva hot smokescreen. The two men did not acknowledge each other's presence, nor even linger with their glances. It was neither the time nor the place, because Oscar knew the security cameras had eyes glued on his every move. He slowly walked over to the bar and slid out the one remaining seat left. Coincidentally, it was about two seats over from where Jimmy and Vanessa sat, with an older couple nestled between them.

Mick wandered over with a frown on his face. He grabbed a coaster and set it in front of the detective and asked Oscar, "If you are on duty, then you might want to rethink your choice of places to drink tonight."

"When I saw the look on your face, then I just made a last-second choice to return to duty. Therefore, yes, I am on duty and as far as I know, I can order a soda. Right? Lemon-lime. What is it . . . like fifteen bucks?" Oscar said as he pulled out his badge and displayed it for Mick to study.

The older couple looked over, as did Jimmy and Vanessa, but no one spoke or commented. Jimmy grabbed Vanessa's hand, and he squeezed it, and while she thought that Jimmy's reaction to the presence of the detective to be a little strange, Vanessa took that as a sign not to comment on the situation.

"Usually, it is two bucks. For you, it is twenty," Mick answered him sarcastically as he grabbed a glass, dipped it into some ice and grabbed a dispensing wand to fill the glass with soda. He spoke while preparing the soda, "I will save you the words with the line of questions and get right to it. I did not know the guy killed in the robbery. We really never crossed paths. As far as his brother goes, never knew the guy. I think I passed him once or twice when I saw him parking his car when he arrived for his shift and I was leaving for the night. He worked midnights and was just a maintenance helper. I only have the highly experienced maintenance guys come by and repair things for me here. I have complicated stuff, like refrigeration issues. The brother changed light bulbs and swept up floors. He was at the low end of the pole around here. Minimum wage dude. With that in mind, here is your twenty-dollar soda and goodbye and get lost. Ya have my best wishes for a shitty life working as a shitty copper."

Mick delivered the glass of soda and seemed more than happy to end the conversation.

Vanessa leaned in and whispered to Jimmy, "That policeman is investigating the death of Rob. Mick is stonewalling him. Told you that Mick was creepy. Should I tell the policeman what I know about Rob and his brother, Ken? I mean, I do not know very much but it sucks that Mick is being so mean to a policeman."

Jimmy did not want to or need to dwell on what was happening on the exterior for Vanessa, but on the inside, he was fuming. He just needed to remain calm and cool. He did it the best way that he knew how to divert the attention—he took a long swig of Scotch and then placed the glass down on the counter. In his heart, he loved the fact that Vanessa showed her inner compassion, and he loved the fact that she sided with the law. That confirmed to Jimmy all that he needed to know.

Now, it was time for a diversion laced with confirmation.

He then leaned over, gently grabbed Vanessa by her face with both of his hands and whispered, "As I said, baby, the night is long. Don't worry about that creep and that mess over there. That policeman looks as if this is not his first gig. He will be fine. Tonight, needs to be 'bout us." He then planted a long and romantic kiss on Vanessa. A kiss that not only took her by surprise, but once the shock wore off, she relished in. It was a glorious first kiss, and the meeting of their lips sent shock waves throughout both of their bodies.

Despite the evil and the deceit, the air filled with unmistakable magic.

It is amazing what love can overcome.

For Jimmy, the kiss was more than just sweet and glorious lips and a mouth that was warm and inviting, the kiss turned out to have perfect timing. The older couple sitting next to Jimmy and Vanessa smiled at the reaction to the tension. They nodded their heads and kissed, too.

Detective Oscar Campenella was a professional and a top-notch detective. He knew when to dig in, when the sores and pain of evil were wide open and when the uncertain wounds ran deep. It is then that the goodness of humankind can overcome evil. When love as exemplified by couples kissing can overcome the burning desire to pervade the world with greed and malice.

Mick had made a miscalculation and stumbled upon his words. Oscar made a note and without hesitation, the good detective pounced on Mick's error and the detective dug in hard.

"So, you are the hot shit, top notch, polished up bartender in a hot shot place like this dump and ya know nuthin'? Interesting. Let me ask you this. Since the brother has not shown for work in a few days, I need to ask ya. Did he drive his car to work? Did you pass each other more than just once or twice? Tell me where he parked his car when you saw him. Maybe in an employee parking garage or a parking lot? Ya just said the only reason ya knew this guy was when ya saw him park his car. Interesting, cuz, I cannot find his car anywhere. Maybe it is parked here?"

Jimmy watched as the detective's question struck a cold, hard nerve within the mind and heart of Mick Malzoni. The good detective nailed into a nerve.

The brother's car!

You could tell by the look upon Mick's face that no one, including Mick Malzoni, or anyone else in the operation had even thought to check for the car parked right here under their noses. A car, which might have clues. After his brother died, there was no way in hell that Ken Mercurio would use his own car to escape. Everyone, police, mob, and otherwise, was looking for this guy. There was no way that Ken would use his own car. Oscar was a sharp cookie and now Mick squirmed at his obvious misstep. The creepy bartender worked as hard as he could to hide the fact that the car could be a missing link.

Mick recovered and leaned in while saying, "That drink is twenty bucks. Pay up, asshole. I do not know. You are the detective . . . so . . . figure it out on your own. Get lost."

Oscar leaned in close while reaching for some dollar bills in his pocket and tossing them on the counter of the bar.

"Might be twenty there, or there might not be. If it is short, my suggestion is to call the police and report me as a dine and dash. Asshole. You have just given me what I needed. A reason to call this a homicide rather than a murder during a robbery. I will figure it out. You can bet on that, hot shot. Bet ya swinging ass on it."

Jimmy covertly smiled, and Vanessa and the older couple remained horrified. Oscar and Jimmy tried hard not to lock eyes as the detective stormed off, but Jimmy knew that the war was on now. No more playing around and smooching it up with a gorgeous woman.

It was time to lock and load.

Jimmy carefully watched as Oscar made his way to the lobby front desk, no doubt to find out where the hotel and resort employees parked, and Mick allowed his emotions and his fear to overcome him. When Mick quickly moved to use the landline telephone, Jimmy knew it was time to jump into action. Jimmy made a quick note of the position of the sunglass case on the bar, and he was sure that the bug was in the perfect location to pick up the conversation during the telephone call. With a quick touch to the case—Jimmy flipped the tiny power switch into the "on" position.

"Vanessa, time to break the seal, honey. I will be right back," Jimmy said, as he double-checked the position of the bug, jumped off the bar stool, and headed for the direction of the men's restroom.

Vanessa reached out and held Jimmy's hand as she gently said, "Don't be gone too, long."

The drinks were now in full-effect on his date, but Jimmy shook off the waves of alcohol as he walked quickly to the restroom. He reached in his jacket pocket, carefully took out the eavesdropper and once he banged through the door of the men's restroom, checked it for occupancy, he made his way to the inside safety and seclusion of a stall. Jimmy was in luck, because he was the only occupant in the restroom. Once Jimmy hid within the stall, he flipped the switch on and placed the earphones in his ears. A careful listen. At first a little static, then a clear signal.

Ah yes, technology. . ..

"Yeah, shit, I know, I know, but none of us thought of it 'til now! I dunno. He is a friggin' detective and apparently, we underestimated him because he is damn good at what he does. I spilled the words outta my ass, and he latched on 'em. Yeah, I know that it sucks big time. I might add that this dude is on his game. He is the real deal. No dope. Now, we are in some deep shit, because his car *could* be there. Hell, for all we know, the shit that Tony Junior needs is there. Right under our noses. You guys have the cameras! I can't even be sure which car would even be his, but detective shithead knows. He is at the front desk right now, no doubt trying to figure out where employees park. Ya needs to, get offa ya asses and tail 'em. Ya might have to whack him if he finds it for us and before he finds the shit, we should'a found. Messy, but ya do what ya got to do, or Tony Junior will be whacking us. If and when ya whack 'em, drag his dead ass far away from Clinton City. Dump the body in Philadelphia for all that I care."

The call ended and Jimmy knew that he had to act fast and smart, too. Oscar was going to head for the employee parking and if Ken Mercurio's car was there, and Oscar began to check it, then it could become mean and ugly very quickly.

There was no time to delay. Forget pretending to be Jimmy O'Shaughnessy. It was time to be Jimmy Reeves and trust his new gal. Even though they just met, Jimmy already knew that he loved her. Now he needed to trust her and protect her too. Once again, he always went with his first instincts. Jimmy needed to beat the henchman or henchmen to Oscar, and Jimmy needed to know where employees parked their cars. Vanessa was an employee, and she knew where they parked and how to get there. Jimmy shut off the eavesdropping device, tucked the earphone and device into his jacket pocket, and he quickly moved into action. Jimmy walked briskly to the bar. He spotted Mick, looked up at him and Mick realized that he had returned from the restroom. Time to roll this into something else, and divert any suspicion whatsoever from their leaving shortly after Detective Campenella's departure.

Jimmy leaned over; he passionately kissed Vanessa and said loud enough for Mick to hear him, "C'mon, baby. Grab ya purse there. Time to split and head for my room."

"Ah, your room, Jimmy? I am falling for you, but I am not sure that I am ready. . .."

Jimmy ignored Vanessa's question, and he passionately buried his lips into hers once again and cut her statement off before she could complete her thoughts. After a deep and long kiss, Jimmy reached in his pocket, peeled off four hundred dollars and held the wad of money up for Mick.

"This good? Are we cool? We have to move the action sum place a little more private. Like my bed in my room, that is."

Mick's face displayed his dismay with the words and the implications of the plans that Jimmy and Vanessa had, but when Mick spotted the money and considering that the amount of money was about two hundred dollars more than the actual tab was, Mick quickly nodded. For Mick, the money overcame his jealousy. Besides, right now, Mick had more important things on his mind other than the fact that this annoying playboy was about to score with gorgeous and sexy Vanessa Michaelson. Jimmy tossed the large wad of money on the counter, took his drink glass and swigged the last drop, and he scooped up the sunglass case and dropped it into his pocket. Jimmy then gently took Vanessa by the hand and then once she landed on her feet, Jimmy watched her grab her clutch, he carefully wrapped his arm around her waist to steady her, and Jimmy led her out the front entrance. Poor Vanessa still had no clue of what was going on, and the alcohol might have dulled her senses for a moment or two. She was certainly glad that Jimmy was holding her steady, too.

Before she could even react and answer, Jimmy leaned in, kissed her cheek, and then whispered to Vanessa in a deep and serious tone, "Listen, to me, baby. Carefully. Do you know the quickest way to get where the employees park their cars?"

Vanessa sensed the complete change in Jimmy's demeanor and while she did not completely understand what was happening, she felt the urgency. The young woman was also very smart, and she quickly connected the dots with the exit of the detective investigating the death of Rob Mercurio and Jimmy's sudden change from a dashing playboy into a serious man. A man who suddenly seemed to have a serious mission at hand. Vanessa felt an even stronger attraction to Jimmy now, because for reasons that she could not place right now, this change had immense appeal to her. In her heart, she suddenly knew that Jimmy was not exactly who he had initially appeared to be.

Vanessa felt some fog clearing from the alcohol as well as the romantic haze and she nodded while answering, "Why, yes, of course. I am an employee. That is where I park."

"Okay, good. Please, you need to get me to the employees' parking lot or garage as soon as you can. Don't look back, just kiss my cheek and laugh. We need to pretend that we are just impassioned lovers heading as fast as we can to a room in order to make love."

Vanessa almost stopped and paused, but something inside of her told her to keep walking and she nodded. Trust, love, and her instincts took over.

She whispered back, "Jimmy, I thought *we were* going to your room. I thought *we were* going to be lovers and we would make love. What the hell is going on?"

Jimmy remained loving, but extremely serious, and his voice was contained in a low whisper, "All in good time, baby. Right now, keep walking, Mick is watching us. I can feel his eyes burning. I am going to pat and squeeze ya hard on your gorgeous ass. Take it in stride and keep walking. The parking, baby. Quick. Trust me. Do you trust me? I am so sorry for all of this. I will explain, but quick, baby, get me there."

Vanessa now shook off all the fog, and she nodded her head while saying, "I do trust you. I am not exactly sure what the hell is happening, but I am with you. I know the quickest way. Take my hand and walk fast. Please hold me up, Jimmy, because my head is swimming with booze and confusion."

"I gotcha, baby. I gotcha tight."

Vanessa looked up at Jimmy and she did not have to pretend to force the stars into her eyes while saying, "Thanks for the ass squeeze. Your hands are amazing and my loins are melting. Very enticing as a hopeful prelude. I can easily pretend that I cannot wait to get to the hotel room, mostly, because, well, it is the honest truth."

Jimmy noticed that Detective Campenella must have obtained directions from the front desk clerk, because he was already gone. Time was now ticking, and Jimmy now knew that he not only picked the right woman, but he was madly in love. Vanessa kicked it into high gear and Jimmy's only hope was that one of the security cameras did not detect them in their pursuit of Oscar and, as a result, they would dispatch more henchmen for Jimmy to deal with.

"Do youse guys park in a parking lot or in a garage, Vanessa?"

"In a garage. C'mon, Jimmy, this door leads to a shortcut to the garage, but it also brings us to the adjoining lobby, so it looks as if we are taking the elevators to your room."

Arm-in-arm they walked down a short corridor, Jimmy scanning the area for the presence of security cameras while appearing to be innocently snuggling with Vanessa.

They were in luck. There were some cameras mounted in the elevator lobby looming ahead of the couple, but before they reached the range of their viewpoints, Vanessa dropped their clasp and whispered, "Here, Jimmy. We can duck in this door and it brings us to the parking garage."

Vanessa led the way as Jimmy nodded, and they slipped through the door into an interior staircase. Once they passed through the door and it closed behind them, Jimmy placed his hand on Vanessa's arm to prevent her from walking any farther.

He held her tightly and said just above a low whisper, "Wait. Hold on. Stay here. Let me study this for a second." Vanessa sensed the situation; she stopped dead in her tracks, nodded, and studied Jimmy's eyes as his eyes scanned the entire staircase. First, he looked all around for cameras, and then his eyes looked at the staircase leading to the floors above them.

Satisfied, Jimmy pointed at the door ahead of them and whispered, "Is it this way to the garage?"

"Yes."

Jimmy nodded, let go of her arm and whispered, "Stay with me here. Most of all, please, remember that I am a good guy."

He opened his jacket and Vanessa held her hand over her mouth to prevent a gasp from escaping as she watched Jimmy pull out his twenty-two-caliber handgun, he then reached into a pocket, pulled out a silencer, and screwed it on the barrel on the gun.

"Follow me, listen to me, and watch my hand signals. Palm up means dead stop. Palm down means slow crawl. I have a feeling that I will need your assistance with disabling some security cameras."

Vanessa nodded, and she stayed close by Jimmy's side as he slowly opened the door to the parking garage. He poked his head out while holding the gun in his other hand. His other hand was palm up. A quick scan and then palm down, and he waved Vanessa ahead. Vanessa's heart was virtually pounding out of her chest, but she stood by her new love. They took a few steps into the garage, Jimmy looked up and sure enough, there was a camera mounted a few feet away and about seven or eight feet above their heads. Jimmy once again stopped their progress with a hand signal and gentle touch on Vanessa's arm. He waved to indicate for them to duck down next to a car parked close to the door and out of the range of the camera. Jimmy looked at the camera, and then he knelt down, carefully set the gun down on the floor of the garage and pointed at it for Vanessa to be aware of the gun's presence. She nodded that she understood. Jimmy then pulled the leg of his pants up to expose the tool kit strapped to his leg. Vanessa withheld her words. It might have been the shock and horror at the scene unfolding, or it was just her trust and honor for Jimmy right now, but she only watched and did not utter a sound or a word. Jimmy opened the tool kit, pulled out a small pair of wire cutters, then closed the case and placed it back into the holster strapped to his leg.

He handed the cutters to Vanessa and spoke in a low whisper, "Here, take these. Jump up on my back, climb up on my shoulders. When I lift you up and get you close, carefully, and quickly, snip all the wires behind that camera. Stay behind the lens. Quick, we only have a few minutes here."

"Okay, but Jimmy, I have a dress on."

"Yeah, I noticed that. Believe me, I did. Are you commando underneath it?"

"No, but. . .."

"Too bad. Anyway, just get your gorgeous ass up on my shoulders. Gotta suggest that, from now on, ya need to wear pants on our future dates. Better, leave ya dress and the high-heels at home. Sorry, but this kind of crazy bullshit comes up unexpectedly in my life." Jimmy knelt down and signaled to Vanessa to jump on his back.

She kicked off her high-heels, tugged at her dress, pulled it up high enough for her to move comfortably and mumbled, "I will keep that in mind."

With those words, she set her clutch on the floor of the

garage, put her arms around Jimmy's neck and jumped on Jimmy's shoulders. With his enormous strength, Jimmy effortlessly lifted Vanessa up in the air. She reached up and carefully cut through the wires.

Jimmy smiled; this was his kind of gal.

Jimmy dropped Vanessa back down to the floor, and they knelt together next to the car. He took the cutters from her, pulled out the toolkit, and replaced the cutters while scanning the garage for action.

"Great. You are amazing. Perfect ass. Black panties, huh? Beautiful."

Despite the intenseness of the situation, Vanessa smiled and as she pulled her dress back down, smoothed her dress out; slipped her heels back on, she picked her clutch back up, and whispered, "Is there any other color?"

"No. I will get a closer look later," Jimmy said as he picked up his handgun. Then he pulled a card out of his jacket pocket and handed it to Vanessa, along with a few hundred-dollar bills.

"Here. Take this card and this money. Hide behind this car and do not move until I tell or signal ya to. If by chance, sumthin' happens to me, and to Detective Campenella, get the hell outta here as quickly as you can. Do not use your car. Run to the front desk, call a cab, and do not go home. Go to a hotel that is outside of Clinton City and call the telephone number on that card. Tell the man who answers that Jimmy Reeves and the detective got whacked and we are dead."

"Okay. Ugh. Really? Well, okay, I have it. This is a little crazy and hard to follow, but I got it. This is like some crazy-ass crime-scene television show. Reeves? That is your real name?"

"Yes. Please, forgive me for lyin' to ya. I will explain everything. I promise. The man, who answers, will be the Attorney General of the State of New Jersey. The highest officer of the law in the state. He is my boss."

"Are you a police officer?"

"Honestly, no. For lack of a'nudder description, I am an assassin. Sorry, but I am. Vanessa, from here on in, I promise honesty. Always."

Jimmy held Vanessa tightly as he studied her eyes for a reaction to his testimony and to the fact that until now, he had done nothing but lie to her. She did not react; instead, she only displayed trust and love from her heart, with all of those emotions displayed through the passion in her eyes.

Vanessa nodded her head and whispered, "Kiss me, Jimmy Reeves. Tell me that nothing will happen to you. No, in fact, promise me."

Jimmy did not answer her request for a promise as to his fate, instead he smiled, he gave her a kiss, and then he signaled for her to hide. Jimmy watched as she scampered off behind the car and Jimmy smiled; this was his kind of gal.

Now, confident that Vanessa was secure and safe, Jimmy then scanned the area; jumped up and silently and in full stealth mode, Jimmy ran to another hiding spot behind a car where he could obtain a longer look across the parked cars. Sure enough, about fifty feet away, Jimmy spotted Detective Campenella checking out an older model four-door sedan parked on the right side of the garage. He was intensely looking the car over; his head was down and he was not paying attention.

In his head, Jimmy thought, "Classic mistake. Head is not on a swivel."

The Marine Corps training kicked in and he crept slowly between cars, darting from cover-to-cover, while carefully watching a door opposite where the detective was scanning the vehicle as it slowly opened. Jimmy slipped down next to a car and silently watched and waited. First, a gun barrel equipped with a silencer appeared, followed by the slow appearance of a hand and an arm. Then a black-suited henchman appeared, with his eyes locked upon the detective, and the gun that he held stayed directly aimed at the detective. A detective, who was deep in thought, oblivious to the danger about to strike. The henchman slowly allowed the door to close behind him, and it closed without a sound. Jimmy knew the gun that he held was a forty-five and at this range, it was a quick kill for the henchman holding it. The man slowly walked forward, and he silently moved in for the kill. Immediately, Jimmy recognized the potential assassin as the thug who stood at the forward watch this afternoon.

"So, we meet again," Jimmy whispered.

Jimmy realized that the door had a viewing window in it and the thug must have been watching the good detective for some time while he watched the scene unfold. Obviously, the thug had not spotted Vanessa or Jimmy, and so far, no other thugs responded to the now dead camera. Perhaps the eyes behind the cameras thought their own man disabled it. Jimmy now was confident that no help was on the way. This thug was their primary killer and he was on his own to take out the detective before Oscar found any trace of evidence before they did.

Within a few seconds, Jimmy processed the scene.

He could take the thug out with a surprise attack from behind, a head shot and a quick kill with his twenty-two, which required a close-range headshot for a clean kill. Another option was the nine, and he could nail the thug from where he knelt with a one shot, one kill. That would blow it all because Oscar would never be able to explain how the thug ended up dead, with bullets from a gun other than his own, and Jimmy knew that Oscar's chain of command was all on the Michanetti payroll. Moreover, Jimmy would blow his cover and the case might be a dead end. Still, one of his missions was to protect Detective Campenella and right now, the detective was in a world of Hell. No, Jimmy made his choice, and he shouldered his weapon, while drawing his knife from his ankle sheath. He was not going to slit the thug's throat; instead, he knew exactly how to strike a man to render him unconscious with a blow from the blunt handle of the knife.

After all, as he just told Vanessa, he was basically just an assassin.

The thug was now about ten feet in front of Jimmy; he aimed his weapon and, quick as a flash, Jimmy Reeves jumped into action. Like a tiger pouncing on prey, Jimmy ran forward, and before the thug could even turn and react, Jimmy cold-conked him on the side of the jaw and across his neck, causing the thug's head to snap violently. Jimmy had hit right at the sweet spot and it was not a deathblow, just an unconscious blow. Jimmy took the weapon out of the thug's hand. As the man's knees crumbled, his eyes rolled in his head and he lost consciousness. Jimmy slowly eased him to the floor of the garage and as he did, he looked over to Oscar, who had now spun quickly around when he heard the disturbance, swung his jacket open and pulled out his service revolver.

When the good detective spotted who it was that was in the process of saving his life, he smiled, shouldered his weapon and said, "Muchas gracias, mi amigo! Nice to meet you in person, Jimmy Reeves. Your reputation precedes you and I can now see how and why you earned it. Thank you for the save here. I owe you."

"You owe me nuthin'. We are a team. It's my job to save ya ass. It's ya job to figure this shit out. Better, cuff this bad boy and call for a black and white patrol car, Detective Campy. I hope they are not all on the take in your department. We need to split before he wakes up. Nice to meet ya too. Did my boss, maybe, kinda, sorta, tell ya to keep ya head on a swivel?" Jimmy asked as he knelt down and slid his knife back into the ankle sheath.

Oscar walked over to Jimmy, while taking his handcuffs out of the belt holster, and as he walked, he admitted, "He did indeed. I screwed up by being too engrossed in finding the missing brother's car. I already called for a patrol car before you and the bad guy here arrived on the scene. I called my crime scene investigations team, too. Not sure, who will show up with the patrol car, but the techie guys are on my side. They are cool, but as of late, it is very hard to tell the good guys from the bad guys these days, but I think they are cool. Help will be here shortly. After we check this car here while it is in place, we are impounding it and towing it for a complete dissection. I have to find this guy. Soon."

Jimmy nodded his head, watched as the detective rolled the unconscious man over, checked for the location of a trickle of blood from the thug's skull, and then he cuffed him.

"I had better call for an ambulance for this dude. He is still alive, but he is out like a light."

"He will be fine, Detective Campy. Just a headache for a few days. I did not want to kill 'em and cause ya too much explaining." Jimmy then turned and waved in the direction of where Vanessa was hiding and shouted, "C'mon over, Vanessa. It is over, baby." While Jimmy spoke, he constantly scanned the garage and kept a close eye on the doors leading to it. He also kept his thoughts on his handguns, and his eyes and ears remained alert for any arrival of backups, but it was very quiet. Jimmy surmised that the hidden thugs might have thought that by now, the good detective was out of the picture, and the camera disabled by their own man to prevent any evidence from recording.

The two men watched as Vanessa stood up from behind the car and she ran over, or ran as best as she could, wearing a skin-tight black dress and high-heels.

Detective Campenella mumbled, "Oh my, Jimmy. Your assistant is quite gorgeous. I saw her with you at the bar, but I thought that she was part of your act. I guess the movies are correct. The muscular hero dude always gets the beautiful chick."

Jimmy smiled and said, "Not always. Honestly, this is my first time with one. But damn, she is gorgeous. Gorgeous, and despite being kinda restricted with that dress painted on her, amazin' body, she is quite capable too."

Vanessa arrived on the scene, Jimmy wrapped his arm around her, and pulled her tight into his body, while asking, " Are you, okay?"

"I am now," Vanessa said, while standing on her tiptoes and kissing Jimmy's cheek.

"Vanessa Michaelson, meet Detective Oscar Campenella. Detective Campy will be ya name from now on. Ya last name is too damn long for a Paterson, New Jersey guy to say. Vanessa is part of the team. How shall we say? I deputized her."

Oscar reached out his hand. Vanessa did the same, and they shook hands while the detective said, "Nice to meet such a lovely deputy. Welcome to the team and thank you."

"Nice to meet you too, Detective Campy. All I can say is that this is one hell of a first date with this guy."

"I can see that. Say, Jimmy, since you are a jack-of-all-trades, can you get me in this car? I cannot get the lock picked."

"Really? Are you a rookie or sumthin'? Let me show you how ya open car doors in the hood. We have no time for picking locks. C'mon, Vanessa, ya have the skinniest arms out of all of us. Open the lock on the door, please, baby."

Jimmy reached again for his knife; he walked over to the driver's side of the car, with Vanessa and the good detective both following him. He waved for Vanessa to stand back and with one quick motion; he plunged the blade of the knife into the rubber gasket on the top of the window on the driver's side door and pried at the top of the glass. With his free hand, Jimmy pulled the window away from the frame and then motioned for Vanessa to open the lock. She slid her arm down inside the window, pulled the lock knob up and in seconds, the door was open.

Oscar shrugged his shoulders and mumbled, "That was easy. I guess that I am a rookie."

The wail of police sirens in the distance told them that the patrol car was close, and upon hearing the sirens, Jimmy patted Oscar on the back and said, "Time for us to book out of here. Their token security punks will be here any second now for damage control, now that the police cars are on the scene. Can't have all these high rollers and payin' guests think that this joint is a den of sin. Let's plan on a phone call at the number we worked out—say, around fourteen hundred hours tomorrow. Ya better call Chuck in the morning, too. See ya."

"Will do. Thanks again, Jimmy. And one more thing. That punk-ass bartender, Mick . . . when it gets down to knuckle time, he is all mine. Once more, I owe you both."

"I will make sure you get the first licks on 'em. 'Member, ya owe us nuthin.' Hope the car has the clues ya need. We are gone."

With a wave, Jimmy grabbed Vanessa's hand and the two of them quickly moved to the staircase from where they entered the garage and they disappeared into the night.

Once in the staircase, Vanessa watched as Jimmy carefully checked it out before proceeding and when Jimmy suggested they take the stairs, she asked, "Where are we going?"

"To my room, of course."

"Good. First, I need a few belts of Scotch, and then you need to tell me exactly what the hell is going on here. I am telling you, Jimmy, whatever the hell your name is—that your handsome and dashing ass better have a damn good explanation for the lies you told to me. Then, we can, well, see where we end up."

"Works for me, baby. Especially the ending part."

"Oh, and by the way, I want a few licks in on that creepy Mick, too. I am gonna kick his friggin' groin in while wearing my best high heels. Furthermore, just to let you know, since honesty now rules our lives, well, I never even have tried Scotch whiskey. Nevertheless, what the hell. After tonight, and the wackiest first date in the history of the world, I might as well give it a shot. After all this secret agent bullshit and mayhem, I guess a few belts of Scotch are not going to matter too much."

Jimmy stopped on a stair, turned, and smiled at Vanessa. He then leaned in, grabbed her around the waist, and pulled her in for a long and deep round of kisses. These were not only kisses of passion, but they were kisses that resonated with love and elements of trust.

When they finished, he whispered, "Yeah, no doubt, for sure, you are my kinda gal."

Chapter 7

Hold a Glass over a Flame

Jimmy Reeves and Vanessa Michaelson stood in the hallway, directly outside the door of Jimmy's hotel room. He carefully checked the hallway of the hotel where his room was located and he made sure that it was clear of any other persons. When Jimmy was convinced that no one else was in the hallway, Jimmy gently held Vanessa back with his arm and then he waved for her to stand to the side of the door, drew his twenty-two-caliber handgun from out of its holster and once more, screwed the silencer onto the barrel. He put his finger to his lips in a motion for Vanessa to remain quiet. Vanessa nodded. She carefully watched Jimmy put the key in the door and slowly opened the door to the hotel room, while keeping Vanessa behind him with a hand motion and his gun drawn and pointed ahead. Jimmy's palm was up, and Vanessa carefully watched and studied his hand signals. His eyes immediately caught a glimpse of the piece of thread that he planted earlier on the carpet right below his foot. Jimmy scanned the room, his gun drawn and his body down in a huddled position. With catlike quickness, he searched the hotel rooms, first the main room, then the bathroom, then the side rooms, the closets and all of them were clear, but his tattletales told him that his instincts were correct. They searched his room earlier tonight, and he passed their inspection.

Convinced that all was well, he put his palm down, then waved Vanessa in and holstered his gun, while reaching to close the door behind her. He put the "Do Not Disturb" sign on the doorknob, closed and flipped all the locks on the door, and swung the deadbolt over in place. Vanessa carefully stood and watched with interest and some elements of bewilderment while Jimmy went to the safes and checked for the disturbance of the Tattletales, and then he scooted over to the desk drawers and checked. All the money and items in all the locations were still in place. They had only checked and searched, but they had stolen nothing. 'Interesting,' Jimmy thought. He then scooted over to the end table drawer next to the bed. Yes, they checked there too. Finally, he checked the field glasses and yes, indeed, they moved from the original position that Jimmy placed them in.

"What are you doing, Jimmy? What are those little threads that you keep picking up and looking at?" Vanessa still stood in the same place and watched Jimmy work. It was as if she was afraid to move too much until Jimmy told her that all was well.

"Tattletales, baby. They are small threads that I put in strategic locations on the doors and ledges to tell if someone searched and checked the room. When ya open the doors and drawers, they move and tell their tale. They searched everything and determined that I was not who I really am. Shows ya how smart they are. Huh?"

Vanessa remained puzzled but slowly the dots began to connect.

She asked, "They searched your room? Who did so? Why? We cannot randomly enter a person's room. Not without announcing beforehand for housekeeping or maintenance duties."

Vanessa's eyes were wide and her voice full of passion while she recited the proper rules that she knew by heart from her employment training. Rules that she now knew in her heart the evil inner workings of her place of employment broke on a regular basis. Still her reciting of the rules went on as if to convince her soul that there was some error and this was not what it seemed.

"Or for good cause or an emergency, or in order to fulfill a guest's request. It is against the rules. Yet, I have a feeling that creepy Mick was behind this."

"Baby, I hate to tell ya this, but not too many people around here follow any rules. Killing a police detective who is investigating homicides is against the rules too. Your workplace is not what it seems to be, it is a dangerous place, a front for the mob operating out of Clinton City. Creepy Mick is the boots on the street. He is a front-line commander for a very dangerous and powerful crime boss. Mick ordered my room searched to check out what he might extract from me, but also to check out my story. He runs the daily game here. That is why he is untouchable to the general manager. A manager who I suspect is not entirely innocent and might be a bad guy too. Right now, I collect the intelligence and let Detective Campy and my boss solve the crimes."

Vanessa shook her head and then finally moved from the spot where she stood for so long. Jimmy embraced her, and she rested her head on his chest for a few moments. She was deep in thought.

Jimmy let go of Vanessa as she suddenly exclaimed, "Wow! I knew there was some crazy stuff going on behind the scenes here. All the staff sense it and know that where there are such wealthy and powerful guests staying and huge money flowing, there are always people with their hands in the till, but wow. The mob. Really?"

"Yeah, I am afraid so there, gorgeous. This place is super-fancy, but it is just a front for some pretty shady operations, Vanessa. Have you ever heard of a man named Tony Michanetti Junior, or for that matter, senior too?" Vanessa pursed her lips together while she pondered Jimmy's questions.

"I am not entirely sure. I have heard of a man named

Tony, and I think that I saw him tour the property one time. He had a team of black-suited men surrounding him and Mike Spence told all the staff to be on our best behavior because Tony was the actual owner of the Casa Al Mare. Not sure if that is the same Tony because his last name was never mentioned. I only saw him from a distance. I would recognize him though if I ever see him again. He was short, dark and his eyes broadcasted evil. He was another creepy dude."

"Well, darling, that sounds like a match. Michanetti Junior is the son of one of New Jersey's most notorious mobsters. He has followed the family traditions."

Vanessa shook her head, folded her arms, and seemed quite disgusted.

With the same look of disdain on her face, Vanessa said, "Makes sense now. All these high rollers all around. And that sleazy Mick and his disgusting suggestions to me. Suggesting that I could be a paid escort and a classy prostitute and he will be my pimp. Shit. What a mess. I really need that drink now, Jimmy. The adrenalin of tonight burned the martinis away."

Jimmy nodded and walked over to the wet bar. He scanned the Scotch bottles, selected one of the finer single malts, and poured one glass for Vanessa and for himself too. He poured them neat.

"Here. Cheers, baby. It is all over now. This can be our time now."

Vanessa set her clutch on the counter of the wet-bar. She took the glass and they touched glasses in a toast, while Vanessa stared at the glass.

"I usually like ice in my drinks."

"Not that drink, baby. That is a fancy-ass single malt, baby. Chillin' changes the taste. Drink it neat. Besides, ya a hot chick anyway. No sense it coolin' ya down."

Vanessa smiled and took a sip of the drink. Her face screwed up at the first taste of the Scotch.

"This tastes like cough medicine, Jimmy."

"Keep sippin' it, Vanessa. Your taste will adapt and it will be magic. It will change your life."

Vanessa seemed as if she would try Jimmy's advice. She walked over to a chair in the room and then she set the glass aside.

With a stern look on her face, Vanessa said, "It is time for you to tell me the truth. Everything, Jimmy. No more lies. I am exasperated with all of this. One minute it is the glorious romance, top-shelf drinks, starry-eyed kisses, you are a handsome and dashing playboy, and the next minute, you are some kind of badass secret agent guy pulling weapons from hidden crevices within your glorious body. Then, I am in the middle of it all and deputized as some honorary secret agent woman helping the good guys defeat the bad guys! What the hell is this, Jimmy?"

"I am sorry, baby."

"Are you?" Her gorgeous eyes had a burn in them as they narrowed.

"I am. I will explain."

"You bet your amazing ass that you will explain."

Jimmy set his drink aside, pulled off his suit jacket, and set it in a chair. From the pockets of the jacket, he carefully removed the various tools of his profession. Bugs, the eavesdropper, the silencer, and all the rest of his gear. Vanessa did not speak, but she sat sipping her drink and she watched as he carefully removed the handguns from their shoulder holsters and set them aside on the desk in the room. He loosened his necktie a little, then took off the shoulder holsters and set them on a table in the middle of the room. He then picked up the suit jacket, reached into the special hem, and removed all the various items stowed in it and set all of it aside on the bed. Jimmy picked up the handguns. He set the nine-millimeter handgun on an end table next to the bed, the twenty-two handgun, along with his drink; he carried and set it on a table, next to a chair that he sat in. A chair right next to where Vanessa sat.

"My goodness. That was amazing. I am surprised that you could even walk, nonetheless run, with all that stuff on your body."

"I have had a lot of practice of walkin' runnin' and doin' other stuff with the gear on me. Where do ya want me to begin?"

"Where you want to, as long as it is the truth."

Jimmy nodded and picked up his glass and took a sip. He began to tell his story, "Once more, James Reeves is my real name. No middle name and I prefer Jimmy for my first name. I grew up in north Paterson, New Jersey. Ain't no James in the hood, only Jimmies. Tough, and rough, neighborhood. A very poor family, but hard working. My old man was a car mechanic and my mom worked in a supermarket as a checkout gal. They are both gone now, but they were good parents. They did what they could for me. It is just me, no brothers or sisters. Made it through high school, barely, but I made it. I was a good athlete, but never played any organized sports. Despite the pressures, I kept out of trouble. No drugs, no crime. I was a tough kid, but honest. Various kinds of turmoil were ragin' on, and since life seemed to be a dead end for me, I enlisted in the United States Marine Corps. In basic training, they found that for whatever reason, I was a crack shot with a rifle. They trained me to become a sharpshooter and sniper and soon, I was in country creepin' around behind and in front of enemy lines with special ops. Every day, it was my job to stalk and then pick off the enemy. Enemy officers were my assignments. When I shoot, well, I do not miss. Ever. Officially, the records report, seventeen enemy officers killed, unofficially, it is more like thirty. Sorry, Vanessa, but I am not pullin' punches. I am an assassin."

The young woman did not react to Jimmy's testimony; she took another sip of her drink and studied Jimmy's eyes. He could not help but to admire how gorgeous she looked while sitting there. He knew that she was gauging what he was telling her for the truth, and Jimmy did not hold back in telling it. Vanessa was too special to pull any punches with or twist anything around to make it less than what it is.

"I did three tours in country. The enemy put a bounty on my head and ambushed me many times to wipe me out. A few times, it came down to hand-to-hand combat with hired killers on their side tryin' to collect on my head, but I took 'em all out and made it. Have me a ton of scars from gunshots and knife wounds, but I am alive. After a few of those attempts to rub me out, the Marine Corps finally sent me home. I stayed in for about twenty or so years, made Gunny rank, I have all kinds of awards, medals, decorations, ribbons, and other bullshit, and worked as a trainer for sniping. I earned a decent pension from the military, and I make a good buck now too, so money is not an issue for me. After I retired, since there are very few honest civilian jobs for assassins, I took a job as a personal bodyguard, driver, and kinda the unofficial informant while protecting two high-powered attorneys in Paterson. They both were prosecuting attorneys going after mobsters. Very dangerous mobsters. With my background, I kinda became involved in helping to collect evidence for cases as well as keepin' them safe. We had a few shootouts over the years with bad guys, tryin' to nail my bosses. I held my own and took the bad guys out of this world. I earned a reputation of a guy that never misses. Ever. The attorneys, well, one is Charles McCracken, and his partner at the time was, Gordon Tolland Senior. They both became special prosecutors, and I stayed on with them. Tolland Senior passed away from cancer and his son took over as Mr. McCracken's partner. Then when Chuck McCracken retired and Gordon Tolland Junior became a New Jersey senator, I worked for Senator Tolland as his driver and bodyguard." Jimmy stopped speaking and took another sip of his drink. Vanessa still had not said a single word, and Jimmy grew concerned that he already had lost her.

"You, okay? Am I ramblin' too much?"

"No, Jimmy, not at all. It is all quite fascinating. I must say that I am sorry to hear of your parent's both passing away. It must be difficult to be alone. Please, I know there is much more. Yet, I must point out the fact that you only killed bad guys."

Jimmy shrugged his shoulders and mumbled, "I guess, depending on which side ya were on."

Vanessa did not speak, but instead, she gave a symbolic wave of her hand in the air to indicate for Jimmy to continue with his story.

"Thank you. Okay, so now, Chuck McCracken, Gordy Tolland, and Mrs. McCracken, they are now my family. I have no livin' blood relatives. I am part of their family now."

"I understand, Jimmy. I sense your intense honor and loyalty to them all. It is glorious," Vanessa said with a smile and a look of admiration mixed with a strong dose of love planted on her face. It seemed as she was slowly softening in her demeanor as Jimmy told her everything about his amazing life and careers.

Jimmy returned her smile, and it seemed as if for the briefest of seconds, the battle-hardened heart of Jimmy Reeves melted just a little more.

Recovering, he continued with his outpouring, "A few years ago, maybe two or so years ago, there was this high-profile case that Gordy became embroiled in and it involved corruption in high places. Mr. McCracken always stayed close to Gordy, even after retirement, as his friend and consultant, and he helped solve the case. Mr. McCracken ain't no ordinary attorney and he tends to get involved in things and solve crimes on his own. We sort of had help from this friend of ours, a strange sort of guy, not sure who he is, but anyway, Gordy came out of the situation politically untouched, Mr. McCracken solved the case, became appointed to the attorney general position and I stayed on with him. Gordy, well, he is now a United States senator."

Vanessa leaned forward in her chair. It seemed as if she recalled the case.

"I think I saw that on the news! Fascinating. I do know who Senator Gordon Tolland is too."

"Yeah, not surprised. It was some unbelievably crazy business. The head of the crime family that was workin' the corruption was Tony Michanetti Senior. He avoided Mr. McCracken's prosecution, but shortly thereafter, turned up missin'. We are not sure, but we think the stranger, our friend, might have had sumthin' to do with his disappearance."

"This stranger, he is a good guy? Is he a federal officer or some type of undercover officer?"

"We are not sure of exactly what his title is, Vanessa, but he is a good guy. In fact, he is a very good guy! It is all quite strange cuz, he seems to have unusual powers. Let's leave it at that. I cannot tell you much more about him. I never met him, but Mr. McCracken has. He helped him solve the big case, and he mysteriously showed up here in Clinton City to offer advice and assistance to Detective Campy. He showed up when they murdered Rob."

Once more, Vanessa could not hold back her fascination with the testimony and Vanessa almost shouted out, "Fascinating. By the way, you were correct. Suddenly, this Scotch is magical. Refill, please?"

She held the glass up with a smile and the light of the room, reflected her face and the glint of the earrings in her ears. She was exceptional in so many ways.

"Gotcha covered. Told ya. It grows on ya," Jimmy said as he stood up, took her glass and walked over to prepare her another drink at the wet-bar.

"So, Rob *was* murdered. It was not a robbery. My sense

told me there was more to it than just a random robbery. From what I knew of him, which actually was very little, other than a few bucks in his wallet, it seemed as if Rob had very little to steal."

"Yup. Somehow, it is a mob rubout. However, for now, we cannot figure out as to why he ended up filled with bullets and with his fingers chopped off on his left hand. Everything that Campy has found until now, tells us that Rob was a good guy."

Vanessa gasped at the description of his gruesome death.

Recovering, Vanessa agreed, "How awful. He was a good guy. No doubt that he was. As I told you when we first met, I always liked him very much. He was respectful. His brother is a jerk. However, Rob was a good guy."

"Yes, we need to speak about the brother. Ken, I think, his name is."

"I did not know him too well. Yes, Ken is his name. He worked in the maintenance department but worked late shifts. I heard that he had a bad drug habit with coke or maybe even heroin. He might have had a girlfriend who worked here as a housekeeper, but I am not too sure. As I said, I did not know him. I only know the hearsay from other employees. He has not been to work since Rob died. That is nothing new. He often was a no show. Another jerk that I am not sure how he kept his job. However, it all is becoming clearer now. The general manager, Mike Spence allows certain people to ride all the time. Strange."

Jimmy nodded and said, "Thanks for the info. Yes, Ken is the key. That is why Detective Campy was so excited to find his car. Ken is missin'. What is da deal wid Spence? Good guy? I think not. He is in a high spot here as the general manager of dis here joint."

Vanessa could not help but to smile at how Jimmy's strong New Jersey accent occasionally kicked in and out. He cut off, and he chopped up and twisted the pronunciation of words as his level of excitement changed. His hard, New Jersey accent was a huge part of his appeal.

Vanessa answered Jimmy's question with an explanation of her opinion of her boss, Mike Spence.

"He is always nice to the desk staff. Strange, but he was never really a general manager of a hotel before he came to Casa Al Mare. He is an accountant. Spends all his time, in general ledgers and lets the department managers run the hotel operations. I do not think he knows too much about the hotel business. He is a spreadsheet guy."

"Makes sense, baby. Bad guy. Spence is how they wash da money through as he cooks the books." Vanessa listened as Jimmy continued to explain, "Anyway, Tony Senior has a son. Tony Junior, and we think, when his old man disappeared that he fled to Clinton City to set up a new base of operations. Drug running up and down the shoreline outta here, fencing stuff, illegal gamblin', high-end prostitution, they have their fingers in all kinds of things and this here, fancy joint allows them to launder the cash through the books. Hell, even your valets parking cars out front here are plugs for weed and pills. Lots of dead people showing up here as of late, both drug overdoses and murders. I am sure you see it on the news here."

Vanessa nodded but did not comment. Her eyes studied Jimmy while the big man continued to prepare her drink refill. She enjoyed studying his every move. Just the hard manner that he moved and his muscles rippled made Vanessa glow with passion. She could not help it. The man captivated her. Jimmy continued to explain while replacing the cap back on the top of the Scotch bottle.

"Detective Campy's old man was a detective in Paterson and he is retired now, but still pals with Mr. McCracken. The Clinton City police department is full of corruption, and Detective Campy is an honest cop. He asked his dad for advice and his dad told him to call my boss for assistance. Well, that started the wheels in motion. When my boss heard about all the police corruption, Tony Junior hanging around, this fancy joint, and then our friend, the stranger showed up, he sent me down here, on how, do I, say it? A vacation."

Jimmy handed Vanessa the drink, and he smiled, "That part was not a lie. I am on vacation."

Vanessa laughed as she took the drink, and said, "Some friggin' vacation. Therefore, you are protecting the detective, while posing as some playboy on a vacation, while simultaneously being the good guy with all the muscles and secret weapons. In reality, you are actually an inside plant working as an informant for Detective Campy and your boss, as well as a bodyguard. I get it now. Nevertheless, you have to tell me. Did you ask me for a date and come on to me just to use me for information? Because I have to say, you are one hot dude. Honestly, this tale of truth and madness, mixed in with your military career and the secret agent stuff, just makes you even hotter."

Vanessa set the glass down on the end table and pretended to fan her face. Her humor was intact, but the humor had layers of truth in it.

"Hotter than Hell. It is as if I am in some spy movie or something. Damn, I am just a hotel desk clerk. The most excitement that I have is when a pen runs out of ink on the job and we have to go get another one. I am used to meeting all the high rollers and movie stars. Most of them are stuck up jerks. Today, I met the socialite, the famous woman, Ms. Hillary Thornburg. She checked in and I have to say, she was really nice to me. We are going to meet for drinks on Wednesday. I opened the store for her to buy some film. Apparently, she is now some, big-shot photographer. She bought a teddy bear for her niece's birthday and she is going to meet me and have me ship it to her. She is stunningly gorgeous, but she was wonderful to me. Hillary was very down to Earth and when she asked why I was so excited, I told her that I had a date with you tonight. A handsome, hot, older guy that I fell for within a few minutes."

Vanessa stopped speaking, and she nervously fiddled with her drink glass and then ran her fingers through her hair and allowed her eyes to first fall upon the bed and then the rest of the room before settling upon Jimmy Reeves. It seemed as if for a moment or two, her mind wandered with possibilities and that she felt as if she allowed her heartfelt feelings about Jimmy to escape too soon in their relationship. However, Vanessa was not going to stop speaking from her heart. Not now. Not after all that this evening had brought to both of them.

"Jimmy, honestly, I never do this. I mean, fall for a man so hard and want to come to his hotel room and make love to him. In fact, I want to make love to him all night long. Maybe forever. But then again, I never met Jimmy Reeves until now."

Vanessa now set her drink glass down on the table and while her eyes studied Jimmy, she nervously fingered her earrings.

With her voice laced with some anger, Vanessa said, "Hillary gave me good advice. She told me to be careful, because the stunning and dashing men always seem to have an entourage of other women on their arms and in their beds that they conveniently forget to mention to you. In my wildest dreams, there was no way for us to have guessed, your actual occupation or motives. No, you might not have an entourage of women hanging on you. Instead, you are a walking time bomb full of weapons and muscles! You lied to me and while I do not see other women, you sure have a shitload of weapons and secret agent gizmos and gadgets attached to various parts of you. I have to know, Jimmy, was I just a ploy to gain inside information?"

Above everything else that Jimmy Reeves was, his honesty was above reproach. He felt terrible about the initial lies, but he was on a case. It was part of the job. He stood in front of Vanessa and set his glass aside. Her eyes begged for a response, and Jimmy knelt down in front of her and motioned for Vanessa to take his hands. She did so and waited for the answer.

"Yes. Initially. At first, I thought you were perfect for some good company and for some inside information. I knew that I won ya over and I felt your honest heart. It is my job, and I had to start sumwhere, baby. I met you and the wheels spun. But, please, believe me with all my heart that as soon as I got to my room, I regretted it. Guilt hung all over me, and I could not shake you from my mind. You took my heart over and I tried so hard to concentrate. I mean, this shit is not stuff ya play at. Jimmy Reeves needed to stay focused on the mission, but ya were all around me. I was just doin' my job. I knew that we connected and planned to clue you in just as soon as I put the pieces together."

Jimmy squeezed her hands harder and then gently ran one thumb over the top of her right hand. He studied her eyes while remaining kneeling in front of her. Vanessa did not react.

Jimmy continued to explain, "The bar scene, before it turned crazy, was amazin'. I fell in love with you tonight. Within a few minutes, I did. I swear to you. I did not want to, but I did. Jimmy Reeves don't ever fall in love. Ever. But, I did. Honest."

Vanessa let go of Jimmy's hands and he stood up. Her eyes told of a struggle, and some hints of tears appeared in the corners of them. Vanessa took the glass and this time; she took a very long sip. She almost finished the Scotch, and then she set the glass aside.

"Do you kill people often?" Vanessa asked. "I mean, as in once a week or something like that?"

"No. But ya never know what comes up. I do my job. Sometimes, it calls for violence. It is my job and there are a ton of bad guys out there."

"Do you have any women in your life, Jimmy Reeves?"

"No. I only date on rare occasions. I think that my work is my life. Until tonight that is."

"Ever married?"

"No, just to the Marine Corps, if that counts. You?"

"No. I am careful about dates. I had a steady boyfriend for a year or so, but we broke it off about six months ago. He turned out to be a handsome, but an immature punk and all he wanted to do was make love in his crummy apartment and take my money to spend on weed. He had no job, was stoned all the time, and he became very clingy and annoying. I dumped him and kicked him out of my apartment. Have never seen him since then. So, tell me, with your hot body and smoking good looks, do you lure women into your bed all the time for sex?"

"No. Never. I bought condoms yesterday for a prop. Put them in the end table drawer for the thugs to find to keep up wid the playboy image bullshit. Took two of 'em and chucked them out so it looked as if I was already into the women here. I did not even know what size to buy."

"What size did you buy?"

Jimmy smiled and said, "Extra-large. I guessed but, ah, well, I did not actually measure."

With those words and his display of openness, Vanessa's eyes dried off the hints of the tears and she seemed as if Jimmy's honesty and somewhat innocent testimony struck a chord with her. Another long sip and she emptied the glass. She softened even more now and allowed her eyes to go up and down Jimmy's body.

She smiled, before finally saying, "I have a feeling they might just fit. Barely. How old are you?"

"Forty-nine. Be fifty in three months. You?"

"I am, thirty-seven. Really? You are almost, fifty? My goodness, what a man you are. You look as if you are no more than forty at the most."

Jimmy smiled and said, "Thanks. Is my age an issue? After all, we fit within the rule. Ya know, half ya age plus seven. We make it by a few years. Do you forgive me? Ya gotta tell me. This is all tough to take, but I have spilled my guts wid da truth here, baby."

Vanessa stood up and did not answer Jimmy's question or comment on his statements.

She picked up her empty glass, stuck it in Jimmy's hand and said, "Rules and bullshit, like that mean nothing. Your age means nothing to me. It is not a factor in anything. Only the age of your soul and heart matter. I have to pee. Refill, please. This Scotch stuff is heavenly. You are correct. It is a life-changing experience."

Jimmy took the glass and watched as she swayed off to the restroom. He could not help but to think that her rear view was almost as extraordinary as the front view was.

He whispered, "Yeah, no doubt, you are my kinda gal for sure."

Jimmy was upset that she did not answer his question, but in his heart, he hoped that his display of honesty had won her over. Obviously, the last thing that he wanted to happen was to lose her. Above all, he had a job to do, and he did not plan to fall in love with her, but he had. So, Jimmy Reeves needed to tell her that.

The truth.

Jimmy finished his drink and thought, 'Damn, he had sucked down so much alcohol today, but still was mostly sober.' Just now, he felt a little of the Scotch working at him, but for the most part, he was only slightly buzzed.

Jimmy walked to the wet-bar, turned his back, and rinsed out Vanessa's glass to refresh it. He heard the toilet flush, the sink run, and the door to the restroom open. As he prepared the drink, he felt Vanessa's arms reach around him and she pulled him in tightly and rested her head upon his back.

He heard her whisper, "I forgive you. I feel your

incredible honor and thank you for all that you told me. I know that you trust me because you would not have told me all that you did unless you did so. I know that your dishonesty was only because of that same honor and in order for you to do your job. Something or someone very powerful has brought us together, Jimmy Reeves. I feel it and you do too. I have waited for you and now, for some reason, we are together. For not only this mission, but for our love."

Jimmy turned around and pulled Vanessa in tight to him. He gently pulled her face up to his, and they kissed.

"Damn, Jimmy, we can get wasted on the taste of the Scotch on our breath and lips alone. Whiskey-laden kisses. Very tasty and sexy too," Vanessa kidded with Jimmy as they broke away and he handed her the refilled drink glass. Vanessa took a long sip and studied Jimmy carefully. It was now all different. Her loins now ached for this man. Even more than when they sat at the bar together. It was a combination of his sexiness, his appearance, his voice, his honor, his truth, and his integrity. She knew this was a special man. A good guy, fighting evil in this world. Even if they just met, Vanessa could tell that she wanted to be a part of him now and forever. The attraction and love overwhelmed her. Vanessa stood silently in front of Jimmy while she carefully studied him. Her soul was now calm, and only her heart was speaking to her.

The earlier martinis now mixed in with the Scotch and her head swirled a little. She thought, 'Was it the drinks or was it love? Or was it a little of both?'

Somehow, someway, this was all fate. Who was driving all of this? She was not sure, but she knew it was fate for her to meet Jimmy and to be involved in what they were now all working on together. For them to be a team and be together in both love and in life.

'It is love,' Vanessa thought.

Vanessa set her drink glass on the counter of the wet-bar

and gently took Jimmy's drink out of his hand and set it next to her glass. She felt waves of desire and seduction work over her body and her mind too.

She gently whispered, "Enough Scotch. Time to work our own magic, Jimmy Reeves."

They kissed again, long and deep, and they lingered for a long time, hanging on each other's lips. While they lingered, Vanessa worked at the necktie around Jimmy's neck and she loosened it all the way, then pulled the knot apart and tossed it aside. She then worked at his shirt as they kissed again. Slowly and seductively, she undid each button individually and when it was completely unbuttoned and loose, she pulled it off Jimmy. Vanessa then rather forcibly pulled the tail of the shirt out of his pants and when it was loose and free, she tossed the shirt aside too. Vanessa was now breathing quite heavily, and Jimmy gently stepped away from her.

She stood back and listened, then watched as Jimmy said, "Wait, baby. Wait, I gotta get rid of these."

He went to pull off and over his head, the small knife and dog tags that hung around his neck and rested upon his chest, when Vanessa stopped him.

"Lose the knife, Jimmy, but please, keep the dog tags. They display your honor."

Jimmy nodded and loosened the knife from the chain and carefully set the dangerous and sharp weapon aside. He now stood bare-chested in front of Vanessa, she breathed deep and heavy, her desire increasing with each breath, and Vanessa slowly worked her hands over his chest, feeling his power, and his remarkable muscles. She lingered with her fingers, while gently feeling a heavy scar on his left shoulder, and took note of what was an obvious gunshot wound, but Vanessa did not mention it or dwell upon it.

"What a remarkable body. The muscles reflect your strength and profession, Jimmy. You are amazing."

She plunged her lips into his as Jimmy slowly worked his hands around her waist, then he gently pulled at the hem of her skin-tight dress and worked it up her body. He slipped his hands underneath the dress, grasped the opposite sides of the top of her panties with his two thumbs and slowly worked them loose, pulled them down and off her body. Vanessa helped Jimmy pull her panties down the last few inches and then, while keeping her lips locked onto Jimmy's lips, she stepped out of them one leg at a time. She kicked off her high heel shoes and then with the big toe of her left foot, she hooked the panties and kicked them aside too.

They stopped kissing for a moment. Vanessa braced herself with both hands firmly planted upon Jimmy's mighty chest and asked, "Do you still want me not to wear dresses on our dates, Jimmy Reeves?"

"No. In thinkin' 'bout it and weighin' it all over, dresses work out just fine. Gives, my hands quick access to your amazin' ass."

Vanessa laughed, as she worked at the hook and loop on Jimmy's pants at his waistline, and loosened his pants. Jimmy quickly let them slide down to his ankles. He then reached down, unzipped the side zippers on his boots, pulled them off and tossed both of them off his feet and aside. He stepped out of his pants and tossed them aside too. Vanessa had unzipped her dress and slowly and seductively, she dropped it and stepped out of it, while allowing it to tumble down to the floor and all around them. She quickly undid her bra and tossed it on the floor, and her breasts tumbled into Jimmy's waiting hands.

Vanessa now stood gloriously naked in front of Jimmy. She was a flawless goddess. Perfect breasts, with nipples full of bursting desire, and glorious curves displaying flawless and glowing skin.

They embraced, and she gasped as Jimmy let go of her breasts and he grabbed her perfect backside with both of his hands firmly planted upon her bare cheeks and forced the hardness of her glorious breasts into his massive chest. She could feel his desire now, pressing into her waistline.

As they kissed, Vanessa worked Jimmy's underwear off his body, and instantly, she held his erect and throbbing manhood in both of her hands.

In a throaty whisper she growled, "My goodness. I hope those condoms fit. I knew you would be beyond glorious, but my goodness. . .."

Within seconds, the two lovers had worked their way over to the bed. Jimmy forcibly swept the items aside that were resting on the bedcovers and they flew in the air and landed onto the floor. Vanessa and Jimmy locked as one into each other's arms and they tumbled together into the bed. Immediately, they were deep in the throes of indescribable passion and heaving deep breaths of love.

"Jimmy, I can't wait. Please, fall into me right now," Vanessa pleaded with her lover.

Jimmy reached for the end table drawer and grabbed the box of condoms.

It was time for a test fit.

How ironic it was that what was originally a prop, and was just another part of the game, had now become a reality. Then again, this entire night was a remarkable and fateful adventure. While the two newfound lovers began to make endless love, the night seemed as if it was not really ending. Perhaps, the reality was that this was just the beginning.

It was now about one in the morning, and down on the first floor of Casa Al Mare, at the bar in Reflections, Mick Malzoni, worked on closing the establishment for the night. Last call here was at two in the morning. The other two restaurants within the hotel and resort would stay open a little later, but for Reflections, it looked as if it would be an on-time closing tonight. With only a few hard-core drunks at the bar, along with some wealthy rich kids spending Daddy's dough in the dining area, there was little activity left in Reflections for tonight. You could also count the young couple who sat in a dark corner of the dining area, in a drunken buzz. They had been there for hours, laughing and drinking, and right now, they really needed to go to their room because the woman's date could not stop plunging his hand down into her low-cut neckline and feeling her breasts.

Other than the lust-fest and the drunks, there was little business left for tonight.

Even the piano player went home an hour or so earlier.

It had not been a good evening for Mick. Despite the nice "sales" he made on a few hook-ups for not only the businessman with the huge belly, but with another loser elderly man, who paid a tidy sum for a night of adventure with one of his hotter chicks, Mick, was licking his wounds over the loss of one of his best men. How it all happened, and all went down, Mick could not explain . . . but it did. He underestimated the detective's ability. Mick really thought he was just a chump, but somehow, his man ended up out like a light, arrested for attempted murder and in the clink and the detective walked away unscathed. It was a huge screw-up and they would need to prevent the media from running this story, which was easy for Tony Junior to do, but worse of all; Ken Mecurio's car was now in the hands of the law. When the camera went out, his watchmen in the security booth thought it was their own man taking out any potential evidence and they should have checked, but they did not. Too many mistakes and he knew that he was going to hear it from Tony Michanetti Junior. Mistakes did not go over well with Tony Junior. Mistakes had a bad habit of causing not only unemployment but also a lot of pushing up of daisies. Mick knew he was a key member of the organization and although he was not the direct cause of the screw-up, it would not go over well. Not with the organization still missing about ten million dollars of street value heroin out there somewhere, along with a wad of cash for a recent deal of another million or two. Ken Mercurio was missing too, and right now, all indications pointed to the fact that Ken was the key. Mick knew that they had to find him quickly or it would be Hell to pay for everyone. Just to add to Mick's anger and add another blow to his operation, Ken's girlfriend, Donna Eardley, was a no show as of late too. Donna was a hot chick, perfect body and a wild gal in the sack and in high demand for high-end prostitution with some of Mick's wealthier clients. Donna occasionally "worked" as the most beautiful housekeeper on the Casa Al Mare housekeeping staff.

She did not clean many rooms, but she sure cleaned out some wallets.

Mick pondered the evening's events and he began to clean up the bar and prep areas for closing. Hell, he even had to suffer through watching the Casa Al Mare's hottest chick of them all, even hotter than Donna was; Ms. Vanessa Michaelson, go off to spend the night with that rich Irish bum, Jimmy. Made his blood boil to think that they hooked up right under his nose. Even though he knew it would have been a stupid mistake, Mick regretted not telling his men who searched Jimmy's room to lift a few bucks from the stash of dough the jerk tried to hide in his room. He had tried everything to get in Vanessa's pants, as did every other male working here, with not even a ripple of attention from her.

She is a knockout.

Oh well, at least, Jimmy throws money all over the place. Mick will get some of Jimmy's dough anyhow. The two hundred dollars that he gave Mick for a tip was very cool. He will be gone in a few days and Mick could resume his pursuit of Vanessa after Jimmy was out of the picture.

The telephone rang at the end of the bar and Mick tossed his bar rag aside and walked over to the end of the bar to answer the phone. There was no need to lower his voice. The only two patrons, remaining at the bar and nearby the telephone, hung over their glasses virtually passed out in their respective drinks. He would have to get a houseman to bring them to their rooms. Tomorrow morning for them was going to be Hell on Earth.

"Really? Coming this way? Now? What do you mean he just suddenly appeared? You did not park his car?"

It was the night shift supervisor of the valets, Michael, calling Mick to report on an incoming guest.

"Okay, I think that I get it. Let me repeat, so I have it right. He is a walk-in from the street at a little past one in the morning. A big guy, dressed all in black, with a big hat on his head. What do you mean he is a huge guy? How huge is huge?"

Mick paused to listen to the answers.

"Shit, c'mon guys, ya gotta turn assholes away before they get in. I will take care of it. Bullshit, I swear, this is all bullshit tonight. You guys need to get on the stick."

Mick listened for a while to Michael and the details of his report and after carefully listening to him; he double-checked what it was that Michael said to him by repeating the details. The report seemed very strange.

"You tried to stop him and he did not stop or even answer you, huh? He wears shiny black boots with metal tips and they click on the floor. Really? What the hell? Is this some kind of joke or what? Is Mario around? Make sure he is packing and send his big sweaty ass over here to sit in the dining room, sweat, and watch. I might need him to bring some drunks to their rooms anyhow. It will be cool. We can roll them for a few bucks and they will think they lost it in a drunken stupor. Yeah, bye and get your shit together out there."

No sooner than a second or two after Mick hung up the telephone, he heard a strange noise. At this time in the early morning, both Reflections and the hotel lobby were very quiet. There were very few people milling around and the noise resonated all around Mick. It was the sound of a loud, clicking noise, somewhat, as if a small hammer was gently tapping on a piece of metal. The noise was rhythmic in its beat, as if the person making the noise was keeping time to music. Mick realized that the source of the noise was what Michael described to him on the telephone. It was the approach of this strange and huge man, dressed all in black, wearing boots with metal tips on them. This stranger was walking this way, and Mick tried hard not to allow the sound to unnerve him. He looked across to the hotel lobby and even the desk clerk remained mesmerized by the sound, as well as an older couple who were holding hands while strolling through the lobby.

The clerk and the couple could see the man, but Mick could not see the source of the ominous sound.

Mario, the obese henchman, slipped in from the back of the house, and he too stopped when he heard the sound of the stranger's boots striking the floor. Mario shrugged his shoulders, looked at Mick, and waited for instructions. Mick waved at the dining area and put his fingers to his eyes as a signal for Mario to watch the scene unfold. Even the two drunks looked up and in a haze of a drunken stupor; they wondered what the noise was that currently echoed throughout the area.

One of them even managed to mumble before fading back into a drunken haze, "What the hell is that friggin' weird-ass noise?"

"Click, click, click."

The sounds of his boots grew ominously louder and closer and as they did so, Mick checked under his suit jacket to ensure that his weapon was there.

It was.

Mick looked up, as did everyone inside of Reflections, when the clicking noises stopped and the source of the noise appeared. The rich punks partying in the dining room stopped laughing, drinking, and carrying on in order to look up. The hazy drunks at the bar wobbled their heads and did their best to focus their eyes to see. Even the young couple stopped their playful petting to see who, or what, was standing there. Mario sat in his chair in the dining room. He sat silently watching, sweating his usual drops of sweat, and he nervously fingered the weapon inside his suit jacket. No hair-triggers allowed.

Standing silently in the entrance to Reflections was a very tall, lean, yet very powerfully built man. He was standing ominously there in front of Mick, Mario, and the remaining guests. The man showed no emotion, nor did the stranger say anything. The silent and immense stranger standing in the entrance to the bar and lounge, was dressed all in black, he wore a black vest, covering a perfectly pressed, black buttoned-up shirt, and his sharply creased, black trousers had no ripples or wrinkles. On his head, he wore a wide-brimmed black hat and on his feet, he wore highly polished black boots. His attire was immaculate. Nothing was out of place on the man; even the hair on his head that Mick could see from under the wide-brimmed hat was perfectly groomed, trimmed neat and clean along the edges. His face sported a black beard and full facial hair and once again, it was neat, clean, and trim. His eyes were a piercing black, and they slowly scanned the room, then the bar and the area all around him. You could barely see his eyes working the room from under the brim of his hat, yet they moved, and it was as if the stranger was carefully studying his surroundings. The look in his eyes alone sent waves of shivers down the cocky bartender's spine as well as every other person who now gazed upon him.

He was the quiet stranger in the black hat.

He moved again, walking slowly to the end of the bar,

his boots clicking along the floor and when he selected a bar stool and sat down at the bar, most everyone returned to their own individual worlds, the silent stranger was immense, unusual and different, but he was just that. An unusual stranger. Simply, a man stopping by for a late night or actually, early morning, sip or two of his favorite libations. . ..

On the other hand, was he?

Everyone returned to his or her worlds. Except for Mick and Mario that is. Mick grabbed a coaster and slowly walked over to where the stranger sat. He did his best not to focus on his appearance or the possibility of who this strange man was or is.

"Last call is at two. You have a little bit of time. Welcome to Reflections. What brings you in here? Are you staying here, or do you want a drink before you check in? I have never seen you here before. Or have I?"

Mick could not help but to think as he studied the stranger's dark eyes that this man seemed as if he traveled from somewhere out of the past. His attire, his dark appearance, it was all very unnerving.

The stranger did not answer Mick's questions; he simply spoke in a deep, low, but melodious voice, "Your best Scotch. Triple pour. Neat."

Mick was immediately miffed that the stranger ignored his questions and now, he felt brave enough to challenge the stranger's request, and of course, pocket a few extra bucks, too. He looked over at his selections of Scotch, walked over to one bottle, picked it up, and held the label out for the stranger to see it.

"This is our best. Single malt. The best on the planet. A triple will cost ya one-hundred and seventy-five bucks for one drink. Do ya have that kinda dough, pal? That is a fortune for one drink."

The stranger said not a single word. He reached into the pocket of his vest, pulled out a large wad of bills and peeled off two crisp, one-hundred-dollar bills and laid them on the counter without saying a single word.

"Plus, a tip, and a surcharge for washing ya glass, and the lateness of the hour. Pal."

Mick was feeling it now. Back to being cocky.

The stranger dropped another one-hundred-dollar bill on the bar and still said not one word. His stare did grow in intensity and Mick knew that he had better not test anything beyond this point.

With a smug and weak smile, Mick took the bottle and poured the drink.

While he poured the drink, Mick said, "Since ya decided not to talk too much, then I have to be sure ya can pay before I pour. I am sure ya understand. Pal."

Mick walked over and set the drink in front of the quiet stranger and he reached for the money. When his hand was on the money, quick as a flash, the quiet stranger grabbed Mick's hand, and immediately, Mick felt as if all the strength and all of his spirit left his body. Mick's knees buckled, and he found it difficult to remain upright. The evil bartender and want-to-be thug reluctantly looked up and into the stranger's eyes. The stranger's eyes burned and it felt as if he could see straight through to Mick's soul.

The stranger spoke, once again in his low, powerful, yet melodious voice, "Please, I need to advise you that I am not your . . . pal."

Mick tried to recover as the stranger let go of his hand and Mick looked over to Mario to signal to him that he might want to hustle over and sit at the bar. Mick's breathing was deep and hard, and his heart felt as if it would pound right out of his chest. He swallowed a load of bile that spit up into his throat.

The stranger reached for a candle that was burning merrily on the bar counter. A little candle in a golden glass, a happy display of ambiance. All the tables had the same candles, and they sat in various locations on the bar.

Mario heeded the signal from his boss and he stood up and slowly wandered closer to the bar.

The stranger did not turn around nor did his eye's move, but as he pulled the candle closer, he said, "Tell, Mario, to sit back down. I can assure you that he will be of no assistance. I will vaporize, Mario, right before your eyes. A pile of ashes and dust will remain as a sad reminder."

Mick felt another shiver down his spine, and with his eyes, he stopped Mario. Mick almost drew his weapon, but he stopped as he watched the stranger pick up his glass of Scotch and he held it over and within the flame of the candle. The glass grew hotter and hotter and you could see the alcohol slowly begin boiling and smoking in the glass. Yet the stranger remained unscathed. Remarkably, his flesh did not burn! The Scotch whiskey was boiling in the glass and he continued to hold it in his hand without any ill effects. Mick was now horrified, as was Mario, but the rest of the guests remained oblivious as to what was occurring.

"Hold a glass over a flame, Mick Malzoni, and you will burn. Right now, you are about to burn."

Mick Malzoni was beside himself in fear and apprehension and Mick began a long rant, "Just who the hell are you? How are you not burning and screaming in pain? Do you have some kind of a special glove on or what? What the hell is this bullshit? Are you threatening me? Do you know who runs this place? I can make one call and you will be a part of forgotten history. We will cut your tongue out and feed it to you for breakfast and then slice the rest of you up in a million pieces."

"Good luck with that. Besides, you are making an assumption that I have a tongue," the stranger said with a smile and with one quick motion and to the added shock and horror of Mick and Mario, in one gulp, he tilted the glass and swallowed the remaining amount of boiling Scotch. The stranger's eyes focused intently upon Mick, and the dark stranger opened his mouth and let out a large puff of smoke. Suddenly, Mick felt the air around him turn cold, almost a deep chill, and Mick shivered violently for a few seconds, until the temperature returned to normal.

"I ask you again—just who the hell are you?" Mick managed to ask between body-wracking shivers and the horror that was now permeating his soul.

The dark stranger gently placed the glass back on the counter and said, just above a whisper, "I am who you want me to be and what you can never imagine that I am. Make your call, I can assure you that ten thousand, Tony Michanetti Juniors and your teams of henchmen will not be enough. Your empire of evil will vaporize, like that whiskey in that glass did. With a simple stomp of my boots upon the surface of your angry world and a wave of my hands, I will turn all of you into dust. Then, you will visit Hell and experience the fury and agony of it. Mark my words that the night and the darkness are now closing in and around you. Be very afraid, Mick, very afraid. Because you, unlike me, burn when you hold a glass to a flame for too long. You have held your glass within the flame for far too long now. Your evil, invoked a response from the good of this world and from beyond this world and we are unstoppable. I will return and it will not be so easy next time. The time to repent is now. Right now. Heed my words or feel the burn. Your choice."

He stood up, pointed at the money, then to Mick, and turned and walked away.

Mick did not move, nor did Mario. They both stood there shocked and amazed while listening to the distinct click of the metal tips of his boots striking the floor. They stood frozen in motion while the sounds of the stranger's boots striking the floor grew softer in volume. They stood in horror and listened in fear until the sounds finally faded away and they could no longer hear them.

Chapter 8

The Pieces Begin to Fit

Jimmy Reeves and Vanessa Michaelson made love for hours and hours. All Vanessa could think about now was how the older men *are so* experienced. Jimmy was beyond an amazing lover. The man turned Vanessa inside and out, over and over, endlessly. They made love throughout the night and into the early morning hours. Occasionally, they stopped, talked about every subject imaginable and basked in their love as they spoke their minds and shared their hearts. Then, once again, the two lovers fell into each other's arms and made love for more hours on end. While exhausted in each other's arms, the two impassioned lovers finally fell asleep. They spent their seemingly endless energy after the marathon display of lovemaking.

One thing for certain was that Jimmy Reeves needed to purchase another box of props. . ..

When the early morning light stole away their glorious night and the flickers of sunlight dashing on the floor of the hotel room and across their faces, finally caused the two exhausted lovers to wake. It was now a night and a day to remember.

Epic lovemaking. Nothing went unexplored.

Jimmy shook the cobwebs of love, and honestly, some Scotch out of his mind. He glanced at his watch.

O-eight-hundred.

He was on schedule with the time, still exhausted from the intense lovemaking, but in his heart, he was bursting with love. Vanessa had her head tucked under his arm, and her eyes opened wide when she sensed Jimmy stirring.

"I hope that I heard you correctly, when you said, you had off of work today," Jimmy quizzed his still sleepy lover.

"Oh my, I do not want to move. It is so safe and warm within the folds of your arms." Vanessa rolled over and she had to face reality. With a rub of her eyes Vanessa replied, "Yes, my love, you heard correctly, but I have a ton of errands to run. Mom and Dad will be worried if I am late. I told them that we would go food shopping around noon today. I left a cushion in the time because I kind of thought in my mind and actually in my heart, I felt that it would be a late night." Vanessa laughed, rolled her eyes and gently reached out and she fondled Jimmy's manhood under the covers while she stated, "That is a friggin' understatement."

"No doubt, baby. C'mon. Let's take a shower. I need a few gallons of coffee too," Jimmy said as he loosened his entanglement with Vanessa.

Vanessa watched his glorious, muscular body ripple and move, while Jimmy threw the covers off and he began to get out of the bed. Vanessa felt it once again. There was no satisfying her Jimmy Reeves urges. She reached out, placed her hand on his shoulder, and promptly stopped Jimmy from getting up.

"Not yet, big guy. I felt you awaken in my hand. Your stamina is unbelievable and my love for you is overwhelming me. One more time and once more in the shower too."

Remarkably, Jimmy's stamina was seemingly endless because they made love a few more times, once in bed and twice in the shower.

They enjoyed breakfast from room service, drank what seemed as if it were gallons of coffee, and then finally, they dressed and prepared to part ways. It was a painful parting, and as a prelude to their parting, Jimmy gave Vanessa some detailed and intense instructions on how they needed to proceed from here on in their lives.

"Trust no one, baby. No one. Head on a swivel. I want ya to be always lookin' around ya," Jimmy carefully and rather strongly told Vanessa as she watched him dressing in another black suit and, once again, he donned all of his weapons and assorted gear. This time, he also held his mini-camera and a small voice recorder in his hands and Vanessa carefully watched him as he took a small phono wire and plugged the two pieces of electronics into each other. He then stashed them both in his endless hidden pockets. Vanessa did not say a word. She found this all fascinating as she watched and simply studied her man. It was quite obvious that he planned to record a conversation during the day, and Vanessa was slowly learning that there always was a good reason for the things he did and what he planned.

"Are ya busy all day with your mom and dad, baby?"

Vanessa nodded and explained, "Sorry, but yes. I promised them. You know, to run them around town for errands on my day off. They are older now and Dad only drives if he has too. I should be free by dinnertime. Okay? Maybe around six? By then, I will be more than ready for some additional . . . quality time."

Vanessa winked and posed seductively, and Jimmy sighed.

"Keep doin' that, baby, and ya parents are goin' to be late for food shopping."

"Sorry. I will stop now. I will meet you here in the room, at say, around six or so?"

Jimmy continued to dress and while Vanessa watched him pull on his boots and zip the side zippers up, he said, "No need to be sorry. Ya gotta take care of ya parents. Very important. Wish I had mine around to take care of 'em. Just come up here to the room at six. Remember this . . . if all is clear and you are okay, three knocks and a pause, then two knocks. If it is anything else and you signal me with a different knock . . . do not worry, I will still come out of the room, but da bad guys will regret my answering the door. Understand?"

Vanessa nodded to indicate that she understood his instructions.

"Great. My kind of gal. You are amazin' in every way. I think we need to keep phone calls to a minimum. When we do talk, please, keep it to landlines only. Smart phones and texting are not gonna be cool, except in a dire emergency. I don't trust nuthin' around here."

"I understand, Jimmy. Six o'clock it is. Special knock. Three knocks and a pause, then two knocks. I will be careful and I know the tag line now. Head on a swivel."

"Perfect. I have to show you where I have some other stuff stashed. If sumthin' does happen to me, well, ya know the drill. Find Campy and call my boss. Let me show ya this stuff."

"More stuff? Wow, fighting bad guys takes a lot of stuff."

Just in case, he carefully showed Vanessa where he hid the backup weapons in the room and where he hid all the money and other items. He also gave Vanessa the spare key to his sports car.

After the tour of the hiding places, Jimmy smiled as he stuffed the long knife into his ankle sheath and said, "That's my gorgeous gal. Ya got it now, baby?"

"You will be careful, too. Right? I know you are the legendary Jimmy Reeves and all of that, but please promise that this will all turn out okay."

Jimmy smiled and his smile melted her heart. His honor projected as if it was a beacon from his soul.

"I promise. So far, at least with the ones that I have met, I gotta say that these punks are dangerous amateurs. I will be careful. Always. C'mon, are you ready? I will walk you to your car."

Vanessa smiled, nodded, and barely mumbled, "Okay." It was painful to leave him. How she hoped that her man was correct in his assessment of the situation. She realized that last evening was exceptional in many ways but one of them was because Jimmy Reeves seldom, if ever, took a day or night off, and deep down, he was such a caring and honest soul.

Vanessa tried hard to focus, and she knew that it was now *their* job, from here on in, they were a team in love and in life, and she knew that he was the best of the best, but she still found it very difficult not to worry about her lover. The two of them confirmed their plans to meet for dinner early this evening, and they reluctantly parted ways with gentle caresses, kisses, and a long goodbye. Jimmy stood, watched and waited, until the taillights of Vanessa's car disappeared from his view and he was sure that Vanessa was safe and secure in her car and heading for home. It felt very strange to be in the employees' parking garage, especially in retrospect of what occurred there during the previous evening. Jimmy glanced at his watch and made a note of the time. He had some hours to kill before he had to head out to the pay phone and make the call to Detective Oscar Campenella at fourteen-hundred-hours.

He missed Vanessa already, and she had only been gone for a few minutes. He knew that he probably should not do it, but a Scotch right now, sure, would taste good. A Scotch and one of those fancy cigars.

Yes, indeed, they sure would taste good.

Detective Oscar Campenella was hard at work. It was still early in the day, but the good detective was investigating a major clue. When the forensics team crawled all over Ken Mercurio's vehicle, it was remarkably clean. Amazingly clean and void of almost everything. The crime scene techies were able to lift fingerprints from the door handles of the car. One was Ken Mercurio's print and the other fingerprint came back to a Miss Donna Eardley. Miss Eardley had some minor busts for drug possession and one arrest for suspicion of prostitution, but the judge threw the charge out of court for lack of evidence and dropped the charge.

It was always interesting in Clinton City. Even from the bench, it was difficult to tell where the good guys began and the bad guys ended.

Ken's arrest record was endless. He was always in trouble, with mostly drug possessions, but some minor arrests for theft too. Drug habits are expensive.

The search of the car found an electrical utility bill, crumbled up and stuffed under the passenger's seat. The utility bill confirmed what the arrest records showed; the address of Miss Donna Eardley was the same street address of the apartment house where they gunned down Rob Mercurio in the hallway.

Finally, the pieces began to fit in this case. Ken Mercurio had a girlfriend and in looking at her beauty displayed in her mug shot, combined with the arrest for suspicion of prostitution, something told Oscar that Miss Eardley "worked" at Casa Al Mare too. Maybe the judge was one of her clients.

Yes, now the trail was growing hotter and Detective Oscar Campenella was licking his chops to search the apartment of Miss Donna Eardley. Especially, when Oscar recalled that the one neighbor who did make a little type of statement, told the police officers, "That he thinks the dead guy lived a few doors away and he would occasionally come and visit someone who lived here."

Oscar surmised that Rob came to visit his brother and Miss Eardley and met his sad fate in the hallway of the apartment where she lived. The questions remained; of exactly what Rob was doing when he visited and why they murdered him. The quiet stranger in the black hat had told Oscar that Rob was a good guy, therefore Oscar assumed that the older, good, brother took the bullets for the younger, bad brother and his girlfriend. Yet, he could not find the car with the broken taillight, the shoe with the blood, nor could he find Ken and his girlfriend. He was sure that Jimmy Reeves might be making headway as he probed the inner depths of the layers of crime that lurked with Casa Al Mare. But at this point, it was not enough to bring the empire down. It would not even make a dent.

Earlier this morning, Oscar called Attorney General Charles "Chuck" McCracken from the prearranged secure telephone and gave Chuck the latest lowdown and progress. Chuck was well pleased with the tale of how Jimmy Reeves saved the good detective from a horrible fate, and he sang the praises of his loyal bodyguard. The attorney general agreed that the team was making progress but had some ways to go. He reported that his task force was also gathering mountains of evidence on the hidden layers of corruption, but they too were some ways away from making any arrests or bringing in charges.

"Keep digging, Detective Campenella, keep ya head on a swivel, too. I guarantee that Jimmy will find some good stuff out today. I can feel it and don't forget the stranger is out there too. Patience, Oscar, it is just a matter of investigation and some digging time now. The pieces are beginning to fit. The fact that they sent a hit man on ya ass, shows that you are poking around in the right spots. Ya got their attention and pissed them off, too. Keep digging."

The thug who Jimmy took out last evening proved to be another loser with a long rap sheet. When he finally woke up in the hospital and the doctors released him for booking and processing, the thug would not say a word. He was going to rot in jail. There was no way that the operation would bail him out, and no way was he going to sign his death certificate by flapping his jaws. He failed in his mission and he is now expendable anyhow. His best hope is to go to the clink for a few years, keep his mouth shut and hope that his silence will earn him a few bucks and a new life on an island somewhere. Right now, the thug was a dead-end, booked on attempted murder of a police officer, illegal weapon possession and other charges that would send him away for a few years. Even if Tony Michanetti Junior and his operation paid off the right judge.

As of late, Detective Oscar Campenella danced carefully around his chain of command. Right now, he had little choice but to approach Lieutenant Davis and ask that he sign off on the paperwork to begin the request for a search warrant for the Eardley apartment. Unlike the stall tactics that Lieutenant Davis implemented on his first request for a search warrant for Rob Mercurio's apartment, he was mildly surprised when his commanding officer, Lieutenant Davis immediately signed off on the paperwork and allowed him to seek a judge for final approval of the warrant. Oscar had surmised that the lieutenant stalled the first warrant just long enough to allow the thugs to check the apartment and ransack it before Oscar and the forensics team could arrive. A feeling of disappointment grew inside of Detective Campenella because of the quick processing of the warrant request by the officer. It might mean they are too late on this search too.

In the meeting, Lieutenant Davis seemed very quiet this morning, especially when he heard that his own homicide detective survived a hit attempt. Oscar knew that his boss was on the take and the news must have reached him that Oscar was growing closer, and now it was going to get dicey.

A few hours later, after a grant for the warrant from the bench, Oscar, and his crime scene team arrived at the apartment house, found the superintendent of the building, showed him the warrant and now they were about to enter the apartment of Miss Donna Eardley.

When the superintendent went to put the master key in the door lock and opened the apartment door, he turned and said, "It is open already. Someone blew the lock out."

It was then that the good detective and his team knew that Tony Michanetti Junior and his team of assorted thugs had beaten the good guys to this one too. Oscar's gut feelings of earlier today when Lieutenant Davis processed the paperwork so quickly were correct. He felt his spirit sink. Another dead-end. Sure enough, they turned the apartment upside down.

Totally ransacked. If anything was here—it was gone now.

Detective Oscar Campenella put his hands on his hips and shook his head while telling the head technician of his crime scene team, "Shit, well, damn, this sure sucks. They beat us to this one too. Please, guys, do what ya can to find something, but I have a feeling this is just another dead-end."

"Sorry, Detective Campenella, but yeah, it looks like a mess. We will comb it. If we find anything, we will give you a shout right away."

Oscar patted him on the back, mumbled, "Thank you," forced a smile, and slowly walked out into the hallway. He knew why his boss was unconcerned about the search warrant, because he already knew that the bad guys had been there. His head was down, he was deep in his thoughts and Oscar knew that right now, his hopes might all lie on the broad shoulders of Jimmy Reeves, his new girlfriend, and of course, he could hope and pray that somewhere in the shadows lurked the quiet stranger in the black hat. He surely needed a dose of his magic, or whatever it is that he brings with him, right now. . ..

In a seedy, greasy spoon diner, lost on a dusty side road off of Highway 1, in a New Jersey shoreline town about twenty miles north of Clinton City, Ken Mercurio and Donna Eardley sat at the counter and shared a breakfast of four pieces of toast with jelly and one cup of coffee. They had to share the meal because they could not afford individual meals. The money was now drying up and their attempts at finding jobs to earn a few dollars had met with dead-ends. Ken needed a fix, his body at times trembled and shook and, right now, his health was not well. Donna tried to get him to eat more than a few bites, but he only picked at the food. Drugs ravaged Ken, and the years of abuse now caught up to him. Donna knew that she could earn some money with her body, but that was going to be a last resort. When they fled Clinton City, she vowed to give that life up. Especially after what Rob did for them. How Rob gave up his own life to allow them to escape the horrible life that they had made for themselves.

Donna loved Ken, for what reason, she did not know, but she did. Love often has no reasons or boundaries. Now, if Rob died for them, the least they could do was to try as hard as they could to make a new life together. The problem was that when all you have is dust, then it is very difficult to make something else out of it.

For years, Ken was an employee at Casa Al Mare while he worked at his "actual" job as a flunky who ran drugs up and down the New Jersey shoreline for Tony Michanetti Junior's operation. Ken carried drugs, the cash from the sales, and worked massive amounts of evil as a drug runner and operative. As of late, the operation trusted him with more and more runs, and they were runs of greater amounts of drugs and deals involving larger amounts of cash. Ken proved that despite his drug issues, he was a reliable runner. He mostly worked for the free fixes, yet they did throw him some cash too. Donna worked as a housekeeper on the staff and she earned extra money working as a prostitute for that disgusting Mick Malzoni and his endless stream of horny, old, wealthy businessmen. It was a disgusting life and when Rob finally realized that the two of them were deeply in love and wanted out of the horrible life that they made, he stepped in and helped them. The only trouble was, when Rob covertly intercepted the last run that Ken made and captured the heroin and the cash that Ken was running, Rob trusted the wrong person in the wretched Clinton City Police Department. Lieutenant Davis was as corrupt as they come, and when Rob went to him to spill the beans, he ended up dead.

Dead, because of Donna and Ken's crazy lives and poor choices. It was heart wrenching.

The only mystery that remained was where Rob hid the money and the stash of drugs. Even Ken did not know. What a mess it now was, and now, Ken was sick as hell from opiate withdrawal and brokenhearted over his brother's death. Without a fix very soon, Ken would be in the throes of withdrawal and quite possibly dead. The money was almost gone, and they were quickly running out of options.

Almost.

In this world, there are many mysteries. Because, within the darkness of the evil that for some reason seems as if it pervades humankind, there are rays of light and truth and goodness. The greatest mystery is from where these rays of light and hope and joy come from. Perhaps they are the result of answered prayers to Heaven or perhaps; they are actually a manifestation of the spirits of all the good and kind persons of the world and beyond. Yet, in desperate times, it is comforting to know that hope and goodness does exist, and forever, it will fight the forces of evil. As long as the power of good remains, then evil will never reign.

Ever.

The door to the diner opened, the few patrons inside,

and the servers could not help but to look up and notice the man who entered the establishment. It was impossible to ignore his presence.

Standing silently in the entrance to the diner, just inside of the doorway, was a very tall, lean, yet very powerfully built man. The man showed no emotion, nor did the man say anything. The silent and immense stranger standing in the entrance to the diner was dressed all in black. He wore a black vest, covering a perfectly, pressed, black buttoned-up shirt, and his sharply creased, black trousers had no ripples or wrinkles. On his head, he wore a wide-brimmed black hat and on his feet, he wore highly polished black boots. His attire was immaculate. Nothing was out of place on the man; even the hair on his head that a person could see from under the wide-brimmed hat was perfectly groomed, trimmed neat and clean along the edges. His face sported a black beard and full facial hair and once again, it was neat, clean, and trim. His eyes slowly scanned the diner as if he was making sure that this is where he needed to be at this moment. You could barely see his eyes moving around from under the brim of his hat, yet they moved, and it was as if the stranger was carefully studying his surroundings. He had dark and piercing eyes that sent shivers down the spines of the patrons of the diner, as well as the staff.

The quiet stranger in the black hat had arrived.

It was as if he magically appeared on the scene. In order to gauge where he was and what he was searching for, the eyes of the stranger continued to scan the entire diner until they stopped and focused on the front counter. The door to the diner, slowly closed behind the stranger and when it closed, the stranger walked quickly over to the counter of the diner and as he walked, his boots made a loud and distinct clicking noise as the metal tips of his boots struck hard upon the diner's floor.

Everyone in the diner followed him as the stranger

selected a counter stool right next to Ken and Donna. When he selected a stool, and sat down at the counter, everyone returned to his or her own individual worlds. The silent stranger was immense, unusual and different, but he was just that, an unusual stranger. Simply a man stopping by for a cup of coffee or a hearty breakfast as he passed through their lives.

Maybe.

"Hello. What will you have? Are you just passing through? Never saw you in here before now and I certainly would have remembered such a striking and handsome man," a middle-aged, but worn-out looking server said as she walked over to serve the stranger. Her hair wound up in waves upon her head, she had a drinker's look in her eyes, and a nametag that pronounced "Sally" in block letters pinned in a sideways tilt upon her uniform breast.

He looked up and said, "Coffee. Black. Please, serve these two next to me, a decent breakfast. Each of them. Here." He reached in his vest, pulled out fifty dollars, and laid it on the counter. "Keep the rest of the money for your gratuity."

Sally's face lit up and with a loud, "Yes, sir," she marched off with the fifty dollars and the order.

Ken and Donna looked at each other and they too studied the quiet stranger.

The stranger said not a word, and he only stared straight ahead without even moving his head or his eyes.

Donna said, "Thank you. That is very kind of you. We are a little down on our luck. It seems as if no one cared until now. That is very kind of you to buy us a decent breakfast."

The stranger still did not react or say a word.

Sally delivered the black coffee with a smile and a push at her brassiere in a futile attempt to improve the shape of her sagging breasts, and a flash of her eyes to the handsome, but silent stranger. To her disappointment, he did not react, but he reached down and took a long sip of the coffee.

Sally turned to Ken and Donna and reported, "Your breakfast will be out in a bit. Giving you the works, Eggs, bacon, pancakes. The works. Anything else, there, handsome? I need to tell you that I am on the menu too."

The stranger did not answer.

When he only sipped his coffee and did not answer, Sally shrugged her shoulders and mumbled while walking away, "Oh, well. I guess not. When you look like he does, I guess you have your pick of 'em. Breakfast will be out in a minute or two."

Ken and Donna did not know what to say or do, and Ken tapped his girlfriend on the arm as an indication for her to lean in and listen to his whisper in her ear. Ken saw the stranger's eyes flash over to them.

The mysterious stranger had spotted Donna lean over and before Ken could speak, the quiet stranger in the black hat said, "In life's most desperate moments, there is always someone who cares, even if you think you have run out of hope. Now, there is a better way, a voice in the wilderness, a light to guide you. Your brother is in a grand place right now. He wants you both to be happy. To be finally free and for that, he gave up his life on Earth for you two to share love and hope."

Donna and Ken sat stunned as he continued to speak in his low and melodious yet powerful voice. "You need to return to Clinton City. It is your only hope. Eventually, they will find you and Ken is too ill for this to perpetuate."

The stranger reached in his vest pocket, took out the business card of Detective Oscar Campenella, and handed it to Donna.

"When you return, call this man right away. He will protect you. He is an exceptional man. Call him from a pay telephone, be smart, be brave, and be safe. Trust only this man. His team is in place now and they are beyond reproach. He will make sure that you are both safe. You owe this to, Rob. You owe him this to make it right and true. You need to face the truth because the truth will not fail you."

The stranger leaned in and Ken and Donna could see his dark eyes peering out mysteriously from under the wide brim of his black hat. His eyes were dark and piercing, but his eyes broadcasted hope and love.

His voice grew softer and a faint smile appeared on his face as he said, "Remember that lovers and friends love at all times, but a brother is born for loving through adversity. Your brother did so, and he still does. Now, please, do what is right and true and trust that he did not die in vain. Your life can and will be grand. Despite the grief of this day and the pain you feel right now—I can assure you both that a renewed life is ahead of you now."

He stood up, reached once again in his pocket, pulled out a few hundred-dollar bills, and set them in front of the stunned couple. He pointed at them and then to the money and tipped his hat and went to turn away.

"WAIT! How do you know all of this? Who are you, dark stranger?" Donna asked.

The stranger stopped, turned around and said, "I am who you want me to be and what you can never imagine that I am."

Once again, he tipped his hat, smiled, and walked briskly away with his boots, making the distinctive clicking noise as he traveled quickly toward the door. He opened the door and disappeared, leaving the two young lovers stunned while remaining alone in their thoughts. They grasped hands, turned and sat in silence while watching him through the large front windows of the diner, until he disappeared from their view.

Jimmy Reeves sat on the main balcony of Casa Al Mare, sitting in a soft chair overlooking a glorious ocean view. It was a bright and beautiful day, not too hot and not humid at all, but still, the warm sunshine worked at his dark suit, but a glorious ocean breeze that cooled the air just perfectly helped to offset it. He wore his ever-present sunglasses and for the most part, he sat motionless and quiet, while pondering his next move. He now returned to playing the role of Jimmy O'Shaughnessy, the rich and carefree, womanizing playboy. A man on vacation, spending money like a drunken sailor just hitting port. Despite his best intentions and better judgments, he sipped an early morning Scotch, and he puffed on one of the glorious cigars that Vanessa had Renaldo bring to him yesterday. He was playing it up big-time, acting as if he was King of the World. He had worked a deal with the houseman, Renaldo, to carry drinks back and forth for him, so he did not even have to move out of the chair and away from this glorious view. His mind could not stop with thinking about Vanessa, but he knew she had commitments today, and he had a job to do. Soon enough, they will see each other, and he was quite sure that they would engage in more lovemaking. He never met a finer woman, smart, keen, gorgeous, an amazing lover and above all, Vanessa was honest and trustworthy. Jimmy Reeves, the man with never-ending missions of good over evil, had stumbled. For once, the great Jimmy Reeves crumbled into a pile of emotions. He was madly in love. The best part of all of this was that lust did not drive his desire. It was pure love. Jimmy had finally found a purpose other than work in his life. He was ready to commit to her fully in just a day or so of their meeting. It was crazy, mind numbing and beautiful. Above all, it was fate. No doubt Vanessa was correct. It was as if someone, for a good cause, somehow predetermined all of this.

"I am so very sorry, Mr. O'Shaughnessy, but I was just

informed that Ms. Hillary Thornburg, had made an appointment to use the balcony for a photographic shoot and with regret I must ask you to relocate to the other balcony."

Renaldo appeared, and he was explaining something about moving Jimmy's location, while a gorgeous, tall woman carrying a camera tripod along with two housemen from Renaldo's team who were carrying an assortment of cameras and photographic equipment appeared behind him.

The woman cut Renaldo's speech off by saying, "Oh, please, nonsense, Renaldo. I am not privileged. He was here first. Please, he can, and he will stay. Such a handsome man too, enjoying a glorious day with a cocktail and a fine cigar. My goodness, it is my pleasure to share the balcony with such a fine and handsome man."

Jimmy smiled and stood up to greet the woman as his eyes studied her from behind his dark glasses. She was amazing. Perfect in every detail. Her figure, face, and brown hair with auburn highlights that glistened in the sunlight. Hair that tumbled around her in gentle waves. She stood stately and proudly, glowing in front of Jimmy with long legs, and dressed in perfect attire, while wearing skin-tight white jeans and a light-blue summer button-up blouse, open just enough to catch hints of some glorious cleavage. Pearls in her ears and a matching pearl necklace tumbled into the hints of her breasts. She too, wore dark sunglasses and even if Jimmy could not see her eyes, he knew that Hillary was studying Jimmy just as he studied her.

"Are ya sure? I can move outta here if ya need me to. The cigar might bother ya too." Jimmy placed the cigar down in an ashtray and went to grind it out. "Ya don't want my ugly puss in any of ya pictures."

Hillary reached out and extended her hand to shake Jimmy's hand as she laughed and said, "Well, with that accent, I know you are from New Jersey. There is no need to ask where you are from, Mr. O'Shaughnessy. Please stay. The cigar smells glorious. You have anything, but as you say, an ugly puss. You are stunning. Instead of staring through my camera lens, I might spend the morning staring at you. I will enjoy the company and listening to such an extraordinary accent. Even though Renaldo told you my name and I know yours, please, a formal introduction is in order. Hello, I am, Hillary Thornburg."

"Oh, well, thanks for the compliment. Ya quite the looker too. Nice, ah, ah . . . pants. Nice to meet ya. Sorry for da growl and horrible accent. I am a Jersey guy for sure. No hiding it. Yes, I am, Jimmy O'Shaughnessy. Nice to meet ya, and please, call me, Jimmy."

Hillary smiled at his cute stutter because she knew that Jimmy had tried hard not to focus on her perfect backside stuffed into the white pants.

"Thank you. They do fit rather . . . well. Especially in the ass." She winked at Jimmy and continued, "Yes, they are designer jeans from my own collection. I think your accent is amazing. Very manly and super sexy. Da growl. I love it," Hillary purred as she still studied Jimmy. Hillary waved her hands in the air and proclaimed, "No apologies are necessary. I will call you, Jimmy, and please, call me, Hillary."

While Jimmy watched, Hillary directed the housemen as to where to place her equipment and she smiled and reached into her purse and gave them all generous tips for their assistance.

"Renaldo, please bring, Jimmy, another drink of what it is that he is sipping and bring me some champagne. My brand. The bartender will know which one."

"Of course, Ms. Thornburg. Right away."

"Hey, dare, Renaldo, put it all on my tab."

Renaldo stopped. He smiled and at first, he looked to Jimmy and then to Hillary and shrugged his shoulders.

"C'mon, I get the first round. Is it a deal, there, Hillary?" She laughed as he stood there in front of her, waiting for her answer.

"Deal," Hillary agreed.

She did not want to, but she could not help but to think, my goodness, this man is amazing. Handsome was not a good description. It was more like smoking hot. He was older, but in amazing shape. The looks, his fine trimmed dark beard and facial hair, his muscles and build, he is like a tank. The accent, tall, powerful, the suit, the entire look. Her eyes were fixated on him and she felt her loins ache a little. My goodness, what must it be like to spend some quality time with such a man?

Hillary returned to reality, and she began to set up the tripod and as she did so, Hillary tried to get to know Jimmy a little better, "So, what is your drink of choice, Jimmy?"

"Don't know the name of it, but it is their best Scotch. Single malt. Neat." Jimmy recalled Vanessa's testimony of last evening upon trying Scotch for the first time and he smiled as he repeated the words, "Honest, ya should try it cuz it is a life-changing experience." Jimmy took a last drag on the cigar, set it down in the ashtray, and snuffed it out.

"Really? Perhaps, I need to trade in my champagne?"

"Ya might want to consider it. Say, can I help ya set up stuff? I don't know shit 'bout photography, but I am good with my hands."

"I bet you are, Jimmy. I have no doubt that is true," Hillary said with a wink. "Well, yes, you can grab that camera bag over there and please, bring it over here. Thank you."

Jimmy laughed at the play on the words and he slowly walked over to the camera bag and grabbed it. As he brought the camera bag over to Hillary and handed it to her, Jimmy thought how this was; some knockout chick and he needed to play the playboy role, but very carefully.

Jimmy recalled Vanessa telling of meeting this famous socialite named Hillary Thornburg, and Vanessa liked her and enjoyed her "Down to Earth" ways. Obviously, this gorgeous chick in front of him right now was one and the same. Vanessa and Hillary had made a date for cocktails after work tomorrow and Vanessa seemed very excited about meeting the famous Hillary Thornburg. Jimmy agreed that for a fabulously famous and wealthy chick, she was open and honest, and while he tried hard to ignore her coming onto him a little, he knew to be very careful here. He almost mentioned Vanessa but decided to play it close to the cuff for now and see what might come out of this conversation and meeting. Jimmy was sure that this woman of fabulous wealth had no criminal ties, but he trusted no one until he verified the trust. Admittedly, Jimmy Reeves knew nothing about movie stars or wealthy socialites, yet he had to agree that Ms. Thornburg was very likable.

Besides, she was amazing on the eyes too.

Renaldo graciously delivered the round of drinks and as Hillary and Jimmy toasted to the day, and they each took long sips, Hillary said, "So, Jimmy, tell me your story."

Jimmy stood next to Hillary, smiled and thought, 'Wow! Damn! What a loaded-ass question! If only he could tell her his story!' He lifted his sunglasses off his eyes for a second and rubbed at his eyes while pondering the question.

Hillary quickly placed her drink on a nearby table and she grabbed Jimmy by his arms and almost shouted, "Wait! Don't put your sunglasses back on your amazing face."

Jimmy was surprised as Hillary zoomed in and carefully studied his eyes.

"Ah, okay," Jimmy mumbled. Hillary looked deep into his eyes and Jimmy tried hard to hide his embarrassment by the study and attention.

"Amazing eyes. Steel gray with blue along the edges. I want to do a photographic shoot on your eyes alone."

While studying Jimmy's eyes, Hillary suddenly recalled yesterday and the words of her new friend, Vanessa, "He is stunning. Kinda oozes sexiness. He has a gorgeous build. I swear even with a baggy shirt on, you could see that his muscles have muscles. And he has these glorious and truly amazing eyes, steel grey with blue highlights. I have never seen eyes like his eyes. Chiseled features, with a full beard. Black hair with just some licks of grey here and there. Geez, he is hard to resist! He is older than I am, too. That is the best part because I am so tired of the immature, younger men that I have dated as of late."

Hillary smiled as she made the connection and for the briefest of moments, Hillary thought, well, sorry, Vanessa, but I am Hillary Thornburg, the world-famous socialite who can have any man that I desire. You are cute, maybe you are gorgeous, but we need to call it what it is. You are a poor gal working as a desk clerk at a fancy hotel. This man is special, and I am going to grab him out from under you. However, something recently had changed within Hillary Thornburg. She did not have an explanation for it yet; she only knew that something had changed with her attitude as of late. Instead of trying to steal Vanessa's man, Hillary felt a huge sense of loyalty to Vanessa and within a second or two; Hillary decided to test him for his commitment. Her assumption was that Vanessa and Jimmy did share the date planned for last evening, and while Hillary did not know how the date went, she sure could test this handsome man for a little tease and see if he is just another player or not. After all, her own advice to Vanessa was for her to be careful with her feelings around this dashing playboy. Their plans included some cocktails after work tomorrow, so she could make sure that Vanessa knew the truth about her new man.

Hillary did not realize that despite her stunning beauty, her immense wealth and her fame, Hillary was testing a man beyond reproach.

"Thank you, Hillary. A few people have told me that my eyes are an unusual color. Even by an eye doctor once. I think that I inherited the color from my old man. He had the same color eyes. Here is your camera bag." Jimmy smiled and placed the sunglasses back over his eyes. "As far as the photos go, nah, I am not much into people taking my picture. Besides, in a few hours, I have to run out of here. I have things to do this afternoon, but thanks."

Hillary decided to turn on the maximum sex appeal with a little bounce and sway and an invitation too. She squeezed in closer and made sure that her blouse tumbled open to reveal a bit more of her attributes. Hillary could not really follow Jimmy's eyes under his dark glasses to see if he caught a glimpse of her chest, but Jimmy remained locked on her eyes for a few moments, and then he even looked away and reached for his Scotch glass sitting upon the table in order to take a sip.

"Oh, too bad. Maybe when you get back, we can share some drinks together, and catch a bite for dinner. Afterwards, we can go to my room. I have an amazing view from my room. The balcony there is fantastic, and it faces west. The management set me up with an exclusive penthouse room and a spectacular balcony. We can enjoy the sunset and some other things . . . together."

Jimmy nodded his head, smiled, and took another sip of his drink. He studied Hillary for just a few seconds and despite her looks and he was sure of her other "attributes" she did not hold a candle to Vanessa. No, Jimmy Reeves was now a one-woman man.

After his careful study and thoughts, Jimmy said, "That is very nice of you. You are a gorgeous chick and I am sure that you do not or will ever have many men refuse you on invitations such as that one. I am sure it is a great view in your room and yes, we can share a drink or two in one of the lounges, but just so ya know, I am in a committed relationship. We are in it for the long haul. Forever. Yeah, it is gonna be forever. But, hey, no sweat, we can be friends, talk, and hang out, but we just gotta be friends. I gotta be honest and upfront, cuz, I have this amazing and awesome gal that I am with now and forever. She is incredibly special and I am just wild about her. Just want ya to know that upfront."

Hillary smiled; she now knew that Vanessa was indeed a very lucky young woman. She set the camera bag down on the table, unbuttoned the straps, and pulled the camera out of the bag.

While Hillary worked with the camera to set it upon the tripod, she said to Jimmy, "I appreciate your honesty. Your gal is a lucky woman to have such an honest and committed man. Especially, one who looks like you do, Jimmy. I would still love to do a photo shoot on your eyes and yes, we can be friends. Company would be nice. Very nice. I seldom encounter such honesty in a man. Especially a man that I invited to spend time with me. Most of them are pigs. It is amazingly refreshing. Then, again, this entire vacation has been an eye-opener for me. A change of direction. An adventure of the sort that I really required in my life. Maybe we can meet in the lobby around four o'clock or so?"

Jimmy nodded, and he walked over to where Hillary was now mounting the camera onto the tripod and said, "That's great. It is a very cool place here. Can't pronounce the name of this joint too good, but it is very cool. Sure, sure, sure. We can hang out. It'll be fun. That works. Now, I will tell ya a little 'bout me, but I ain't all that exciting. I am kind of interested in how this camera stuff works. I might take a few photos of stuff someday. Maybe, I can learn a thing or two."

Hillary completed the camera mounting and double-checked the mount to make sure the camera was secure and tight. She then motioned for Jimmy to pick up his Scotch and she walked over and picked up her drink.

Hillary was satisfied with not only Jimmy's response and faithfulness to his woman but also in the changes in her own demeanor and behavior. The "old version" of Hillary would have run ramshackle over the top of Vanessa and, to a certain extent, this handsome and sexy man too. Used him for some good company, some casual sex with no commitments, then moved along. This was now the new Hillary Thornburg, and while she had no explanation for the changes that she felt, she had a new commitment to redirect her life, to care more, to create art through her photography and a new direction and purpose.

They toasted again and touched glasses as Hillary said, "Here is to a great day and to being friends. I will be happy to show you a little photography and listen while you tell me about your not so exciting life. Believe me, people think it is glamorous to be Hillary Thornburg, but it is not so special. I have a feeling that I am going to be very happy to hear your story and that I am going to be very thankful that I met you today, Jimmy. Very thankful."

Jimmy sipped the drink and mumbled, "Okay. Well, maybe. . .."

Hillary and Jimmy shared a few more drinks; lots of good conversation and she did show Jimmy the ins and outs of photography while taking many digital photos with her newer cameras and shooting many rolls of film with the older models. Hillary snapped endless pictures of the ocean view from the balcony. Jimmy gave her his now slightly well-worn story with the playboy from the wealthy family angle. He was still not very comfortable spinning the yarns with people whom he enjoyed company with, but he now knew that it was just part of the job. When his time grew short to leave and make the prearranged telephone calls, Jimmy promised to call Hillary when he returned and they could catch some more drinks and pass some more time at one of the lounges.

As Hillary watched Jimmy walk off the balcony and

through the main hallway while heading for the front door, she could not help but think as to how lucky a woman that Vanessa Michaelson was. The man was an amazing package, toughness, sexiness, handsome and charismatic all in one six-foot-five hunk of man.

"Hey, Teddy, how goes it today?" Jimmy asked the Head Valet as he walked out to the front of the hotel to request that the valet crew bring his car around.

"Oh hey, Jimmy. It is going all right today. Nice day, lots of pretty women around and the tips are decent. Hey, heard ya doin' well too. Ya managed a date with that hottie, Vanessa, and now ya spendin' time with that gorgeous, famous, rich chick that is on the cover of all the magazines." Teddy smiled as he overflowed with admiration over the rumors of Jimmy's reputation with the women.

"Vanessa is amazing and all the guys around here have tried to date her, with no luck. One day here, and ya already all over her. Lucky dude. But I guess that is why ya Jimmy and I am, not."

"Well, yeah, ya know, how it is sometimes. . .." Jimmy's voice trailed off as he was just about to toss the keys to his car to the admiring Teddy. His eyes caught a large, four-door luxury sedan parked in front of the entrance to the hotel. Blacked out rear windows, and a broken rear taillight and some damage to the rear driver's side of the vehicle. He tried hard not to focus too sharply. Teddy was watching and a quick scan of the front of the hotel revealed a new forward watchman standing guard stoically in the usual post. Jimmy certainly knew what happened to the former watchman.

He suddenly came down with a terrible headache.

The replacement henchman was a shorter, rounder thug with a heavy face and a wide girth. He hid behind his sunglasses, sweating profusely while looking as if he was an overstuffed sausage inside of his black suit.

From his initial debriefing with Detective Oscar Campenella, and Chuck McCracken, Jimmy knew that one of the missing pieces of the puzzle was a luxury four-door sedan. The presumed getaway car. A car with damage to the rear taillight and to the rear driver's side of the vehicle. A vehicle that the dark and quiet stranger, their friend and ally, clued the good detective in on to some details of its existence. A car that the good detective currently had had the broken pieces of the taillight and paint samples held for evidence.

Jimmy shifted gears and played the role. He pulled the case for his sunglasses out of his pocket, fiddled with it, and exposed the electronic bug to pick up the conversation. He then reached in his pocket, flipped the eavesdropper switch to the "on" position, and then turned on the micro-recorder. They were on the air and Jimmy had a feeling that this conversation might come in very handy down the road.

"Oh shit, too bad, there, Teddy. A guest's car all smashed up in the back. I guess these tight parking garages are tough to park all these cars inside of without a few accidents here and there. 'Pecially, a big one like that there, fancy wagon is. Beautiful car too, man, that sucks." Jimmy pointed at the car as he commented to Teddy as to the misfortune of the damage to such a fine vehicle. Jimmy then added to the smokescreen, "I hope nuthin' happened to my wheels, Teddy." Teddy looked over to the sedan and out of the corner of his eye, Jimmy watched the forward watchman, glance up when he heard the conversation about the car.

'Careful now,' Jimmy thought. 'Play it cool.'

The thug only briefly looked over and listened and when he heard it was just car talk, he went back to sweating in the sun.

"Nah, Jimmy, ya car is cool. That is not a guest's car. It is one of our own cars. The owner of the resort keeps a few of them around, ya know, to use for his own use, or for hustling fancy guests around. One of our drivers was a jackass and was down in the city da udder day. The jerk backed into sumthin.' I am havin' one of my drivers take it down to Danny's Auto Body Shop down the main road a piece to have it all fixed up," Teddy explained with some handy information and Jimmy quickly processed it, he hoped the recording came in loud and clear and he made a mental note of the license plate information. Now, if he could just lose Teddy, pull out the miniature camera and snap some pictures of the car in place here in the front of the hotel, the damage, and the license plate, all without the forward thug and the security cameras spotting him.

"Oh yeah, okay, that's good. Danny's auto joint, huh? I might have a little hood nick on my wheels. Gotta check, but I think a rock kicked up on the parkway on the roll down here. Maybe this Danny guy can touch it up for me. He is close?"

"Oh, yeah, he is topnotch, Jimmy. When we git a dent or a nick on a guest's car, he takes care of it right away for us. He is the best. Yeah, easy to find. Ya just go right down the main drag here about five miles. Southbound, make a left out the driveway and just keep going. About a mile before the beach exits. Tell 'em I sent ya down there."

Jimmy nodded and tossed Teddy his car keys. Time to lose the loose-lipped kid.

"Hey, thanks. I will check it out, Teddy. Gotta roll out now. Have a chick that I am meetin' for some lunch and some drinks. Can ya bring my car around for me?"

"Sure, Jimmy," Teddy deftly caught the keys and sprinted off and Jimmy was in luck, because just as Teddy took off, a guest rolled up in a long sedan and stopped between the damaged car and the hotel front entrance. Jimmy watched as another valet sprinted out to attend to the new arrival and when he was satisfied that the car blocked the view for the thug, Jimmy pulled out his camera and with a few quick shots from the side of his hip, he pointed and snapped away. As he slipped the camera back into his jacket pocket, he thought how Hillary would be proud of his newly acquired photographic abilities.

Teddy pulled the sports car around, Jimmy tucked a fifty-dollar bill in his hand, and he jumped in the car and took off. He was still playing the playboy facade to the maximum, and as Jimmy went through the gears and brought the high-performance engine up to speed on the main drag, he felt as if finally, some pieces of the puzzle began to fit. He would drop a few coins with Detective Campenella and maybe the car that he just stumbled onto, will unlock some more clues.

Jimmy revved the engine up, shifted into a high gear, blew the doors off some slow pokes and slid into the passing lane.

While he cruised along, Jimmy's mind raced with a million thoughts.

'Detective Campy, how his boss was faring without him by his side, the mission, of how he wanted to take out Mick Malzoni and the rest of his punk ass thugs and primarily, of course, there was this dinner date he had tonight with this amazing gal, with sparkling eyes, a golden smile, a courageous soul and a perfect laugh.'

Chapter 9

Jimmy Reeves' Time

Jimmy Reeves stopped at the payphone, fished some coins out of his pocket, dropped them in and right on time, he made the call. Fourteen hundred hours. Jimmy was always spot on, and so was Detective Oscar Campenella. No doubt, they made a good team. Oscar answered on the first ring, and the conversation was rolling. They covered it all very quickly, the news of the thug that Jimmy took out, the dead-end on the apartment search of the girlfriend, the fact that she was apparently working under the slime-ball auspices of Mick Malzoni, servicing his clients and all the other details. Jimmy then told Detective Campenella the details of finding the car. Jimmy carefully explained where the car was located, and where it was that the car was going to for repairs, in hopes that the good detective and his team of techies could find it.

He gave him the license plate information.

"New Jersey tag. Nine-five-six, India, Alpha, Zulu," and the full description of the vehicle.

"Shit, man, great work, Jimmy. And you have pictures of the car parked in front of the hotel and a recording of what happened too. You are the real deal. I am going to call your boss and receive some marching orders on this one. I think that I have probable cause to search the vehicle right now, but I need to make sure we do not make any missteps at all. Attorney General McCracken will most likely agree with me, but still instruct me to get a search warrant, just as

I did for the apartments. We might need to go out of the county for this warrant. Have to get away from the madness and find an impartial judge."

"Yeah, no, missteps, Detective Campy. None. My boss is the best in the business. He will guide ya. What else did he tell ya?"

"He said that you saved my ass, and I needed to keep my head on a swivel. These are the ultimate bad guys."

"Some of them are bad ass and some of them are punk amateurs, but, yes, head on a swivel, Campy."

Jimmy laughed. Yes, indeed. Chuck McCracken was the best.

"Seriously, you did save my ass, and thank you once again. I learned my lesson. Head on a swivel from here on in. He also reported that the special task force was closing in on the corruption. There were numerous inflated accounts in a variety of banks. They need a few more pieces of the puzzle and they might have enough to nail many of them. It will come down to him assigning a special prosecutor and most likely using the New Jersey State Police to help us close this mess out at the end. By the way, Jimmy, have you heard or seen anything of the mysterious and often, quiet stranger?"

"Nah, in fact, ya know, I have never met him. Seen him from a distance, but never met him. Don't worry because he is out there. Watching and waiting for the right moment."

There was a long pause on the telephone, as if the good detective was trying very hard to assure his soul that Jimmy Reeves was correct. It was a comforting thought indeed, to know that out there somewhere, the quiet stranger in the black hat was on their side. Somewhere.

"When we find the car, we search it, or even impound it, then, it might point a finger to you, Jimmy. Depending on if that valet kid is a dope or not, they might start to put some pieces together. As all of this madness winds down, it is only a matter of time before your cover is blown and all the darkness closes in on us. It is going to get dicey as hell."

This time, it was Jimmy's turn to pause as he deposited more coins into the pay telephone and he thought about what Oscar just said. Jimmy felt his muscles ripple, and a smile came across his face.

"Then, I will be ready. It will be time to be Jimmy Reeves and not, Jimmy O'bullshit. I do my best work when it is dicey, Oscar. My best work when it is Jimmy Reeves' time."

"I am sure that you do, Jimmy. It is very comforting to know that Jimmy Reeves is on the job. I have the landline number for the front desk of the hotel and your room in my wallet. When it all goes crazy, we might need to take some chances and use the conventional communications."

"Yeah, maybe, but carefully. I have it worked out now. I do have some backup communications too. If we need them, I can break it all out. Chuck can explain more about that if it comes down to using it. Our plan sounds good. When ya can, give me an update on the car, so I know if they are putting some pieces together and whether they are gunnin' for me or not. Vanessa will be working the front desk tomorrow, so that might work out for us if ya call her there. Head on a swivel, Detective Campy. Make sure ya are always packin'. Take good care. Be in touch."

The two men hung up on the call. Jimmy briskly walked back to the sports car while keeping his head on a swivel. He climbed in the car and checked his watch. He had enough time to head back to the hotel, wash up a little, meet Hillary for a few drinks, and relax before Vanessa arrived. Jimmy's plan was to grab a few drinks with Hillary in Reflections, not at the bar, but at a table, and as he did so, he would carefully watch Mick Malzoni to pick up some more observations and angles. Mick was a grimy dude and Jimmy badly wanted to take out Mick Malzoni. He was very high on the "inflict pain" list for Jimmy

Reeves. Very high. This evening's meeting with Hillary was to spend some time with Vanessa's new friend and his friend too, but he also wanted to gather some more information and observations too. Something told Jimmy that Hillary Thornburg was going to be not only fun and easy on the eyes, but an ally too.

Another nagging thought was that Jimmy knew in his heart that Detective Campy was correct. Things were about to become very dicey.

Jimmy pulled the sports car back in front of the hotel's entrance, and Teddy and his team of valets frantically dashed out to meet and greet him. It was quite amazing what a remarkable level of customer service that the feeding of fifty-dollar tips could manage to inspire. Jimmy jumped out, flipped the car keys to Teddy, and handed him another fifty-spot. Teddy shouted out a loud, "Thanks" but Jimmy was in "ultra-cool" mode so he just nodded and continued his way into the hotel. Within a few steps of the front door, Jimmy carefully gauged the situation. So far, everything was quiet on the Casa Al Mare end. The valet team was still falling all over Jimmy to provide service.

Playboy Jimmy O'Shaughnessy, that is. It was not yet Jimmy Reeves' time. However, things can change in a hurry around Jimmy and around Casa Al Mare.

Jimmy's head was up and on a maximum swivel as he scanned the surrounding area, then the security cameras, and finally, he counted the number of valets. Three men in total. He could easily take three men out if he had to. Although it seemed normal right now, Jimmy was practicing, refining his senses and moving into a full-alert mode. In his mind, he played out how the attack would occur and how he would kill them all.

Okay, no, wait, four men—because there was a black-suited guy just inside the hotel entrance. Immediately, Jimmy went on high alert. There remained no break in his stride, or his facial expression, but something was different here. Jimmy's senses could smell trouble brewing. It was a combination of his training as well as his naturally keen senses and aversion to evil. Behind his dark sunglasses, Jimmy scanned the area with another quick assessment of the area and the front entrance.

There was no forward watch outside the building and front entrance. Only a henchman inside the front door. Something changed and for some reason it did so. The obese, sweaty henchman was gone. Off duty. He was off sweating someplace else. His replacement seemed a bit more formidable, as well as considerably less sweaty. The new forward watchman was a large and very muscular man, with a sneer on the corner of his upper lip, and a standing posture that broadcasted cocky. He had dark sunglasses on that successfully hid his eyes but even with the dark sunglasses on, Jimmy could tell that he stared stoically ahead in Jimmy's direction. Jimmy felt the stare and the burn. He carefully watched while Jimmy approached. The ripple and bulge under his tight suit jacket revealed which shoulder his weapon was on. These guys all wore their suits far too tight. This was unusual. The forward watch was generally just a single henchman standing on the outside, but even so, Jimmy remained confident that in a flash, he could take out the entire gang of thugs. Chances are that of the valet team, only Teddy carried a weapon. Jimmy suspected it was a small caliber handgun in an ankle holster. His eyes darted around for bystanders and civilians, as well as potential areas and objects to provide cover. In a mere second or two, Jimmy had a plan.

While Jimmy walked into the front entrance, the large man reached out and grabbed Jimmy by his arm. Usually, in these instances, the first reaction by Jimmy Reeves would be a simple defensive move and the man's arm would be broken in two, but right for now, this was not Jimmy Reeves. This was Jimmy O'Shaughnessy. Jimmy cooled his inner hostility by reminding himself of his current identity. It was still too early in the game to blow his cover, but he had to defend himself and the way that he had been strutting about the past few days implied that Jimmy O'Shaughnessy was no pushover. Jimmy could feel the eyes of everyone watching this scene unfold, Teddy and his team, and the eyes behind the cameras. With a slow gaze, first into the sunglasses of the man holding Jimmy's arm, then down to the man's grip on his arm, Jimmy stopped in his tracks and waited for the next move. The henchman was large; not quite as tall as Jimmy was, but he looked powerful and muscular. However, he did not match the size or the power of Jimmy.

"Don't I know you?" The man asked, while keeping his grip on Jimmy's arm.

"I never met you before in my life." Jimmy answered while still gazing at the grip on his arm.

"You are Jimmy from up north in Paterson. Right?"

"That's right, Jimmy O'Shaughnessy. Who the hell are you?

"Hotel security."

"That so? Do you always make a habit of forcibly grabbing guests to your hotel and resort by the arm and asking them stupid-ass questions?"

"As I just said, I think that I know you. I ain't exactly sure you are a guest. Kinda think you are someone else. Do you have a problem with that . . . pal? If ya do, then I gotta ask ya point blank . . . whatcha gonna do about it?"

Jimmy violently shook his arm, the man stepped back, and the action caused the thug to lose his grip on Jimmy's arm. Jimmy straightened his tie and jacket out and then he stepped very close to the "hotel security."

"First off, I am not your pal, and second, I am a guest here. Third, go ahead and touch me once more and I will pull the knife out of my boot and I will then peel you like a friggin' banana. I will start at the top of your head and in slow, painful and agonizing, slices . . . I will peel the skin off your entire body. Then, when I have you bleeding, peeled, and exposed, I will pick your sorry ass up and throw you through the front glass of this hotel. Right here and right now, in front of everyone here at this fancy hotel and resort. Hotel security will go down and it will be one helluva hurt on ya dead ass. So, point blank, asshole, I gotta ask ya. Does that answer your friggin' question?"

The henchman stood stiffly, and he did not say a word. Beads of sweat appeared on his forehead and his head darted around the area and then his eyes, behind the dark sunglasses, landed on Jimmy's face. The thug cautiously and slowly took one-step back. He sniffed, and he nervously wiped his nose with some loose fingers and with the palm of his hand. The henchman looked carefully at Jimmy, and then he looked at Teddy and his valet team standing a few feet away. He then shook his head a little, turned, and walked slowly out the front door to join his cohorts in madness.

"Big talk and no action. I figured as much. Ya just a blowhard jackass with an asshole that talks bullshit. I guess that I answered your question. I gotta say that it is a wise decision on your part to walk away while ya sorry ass is . . . intact," Jimmy said as he briskly walked away and headed for the front lobby.

Yes, indeed, it was now Jimmy Reeves' time.

While Jimmy walked to the front desk and left the stunned thugs and valets behind him, he knew that Detective Campenella was correct and as they moved closer to ending this case; it was going to become quite interesting. No doubt, that thug had some recollection of Jimmy from his days in Paterson and his previous adventures and reputation. Perhaps he served as a thug and henchman for Tony Senior or another crook, and somewhere they crossed paths. Regardless, Jimmy knew his cover might be blown, and he needed to move in delicate circles now.

While he approached the front desk for them to ring Hillary's room phone, Jimmy hoped and even prayed that Oscar would quickly obtain the warrant for the vehicle search and his team could discover some solid evidence that would turn the tide of this battle in the good guy's favor. Sharing some drinks and hanging out with Hillary would be a good idea to perpetuate his playboy image and to keep his eyes on Mick. The chess game continued, and if Jimmy could watch and observe some more of Mick's operations, he might just gather some more evidence.

With his reputation fortified, Jimmy approached the front desk, moved onto the next phase of the mission, blew a smokescreen, and provided a little damage control too.

"Hey, how's it goin'?" Jimmy asked the young man on duty at the front desk. "Ya hotel security guys are kinda aggressive and uptight here today. Ya can forgive me if I don't tip 'em and thank me for not kickin' his sorry ass in front of payin' guests. Could you please ring up Miss Hillary Thornburg's room and tell her that Jimmy is in the lobby?"

The young man nervously adjusted his necktie and said, "I apologize for the security's, ah, ah, overly cautious approach."

"Apology accepted. Not sure, what the hell that means, but whatever. Forget that jackleg out there. He can go clean out his underwear now. Right now, I got better things on my mind. I got me a hot date with a super, hot chick."

"Of course, Mr. O'Shaughnessy. Ms. Thornburg told us that you would be calling," the front desk clerk answered as he looked up the room number and made the call. Jimmy glanced at his watch and it was approaching four in the afternoon. He had enough time to have a few drinks with Hillary, collect some intelligence, and then head for his room and wait for Vanessa. Jimmy thought how it would be so wonderful to see his gal. He missed her.

Jimmy was glancing in the window of the lobby store that remained closed when he spotted Hillary step off the elevators and into the lobby. She looked quite stunning, dressed to the hilt in a tight black dress, with her usual matching pearl necklace showing off her plunging neckline and bulging cleavage. The pearls in her ears danced underneath her hair as she swayed and bounced across the lobby floor.

"Good afternoon, Jimmy. I trust that your business was rewarding," Hillary proclaimed as she leaned in and kissed Jimmy on his cheek. Her perfume filled the air and seemed to swirl around Jimmy as if it was a thundercloud before the deluge. The fragrance was some type of intoxicating bouquet that lured a male in and brought him to his knees with the impact of the alluring scent. It was a perfume full of sexiness and it broadcasted a web of potential romance.

"Hey, Hillary. Let's just say it was an unusual afternoon. I hope the seeds that, I planted will grow into sumthin' productive. I hope. How about you?"

She smiled and took his arm as Jimmy pointed to the entrance to Reflections and she reported, "Honestly, I drank too much champagne, but it inspired me to try some new angle shots, as well as, some unique lenses and filters. I was quite loose-minded and might have been wide open due to the bubbles. As you just said . . . and I echo . . . I hope. When the film returns and I have time to download the photos to my laptop, then we will know. That is the mystery of photography, you never know until the film returns or the computer screen dissects the shot. It is as if you are meeting a new lover. There is an air of mystery to the new love until you make the final connection. If you know what I mean." Hillary tightened her grip on Jimmy's arm and chuckled a bit at the actual meaning of her words.

"Nice analogy. Amazing visuals in my mind. Anyway, it works for me. Let's get a table. The bar seems stuffy." Jimmy waved and nodded to Mick Malzoni, who stared daggers at Jimmy.

Immediately, you could tell from his face that the sight of Jimmy courting another gorgeous woman on his arm was enough to set him off again. Vanessa was bad enough. Now he had the world-famous socialite hanging on his arm.

Mick feebly waved back and put up a phony front. "Hello, Jimmy. Hello, Ms. Thornburg. Welcome to Reflections. Please pick any table that you like. I will send the server over right away. I am going to assume it will be your usual Scotch poured neat and the finest champagne for the lovely woman?"

"Yeah, Mick. The Scotch is good for me. Hillary?"

"No, for now, screw the bubbly bullshit. I think that I will have the Scotch too. Same brand as you drink. Neat. I hear that it is a life changing experience." Hillary laughed and leaned playfully into Jimmy, and Mick nodded and went to prepare the drinks.

The grimy bartender mumbled, "Sure. We will have them right up for you."

Jimmy thought how Mick would gladly pour poison in his drink if he could only get away with it. Hillary might have been lucky enough to have a family of incredible wealth, but she was not just a gorgeous face and perfect body, flitting about her life. Instead, she was very keen and quite perceptive.

While Jimmy held out her chair for her to sit at the table, she leaned in and said to Jimmy, "My goodness, the bartender is a little less than pleased to see you. Did you pee in one of his drinks or what?"

Jimmy made sure Hillary was in her seat and tucked in. He walked around and sat opposite her and with a coy smile on his face, he answered, "Yeah, he is not my biggest fan. I think that I stole his gal, and he knows that I am on to his ways."

"Ways, Jimmy?"

"Yeah, he is a player. A very grimy dude. Please steer clear of him, Hillary."

"Oh, I will. I have seen a million of these kinds of guys and I usually have my bodyguard with me, but this trip is solo. Thanks for the advice."

Jimmy nodded and thought how this was the one trip that you should have had your bodyguard with you, and how she might have seen a million grimy dudes, but Mick was a little higher level of grime.

An older, but immaculate, and elegant female server with a gentle hint of a Spanish accent promptly delivered the drinks with a smile and a perfect presentation and introduction. The server graciously timed her exit after assuring Hillary and Jimmy that she would promptly take additional orders for drinks or food requests.

"While I sit here and study you, I must stick to my original opinion of your look. You still look as if you are the perfect male model, Jimmy. Please reconsider my offer for a photo shoot. You are stunning. Perfect. Your facial structure is amazing. The look is of the consummate experienced male, sitting where he wants to be in this life. Very self-confident and it projects in your amazing sexiness. The beard, the build, the eyes, the look. Amazing. You would make women melt. Perhaps, earn a small fortune on top of the fortune you already have earned. I guess that is the downfall to my offer since you do not need the money or desire the fame."

Jimmy raised his glass and smiled while thanking Hillary and avoiding responding to any of her statements.

With a graciously whispered, "Thank you," Jimmy followed up the thank you with a toast, "well, here is, to stunning. You are a gorgeous woman, gotta say that ya are second only to my own lovely and gorgeous woman. Anyway, cheers."

Hillary smiled at his honor and loyalty. Even dressed to the hilt and with her onslaught of sexiness, Hillary could not break this man. This was a strong and very unusual man. Hillary was used to staggering men with her allure. As the first few sips of liquid magic trickled down and flowed into her system, Hillary allowed her soul to open, and to expose just a little self-examination. Hillary had to admit that despite her new approach to life and her connection to Vanessa, she dressed in this dress and put on the maximum allure in a final effort to overcome the unreachable Jimmy O'Shaughnessy. This man was very special and rare. He was worth a last try. No offense to Vanessa, perhaps, it was just a bit of egotistical boasting for her own means, but now, Hillary conceded defeat. Vanessa had a keeper. He was obviously deeply in love. They toasted, and each took a deep sip.

"So, how's the Scotch, Hillary?"

"Wow! At first, it sucks. It tastes like cough medicine but as it flows in and around it is, ah, well, kind of life changing. . .."

"Yeah, well, wait 'til it works some inner magic. Ya will be howling at the moon. Say, Hillary, I have to say working with you today, I might get into this photography stuff a little bit more. Please tell me more 'bout how ya take close-up shots. I took some pictures this afternoon with a point and shoot. Tell me, 'bout the best camera for me to use for close shots."

Hillary's face lit up as Jimmy dove into her favorite subject, and she picked right up on the subject matter while giving Jimmy some pointers. The server returned a number of times. She brought refills and the conversation was engaging, and Hillary energetic and of course, very appealing. Jimmy was interested in the subject and in Hillary's expertise, but while she explained the nuances of macro photography and he admired her beauty between sips of life-changing magic, he kept an eye on Mick Malzoni.

A very close eye.

Mick was busy, it was still early for the bar and lounge scene, but Mick was running around quite a bit. He worked a few whispered deals with some businessmen that Jimmy was sure were some covert deals for some escorts and "company." Even after some very careful observations, in between the engaging conversation with the amazingly stunning Hillary, Jimmy had no significant new items to work with right now. Jimmy listened and engaged in the conversation, but all the time, he watched and knew in his mind that Mick was a little nervous. He was not quite as cool, calm, and cocky, as he was the night before. He was on edge.

Something or someone had rattled his soul.

Jimmy could tell. Part of his training was to observe and to record the enemy's behaviors and patterns.

Mick took a phone call and Jimmy watched his eyes glance over to where Hillary and Jimmy sat. By the reactions of Mick and his eyes darting around, Jimmy was quite sure that the phone call was from the forward watch. His henchman was reporting on the conflict Jimmy had with them at the front entrance. Jimmy was also quite sure that his cover was blown, or at least in question now. Mick glared in the general direction of Hillary and Jimmy while speaking on the telephone and he tried hard not to allow his eyes to meet with Jimmy's eyes. Right now, Jimmy knew that if he had blown his cover, then the burn in his own eyes would establish the ground rules. Jimmy wanted Mick to know that right away he was going down. Mick was target number one. When Mick hung up from the call, it was easy to tell that he was very uneasy and uptight.

Between the cat-and-mouse game, the uneasiness and the covert phone calls, Jimmy did notice that Mick seemed to keep a little notebook that he kept by the telephone. He would often work a deal with some sloppy businessman or on the telephone, and then he would often run over to the notebook and jot down some information. Jimmy was sure that was how he tracked his arrangements and deals and filtered the extra money in the till to Mike Spence for burying into the legitimate bar operations. Potential evidence. How he would like to get his hands on that book.

"Jimmy, have you traveled much? I am sure that a man of your circles and means might have logged a few miles." Hillary asked, and her eyes sparkled in the light of the lounge. Careful now, Reeves. The liquid magic loosened her inhibitions, and he needed to make sure it did not loosen his inhibitions, as well as his lips too.

"Oh, a little. I did a visit or two of the Middle East, in the desert areas of the world. Here and there. For some reason, I seem to enjoy desert tours," Jimmy strategically replied.

After all, it was not a lie.

Before Hillary could dwell too much on the reply, Jimmy spotted Mick finish speaking with a middle-aged man sitting at the bar, take a wad of dollars from the man, deposit them in the register and then walk over to his notebook. Mick made a note in his notebook and he left the book on the far end of the bar. Right in the direct path to the restroom.

Jimmy thought, "These guys are such careless suckers."

Time to move, but carefully. The security cameras were all watching and always-on duty. Jimmy stood up and excused himself to pay the restroom a visit.

"Oh, I have to go too, Jimmy. Besides, we need refills."

Jimmy stood up, walked over to Hillary and assisted her exiting the table.

She grabbed her purse, put her arm inside of Jimmy's arm and while they walked, Hillary leaned in and whispered, "Time to have some fun with Mr. Gloomy. This guy is such a slime ball. Let's see if we can captivate him for a little tease and have some fun."

Hillary tugged at her neckline and forced her dress down a little farther into her amazing chest. This gal was a ton of fun, and Jimmy thought how this little diversion was exactly what he required! This was all falling perfectly into place. While they approached the bar, Hillary broke off, and Jimmy's eyes darted to the notebook and then to the security cameras, then to Mick, and finally to Hillary. The stunning woman leaned over the bar right near the end and waved to Mick. Her dress fell all around her amazing cleavage, her hair tumbled in waves of desire, and her eyes sparkled. There was no way in hell that either Mick or the eyes watching through the security cameras focused on anything other than the stunning and captivating Hillary Thornburg.

"Yoo hoo! Micky, baby. I am in such need of *your* services. Please be a doll and send over some refills for Jimmy and me. I am dry and you do not want me dry. Do you? We are scooting out to the restroom, but please be a dear and refill me. I mean . . . refill us. Will you?" Hillary wrapped Mick around her finger and melted him with her looks and her suggestive words. As soon as Mick turned and spotted Hillary's maneuver, and Jimmy saw his eyes glued upon her, and her overly exposed chest, Jimmy slid in behind her so that Hillary blocked Mick's view and in one quick motion, Jimmy snatched the notebook off the counter of the bar. He slid the notebook into the pocket of his pants and then, comfortably and tightly, leaned into Hillary with some heavily romantic inclinations. All under the pretense of ticking Mick off even more. Hillary was loose from the Scotch and she was having fun with Mick, but Jimmy was covertly working on the mission. Hillary conveniently fell into place as being the perfect partner for this part of the mission. Hillary was having fun, and she had no idea that it worked Jimmy's plan to perfection. Hillary reached over, put her arm around Jimmy, pulled him close, and gave him a sloppy kiss on the cheek.

She was very cool.

Mick nodded and even though he was enraged with Jimmy, he turned on some more phony charm.

"Why, of course, Ms. Thornburg. Refills on the way. Dry is . . . very unacceptable. Refills are on the way, immediately."

Hillary nodded and winked. She pulled and tugged at Jimmy, and they walked arm-in-arm to the restrooms.

"This is such fun, Jimmy. That bartender is a grimy one. His eyeballs almost fell out of his evil head. See you in a few minutes. If you were not so dedicated and amazingly and deeply in love with that very lucky woman, I would invite you in and lock the door behind us. That Scotch has gone straight to my head and I am on fire. What we could do within a few minutes would be remarkable."

Hillary playfully slapped Jimmy on the backside as she wiggled off to the women's room. Jimmy laughed at her humor and her amusing personality. But now it was time to get to work.

Quickly.

Once in the restroom stall, Jimmy flipped open the notebook and scanned it. Names, dates, phone numbers, the names of women, the time, and most of the money exchanged during the deals. Mick was such a punk and in the big picture, such an amateur. But the jackass did keep meticulous records. Jimmy gasped as he noted that some of these dopes paid up to eight thousand dollars for one night with a lovely woman.

Oh well, evil knows very few boundaries.

Jimmy took the camera out and began snapping each page as quickly as he could. How he wished that he could use some pointers that Hillary provided on macro shots, but his camera was not very sophisticated. He snapped off each page until the camera and the time told him that he was at the end of the line with the storage and the minutes. He did not capture all the pages, but he certainly captured the majority. Out of the stall he rolled the camera back in his pocket and the notebook tucked in his hand and concealed. The replacement of the notebook without detection was going to take a tricky and strategic maneuver. Jimmy might have to step up the "playful" notch just a hair or two. Luckily, Hillary Thornburg was playful and perfect for his next move. Hillary walked out of the women's restroom a few seconds after Jimmy arrived. She smiled, and her face lit up at the sight of Jimmy.

"Sorry. I had to make myself beautiful. I had to retouch my makeup. Were you waiting long?"

"No, and you did not need any touch up. You were and are quite gorgeous, with makeup or without."

Hillary swooned at the comment and smiled. She then locked arms with Jimmy.

Jimmy whispered, "Sorry to do this to you and perhaps, I can explain someday soon, but honestly, we are just friends. For many reasons, I have to hand this creepy dude his head on a jealous platter and have a barrel of fun with him. Please, just go with it," to a stunned and slightly perplexed Hillary, while Jimmy leaned in and passionately kissed Hillary on the lips. At first, Hillary remained perplexed, and then as the warmth of their kiss deepened, she groaned, opened her mouth and danced her tongue with Jimmy's tongue, leaned into the kiss and thoroughly enjoyed it. While kissing, and while Jimmy was sure that all eyes locked on their incredible kiss, it was Jimmy's chance to maneuver under the cover of sharing some passion with the gorgeous Hillary Thornburg. As they kissed, Jimmy leaned in and strategically slipped the notebook right back where it was at the end of the bar. It was a perfect placement, and the notebook landed in almost the exact spot from where Jimmy removed it. After they kissed, and Hillary slowly recovered from what she felt was the greatest kiss in the history of the world, Hillary moved, and she bounced and swayed with amazing allure. Hillary caused every male within twenty miles of her to fall to his knees and beg for mercy. Even if one of the most unlikely events in the history of the world occurred, and someone's focus was not on Hillary Thornburg, there was little chance that anyone could have seen Jimmy's quick maneuver in replacing the notebook. Hillary's amazing appearance, her glorious figure, and their passionate kiss had blocked their view.

Mick's eyes burned a hole into the air. The smoke rose from his head and out of his ears. It was perfect, and Jimmy basked in the delight of making Mick Malzoni as uncomfortable as possible. Mick was teetering on the edge now and Jimmy was ready to push him as hard and as strongly as he dared to without causing an eruption.

Moreover, if it did erupt, then Jimmy would gladly handle it.

It was Jimmy Reeves' time.

Hillary leaned in as they approached the table and she whispered, "I know that we are just friends and this is such fun and the kiss was all in jest to have some more fun with Mick, but my goodness, Jimmy, you just melted my panties." With a wink, she added, "I can easily show you a glimpse and prove it too."

Jimmy smiled, but he had no comment.

'Steer clear of that one, Reeves' was his only thought.

The refilled drinks were at the table and they shared a few more laughs, some more conversation, and the time passed rather quickly.

Jimmy glanced at his watch and announced, "Hillary, this has been a blast. Ya da bomb, but I gotta get back to my room, wash up, and wait for my woman. I have enjoyed this very much and you are a great friend. I hope we can stay in touch and be friends. I will pay the tab. My treat, please." Jimmy waved for the server, and she quickly scampered over. "Please, bring the check. Ya been great. The greatest server and such a fun time. We sure cooled old hot-shit, Mick, didn't we?"

It was easy to tell that the server wanted to agree with

the comment, but she only smiled and held her tongue.

After the server left, Hillary leaned back, smiled, and said, "Of course, we are great friends. I will give you my card and please stay in touch." Hillary handed Jimmy her card and Jimmy did the same. "I will say it once again, that woman of yours is the luckiest woman on Earth. I have to say this, because I have no panties left, but if by chance, something changes, then I am in room four-twenty-two. On the other hand, we could meet on the moon. Anywhere."

Hillary winked, and Jimmy stood up just as the server arrived with the check.

Jimmy glanced at it and said, "Oh, geez, it is only two-hundred bucks, huh? Hell, here ya go, here is five-hundred bucks. Have an amazing night and pay a few bills on me."

The server smiled widely and for a brief moment, it seemed as if she would leap into Jimmy's arms and give him a kiss. Instead, she repeatedly thanked Jimmy. The big man shook her hand, and he patted her on the back.

"Keep up the good work, honey. You are the best of da best."

Hillary smiled and as the two friends walked away from the server, Hillary commented, "You are so special. You just made her so proud of her job. You gave her honor, and that means even more than the tip does. You are a prize, Jimmy. A rare and precious prize."

Jimmy took Hillary's hand, and they walked by the bar only to once again meet the glare of Mick Malzoni.

"Thank you, Ms. Thornburg," was all that Mick said as he ignored his nemesis. At first, Jimmy ignored the bartender and instead, he pulled Hillary in even closer to him.

In a low growl, Jimmy said, "You have a nice evening, Mick." Jimmy then raised the implications by adding, "I will most certainly have a wonderful evening."

Hillary and Jimmy continued to walk hand-in-hand to the elevator, where they rode the car together until it stopped on the fourth floor. There, they parted ways with a gentle kiss on the cheeks and a promise to stay in touch. While the doors glided slowly to a close and Jimmy admired the rear view of Hillary moving off into the distance. In his heart, he grew very anxious. Anxious, because his precious Vanessa would be arriving so very soon. Jimmy felt as if today was a huge success. He was sure the notebook held valuable evidence and that his time with Hillary was well spent. His fictitious cover might be on the edge, but right now, Jimmy had other things on his mind.

Upon arrival, Jimmy checked his room carefully. No Tattletales today. Housekeeping would have been in the room, anyway. The room was clear and Jimmy showered, changed into casual clothes, a tee shirt, some dungarees and sneakers. He hoped that Vanessa would agree with his plan, order some food from room service and then stay here in order to hang out together in the room. He glanced at his watch. A minute to six and while he prepared a Scotch from the wet-bar, there were gentle knocks on the door. Three knocks and a pause, then two knocks.

This was his kind of gal. She was on top of her game. Always.

Just in case there was an ambush, Jimmy glanced at his twenty-two-caliber handgun on the counter of the wet-bar and Jimmy grabbed the gun while looking through the security peeper in the door.

It was Vanessa, and he scanned around her as best as he could through the security door peeper. The knock indicated all clear and Jimmy breathed deeply and then he relaxed. It looked all clear, and Vanessa looked calm. Gorgeous and calm.

Confident that everything was all clear, Jimmy set the handgun back on the counter and swung open the door. She looked beyond ravishing, and it appeared as if the two lovers were on the same page. She held a large luggage bag, her work uniform and a black dress on a hanger, and her purse draped over her shoulder. She planned to stay overnight and then some. She, too, was dressed in blue dungarees and a casual blouse. Vanessa tossed the bag aside, Jimmy kicked the door closed with his foot, and flipped the locks and the deadbolt closed with a spare hand. They dove into each other's arms, and their lips locked.

"I missed you more than words can ever convey," Vanessa whispered between kisses.

"I missed you too, baby. It was such a long day. Let's vow never to be apart for that long again. Ok?"

She nodded her head in agreement and Jimmy pointed to the wet-bar and said, "Ya must be thinking what I am thinking, cuz you dressed casually. I figured we could get room service and hang out in the room. I need to keep a low profile tonight. I need to fill you in on the latest and greatest. Do ya wanna a Scotch? Did you have a good day with your parents? Did ya get all the shopping done?"

Vanessa smiled, and at first, she did not answer Jimmy's questions and then she whispered, "No Scotch right now. Later. Everything is fine. My parents are fine. Thank you, but you ask too many questions. You are yapping too much. I need you naked. Right now."

Vanessa ignored the rest of his comments about their common manner of dress and staying in the room. Instead, she tugged at Jimmy's belt and pulled it off and tossed it aside. Then she worked at his pants and loosened them at his waist. Jimmy received the message loud and clear and he began to strip his clothes off while Vanessa did the same with hers. In a flash, she pulled her blouse off, unlatched her bra, tossed it aside, and it landed upon the lampshade next to the bed, and there it hung in a seductive display of exploding lust. Vanessa's breathing was heavy, and she rapidly scrambled out of her pants and her panties. Vanessa tossed her panties aside, and they ended up hanging on the lampshade too. Jimmy thought how this woman must have great potential at the shooting range or the golf course.

Within a few seconds of uninhibited stripping of their garments, they both were naked and in each other's arms.

As they tumbled into the bed, Vanessa whispered, "No, no, no, Scotch right now, and hell yes, we are staying in the room. Right now, my love, I need to absorb into you. Scotch later. First, we screw like wild baboons. Then, we will talk and have a few drinks. Maybe, I will let you come up for air long enough to eat. Maybe."

After a few hours of making love, the two impassioned lovers stopped, and they sat in bed, studied each other's bodies, and explored their minds together.

The physical connections are only a small part of true lovemaking. The emotional aspects and exploration of two connected souls are the most important part.

"I gotta clear the air, baby. Confession time, Vanessa. I know you are gonna see Hillary Thornburg tomorrow and I want you to hear this from me first."

For a second or two, Vanessa's heart jumped and skipped a bit. When she heard the word confession and then Hillary's name, she wondered what this was all about now. She was madly and hopelessly in love with this man, and she had shared her heart and her body with him, as she had never done with any man before. Vanessa felt as if his trust and his honesty were both attributes that were never in question.

She pulled at the pillows, set them on the headboard, and stared intensely at her lover.

"Confession? Ok? I think," Vanessa said, with some apprehension in her voice.

"I spent a lot of the day with her."

Vanessa's eyes closed and her mouth screwed up tightly, and Jimmy sensed that Vanessa was thinking the worst, and he gently grabbed her face and kissed her cheeks.

"Relax, baby, it was work related, nothing happened. You are my only love. Now and forever more. C'mon, now, ya gotta relax."

Vanessa opened her eyes and smiled. Suddenly, she felt foolish for doubting her Jimmy.

"I was relaxing on the balcony this morning, smoking one of those fancy cigars you got for me and sippin' Scotch. She came by with Renaldo and his team of housemen carrying camera stuff. Lots of camera stuff." Vanessa sat upright, and the covers slipped away and exposed her magnificent bare breasts.

She smiled as she interrupted Jimmy's story because she could verify the facts, "Yes, Hillary reserved the balcony for a photo shoot of the ocean. She worked it out yesterday when she checked into the hotel. Hillary is very cool and amazing. Isn't she?"

Jimmy nodded and agreed, "She is a very cool chick and gorgeous too. Ya can see why she is so famous and plastered on the cover of all those magazines. She shared some drinks wid me, or actually, wid Jimmy O'Shaughnessy. The other Irish guy within me had Scotch, and she had champagne. Both Jimmy guys don't do bubbles."

Vanessa laughed and agreed, "No. Bubbles and Jimmy and his alter ego, do not seem as if bubbles would make the cut."

Jimmy continued, "I did not think Hillary was on the dark side, but all that dough, all those connections, power, fame and fortune. I still had to check her out, cuz, like they taught me, trust no one. Plus, she was now ya friend, and you was gonna hang out with her, so I needed to make sure. Hillary Thornburg could fund lots of evil stuff."

Vanessa looked as if she never thought of that angle before, but she felt the immense amount of love churning inside of her at the thought that Jimmy was working, but still thinking of protecting her.

"She is cool. No issues, very honest and I agree with you. For some high and fancy chick, she is very down to Earth. Great sense of humor too. She showed me a lot of interesting pointers about taking pictures and I learned a lot of things. I think it could be useful, in my work, ya know—if I had a fancier camera and learned to take better pictures. Very useful. Anyway, we sat for a few hours, drank more than we should have, and I had to connect with Detective Campy, so I split. We met back up later in the Reflections for a few drinks and we had some fun with grimy Mick. I wanted to milk Mick and that scene and Hillary was a great partner in the plan to observe and to gather some more inside information. I have to tell ya, but we kissed on the lips under the pretense of having fun with Mick. But I really needed a smokescreen to cover up some evidence that I hoofed. It is kinda hard to explain, but I hoofed this notebook of Mick's from the bar, took it in the restroom and snapped a bunch of pictures of the pages. The notebook had a bunch of John's names and transactions recorded in it. I needed a diversion to get it back where it was. The kiss worked for a diversion. Sorry. It was just part of the mission and Hillary thought we was just havin' fun' with Mick. Meant nothing, baby. Part of the job. Honest."

Vanessa blinked at the thought of them sharing a kiss, but she nodded as she understood and felt the honesty in her lover's eyes. Vanessa would need to accept that Jimmy using his amazing looks and charm was part of his bag of tricks.

Still, Vanessa had to ask, "Was Hillary a good kisser? I mean . . . was she better than I am?"

Jimmy waved his hand in the air and dismissed the thought, "Nah! Nowhere even near ya. Vanessa, c'mon, now baby, you are everything to me. The greatest kisser, the greatest lover, the smartest, the most gorgeous, and the most wonderful woman on Earth. I know it has only been a few days, but I love ya to the moon and back. Plus, no bubbles for Hillary. This time, Hillary had Scotch, so she was a bit loopy and playful. I convinced her that the Scotch would change her life. She might not even 'member the kiss. She was feeling it all. Anyway, I got lots of good intelligence on that bum, Mick, and I gotta tell ya all 'bout it. Good stuff. Mick is on the ropes. We have 'em on the ropes. I might have blown my cover a little, but I think we are still good." Vanessa looked up at Jimmy with some concern, and she raised her eyes at his comment.

She then asked, "Blown your cover? How so? Is that another reason that you wanted to lie low, tonight?"

Jimmy nodded and said, "Yup. Mostly, of course, I wanted to make love to you all night, but yes. I need to stay out of sight and out of mind tonight. Left Reflections wid Hillary and gave Mick the impression that we were shackin' up. Had to blow more smoke and let it all die down. This afternoon, when I got back here, one of the henchmen met me at the front door and thought he knew me from up north. He might have recognized me, but when he got tough, I shut his ass down. I think it worked for now."

Vanessa nodded again. She was now growing accustomed to the fact that Jimmy's energy and his commitment to honor were nonstop, and the mission enveloped all of his soul.

"On a good note, I found the car that Campy was lookin' for too, so much to tell ya, but first, I wanted to tell ya 'bout Hillary. I wanted to be honest and clear all the air."

Since Vanessa was so intuitive and she knew how sexy and appealing her man was, she nodded in acknowledgement of Jimmy's testimony of the day's events and then pulled Jimmy close and leaned her head on his chest. Her bare breasts rested upon his mighty muscles as she ran her hand up and down his body and ran her fingers through his chest hair.

In a gentle and soft whisper, Vanessa asked, "Okay. I understand. It sounds as if it turned out to be a productive day. You found the car? I need to hear more about the secret agent bullshit, but first, let me ask you. When she first met you, did Hillary come on to you?"

"Yeah, she did. She loved the color of my eyes and made a big deal 'bout 'em. Wanted to do a photo shoot and then invited me to her room to hang out on the balcony and take pictures and drink. She made a huge suggestion that we should do more than just shoot pictures too."

Jimmy looked down into Vanessa's eyes and his lover looked up at Jimmy and asked, "What did you tell her, Jimmy O'Shaughnessy? After all, you were playing the playboy part. And, yes, your eyes are beyond amazing. Surreal."

"I told her the truth. I told her that we can share a drink or two here or in one of the lounges, but just so ya know, I am in a committed relationship. My woman and me, we are in it for the long haul. Forever. I told her, yeah, Hillary, we can be friends, talk, and hang out, but we just gotta be friends. I told her that I gotta be honest and upfront, cuz, I have this amazing and awesome gal that I am with, for now and for forever. She is incredibly special and I am just wild about her. I told her the truth, Vanessa. Told her that I am in love. For once in my life, I am in love, with something other than guns, danger, the military, and missions. I have me a woman to love now."

Vanessa smiled and curled up closer to Jimmy while she gently worked her hands from his chest to his once more growing manhood. In her heart, she knew the mission was part of his soul and it was his job, but his love was hers. She felt his love and vowed never to doubt it again.

"I have heard enough. You *are* mine forever! I wonder if she made the connection, because when we first met, I told her all about you. Even mentioned your eyes to her. She is still my friend, because I cannot blame her for coming onto you. What woman wouldn't? Perhaps, she realized that you were the man that I was meeting for our first date. Regardless, I will find out tomorrow. A rich, glamorous, wealthy, world famous woman, clawing at you, and you picked me. Hillary is a woman who could pick any man in the world and the men run into her arms and dive into her bed. You. Picked. Me. Vanessa, the hotel desk clerk. Enough talking. I will love you forever, Jimmy Reeves."

"You are not a hotel desk clerk, you are, the captivating and gorgeous, Vanessa Michaelson and we are a team. Partners. You just signed up for life with me."

Vanessa mumbled, "Yes, for life and for love too."

Jimmy laughed and pointed at the lampshade that now sported a dangling pair of black panties and a lacy black brassiere.

"Hey, cool décor. I love da lampshades they got in this fancy dump. Can we always have one of those in our house?"

Vanessa looked over at the lampshade and she laughed, too. "Of course, Jimmy. I have a feeling that wearing my clothing around you will be optional."

"Yeah, baby, ya right on wid that one."

With those words, Jimmy rather forcibly, but still carefully, flipped Vanessa over. He tore the covers away from their bodies and he hovered seductively over her gorgeous naked body. One glimpse at Jimmy's naked body told Vanessa that Jimmy was ready.

More than ready.

Vanessa let out with a little gasp of surprise at Jimmy's actions. Then a seductive smile appeared on her face as she opened her arms and wrapped them tightly around her man.

Yes, indeed, it was Jimmy Reeves' time. In more ways than just one.

Chapter 10

Out of Hiding

Jimmy and Vanessa finally stopped proving their love, they ordered room service, enjoyed copious amounts of Scotch and Jimmy discussed all the day's events to his partner in love, in life, and in danger. During the discussion, Jimmy expanded upon the details about the notebook, the vehicle, and Detective Campy's quest for a search warrant. With a hint of a gleam in his eye at the fury he felt because of the incident with the thug, Jimmy explained to Vanessa about how the thug backed off when Jimmy confronted him. They both shared a few laughs when Jimmy told of Hillary's playful toying with Mick and how Mick's eyes nearly fell out of his head, when Hillary showed him a little extra skin. Vanessa found it quite refreshing how a wealthy and famous socialite such as Hillary Thornburg was also possessed such a wonderful sense of humor. It was an in-depth and exciting discussion. He also revealed that he thought tomorrow would prove to be a very fateful day. A crucial day as they waited for the results of the investigation of the vehicle, and Jimmy studied more of the evidence he gathered. Jimmy thought that it was helpful to their cause for Vanessa to be on duty at the front desk tomorrow. She could feed Jimmy play-by-play information of when, and if, something unfolds. Vanessa also agreed with Jimmy to lie low, just in case his false identity was exposed. Jimmy explained that his plan was to stay under wraps until he needed to jump into action. Maybe some gym time, a little run, some weight lifting. Just play it cool for now and wait for Detective Campy to call Vanessa and check in with the full details and the full plan.

Jimmy made a trip to his car, obtained the small VHF radios, and gave one to Vanessa. They were encrypted transmitters with both radios programmed to a frequency assigned to the attorney general's departments. In an emergency, Vanessa could use the radios to alert Jimmy. The radios were perfect for the mission because they fit nicely into Vanessa's purse. The plan was in place. Now it was just a matter of waiting for it to unfold.

After enjoying discussion, sharing their dinner meal and some copious doses of Scotch, the lovers slept soundly wrapped in each other's arms. The lovemaking, the food, the day's events, and the Scotch worked to induce a restful sleep.

When the morning light arrived, and the night faded into spent glory until it returned, Vanessa and Jimmy showered, ordered some breakfast and while Jimmy dressed for working out, Vanessa prepared for work. She had to report at eight in the morning; they walked to the elevator together and parted ways in the lobby, promising to stay in touch constantly. There was no need any longer to hide their romance; most everyone felt that the two of them were an item, anyway. Some people might accuse Jimmy of two-timing with his act on the previous day with Hillary, but the phony antics might help to perpetuate the playboy image, just in case the truth behind his false identity was closing in on him now. Regardless, Jimmy felt that it did not matter much any longer. He knew this was all going to come to a climax today, anyway. He could feel the tension in the air, and he was ready for action.

Time to end this with a win for the good side.

Jimmy ran a few miles, and he worked out in the gym located within the resort of the property. He occasionally stopped by the front desk and checked in with Vanessa. Back in his room, he showered and checked his equipment. He pulled one of the spare handguns from its hiding spot and some spare ammo, too. He was not sure if Vanessa ever fired a weapon before, but he might need to give her a crash course. He broke down his weapons in his room, cleaned and dressed them, and time passed very slowly. It was as if there was a quiet stillness in the air before the deluge. Jimmy knew this feeling well. The silence was too unnatural. He looked at his watch and it was o-eleven-hundred-hours. And by now, Detective Campy must be deep into his vehicle search and the thugs alerted as to the police detective seizing the car. The pieces would come together very quickly after the hierarchy of the mob quizzed Teddy, and the finger pointed to Jimmy.

Jimmy put the "Do Not Disturb" sign in place on the doorknob.

It was now time to dress and to prepare for battle. Jimmy Reeves dressed in his black suit, side-zip boots and he donned all the weapons. No eavesdroppers or recorders on this go-around, just the VHF radio. Once dressed, he set the radio on the desk in front of him and waited for a call.

Jimmy O'Shaughnessy was history.

He was officially Jimmy Reeves.

Detective Oscar Campenella nervously paced the floor of an office located within the local barracks of the New Jersey State Police. He could feel the tension as the scenes now folded into each other and everything overlapped. Attorney General Charles McCracken had arranged for a judge located in an adjoining county to hear the probable cause, and the judge quickly approved the search warrant and impound of the vehicle as part of an ongoing homicide investigation. His team towed the vehicle to the lab and garage and they now poured over it. The news of Detective Campenella appearing with an escort of heavily armed New Jersey State troopers, an elite crime scene team and a warrant issued by an out-of-county judge, must have caused more than a stir in the mob. It probably caused an eruption! The vehicle seizure must have spread like a fire through the mob and the assorted cast of characters. Oscar knew by now that his chain of command was on edge, because Attorney General McCracken assigned undercover troopers to watch them all now for potential flight risks. The silence from the Clinton City Police Department told Oscar all that he needed to know, yet he sat poised for action, when and if they tried to pressure him and shut the good detective down.

Charles McCracken informed Oscar that he felt as if his task force now had enough evidence to bring the entire Clinton City Police Department chain of command down, as well as the mayor and some councilpersons. Chuck had ordered Oscar that he was now reporting directly to the attorney general and for him to use the office and command center at the state police barracks for all his work and communications. The cagey attorney general alerted the New Jersey State Police investigators, and he assigned New Jersey State Police crime scene technicians to assist in the dissection of the vehicle. The attorney general also assigned special prosecutors to review the case. When the lab results came in, the legal team was ready to perform the initial review of the case. Afterwards, they would determine if they had enough evidence to send it to Attorney General Charles McCracken for the final review and ruling to agree to go after Tony Michanetti Junior and finally nail him. The attorney general also spoke with the governor of New Jersey and provided a briefing of the situation, and after receiving permission, Chuck ordered New Jersey State Police troopers to be on standby to step in when required and back up his team with some substantial firepower. Attorney General McCracken was on standby to make his way to Clinton City later today. If the evidence was positive and the special prosecutors and Charles McCracken agreed that it was a solid case, the attorney general was taking a ride along with an escort of New Jersey State Police, and he would arrive, to close the case on the corruption, mayhem, murder, and assorted evil of the empire of Tony Michanetti Junior.

Oscar knew that he needed to communicate to Jimmy Reeves and inform Jimmy of where they now were on the case. He was sure that by now, Jimmy's cover was history, as Tony Michanetti Junior and his gang of mobsters put the pieces together of how Oscar and his team found the vehicle. The good detective needed to check in with him and make sure that Jimmy and Vanessa were safe and on full alert.

Knowing Jimmy, he was sure that he was on full alert, however; extreme danger was now closing in.

Oscar also wanted to hear any of the latest developments at Casa Al Mare. The last thing that he wanted was for the members of the operations to get cold feet and begin to flee. Oscar knew that Jimmy and Vanessa would see indications of that and besides that fact, Oscar was sure that Jimmy might have new evidence. At the very least, he wanted the photographs of the vehicle at the hotel front entrance from Jimmy's camera. He knew that a phone call to Jimmy's room was a very bad idea. He was sure that the mobster's technical team had a tap into Jimmy's room phone. Detective Campenella then recalled that Attorney General McCracken had informed him that Jimmy had high frequency radio equipment to communicate with and that the state police radio operators were equally equipped.

Oscar thought as he listened to the information, "What the hell does this guy not have?"

In looking through his careful notes, taken during the conversation, Oscar found what he needed to do to initiate the communications. All that he had to do was to get a message to Jimmy and use the words, "Four-zero-two-two, Uniform, Sierra, Bravo and the time for a call." Jimmy would know what to do and the police radio operators would know too.

The good detective picked up the phone and called the front desk of Casa Al Mare. He hoped that Vanessa answered.

One ring, two rings, "Thank you for calling the world-famous Casa Al Mare. This is Vanessa speaking."

Now, they were cooking with gas. Jimmy Reeves not only recruited a gorgeous partner for love, but for war too.

"Campy here. Tell him, four-zero-two-two, Uniform, Sierra, Bravo and o-twelve-hundred."

Vanessa immediately sensed the situation, and she carefully noted what Campy told her. Vanessa jotted the info on a pad and then she spoke as if the call was a potential guest calling to request information.

"Oh, yes, I have the information. Availability on May sixteenth. Let me check. How many guests?"

She continued with the pretend exchange, even though Oscar had hung up the telephone call. Vanessa followed through as if the call ended with the potential guest calling back to finalize the reservation. Vanessa hung up the phone, looked over at her partner, and grabbed the notepad and her purse.

"I have to visit the restroom. I drank too much coffee today. Can you cover? Be right back," she said as she hustled off to use the radio and alert Jimmy. Her partner working at the desk nodded and waved to indicate that he was on it.

Once inside the restroom, Vanessa scooted in one of the stalls, opened her purse and just before keying the radio to transmit she thought, 'Two days ago, I was just a hotel desk clerk, making sure the stapler was full of staples and now I am a damn secret agent chick.' Vanessa pulled out the notepad and keyed the radio transmit button, and whispered, "Jimmy. You there?"

Jimmy answered in less than half a second, "Here."

While reading the notes, Vanessa said, "Campy called. He said, four-zero-two-two, Uniform, Sierra, Bravo and o-twelve-hundred. Does that mean something to you?"

"Roger. Got it. Be safe. Head on a swivel. I am here and on this."

Vanessa replaced the radio in her purse and shook her head while speaking aloud to the stall, "Roger? Who the hell is Roger? Some other dude in the mix. I swear, this man is endless with mystery bullshit. Why did I have to fall madly in love with a secret agent, dude? Oh, what the hell. Might as well pee while I am here."

Quick as a flash, Jimmy was walking to his car while carrying his gym bag. The eyes behind the cameras would think that he was loading workout gear and not radio equipment. It was also time to grab his body armor too. Jimmy whispered aloud to himself as he hustled to the car, "Four-zero-two-two, Uniform, Sierra, Bravo and o-twelve-hundred." Jimmy spoke aloud and repeated the information and then he thought, 'A military frequency, very close to the eighty-meter amateur radio band. I did not know the state ops could use that one. Oh well, I can. I still have my Navy Department call sign assigned to me. That is a long ass antenna for that frequency and on the upper sideband too.'

He knew his best chance was to use his micro-tuner and find an antenna for the tuner to adjust the physical length of the antenna to something that he could use. He knew just the object, too. Within a few minutes, Jimmy returned to his room. He grabbed his tool kit, some solid gauge wire, and opened the window. He was in luck; a downspout leading to a long rain gutter was within his reach. Six floors up, a perfect antenna for this frequency. Jimmy leaned out, drilled a small hole in the side of the downspout, screwed a copper lug into the metal, and then attached the wire to the lug. He set up the radio and attached the wire from the "antenna" to the input of the tuner, plugged it all in, and flipped all the equipment on. Now he needed a ground plane. He took his ground plane wire out of the radio kit and Jimmy spread it across the hotel floor, opened the plumbing maintenance access plate in the corner of the bathroom wall, and with the alligator clip soldered on the end of the wire forced wide open, Jimmy clamped the wire to a copper pipe. In theory, he knew that he had all the copper in the facility working as a ground plane. Even at midday on that frequency and with his low power output, his signal should be strong, as long as the tuner could handle the tuning of the rain gutter.

Jimmy looked at his watch. Two minutes to the hour. Wow! Nerve wracking. He spun the radio dial to the frequency of 4022.0, flipped the sideband switch to USB, and keyed the microphone button. Simultaneously, he hit the tuner button and after some clicks, some searching and adjustments, the output meter locked on and indicated a full twenty watts of power output. Success!

Since Jimmy did not know who was to initiate the net, he made the first call, "This is, N-N-N-Zero, Papa, Alfa, X-Ray, listening. Is there a net control on frequency? Over."

Immediately, a station answered, "Roger. N-N-N-ZERO, Papa, Alpha, X-Ray, this is, N-N-N-Zero Gulf, Bravo, Gulf. Net Control for the One-Gulf-One, Bravo tactical net. This is a directed net. Full call signs only. Do you have ritty capabilities? I have one flash precedence message for your station. Over."

"This is N-N-N-Zero, Papa, Alpha, X-ray. Negative. Voice or Charlie Whiskey only. Over."

Oops, a mistake. Maybe he should have checked first. Jimmy looked over at his bag with the radio gear. He had it. Good. Jimmy smiled as he confirmed that he had his Morse code key in his bag. Jimmy knew that his boss never missed an angle. He had pulled a Navy, Coast Guard, or Marine Corps radio operator out of his hat for duty. Most likely, an experienced NAVMARCORMARS operator, Jimmy surmised from the call sign assignment. The protocol was exactly Navy Department protocol, and Chuck McCracken knew that Jimmy remained authorized through NAVMARCORMARS for the use of these military frequencies.

McCracken was brilliant.

"This is, N-N-N-Zero, Gulf, Bravo, Gulf. Roger. Wait one." The radio went silent and Jimmy gathered up a pad and pencil.

"N-N-N-Zero, Papa, Alpha, X-ray, this is N-N-N-Zero, Gulf, Bravo, Gulf. Message follows . . . flash, time. . .."

Jimmy copied the message at a furious pace, and the operator was perfect. An expert op. Jimmy just hoped that he recalled all the NMAT abbreviated text assignments. After the transmission and exchange of the message, Jimmy knew that Oscar was now working at a New Jersey State Police facility. Jimmy Reeves now had the address and a telephone number for a secure line there. Jimmy also knew that the vehicle search was in progress and that right now, Jimmy and Vanessa were in some deep shit. There was no abbreviated text message that translated exactly like that, but Jimmy translated it into, "Jimmy Reeves speak." Jimmy sent some more info in abbreviated text to relay to the good detective that he had more evidence, and to arrange a meeting here as soon as possible. Coincidentally, the meeting time was set for around the same time when Vanessa was off duty and set to meet Hillary. After successfully exchanging the messages, the two radio operators closed the net. Jimmy pulled in the wires, wrapped them back onto the wire reels, packed all his radio gear up and tucked it away in a closet. There was not much need for hiding things any longer. Jimmy was sure that it was all going to blow up very shortly from now. A glance at his watch told Jimmy that it was already o-fourteen-hundred hours, and Jimmy needed to check on his gal. She was most likely antsy from all the secret language that made little, if any, sense to her. Jimmy missed lunch hour with her and she might be on edge. A stroll into the lobby. And some eye contact with Vanessa was all he needed to do in order to check in on her and calm the situation. Oh yes, and a cigar and some Scotch on the balcony would be a nice, added touch. Renaldo would be the man to deliver those key items. It was important to try to make everything appear as close to normal as possible until the time arrived to jump into action.

The phone on Detective Campenella's temporary desk rang, and he knew it was the news that he waited for. Detective Campenella had clued the crime scene team in on the waves of corruption and the danger involved. Oscar trusted his technical team because at this point, he had little choice and the presence of the state troopers watching the operation and added to the mix, made for another level of trust too.

"We hit a home run, Detective Campenella," the lead technician reported as Oscar's heart skipped a beat or two. "Gunpowder residue on the rear passenger's seat, Tony Michanetti Junior's fingerprints all over the same location and get this . . . blood residue on the carpet in that location. The blood is a match to the victim's blood. Whoever sat in that seat, well, they potentially pulled the trigger, but they most definitely, stepped in the victim's blood. All indications are from the evidence all around that area, well, it appears as if Tony Junior was sitting in that seat."

"Great work, great. I hope it is enough. It might be. I would be happier if we found the brother and his girlfriend, the murder weapon, and the shoes, but it might be enough to pull a search warrant of Tony's house to find the shoes. Not my call that is up to the prosecutors and Attorney General McCracken now. Right now, I have to meet up with someone and gather some more evidence to start to nail some other persons involved in this operation. Today is our day. We are gonna shut all of this bullshit down. I might need you to develop film for me, from some kind of spy camera gizmo."

"No trouble, bring it on and we have it covered."

"Great. I think that I can make one or two arrests of some thugs today. Are the state boys sending the evidence reports to the legal eagles?"

"As we speak, Detective Campenella. As we speak."

"Youse guys are awesome. As I mentioned, we are all targets here now. Keep your heads on swivels, thank the team for me, and, please stay close to those troopers. I owe youse guys some cerveza."

"Some what? English please, Detective Campenella."

"Sorry. Cerveza is the Spanish word for beer. I owe you gallons and gallons of beer."

The technician laughed, and he told the good detective, "Yeah, ya do. Shit—you owe us all dinners. The hell with a few beers. And we are all packing and keeping our heads on swivels too. First time since the academy that we carried weapons. I just hope that I remember how to shoot."

No sooner had Oscar hung up the telephone, it rattled and rang again. Oscar thought that it was the head technician calling back to share some additional information with him, but it was not.

A low, female voice squeaked on the other end of the line as Oscar answered the call, "This is, Detective Campenella speaking."

"Detective, this is, Donna Eardley calling. I think you are looking for Ken and for me. We need your help. Ken is very ill and we are desperate. Can you help us? Please. We are so tired of running and we are very scared. Please, tell us you are a good guy."

Oscar almost dropped the phone. His knees wobbled and his voice did too.

Recovering, he shouted in the telephone, "Donna Eardley! Yes! I am a good guy. I will help. Where are you? I will be there as soon as possible."

Oscar turned to the large window in his office. He frantically waved to the state troopers outside his office and caught their attention. The troopers burst into the room, waited, and listened to what was happening.

"We are at a diner, the Regal Star on Route 9. I am on a pay telephone here."

"The Regal Star on Route 9," Oscar waved to a trooper and indicated for the trooper to write while Oscar spoke aloud. The trooper grabbed a pen and pad and began to write the relayed information down.

"Please, give me the telephone number of the pay phone. Okay, slowly now, it is going to be ok, now. Six-zero-nine-two-four-seven-nine-zero-two-two. Got it."

The trooper continued to write.

"Stay right there. We are on the way. I will arrive with about ten, New Jersey State Police troopers. Stay put. Trust no one."

"Okay. Thank you. We will. We have to. Ken is so sick that we cannot go on any longer."

Oscar then had a strange thought. His mind reeled as he asked Donna, "How did you get this number? This is a secure line. How did you know to call me here?"

There was a long pause on the telephone and Donna seemed surprised at the question, but she finally said, "A stranger gave us the number. He told us to call you here. He said for us to return to Clinton City and help you. He said that you were a good man and that we could trust you. Only you. He gave us money, and honestly, he gave us hope. He was very large, strange, but very kind and wonderful."

Oscar smiled because he knew the ace in the deck had appeared at just the right time.

Just as Chuck McCracken told him when this all first began, "He always shows up when we and the rest of the world needs him the most."

"Let me guess, Donna, this strange man, is immense, and he dressed all in black with a wide-brimmed black hat on his head. He wears boots that made a clicking noise as he walks. His eyes are dark and black. Is that the man you encountered?"

"Why, yes, it is. Who is he?"

"A good guy. The ultimate good guy. If he shows up, before we get there, then you can trust him. I assure you that you can trust him. We are on the way."

Oscar hung up the telephone, checked for his shoulder weapon and waved to the troopers while saying, "Saddle up, men. We are rolling. Muster all the manpower we have. And firepower too. The final piece of the puzzle just arrived. Courtesy of the quiet stranger in the black hat."

"Who?" One of the troopers asked as they gathered fellow troopers and ran behind Detective Campenella.

Oscar did not answer. There was no need to answer because they would not understand, anyway.

On the balcony of Casa Al Mare, Jimmy Reeves sat and smoked a fine cigar; he sipped a glass of Scotch and kept an eye on the lobby. He could see directly through to the lobby, and his eyes remained glued on the activity. It was quiet.

Too quiet.

Vanessa had given him an "all clear signal" as he checked with her again in order to calm her nerves. Jimmy was very proud of his woman because she was proving to be rock steady. Vanessa reported that Hillary had briefly stopped by on her way to a photo shoot outing and that they were still on for their cocktails after work. Jimmy could not relate too much to her, but through some strategic wording, Vanessa surmised that Oscar was on his way around the same time. She knew that it was all coming to a conclusion and by the look in her man's eyes; she knew that Jimmy remained locked, loaded, and ready for whatever arrived. Cocktails with Hillary would work out perfectly. Vanessa needed to relax a little. After all, nothing might go down for a few hours. Maybe not even until later tonight.

Jimmy had no idea how long the technical team required in order to check and investigate the vehicle, but he knew that this quiet atmosphere meant one thing; the thugs were working their own plan and all the angles behind the scenes. Jimmy's plan was to join the women later in the evening for cocktails and continue to wait for Campy and for the rest of all this madness to unfold. He did not want to leave his woman out of his sight for too long tonight, but he did need to prepare for the battle that he knew loomed closer and closer and Vanessa had the radio with her too. Jimmy was only a call away, and he needed to suit up.

When he finished the cigar and sipped the last of his drink, Jimmy decided that he would head for his room and double-check his gear. Now might be a good time to test fit his body armor and to make any adjustments. It was just past fifteen-hundred-hours, Jimmy stood up, walked into the lobby, waved to get Vanessa's attention, and he pointed at his watch, then to the upper reaches of the hotel to indicate that he was heading for his room. She nodded and blew him a kiss.

A few minutes after Jimmy left, Hillary rushed in, with a group of hotel housemen carrying her mountains of photographic gear, and she rushed right over to Vanessa. Hillary was full of bluster and enthusiasm.

Her mouth was going a mile a minute, "Oh, what a

lovely day. Great shots of the lighthouses and beach. It was amazing. I will just run up to my room and be right down. We will have such a great time, Vanessa and I have so much to tell you."

"Okay, great, Hillary. I will grab us a table at Reflections. Does that work? I need to change my clothes and powder my nose, but I will be off in a few minutes."

Hillary leaned in and smiled while saying, "Yes! Perfect! Reflections! We can have some fun with that creepy bartender. He is such a grimy guy. See you in a few minutes. I still have to bring the teddy bear down for you to ship to my niece. Honestly, I am not sure where the time is going."

Hillary waved to all the housemen and off they followed her as she made her way to the elevator. Vanessa shook her head at the boundless exuberance of her new friend and thought about how she seemed as if she lost all reservations with Vanessa. They were as if they were old friends. She was even friendlier to Vanessa than she was just the other day when she shopped at the store. It was certainly strange to examine the complete change in her approach and attitude. Hillary could not be farther away from the aloof, world-famous, wealthy, socialite stereotype than she was right now. Vanessa wondered what could have changed her so radically.

"Great news, Attorney General McCracken. We have Ken Mercurio and Donna Eardley in protective custody. We just picked them up at a diner off one of the main drags right outside of the city," Detective Oscar Campenella proudly reported to Chuck McCracken on the telephone as he told the attorney general the news.

"Shit, my goodness! Damn good detective work, Oscar. Your old man was one helluva detective, and now, you are too. Ya did a helluva job here. How the hell did ya find 'em?"

"I didn't. It was just as you told me. The stranger shows up at just the right moment."

Chuck smiled, and he did not say anything for a few seconds before he finally said, "The quiet stranger in the black hat found 'em. That is how he operates. Told ya. Let me guess, these young people met him and he convinced them to turn themselves into ya."

"Pretty much. The young man is suffering with some hard-ass opiate drug withdrawal. He is in the hospital under the guard of many troopers and with the best medical care with some of our finest doctors. We have Donna in protective custody, and she is in good shape. Just emotionally upset."

"Understandable. Bet they have been through a bunch of shit. Running and hiding. Will they talk? Do they know a lot?"

Oscar breathed deeply, and he said, "They will talk and have talked already. Yes, they know a lot. However, Donna says that the dead brother has the golden eggs of evidence hidden somewhere. They do not know where it is. Rob Mercurio hid millions of street dollars in heroin, marked money, books and books of records, names, numbers, dates, and transactions. All of it. All the illegal running that his brother was doing for Tony's operations supposedly recorded in these books. Donna worked as a high-end prostitute out of Casa Al Mare for this crumb named Mick Malzoni. Donna is willing to testify to her role for a plea deal. Mick is the boots on the street running that operation. A mountain of drugs here and it is all hard-core stuff. Mick works the drug procurement, as well as the distribution of the drugs to their dealers up and down the shoreline, selling drugs to the rich and famous within the hotel and resort, and rolling the wealthy for dough after they hook-up with the chicks. Mick often threatens some weaker

Johns with exposure and they cough up more dough. Mick filters the drugs and laundering of all the money through the hotel and resort's books."

"Hell yeah, we can plea out for the chick and Ken too. This Mick guy is an evil dude. A real nice guy, huh? We will nail this Mick's ass. Today. Let's go get him. I despise crooks, connivers, chiselers, and thieves!" Chuck commented, and then he carefully listened to the rest of Oscar's testimony.

"Yes, let's get 'em! He is a badass and a punk. I want him nailed too. Rob wanted to get his brother and gal out of the operation and bring it down. His downfall was in putting his trust in my former boss. He trusted Lieutenant Davis, and that was his downfall. Davis ratted him out and when he would not give up the drugs, notes and money, or tell them where he hid it, they whacked him. It appears as if the mobsters thought Ken and the gal knew where the brother hid the evidence, but they do not know."

"Gotcha. That explains the frantic ransacking of the gal's apartment and the nervous reactions when you found Ken's car. Nice work."

"Exactly, and when Ken and Donna knew they were targets, they took off. We might never have found them, at least alive that is, but the stranger intervened."

"Yeah, he did. Look, I have gone over this with the legal team, they think, and I agree now, that we have enough for arrests and potential indictments. At least, one helluva good try at 'em. It is good enuff for me. If we can get a warrant for Tony's house and find the shoes, we might have him for murder. The murder weapon would be an ace in the deck. At the very least, I am coming down there to nail all the police and the city officials. We have them nailed and the rest of this mess, well, we are looking pretty good. Let's get this Mick off the streets and nail his punk-ass. Shut down that friggin' den of sin, Casa Al bullshitti. As I said, it is not ironclad for an indictment, but pretty good. Plus, ya tell me that Jimmy has stuff too."

"He does, sir, and I have to hustle over there. Right now. As soon as we finish here. Going to bring an army of troopers with me to help him. I have troopers, volunteering right and left to jump in on this mission. More reinforcements coming in from other barracks. Jimmy is there by himself and holding the fort with his girlfriend. It might get rough there in a few hours if it is not already. Finding Donna and Ken delayed me, and Jimmy might be wondering where the reinforcements are. Especially, if they are in it deep right about now."

Chuck paused and laughed. Even in the tension of the moment, Chuck laughed. He thought he heard Detective Campenella incorrectly.

Chuck repeated the word for confirmation, "They? A girlfriend? Did you just say Jimmy's *girlfriend?"*

"I did. She is a knockout too. Lots of courage and a figure and a face like a goddess. Little younger than Jimmy is, but what the hell, who the hell am I to judge? Good for him. After all, Jimmy is the man. All the women chase him all over the place. You can tell that the guy is a legend. She is now his partner on this mission. Jimmy told me that she works at the hotel, but he, in his own words, deputized her. Vanessa is her name, and she was with Jimmy and helped him when he took out the thug who tried to kill me."

Chuck was in shock; he did not know what to say. Jimmy Reeves. Long time bachelor, the man who is always on a mission now . . . with a girlfriend. Oh well, what the hell, he *is* technically on vacation.

"Well, I will be a son-o-a-bitch. Body and a face like a goddess, huh?"

"Oh, hell, yeah. She is beyond stunning, sir."

Chuck laughed again and told Oscar, "Look, stop the sir bullshit. From now on, just call me, Chuck. I am on my way. Get over and help Jimmy. I would not worry too much, ya can bring the army of troopers, but 'member,

Jimmy Reeves *is* a one-man army."

Chapter 11

Heed My Words

"I knew it! I knew that Jimmy O'Shaughnessy was your man. Vanessa, my dear, you are one lucky woman. He is beyond stunning. I knew it when I saw his eyes. I recalled your description, and I knew right then and there. Steel gray and blue. Amazing eyes. Let me tell you that once, I knew he was your man, I tried to test him for you. I pulled out all the stops, bending over with my blouse open and my big twins hanging out, my best moves, perfume, a pearl necklace hanging in my cleavage, multiple invitations to my room, filling him with Scotch and he did not waver. He stoically and proudly told me that he had a gal. He remained loyal and solid. He is in love with you. Madly in love. We had a few drinks and were acting silly. Such a kick he is! We played with this grimy bartender quite a bit and had some fun. Jimmy kissed me while we teased him . . . all in fun, but geez, what a smoocher that man is! I will never forget that kiss, ever. I did not want to wash my lips. He melts your lips, and he heats the rest of you up too. What a man!"

With a flutter of her eyelids, Vanessa commented, "Yes, he explained the kiss. I understand that it was all in . . . fun. You have no idea what he melts. It is not, just your lips. He melts *everything*. The man is the epitome of hot."

Vanessa smiled at her comment and at Hillary's testimony and praise of her beau. Of course, Vanessa already had heard the story from Jimmy, but she appreciated Hillary's honesty and in fact, her looking out for her love life with her "test" of Jimmy. The two gorgeous women both dressed in black tight-fitting dresses, both of them, wearing high-heels and jewelry, knocking the eyes out of every male in Reflections, while they sat at a table within Reflections, very close to the front entrance door. It was a few minutes after four in the afternoon and the same server that waited on Jimmy and Hillary, during the previous evening, delivered two Scotches for the women to enjoy.

Both drinks poured neat.

Jimmy had rubbed off on them both.

"Whooo weee . . . it is getting a bit warmer in here," Hillary commented at Vanessa's comment of the sexy and dashing Jimmy Reeves. Hillary giggled a bit while she faked fanning her face with a napkin. "Screw the bubbles of champagne. Jimmy is correct, this stuff changes your life," Hillary said as they lifted their glasses in a toast.

As they toasted, Vanessa noticed Mick Malzoni run over to answer the telephone at the bar. He said only a few words and then he hung up. Mick came out from behind the bar, frantically waved one of the servers over, and pointed for them to assume his bartending duties. Mick rushed out, and both Vanessa and Hillary watched as he hustled out the front entrance and met a large group of black-suited men in the lobby right in front of where they sat at the table.

"My goodness. I wonder why Mr. Grimy is so upset? He has his head up that small man's ass. Look at him, not so big now, is he?" Hillary commented as they watched Mick frantically explain something with his hands and then nod as a small man, wearing a black hat and a perfectly fitted black suit, reamed Mick out over something. Vanessa studied the smaller man carefully, and her heart jumped in her chest. She recognized the man as Tony Michanetti Junior. She was sure it was Tony Junior, especially after

Jimmy had told her about him this morning. Vanessa remembered him from the tour he took when Mike Spence told the staff that he was the owner. Vanessa knew that she would recognize him if she ever saw him again, and she did.

Vanessa mumbled as she took another sip of the Scotch, this time a longer sip, "Yes, not so brave. It is rather heated. Oh my, that is my boss joining them now."

Hillary watched and said, "Interesting," as she too took a long sip of the drink. Mike Spence led the group over to the store, and the women watched as Mr. Spence unlocked the front door to the store and the men all disappeared inside.

"The general manager let them all in the store. This is fascinating. Why the big deal about the store? All of that yelling and carrying on, just because that short man wanted to purchase a few items from the store. That short man must be very important," Hillary said between sips.

"I am not sure. Excuse me. Please let me see what is happening. I will be right back."

Hillary nodded and Vanessa walked out in the lobby and through the windows of the store. She was in shock to see the team of men ransacking the store! They were turning it upside down. Specifically, she watched Mick and another man, taking knives to the display of teddy bears and ripping them apart. Vanessa knew that they were looking for something and it suddenly connected! Rob was the manager of the store—the mob killed him—the teddy bears that he brought in a week or so before they shot him. The only bear that was different was the bear that Hillary had purchased! Perhaps Rob had hid something inside of the bear! How would he tell which one was which? Yet there was only one girl's teddy bear there. That bear was the bear tucked in a dark corner, so it was different and not easily noticed or even sold. Rob was dead before he could circle back, recover it, or tell someone he trusted where he hid something! On no! The only different bear was now in Hillary's possession!

Mike Spence knew who bought that one particular teddy bear. He was there when Vanessa sold it and Vanessa turned in the chargeback paperwork to Hillary's account with the details of the film and the teddy bear to Spence.

Spence knows!

"Damn!" Vanessa yelled out and as she turned and ran, she thought, 'And I am wearing another friggin' tight-ass dress! Why does this man do this to me? I am swearing off dresses. He can undress me with his eyes. I don't need them. Is this my life from now on, all this secret agent bullshit? What the hell is going on in my life?'

Vanessa ran as best she could in her high-heels, back into Reflections and Hillary jumped up from the table, when she saw the reaction of her friend.

"Hillary, listen to me carefully. Let's down our drinks in one shot, throw the money on the table, and let's get the hell out of here. C'mon! Trust me."

"Oh, ok, Vanessa. I guess. Are you going to meet Jimmy? The trust part, I mean, what is going on? Why are you so frantic? The sex must be great, but my goodness, can't I stay and finish my drink? I mean, why am I coming with you? Does Jimmy have an identical twin? I thought that he said he was an only child and I do not do anything kinky. . .."

Vanessa looked at Hillary and forcibly tugged at her arm. The burn and serious look in Vanessa's eyes told Hillary to stop talking so much because this situation was very serious.

"I need to stop yapping, right, Vanessa?"

"Yes! Shut your million-dollar trap and follow me!"

Hillary nodded while mumbling, "I don't think the work on my teeth was quite a million dollars, but ok, ok let's go."

Hillary tossed wads of money on the table and Vanessa grabbed her by the hand and forcibly pulled Hillary out of Reflections. The women hustled past the store and headed for the elevators. The men were still tearing things apart in the store and if they were lucky, they had a few minutes to make it to Hillary's room before they figured it out.

At least, Vanessa hoped so.

"Shit, how weird. Those men are tearing the store apart. What the hell is going on here?" Hillary asked as she noticed the ransacking of the store and connected the dots with the store ransacking and their frantic exit.

"It is not weird, but it is dangerous. What is your room number?" Vanessa asked as they reached the lobby elevators and she pushed the car button.

"Room four-twenty-two. Okay, I trust you, Vanessa. Something tells me this is not about a hot hook-up. Dangerous? Not sure, what is dangerous. Can you please tell me what the hell is going on here?"

Hillary watched as the elevator doors opened and Vanessa forcibly pulled her into the elevator. "Those men tearing the store apart are really bad guys. I mean, very, very, bad guys and I might be wrong, but they are going to be coming for you next."

"Me! Why? My goodness, I should have listened to my friends and family and brought my bodyguards!"

"You don't need them, Hillary. We already have the best."

Hillary's eyes widened as she watched. While Vanessa pulled out the VHF radio from her purse, Vanessa keyed the transmit button and called, "Hi, please tell me that you are there. Please head to room four-twenty-two as soon as you can."

Within nanoseconds of the end of the transmission, Jimmy answered, "Roger."

That was all Jimmy said and Vanessa calmly put the radio back into her purse while a stunned Hillary

Thornburg watched the scene unfold.

"I thought you worked as a hotel desk clerk?"

"I do, Hillary. I am a desk clerk, but as of late, I have a little side gig too. I am a secret agent chick or something like that. Honestly, other than being madly in love with the hottest man on Earth, I am not really sure what the hell I am."

Vanessa tugged at her neckline, adjusted her hair, and pulled her dress around her waist.

"Oh yes, by the way . . . that was my darling, Jimmy, on the other end of that secret, spy radio thingy. He is on the way. I have no friggin' idea who the hell Roger is. I have not figured that part out yet. Do I look okay?"

"Gorgeous, you look gorgeous. Especially considering that, we just ran like mad fools in our tight-dresses and high-heels across a hotel lobby and my twins ache from bouncing like basketballs. Do your twins ache from running too? Yours are even bigger than mine are."

"Yes, they do. I thought my eyeballs might get knocked out by them because I have a very lightweight bra on tonight."

Hillary nodded and adjusted her breasts and said, "I thought so. Besides bouncing our twins until they ache and endangering our eyeballs, we are now riding to who knows the hell where, for who the hell knows what. Apparently, we are running for our friggin' lives."

"Yes, unfortunately, we might be running for our lives, Hillary. However, Jimmy told me that no matter what, we need to keep our heads on swivels and that we should always stay calm, and luckily, we sucked down a few large hits of Scotch before all of this bullshit happened." Vanessa smiled, and she shook her head a little while smoothing out her dress. Vanessa proclaimed, "Hillary, I am not wearing dresses on dates with this man anymore and I need one of those reinforced bras, too. I have learned my lesson, and to think, I almost went commando for him tonight."

Hillary nodded and looked at Vanessa. She made a spinning motion in the air for Vanessa to turn around, and Vanessa did so while Hillary checked her dress.

"Ya look, great. Great ass in that dress and no panty lines. If I had to guess, I would say that you are commando. Just saying that if I were, Jimmy O'Shaughnessy's woman, I would always go commando. Just saying, because, I would not want to delay a single thing."

"Jimmy Reeves, his real name is actually, Jimmy Reeves and yes, believe me, there is no delay. My clothes literally melt off my body when he is around. I melt in that man's arms. When I hold him, listen to that New Jersey growl of an accent and look into those amazing eyes, my panties feel as if they are going to explode in a burst of flames and my bra is possessed, because it unlatches on its own and mysteriously explodes off my body and flies across the room. My panties and my bra both end up hanging on lampshades. The sex is unreal. He is unreal."

"Lampshades, huh? Wow! Now that is an explosion. Lucky gal. Melting away while the rest of us gals freeze to death in admiration. Reeves? Something tells me that Jimmy is not the wealthy playboy son of some wealthy family in north Jersey."

The elevator doors opened and Vanessa waved to indicate the way, and they began to run once more.

"Hold on to your twins! No, actually to be honest, Hillary, Jimmy is an assassin. A very, very good guy, and incredibly honest too. But technically, he is an assassin."

"Oh, nice to know. I guess someone has to work in that profession. Something tells me that the kiss we shared was not in the name of fun. Oh well. Glad, he is a good guy. That is beneficial for us. The sex is unreal, huh?"

"Beyond, unreal."

As soon as the radio call from Vanessa came in, Jimmy was on his way. He was already suited up and armed to the hilt. No black jacket, just weapons and body armor over his white shirt. He sprinted down the hallway and entered the fire staircase. In two giant leaps, he jumped the stair landings and was on the fourth floor in a flash. He knew that particular room number was Hillary's room. He recalled her joking with him last night and mentioning it.

Jimmy heard the women running down the hallway and he looked up as he stood in front of the room.

"Jimmy! Tony Junior is here. He has his entire gang of henchmen with him and they are all here now! All of them are in the lobby! In the gift store! They are looking for the teddy bears that are sold in the store! Rob must have hidden something inside of a bear. They are tearing the bears and the lobby store apart, and Hillary, well, I think she has the one they want. Her bear was marked differently and Mike Spence will figure it out. We are almost out of time. Something that they need very badly is inside of her bear."

"Gotcha, baby. Stand away."

Jimmy pulled his nine-millimeter handgun out of his holster and he waved for the women to stand away.

Hillary reached in her purse for the room key and said, "I have the key."

Jimmy kicked the door in with one powerful kick.

The door blew off the hinges and Hillary said, "Well, I guess he does not use room keys."

Jimmy quickly checked the room, and then he shouldered his weapon and waved the women into the room.

"Where is the bear, Hillary? Quick!"

Hillary nodded and ran to the closet and pulled the bear down from the shelf and out of the box. She handed the box to Jimmy, who set it on the floor and carefully opened it. Once it was open, Jimmy reached in and grabbed the teddy bear and after examining it and squeezing its body very carefully, Jimmy reached for his long knife strapped to his ankle, pulled it out and with a quick slice, he cut the bear open and the stuffing popped out and all over the floor.

Vanessa leaned in and whispered to Hillary, "I guess we will have to pick out another birthday present for your niece."

"I think you are correct. It is damn sure not going to be a teddy bear."

Jimmy pulled the rest of the stuffing out of the bear, and sure enough, a small cardboard box fell out of the bear and onto the floor. Jimmy opened it and immediately saw that it was the key to a safe deposit box. It had a set of papers with it, detailing the box number, ownership records and the location of the box within a bank in Clinton City. Rob had the evidence locked in a safe deposit box and the key and the papers with the explanation and details hidden in the bear! Jimmy stuffed the key and the papers in his pockets, slipped his knife back in the sheath, and stood up.

"We have to split outta here right now. I only have a sports car and we cannot all fit. Detective Campy and reinforcements are on the way, but we might not have enough time to wait for them."

Hillary piped in, "Jimmy, we can take my car. It is still in the garage by the loading dock. I did not valet park my car because the housemen helped me unload from the photo shoot. It is a large sedan. Quite comfortable and luxurious. Very, very expensive too. At least, our escape will be in top luxury. Here are the keys." Jimmy grabbed the keys, nodded, and they all reached out, grabbed each other's hands, and sprinted for the staircase.

"Sorry 'bout the dresses and high heels, but we gotta take the stairs. Oh, by the way, nice to meet ya, Hillary. I actually am, Jimmy Reeves. Sorry 'bout the lies, the kiss, and deception, it is part of the job. Nothing personal."

"Nice to meet you, Mr. Reeves and yes, no more dresses and high heels when I hang out with you guys. And we both need reinforced bras too."

They made the descent as quickly as they could and when they reached the bottom landing and Jimmy peered out into the garage, he slowly opened the door and spotted the security camera. Vanessa expected Jimmy to ask her to dismantle it in the same manner as before, but to her shock and Hillary's shock, Jimmy turned and instructed them to "Put ya fingers in ya ears and stay behind me and get down low on the floor."

They did so and Hillary whispered to Vanessa, as she tugged at her dress while attempting to kneel, "I understand about the commando part now. Are dates with this guy, always like this?"

Vanessa nodded, put her fingers in her ears and said, "I have only known him a few days, but generally, it appears so."

Jimmy pulled his twenty-two-caliber handgun out of the holster and in one shot, he took out the camera and the bullet knocked the camera clean off the mounts.

"Which way to your car?"

Hillary looked up and pointed and they once more joined hands and ran. Through the garage, then down a long line of cars and around the corner they turned.

As they did so, and Hillary spotted her vehicle, she pointed and shouted, "There! The long black sedan."

No sooner had Hillary shouted, and they all stopped dead in their tracks. Coming out of multiple directions from hiding spots within the garage and from between parked cars were a large group of men. They came out of every direction; Jimmy pulled his handguns, but he did not know which man to fire at first. Assembled, and now standing in front of them, was a long line of about eight or so henchmen and they all pointed their individual weapons in the direction of Jimmy and his women. The group included Mick Malzoni, the forward watchman, the obese, sweaty guy, and front and in the center of them all, stood a short man, with a perfectly fitted black suit on, and a black fedora hat on his head. The small man also had a handgun pointed at Jimmy and his women and a wide smile on his face.

"Oh shit, the short guy is, Tony Junior," Vanessa said as she stopped and spotted the obstacles in front of them.

"I kinda figured that it was him. All these mob bosses have the same types of weasel-faces. He looks like his old man. Stay, cool, 'member what I taught ya 'bout hand signals and everything else and get in behind me here."

Jimmy waved the women in and behind him as he kept both guns drawn and pointed, and he carefully maneuvered and assessed the situation. Even for the legendary Jimmy Reeves, this was a difficult situation. Multiple henchmen all armed with semiautomatic weapons. At best, if he was alone, he could probably take out three or four henchmen, and then dive for cover and battle it out. But with the women to protect, this might be an insurmountable situation.

Tony Junior spoke first, "Well, isn't this nice. We have all of this wrapped up in a tidy, little package of doom. The legendary Jimmy Reeves and his gorgeous women. One is just a hotel desk clerk, a former employee of mine, who would not take her clothes off for anyone, but apparently willingly shed them for Mr. Reeves. And the other one who really wants to bang Jimmy too, is the famous and wealthy, Hillary Thornburg, who foolishly left her bodyguards home and made the mistake of shopping in the lobby store. Sorry, guys, but you have what we need and we will take it."

Tony Junior shook his head rather mockingly and threw his head back as the next words came out of his mouth in the midst of sarcastic laughter.

"And to think, the end of the road for the great, Jimmy Reeves comes so unromantically, in a cement-parking garage in the grit of his beloved New Jersey. At the hands of a fuckin' stupid-ass teddy bear. How ironic and silly! A teddy bear takes out the great, Jimmy Reeves! A man, who survived stomping around the deserts and the jungles of this stinky-ass world, while killing the horrible enemy and serving so honorably in his beloved, United States Marine Corps."

Tony Junior waved his gun in the air and in the direction of Jimmy and for a brief second, Jimmy thought to fire a head shot and take Tony Junior down while he spewed bullshit and was distracted, but Jimmy decided to wait it out. Jimmy thought, 'How all these leaders of gangs and mobsters were alike because the evil dudes always come up with stupid bullshit to spew before the final battle and it always gave the good guy's extra time to think.'

Right now, Jimmy required extra time to think.

Tony Junior continued, "Isn't that what you are about, Jimmy Reeves, the honor of the country and honor of the Marine Corps?"

"You would not understand honor, Tony Junior. Why bother asking?"

"Cuz, I will tell ya, Reeves, honor is bullshit. Honor lies on the cold, dead, bodies, spread on battlefields from here to wherever. Pin medals on the dead and honorable. Medals pinned on their chests will make their deaths honorable. Yes, indeed, honor is for brainwashed idiots who think they can make a difference in a sick and absurd world. Yes, we all know who you are, and no doubt, you are a tough dude. However, it will not help you. Not today. Jimmy Reeves, combat Marine Corps hero, sharpshooter, sniper, a professional assassin, informant, bodyguard, and sidekick to one of New Jersey's finest. Another bum, who I will fill with bullets for one day. Good old, Chuck. Yes, indeed, with Jimmy Reeves outta da way, old Chuck will have a huge target on his old ass. I will be drunk in celebration for days once we plant old Chuck McCracken and he is pushing up daisies."

"You are betting on a win here, Tony Junior. You are

wrong. I am more than just a Marine. I am your worst nightmare. I am a Marine from the hood of north Paterson, New Jersey."

Tony Junior turned to the henchman who confronted Jimmy at the front entrance, and Tony Junior laughed. For a mere second, Jimmy knew that he could drop Tony Junior like a fly with one shot, but that would only serve one purpose, and that would be for Vanessa, Hillary, and Jimmy to die with Tony Junior. This was not a good situation and Jimmy delayed the inevitable a little longer with some boasting to try to scan the area and work out a plan of defense and attack. Hillary and Vanessa were motionless. No doubt, they were terrified, and they hid behind Jimmy. He would willingly die if it meant saving the women, but right now, he could not figure out how to make that scenario happen.

Tony Junior said to his henchman, "The hood produces a hero. Yay, for Paterson! How was he gonna kill ya? Peel ya like a banana, right?"

The henchman nodded to confirm Jimmy's words.

Tony Junior then said, "The sad part is that he most likely has done that before too. Talented guy. You ladies, ya love a killer. That is all he is, a polished-up killer. Not much difference between us. Jimmy kills in the name of good, pure, and wholesome causes. I kill for monetary gain. But, hell, a killer is a killer. Enough of this bullshit. Hand over what was in the bear. I will kill you with a clean head shot, Honorable death for a Marine. I have to admit that I admire your commitment to bullshit. That does not mean that I will not kill you, because I will. Nevertheless, you are a man of strength and a great warrior. However, even warriors die. The women will die too, but not before, we all have fun with those luscious bodies. Ooooh boy, Hillary! Ya thought the tabloids loved snapping ya gorgeous naked ass with that boy toy! Ya dead body on da covers are gonna really sell some copies!"

Jimmy felt his blood boil, and he breathed deeply and thought that with his body armor he could take out Tony Junior, the fat and sweaty henchman, and maybe two more. Then, he could push the women to the ground and battle it out. The odds were very good that once he took out Tony Junior and a few of the key men, the rest might turn and run. Jimmy worked the plan out in his mind. Where the first bullets would land. First, Tony Junior, with a clean head kill, right through his right eyeball and out the back of his head, next, a shot from the nine-millimeter at a calculated angle will blow the fat guy's head off and the bullet should pass through fatty and take out the thug next to him too. The height calculation of the two thugs worked for two kills in one. Then, with two or three squeezes, he would take out Mick and the other forward watch guy. Clean kills, within about two seconds.

It was the only plan that he had now and as Tony Junior lifted his handgun and pointed it at Jimmy, Tony Junior said, "Okay, well even for a Marine from the hood, I guess that all of us were too much for ya. Bye, bye, Jimmy, I will just take the stuff off ya dead body."

Suddenly, there was a loud noise echoing behind Jimmy and the women. The loud noise of a door slamming. Then a strange and different noise resonated throughout the parking garage. This noise sounded very loudly, it was the sound of a loud, clicking noise, somewhat, as if a small hammer was gently tapping on a piece of metal. The noise was rhythmic in its beat, as if the person making the noise was keeping time beats to music.

Mick Malzoni's face spun in horror and he turned to Tony Junior and shouted, "That is the noise of his boots! Shit, man! He is coming! Believe me, this is a bad scene. You think Jimmy is a badass? Well, this really sucks because it ain't gettin' any better because, this dude is super badass and he is not of this world! That is the guy that I told ya about! The stranger in the black hat." Mick turned and pointed at the obese and now very sweaty henchman for confirmation.

He asked, "Right, Mario?"

The obese henchman nodded furiously, and the sweat ran off Mario's forehead like a river in the spring after snowmelt. Tony Junior looked around nervously. Suddenly, he had lost quite a bit of his previous cockiness and self-assurance. Tony Junior did not know what to do or who was coming. The sound was so ominous that it caused shivers up and down your spine. Everyone froze in place in a classic stand off now. Guns pointed, but no one dared to react. The first trigger pull would result in death, and no one was willing to be the first to go. Especially, while the unknown source of the noise grew closer and closer.

Jimmy kept the women behind him and he kept his guns drawn and pointed as the noise grew louder and louder and the source of the sound grew closer.

"I love you, Jimmy," Vanessa whispered to Jimmy.

"I love you too, baby."

"Can I kiss you, Jimmy Reeves?" Vanessa asked.

"Not right now, soon, but not right now, baby."

"Okay and remind me later to ask you who the hell Roger is too."

Hillary leaned in and admitted, "I love you too, Jimmy. I do not stand a prayer with Vanessa being your true love, but if I die, I wanted you to know that. I never really loved a man until now. The rest were all pretenders, but oh well, that is the way it goes. But, now that we all bared our souls, can you tell me, what the hell is that weird clicking noise?"

Jimmy leaned in and said, "I think it is what we would call in the Marine Corps . . . reinforcements. Stay behind me and be ready to run behind those cars on my signal. Get rid of those damn high-heels."

The women quietly and slowly slipped out of their shoes.

"Click, click, click, click."

The sounds grew ominously louder and closer and as it did so, the gang of henchmen all looked to their leader for instructions.

Mick begged his boss while leaning in and pleading, "Tony Junior! Honest, I am tellin' ya that we need to get the hell outta here! He is coming!"

Tony Junior waved for Mick to shut up and then he waved to the fat henchman and said, "You! Get ya fat and sweaty ass over dare, grab one of the chicks, and hold a gun to her head. We might need to negotiate sumthin' here."

The fat henchmen nodded and Jimmy moved into his path and pointed one of his guns at the henchman and the other one at Tony Junior.

"I need to warn ya, fat ass, that I generally don't negotiate anything. Unless you consider me blowing, ya head off from here a negotiation. Gotta warn ya, fat ass, touch any of them and I will put a bullet right through your eyeball, and the other bullet blows, Tony Junior's head into pieces. I assure you that I can shoot two at the same time. I will go down in a hail of bullets, but not before, I take you both with me. Can't ya see that Tony Junior is too much of a pussy to do his own dirty work, cuz, he knows that I do not miss? Ever. Do you ever miss, fatty? Betcha do, so go ahead and try me. Can't ya, sweaty ass see that is why he has not pulled the trigger yet? He knows that I might take a bullet, but before I do, that I will take him out with one shot right through his brain. Like, I said, I don't miss. Ever. And I have help on the way now, and it scares the livin' shit out of all of ya. So, tubby, ya wanna negotiate or what?

The fat henchman stopped dead in his tracks. The sweat fell in great drops and splashed upon the concrete floor of the parking garage.

"Hold on. Stop, Mario!" Tony Junior yelled and as he did so, the clicking noise stopped and a deep, low, melodious voice echoed across the garage.

"The guns will not fire. None of your guns will fire. Not any of yours, but I must warn you that Jimmy's guns will fire. You see, despite what men such as Tony Michanetti Junior, want to tell you and force you to believe, in the end, the good forces of this world always prevail. Hold a glass to the flame and you will burn. I do not burn. You did not heed my words, now, you will pay the price."

Everyone turned to look, and there, standing about ten feet behind Jimmy and behind the women, was an immense man. The lights of the garage cast a mysterious light on his face. You could see his immense frame and some of his features, but the lights caused his eyes to glow as if they were furious beacons in the dim light of the parking garage.

Standing silently in the light of the garage was a very tall, lean, yet very powerfully built man. The man showed no emotion, nor did the man say anything else. The silent and immense stranger standing in the garage was dressed all in black. He wore a black vest covering a perfectly pressed black buttoned-up shirt, and his sharply creased black trousers had no ripples or wrinkles. On his head, he wore a wide-brimmed black hat and on his feet, he wore highly polished black boots. His attire was immaculate. Nothing was out of place on the man; even the hair on his head that anyone could see from under the wide-brimmed hat was perfectly groomed, trimmed neat and clean along the edges. His face sported a black beard and full facial hair and once again, it was neat, clean, and trim. His eyes were black, and they slowly scanned the area in front of him.

He was the quiet stranger in the black hat.

He walked slowly ahead, his boots making a loud clicking noise as they struck upon the cement floor of the parking garage.

The quiet stranger now stood next to Jimmy and the women and he waved his arms in the air while speaking once more, "Please. We will carefully examine this situation. Eight men on your side, and two beautiful women and two of us on our side. One, Jimmy Reeves, and one of, well, let us just say . . . me. I think our odds are superb, but go ahead, Tony Junior, and prove me correct. Order your men to pull their triggers."

Tony Junior's eyes darted back and forth, and Mick Malzoni fell to his knees and covered his head. The cocky bartender, so confident to spread his malice and evil, now on his knees while quivering in fear. In disgust at his cowardice, Tony Junior looked at and he pointed his gun at Mick and pulled the trigger. Once, twice, then three times, and nothing. . ..

Tony Junior was now frantic. He ripped the gun out of a nearby henchman's hands, and he pointed and pulled the trigger of that gun too.

Nothing.

Now, the entire gang stood in fear and it appeared as if most of them were about to turn and run, when the henchman who confronted Jimmy at the front entrance lifted his gun and pointed it at Mick and pulled the trigger.

Nothing.

The quiet stranger now walked forward, and the stranger said, "Now, we can do this the easy way, or we can do this the gruesome way. I could unleash Jimmy and allow Jimmy to work his profession on each of you, but that will be the gruesome way. You see, even before I arrived, I am not entirely sure that you understood how close you all were to death and meeting the flames of Hell. Despite what you thought, you obviously did not know whom you were dealing with. Jimmy was not quite out of options. Instead, I will save you from that sad and gruesome fate. I think we will do this the easy way, because the gruesome way will be too difficult for the good detective, who is about to arrive—to explain. The mess from the blood would be horrific. Please, think of this as if I saved you from Jimmy Reeves, not as if I saved Jimmy and the women."

He lifted his arms and suddenly the air around Tony Junior and the entire gang of henchmen grew intensely cold, and each of them began to shiver in a deep freeze. When they staggered to their knees and cowered in fear, the quiet stranger in the black hat stomped the ground with his right foot, and Tony Junior and his gang of henchmen all collapsed in a heap. It was as if they all fell dead. All of them except for Mick Malzoni, who still sat upon his knees and cried aloud in fear, while rocking back and forth in a wrapped-up ball. For some reason, whatever magic or force that it was that the mysterious stranger conjured up, it excluded the grimy and wretched Mick Malzoni.

The loud wail of police sirens filled the air and suddenly the garage filled with New Jersey State Police cruisers. They all screeched to a halt and out of one of the cars popped Detective Oscar Campenella with his service revolver drawn and pointed at the collection of fallen foes. The good detective stood and assessed the situation and then he looked over to Jimmy, and to the stranger, and the women, and smiled widely.

Oscar holstered his revolver and mumbled, "Should have known. After all, it is Jimmy Reeves and our friend, the stranger. An unbeatable combination."

Jimmy yelled out to his comrade, "Right on time! Nice to see ya, Detective Campy!"

Hillary leaned in and whispered to Vanessa, "I do not want to disagree with your incredible hunk of man, but if the detective and all of those state troopers had been just a few minutes earlier, this entire situation would have been a little less stressful."

Vanessa nodded and added, "Yes, but damn, Jimmy is so sexy."

Oscar yelled out to Jimmy as the good detective laughed and waved, "Gracias mi amigo!" Detective Campenella then asked the troopers, "Which one of you, troopers are in command?"

A trooper waved and raised his hand while saying, "Here, Detective Campenella. I am the troop commander. Master Trooper Lehman, sir."

"Great, thank you, Master Trooper Lehman. Thank you to all of your troopers. Please, call the crime scene team and if you need to, call for a paddy wagon. Handle all their weapons and anything else that you find as if they are evidence."

"We have you covered, Detective Campenella. What is the deal here? I mean, are most of these guys laying here, the perpetrators? Are they mostly dead? Or what? There is no blood, but . . . ah, I mean, do we need the coroner? And who are those people over there? I mean, the one guy is decked out in body armor, he is armed to the hilt and the huge guy in the black hat and the beautiful women?"

Detective Campenella smiled and pointed first at the thugs strewn all over the floor of the garage and the still cowering and crying, Mick Malzoni and then, he pointed over to the stranger, to Jimmy, and the two women.

"Easy to figure out, Master Trooper Lehman. Bad guys here on the ground and very good guys and gals over there standing up. As far as dead goes, well," Oscar looked over to the quiet stranger in the black hat who, of course, said not a word, but he shook his head to confirm that the men were not dead. The stranger tipped his hat and smiled at Oscar.

Oscar nodded, waved, and then told the trooper, "Nah, they are all unconscious. Drugs, man, too many drugs mixed with booze. Bad combination. I will explain it all later. It will be in my report. Wake them up and cuff the bastards up. Cuff them all and arrest them all. Read them all their rights and stuff their sorry asses in the cruisers or the wagon. All except for this punk here because he is mine. Look the other way for a few minutes, guys. Ya not gonna see shit. I think that he is resisting arrest." Oscar smiled and pointed to Mick Malzoni, who was still kneeling on the floor, his head down and cowering in fear.

The commander of the troopers smiled, nodded and playfully covered his eyes while turning to direct his troopers.

Jimmy Reeves shouldered his weapons, turned, grabbed Vanessa, and kissed her as he never kissed her before. He hugged Hillary and then put his arm around Vanessa and turned and stood in front of the quiet stranger in the black hat. Jimmy and his woman walked over to the quiet stranger, who stood and smiled at them both. The quiet stranger pointed in the direction of Oscar and Mick Malzoni.

The stranger spoke to Vanessa, "Miss Michaelson, I do believe that you are second in line to settle a score with Mr. Malzoni. The good detective is first."

Now, it was very clear as to why the stranger excluded Mick from his magical wave of strange forces.

Vanessa turned around and looked in the direction of where Oscar stood over Mick and she smiled. She looked at Jimmy, who nodded, and off she happily scampered to where she left her high-heels and put them back on her feet. She then ran over to where Oscar was standing next to Mick.

Hillary walked over to where the stranger and Jimmy stood and Jimmy put his arm around Hillary's shoulders and said to them, "Watch this."

Detective Oscar Campenella slowly lifted the head of Mick Malzoni by grasping a wad of his hair, and he bent down and stood right in front of his face.

Oscar said with a low growl, "So, we meet again, huh? Ya thug ass punk. Guess what, punk? We did what ya told me to do. We figured it out."

Oscar then made a fist, and he punched Mick Malzoni right square in the jaw. As the thug fell and spun across the floor of the garage, Vanessa walked over, lined his groin up with her right foot, and kicked him as hard as she could in his groin with her best high-heels.

"That is for me and all the other women that you took advantage of, you, lowlife crumb. I hope you rot in jail."

Vanessa hugged Detective Campenella, and kissed his cheek. The good detective motioned for a trooper to cuff, Mick Malzoni, who now rolled around on the ground in a great deal of pain. Together, arm-in-arm, Vanessa, and Oscar walked over to meet the rest of the group.

Jimmy said as he watched the scene unfold, "Yeah, no doubt, that is my kinda gal. What a woman! Courageous, gorgeous, and the heart of a lioness and the voice of an angel. And sharp-ass high heels, too. I am a lucky man."

A joyful reunion ensued. Jimmy introduced Hillary to the good detective and after some hugs and celebrations, Oscar, Jimmy, Vanessa, and Hillary stood arm-in-arm in front of the quiet stranger in the black hat.

Jimmy Reeves turned to the quiet stranger, extended his hand, and said, "I do not understand how you do what it is that you do and I think we should leave it at that. I also am not gonna ask who you are and all of that stuff. My boss already told me enough stuff to satisfy me for now. I—I—mean—I think—that all we need to say is—thank you."

The quiet stranger nodded and, of course, he did not say a word.

While Vanessa tightly hugged her man, Jimmy Reeves spoke once more, "I am not sure that my plan would have worked, but I was ready to go with it, when ya showed up, but I gotta say that it. . .."

To everyone's surprise, the quiet stranger in the black hat interrupted Jimmy Reeves and in his deep and melodious voice, he spoke. Even with the large size of Jimmy Reeves, the stranger loomed over the top of Jimmy, Oscar, and the women.

His face lit up and his dark eyes, once ominous, now

glowed in love, joy, and kindness.

"No, I need to say thank you. This weary world needs to thank all of you, too. Jimmy, I can tell you that your plan would have worked. You see, James Reeves, you are a man with a mission that is blessed by a higher power than any man could ever comprehend or understand. Now and forever, you are a man of honor, who will defend all that is right, just, and kind. All of us, we will stand together. We are all friends forever. You are never alone. None of you. I am always here, watching and waiting from the shadows of this world. You have my assurance that all the good and kind persons in this world are never alone. I guard their souls. I make sure that is always the case. Now and forever, I am watching."

The stranger tipped his hat, smiled and walked briskly away with his boots, making a loud clicking noise as he traveled quickly across the parking garage floor. None of the group made a sound or uttered a word. They still all stood locked, arm-in-arm, heart-in-heart, while they watched and listened.

The stranger eventually disappeared from their sight, yet the group still stood there until they could no longer hear the clicks of his boots upon the floor, and the sound slowly faded away forever.

Chapter 12

The End of it All

One year or so later, at a press conference in a room in Trenton, New Jersey where the air conditioning strained to keep up with the enormous number of persons and broadcast equipment crammed in the room, New Jersey Attorney General Charles "Chuck" McCracken, stood at a podium. Chuck was ready to deliver his statement on the final convictions and the sentencing on the persons involved in what the press and media labeled, "The Casa Al Mare Scandal."

With the microphones dancing in his face, and a multitude of television cameras and other cameras pointed at him, the cagey, old, attorney general stared down at the cameras and faced the music. Jimmy Reeves stood in a corner of the room, alongside Vanessa Michaelson, Mrs. Charles McCracken, Clinton City, Police Chief Oscar Campenella and Oscar's wife and parents, and Ms. Hillary Thornburg.

"Despite the sensation that youse guys and gals in the press want to make out of this, it was not the wild and mysterious scene that everyone thinks that it was. It was an extensive investigation involving many departments over all the state. I want to thank my Financial Task Force, who made all those numbers and bullshit of launderin' dough mean something to this confused old man, thanks to the Crime Scene Investigations Team, the men and women in the labs staring at weird shit under microscopes and stuff.

"Chuck is such kick-ass, Jimmy," Vanessa whispered.

"Baby, he is just startin.'"

"Thanks to the New Jersey State Police, the Military Affiliate Radio System for the Department of the Navy, United States Marine Corps, and thanks to my team of special prosecutors and all the deputy attorney generals. There are more folks out there, but I can't name 'em all. Once I have some Scotch for lunch, then my lips will get looser. Just know that I admire you all and thank you for what you do every day to protect the good people of this state and our country too. You are all hard working, honest persons, who sacrifice so much of your lives and for that and so much more, it is my honor to serve with you all. Youse guys and gals are the true heroes and heroines of this world. Not them movie star clowns all decked out in plastic, not the million-dollar earnin' jackasses, wiggling their silly asses around like drunken fools out on football fields after scoring some bullshit touchdown. I read somewhere that—we make heroes out of the strangest persons these days. No truer words ever written." Chuck leaned in. His eyes grew in intensity, and he waved his hand over the dimensions of the room.

"Youse guys and gals are the true superstars. Puttin' ya asses on the line to protect all of us. Earning a livin,' supportin' ya families, and leavin' it all out there every day to take down the evil and to protect the good. Thank you from the bottom of my heart."

Chuck paused and began to applaud, and the rest of the room joined in and shared in the applause.

When the applause ended, Chuck continued, "A special thanks to the police chief of Clinton City, New Jersey, the former Detective Campenella is now, Police Chief Oscar Campenella. A cop's, cop. A man of honor, courage, intelligence, and above all, incredible perseverance. I had the pleasure of working with Oscar's father when we were all very young, and I have to say that pride does not even describe the feelings we all have for Chief Campenella. The Clinton City Police Department is in the best of hands with Oscar in charge. The reign of bullshit, crime, and terror is over in Clinton City."

Jimmy reached over and the big man almost toppled poor Oscar over as he gripped his friend by the shoulders and congratulated him. Under the watchful eye of Mrs. Campenella, both Hillary and Vanessa gave Oscar kisses on the cheek and then his wife gave him a lover's kiss and he received warm hugs from his parents.

Of all the good people on this planet, the list certainly has the name of Oscar Campenella right near the top of it.

"We nailed 'em all. From the former Clinton City, police chief, to some officers, all the way down to some patrol officers. All of 'em. Beware, jackasses out dare, if ya take a payoff and are a crooked cop, sooner or later, we are gonna get ya ass. We got 'em all and they will all serve time. We nailed all the henchmen of Tony Michanetti Junior's gang. All of 'em doing time with long ass sentences. You name 'em and we got 'em, not a single not guilty verdict on any count. We even nailed the punks parking cars for conspiracy and drug trafficking. Now, the general manager of the hotel and resort, he can practice his accountin' in jail. Got his ass for cookin' books. I am okay with the pleas and suspended sentences for Ken Mercurio and Ms. Donna Eardley. They are gettin' married now. They both have honest and worthwhile, full-time jobs and are doing their best at cleaning up their lives. I wish them all the best."

Chuck was now not only verbal but also, he was very animated in his emotions and he waved in the air and pounded his fist upon the podium. The emotion of the victories was difficult for the old attorney general to hide.

"Most proud of two convictions and the sentences handed down from the bench. First, we got that crumb, punk-ass, Mick Malzoni. His evil ass will do a long time in jail for his role in ruining lives. Guilty on all counts, conspiracy to commit murder of a police officer, sellin' drugs, prostitution organization, illegal weapon possession charges, money launderin' and whatever the hell else, I cannot even recall. Thanks to the great detective work, we found the list of Johns who solicited the high-class escorts and prostitutes there at that fancy den of sin. We even nailed the "Johns" of the hotel prostitution ring, got us some high-powered jackasses and embarrassed the hell out of 'em."

Chuck now leaned into the podium and stared down into the eyes of the entire room. His voice lowered, and the emotion filled his voice.

"Lastly, we nailed Tony Michanetti Junior. I must admit out of the twenty or so charges we brought—that hangin' the murder charge on him for the murder of Rob Mercurio was the most difficult charge of all to make stick. When Tony's shoes entered into evidence and we surprisingly recovered the murder weapon hidden in the bum's fancy-ass mansion, along with the testimony of the fat-ass henchman, who sung like a mockingbird in return for a plea deal and the promise of top-notch, full-course meals in prison, then we turned the tide. The cocky dope thought he was above the law and he was too stupid to ditch the murder weapon. With the rest of the charges on top of the murder conviction, well, he is in for life and five years. Rob Mercurio was a hero. He died with honor in his heart. The evidence we found in the safe deposit box was overwhelming. Not to mention the directions that led us to where Rob hid the huge quantity of drugs that we found and confiscated. Hell, the street values of those drugs reached to the moon in dollars and think about the lives saved. Bye, bye, Tony Junior. Love it, cuz—this is an evil man. I hope that this finally ends the reign of terror and crime from the Michanetti crime family. I hope."

Chuck stood up straight and tall, and he closed his eyes for just a moment before looking down at his watch.

After noting the time, Chuck continued, "Okay, time for lunch and love with my wife and joy with our friends. Plenty of Scotch to celebrate. I am late for lunch at my favorite restaurant, but before I answer one or two, of your stupid, dumb-ass questions, I have to say that, if you are doing evil things in this state and breakin' the law that eventually, we will cross paths. I have eyes out there. Eyes that watch from the dark corners of this world and watch for people doin' the things that they should not do. And these eyes, they are just the same as mine because they belong to a person who thinks just as I do. The both of us, we can't stand, crooks, connivers, chiselers, and thieves!"

Chuck pounded the podium in exuberance, and then pointed out to the media, and said, "You there, kid, with the thick eyeglasses and the pad and the stubby-ass pencil with a worn-ass eraser. Ya look as if ya are reportin' for your high school newspaper. I will take a question from ya. Go ahead, kid. Make it quick, I got Scotch to drink."

A surprised young man stood up from his seat and said, "Thank you. Dwayne Rouchet from the Newark Star Gazette. Is it true that Ms. Hillary Thornburg, the wealthy and famous socialite, was somehow involved in the investigation and your longtime bodyguard and driver, the decorated Marine Corps veteran and hero, Mr. Jimmy Reeves, assisted in the apprehension of the now convicted criminals?"

Chuck smiled and answered the reporter's question without hesitation. "Where da ya guys get this bullshit from? I swear. Look, I told ya guys a million times. Yes, Jimmy was there at the resort and so was Ms. Thornburg and they just happened to both be on vacation. Ms. Thornburg did not bring her bodyguards on the trip, so Jimmy stepped in and provided a little protection. That's what Jimmy Reeves does for a livin' He protects people and does some . . . other things. C'mon, kid, I gave ya ass a chance, can't ya do better than that? C'mon, one more chance."

The young reporter smiled and laughed, as did most of the people in the audience, at the attitude and words of the famous Chuck McCracken.

Once he recovered, the reporter asked, "Okay, well, what about the continued reports from hotel staff of the involvement of the tall, dark and mysterious man dressed all in black and wearing a wide-brimmed black hat? Many of the hotel staff and witnesses swear to me that they know this mysterious man was there on the scene when the arrests occurred and he was somehow involved with mysterious methods of apprehension and control, along with Jimmy Reeves. Eye-witnesses say that the mysterious man is immense in size and that he hardly speaks a single word and one night at the bar, he swallowed boiling Scotch in a glass and did not even get burned."

Chuck shook his head, leaned in on the podium, and frowned.

"How old are you, kid? Your age?"

"I am twenty-five years old, Attorney General McCracken."

"Okay, just outta school? Studied journalism, I bet. Right?"

The young reporter nodded and answered, "Yes, sir."

Chuck stood up taller and smiled, "Boiling Scotch in a glass, huh? No burns, huh? Even I cannot do that and my liver is hanging on by a thread. Seems like a waste of good booze. Mysterious, immense, dark, strangers, in black hats, huh? Goin' around helpin' to solve crimes with the help of courageous ex-Marines, cagey and fearless detectives, and gorgeous and famously wealthy women. Well, maybe. Who the hell knows? I like it and I like you too, kid. Ya gonna have a great career. I can tell. There were many casts of characters passing through the hotel and resort. Maybe the dark stranger was visitin' too. I have a suggestion, kid. Why don't ya use your overpriced education and training and dig a little deeper? Come up with some answers and if it turns out to be bullshit and hearsay, write it as a fiction novel. Yeah, man, it will be a best seller! Crime-fantasy bullshit. Murder, mayhem, mobsters, beautiful women, romance, and courageous heroes, mysterious strangers with unworldly powers and elite crime fighters, all at a fancy-ass hotel and resort along the New Jersey shore. I love it, kid. Cap it all off with the mysterious stranger coming out of a dark corner while wearing his trademark black hat in order to save the day. It will sell millions, they will make it into a movie, and I can have a cameo as Attorney General Chuck McCracken. When ya do make ya millions, 'member me for some royalties, huh? We will smoke cigars, pinch the asses of cute chicks, and drink Scotch together. How's that sound, kid?"

The young man smiled and nodded, and the entire audience broke into hysterics. Chuck was quite the character.

Chuck smiled, pounded the podium, and announced, "That is it for today, folks. Thank you all. Write it as I said it and shock the shit outta ya editors! It is lunch and drinkin' time!"

It was now lunchtime and Charles McCracken, and his wife, Michelle McCracken, sat at an elegantly set lunch table along with Jimmy Reeves, who sat at the table too, along with his fiancé, Ms. Vanessa Michaelson, Oscar Campenella, Mrs. Campenella, the Campenella family and Ms. Hillary Thornburg. They were all nestled into a quiet corner of their favorite restaurant, "Nous Somme Du Soleil."

"Jean-Marc! What the hell is this here lunch special on this stupid-ass sheet? This here one."

Chuck McCracken held the listing of the daily specials

out for Jean-Marc Richard to read and Chuck furiously pointed at one of the items.

The faithful waiter leaned in, looked at the item, and asked, "Sir, in French, or in Spanish for Chief Campenella to translate, or in Chuck McCracken, New Jersey, speak?"

"In Chuck, New Jersey talk! Please."

"Oui. Glorified pork chop bullshit."

Chuck seemed surprised at the identity of the daily special and he sat back in his chair and mumbled, "Pork chops, huh? For seventy-five bucks? I would not have guessed that one." Chuck's voice grew louder, and he spoke to Jean-Marc again, "Oh well, we can decide on food in a minute or two. Right now, it is hard-core booze time! Jean-Marc we are celebratin'! We are gonna need drivers for our drivers today! Please, Jean-Marc, use the house landline phone and make the call for some limos for us. Bring on the best of everything today!"

The faithful waiter stood next to the table and smiled while answering Chuck's battle cry, "Oui. I will make the call. Of course, Mr. McCracken, our best of everything is at your fingertips. We always serve nothing but the finest. Congratulations to you and your team on the latest victory against the evil, bad guys. I knew that Mr. Reeves' holiday at Casa Al Mare would be . . . how shall we say . . . interesting. Will it be the best of our Scotch poured neat, all around? In other words, a little dose of life changing for everyone."

Everyone nodded and answered, "Yes," but when Ms. Hillary Thornburg raised her hand, she surprised her friends by saying, "Oh, maybe, champagne today. This is a celebration and I should. . .." Hillary looked around the table, studying the faces and eyes of all of her friends. She waved her hand in the air and smiled as Hillary said, "Oh no, screw it. Those bubbles suck and give you terrible hangovers. Yes, Scotch, please, dear Jean-Marc. After all, now that I am the proud owner of Casa Al Mare, and for once in my life, I am going to do this on my own without my family backing me up, I can proudly say that drinking fine top-shelf Scotch changed my life. Why change now?"

"Oui, oui, of course, as you wish, Ms. Thornburg," Jean-Marc smiled, wrote on his pad and disappeared. Within minutes, Jean-Marc and his crack team delivered the drinks, and the group raised their glasses in a toast.

"Jimmy, I did enuff jaw flappin' today. Please, you make the toast for us."

"Okay, boss, well, here is to the best people on this planet and here is to vacations. I kinda, sorta like what Jean-Marc just said. They sure are, well, for lack of any other description, interesting."

"I like it. Vacations are interesting, huh? Works for me," Chuck said after a long sip of his drink.

"Ya know, boss, right after we get Vanessa's parents up here and settled into a new place, we are gonna get married. Ya gotta take some time off too, with me for the wedding. We are all gonna have some fantastic time at the new and improved, Casa Al Mare. No crooks allowed. The wedding will be there, then a wild celebration for a few days. You are the best man, and Campy and Gordy are my ushers. We gotta take the time off, boss. No choice on this one."

Vanessa jumped in and offered, "Yes, another vacation, or let me practice my north Jersey accent. A'nudder vacation. Hold on to ya asses, vacation time is here! Hillary is my maid of honor, as well as, the organizer, and Mrs. McCracken agreed to be one of my bridesmaids, so it looks as if you boys are doomed for mandatory vacation time."

Vanessa smiled, and all eyes looked at Chuck, who folded his arms across his chest and frowned at the thought of vacation time looming over his schedule.

"I guess. No choice, huh?" Chuck was not happy with the potential of taking time off with his faithful bodyguard and he pondered the situation for a few moments while everyone watched for his response.

Chuck asked, "Will ya have top-shelf Scotch there, Hillary? Will ya have the best food, and the best of everything? Ocean views from da room wid a balcony that Mrs. McCracken can sunbathe nude on it. Will my room have, one of those giant, fancy-ass soaking tubs, so my old ass can bask in warm bubble baths while I sip Scotch and smoke the finest cigars?"

Hillary waved and leaned over the table while saying, "Of course, my darling, Chuck. The best of the best. Even the bubble baths. World class. Top shelf will not be even high enough. After all, are you kidding me? This *is* Jimmy Reeves and Vanessa's wedding that we are talking about here! And I might just join Mrs. McCracken in a little nude sunbathing on the balcony too and come in and scrub your back, while your old ass soaks in the tub."

Hillary winked playfully at Chuck and then added, "Let me practice my New Jersey speak too. How 'bout dat?"

Chuck slammed his hand on the table and yelled, "Hot damn! When do we leave? Gonna order me a few cases of bubble bath! Screw this work bullshit! The bad guys will still be around when we go back to work. They always are. You know, in thinking about all of this, it might be time to retire to a life of luxury. I ain't gettin' any younger and there is always too little time and too many types of Scotch to sample."

Mrs. McCracken rolled her eyes at her husband's statement and she mumbled, "Oh, yeah, sure. You retired once, and it lasted about three months. Drove me nuts the entire time."

"Just a minute, Chuck, a few more things," Vanessa interrupted the humorous banter, and she smiled while winking at Jimmy. "Chuck, I am quite sure that you have already checked my ass out today, but please, make a note of the tight pants, the classy blouse covered with an expensive cashmere sweater and all the expensive gold and diamond jewelry that I now wear. Classy attire, but seldom, if ever, will I wear dresses and high-heels anymore. At least, not when we are working. It just is so difficult to run in them. Besides, when we are not working, I usually do not wear much of anything. And now that I am onboard here, let me tell ya, Chuck, we all promise to keep our heads on swivels, and yes, we are all packin.' I have the jargon down pat. Just struggle a little with who the hell Roger is and all of that radio, chitter-chatter, bullshit."

Vanessa opened her expensive cashmere sweater, and she exposed a shoulder holster fitted with a weapon and smiled a coy smile. Vanessa then stared down into her expansive cleavage; she tugged at the gold necklace hanging around her neck and pulled the entire necklace out to show everyone the little, sheathed knife attached to the end of the glimmering golden necklace.

Vanessa smiled again and, while shyly giggling, the former hotel desk clerk proudly said, "My darling, Jimmy, bought all of this for me. He picked it all out on his own. He picked out the weapons, the outfit, the sweater, and the matching jewelry too."

Vanessa turned to Hillary and asked, "It does not clash—does it?"

Hillary shook her head and said, "No, my darling, Vanessa. Not at all."

Jimmy leaned in and kissed his fiancé and after the kiss he said, "I told ya boss, this *is my* kind of woman."

THE END

Epilogue

Mr. and Mrs. James Reeves worked their way through a receiving line of guests, friends, family, and other well-wishers assembled in the grand ballroom of Casa Al Mare. The couple had just exchanged wedding vows in a chapel set up within the elegance of the room and now as they made their way as husband and wife, through the seemingly endless line of guests, Jimmy looked over to a corner of the room and he spotted *him* standing there. Jimmy smiled and gently tapped his wife's hand and captured her attention. Jimmy pointed and Vanessa saw him too, and she smiled and waved.

After greeting the last person in the line, Jimmy and Vanessa walked arm-in-arm over to the far corner of the room, where the quiet stranger in the black hat stood watching and waiting.

"I knew that you would be here . . . somewhere," Jimmy extended his hand, and the stranger did the same and the two friends shook hands. After shaking Jimmy's hand, the stranger extended both of his hands for Vanessa to hold and she warmly grasped them. Immediately, an incredible feeling of peace and calm filled her soul. The stranger's dark eyes sparkled, and they broadcasted kindness, warmth, and love.

While keeping the tight and loving grip on both of the stranger's hands, Vanessa Reeves said, "Thank you, for being here to share in our day and our celebration of joy. I knew that you would be here, too. Jimmy and I knew in our hearts that you would not miss this moment."

The stranger did not say a word; he only smiled and nodded in response to her words.

Jimmy said, "I cannot even explain in words the joy and love that I have for this amazing and remarkable woman. Somehow, I know we needed to drive evil away, save lives and end the reign of crime, but in my heart, while I look back on all of this, you had multiple missions. I do not know how you know all of this and do all of this, but you did it all. Your plan was for us to meet, to fall in love, for Hillary to change her life around, for Ken and his gal to clean up their lives and for Campy to be da man. We also noticed the starry-eyed looks in Hillary's eyes as she waltzes around today with Senator Gordon Tolland, and we noticed how Gordy cannot take his eyes off of her, so I gotta say, well, it looks as if romance might be in the air for them too. I might be wrong. If I am, it ain't gonna be the first time or da last. But sumthin' tells me, I am right on this one."

The stranger only nodded to assure Jimmy that he was correct.

Still, he did not say a word.

He remained the quiet stranger in the black hat.

"Well, you can always count on us. We are partners now and forever, in life, in love, and in our missions. My wife signed on to make a difference and Vanessa is my kind of gal."

Jimmy's statement finally invoked a response from the stranger, and he gently let go of Vanessa's hands and pointed to his heart. He then stared off into the space of the room as if he was looking to a faraway place where Jimmy and Vanessa could not see. They both marveled at his handsome face, and they admired how his dark eyes sparkled like beacons of hope.

In his low, melodious voice the stranger said, "I know that I can count on both of you. I will need your assistance. As I will need the assistance of Gordon, Charles, Oscar, Jean-Marc, and Hillary. At times, my allowance for intervention is limited. I see a long and happy life for you both. Wonderful children. The children will inherit their parent's extraordinary looks, their loving and powerful hearts, their courage, and their honor. These fine children will perpetuate their parent's goodness into this world. Now, that you have finally found love and respect, you are both whole. Together forever. Love and respect overcome all. The power of true love and respect is beyond comprehension. Combined, they conquer all the absurdity and selfishness that humankind creates. I can assure you both that goodness and kindness always will prevail over evil. With the souls of good people such as you both are, then goodness will never fail. We will meet again soon, James and Vanessa Reeves. Unfortunately, the evil in this world always tests the good. Until then, keep the faith, love each other with all of your hearts, bodies, and minds, and as you have never loved before and always stay the course. I am with you always, both here and beyond. Forever."

The quiet stranger in the black hat smiled. He nodded, tipped his hat and turned and walked briskly away. Jimmy and Vanessa held each other tightly as they both watched and listened as his boots made the now familiar noises as they struck upon the floors of the rooms.

They watched, enveloped in their love and honor, until he disappeared from their views and the sounds of his boots slowly faded away into the noise of the day.

ABOUT THE AUTHOR

If you ask Paul John Hausleben, he will tell you that he is not an author, he is just a storyteller. His mission is to continue to write and tell stories to warm your heart, make you laugh, and sometimes make you cry, just a little. Most of all, he deals in memories, and helps you to remember the good times of your own life, and the special people who touched you along the way. Paul was born and raised in Paterson, and then nearby Haledon, New Jersey, and began writing at an early age. He revisited a writing career later in his life, and he now is the author of a number of novels, compilations, short stories and audio and video works. Most of his work touches upon nostalgic remembrances of simpler times, and tells the stories of heartfelt, humorous, and special human relationships. Other than writing, among many careers both paid and unpaid, he is a former semi-professional hockey goaltender, a music fan and music reviewer, an avid sports fan, photographer and amateur radio operator. He now resides in Somewhere, U.S.A., but his heart always remains along Belmont Avenue in good old Paterson, and Haledon, New Jersey.

Other Work by Mr. Paul John Hausleben

The Time Bomb in The Cupboard and Other Adventures of Harry and Paul

The Night Always Comes, Another story from the Adventures of Harry and Paul

Reunion, A sequel to the Night Always Comes and Another story from the Adventures of Harry and Paul

The Autumn Collection

The Christmas Tree and Other Christmas Stories. Tales for a Christmas Evening

The Miracle Tree, Another story from the Adventures of Harry and Paul

The Summer Collection

Special Edition: The Time Bomb in The Cupboard and Other Adventures of Harry and Paul

Tales of the Quiet Stranger in the Black Hat

The Return of the Quiet Stranger in the Black Hat

Geyer Street Gardens
Beneath the Mask of a Hockey Goaltender
Another story from the Adventures of Harry and Paul

And a few others too!

You may write to the author at ctte27@gmail.com

Published by God Bless the Keg Publishing
Somewhere, U.S.A.

You may write to the publisher at
Godblessthekegpublishing@gmail.com

"Life's simple pleasures are so often the best ones!"

www.ingramcontent.com/pod-product-compliance
Lightning Source LLC
LaVergne TN
LVHW091032080826
845145LV00002B/466

* 9 7 8 0 9 9 8 6 3 0 0 3 8 *